FROM

Paris

With Love

With Love
COLLECTION

February 2017

February 2017

February 2017

March 2017

March 2017

March 2017

FROM

Paris

With Love

**JENNIE
LUCAS**   **KATE
HARDY**   **MERLINE
LOVELACE**

MILLS &
BOON

HarperCollins
PUBLISHERS
Since 1817

First Published in Great Britain 2017
By Mills & Boon, an imprint of HarperCollins*Publishers*
1 London Bridge Street, London, SE1 9GF

FROM PARIS WITH LOVE © 2017 Harlequin Books S.A.

The Consequences of that Night © 2013 Jennie Lucas
Bound by a Baby © 2013 Pamela Brooks
A Business Engagement © 2013 Merline Lovelace

ISBN: 978-0-263-92787-0

09-0217

Our policy is to use papers that are natural, renewable and recyclable products and made from wood grown in sustainable forests.
The logging and manufacturing processes conform to the legal environmental regulations of the country of origin.

Printed and bound in Spain
by CPI, Barcelona

THE CONSEQUENCES OF THAT NIGHT

JENNIE LUCAS

CHAPTER ONE

A BABY.

Emma Hayes put a hand over her slightly curved belly, swaying as the double-decker bus traveled deeper into central London in the gray afternoon rain.

A baby.

For ten weeks, she'd tried not to hope. Tried not to think about it. Even when she'd gone to her doctor's office that morning, she'd been bracing herself for some problem, to be told that she must be brave.

Instead she'd seen a rapid steady beat on the sonogram as her doctor pointed to the flash on the screen. "See the heartbeat? 'Hi, Mum.'"

"I'm really pregnant?" she'd said through dry lips.

The man's eyes twinkled through his spectacles. "As pregnant as can be."

"And the baby's—all right?"

"It's all going perfectly. Textbook, I'd say." The doctor had given her a big smile. "I think it's safe to tell your husband now, Mrs. Hayes."

Her husband. The words echoed through Emma's mind as she closed her eyes, leaning back into her seat on the top deck of the Number 9 bus. Her husband. How she wished there was such a person, waiting for her in a homey little cottage—a man who'd kiss her with a cry of joy at the news of his coming child. But in direct opposition to what she'd told her physician, there was no husband.

Just a boss. A boss who'd made love to her nearly three months ago in a single night of reckless passion, then disappeared in the cold dawn, leaving her to wake up alone in his huge bed. The same bed that she'd made for him over the past seven years, complete with ironed sheets.

I know the maid could do it, but I prefer that you handle it personally. No one can do it like you, Miss Hayes.

Oh, boy. She'd really handled it personally this time, hadn't she?

Blinking, Emma stared out the window as the red double-decker bus made its way down Kensington Road. Royal Albert Hall went by in a blur of red brick behind the rain-streaked glass. She wiped her eyes hard. Stupid tears. She shouldn't be crying. She was happy about this baby. Thrilled, in fact. She'd honestly thought she could never get pregnant. It was a miracle.

A lump rose in her throat.

Except...

Cesare would never be a real father to their baby. He would never be her husband, a man who would kiss her when he came home from work and tuck their baby in at night. No matter how she might wish otherwise.

Because Cesare Falconeri, self-made billionaire, sexy Italian playboy, had two passions in life. The first was expanding his far-flung hotel empire across the globe, working relentlessly to expand his net worth and power. The second, a mere hobby when he had an hour or two to spare, was to seduce beautiful women, which he did for sport, as other men might play football or golf.

Her sexy Italian boss annihilated the thin hearts of supermodels and heiresses alike with the same careless, seductive, selfish charm. He cared nothing for any of them.

Emma knew that. As his housekeeper, she was the one responsible for arranging morning-after gifts for his one-night stands. Usually Cartier watches. Bought in bulk.

As the bus traveled through Mayfair, the lights of the Ritz Hotel slid by. Looking down from the top deck of the bus, Emma saw pedestrians dressed in Londoners' typical festive autumn attire—that is to say, entirely in black—struggling with umbrellas in the rain and wind.

It was the first of November. Just yesterday, the warmth of Indian summer had caressed the city like a lover, with promises of forever. Today, drizzle and rain had descended. The city, so recently bright and warm, had become melancholy, haunted and filled with despair.

Or maybe it was just her.

For the past seven years—since she'd first started as a maid at Cesare's hotel in New York, at the age of twenty-one—she'd been absolutely in love with him, and absolutely careful not to show it. Careful not to show any feelings at all.

You never bore me with personal stories, Miss Hayes. I hardly know anything about you. He'd smiled. *Thank you.*

Then three months ago, she'd come back from her stepmother's funeral in Texas and he'd found her alone in his darkened kitchen, clutching an unopened bottle of tequila, with tears streaming down her cheeks. For a moment, Cesare had just stared at her.

Then he'd pulled her roughly into his arms.

Perhaps he'd only meant to offer comfort, but by the end of the night, he'd taken the virginity she'd saved for him, just for him, even when she knew she had no hope. He'd taken her to his bed, and made Emma's gray, lonely world explode with color and fire.

And today, a new magic, every bit as shocking and unexpected. She was pregnant with his baby.

Emma traced her fingertip into the shape of a heart against a fogged-up corner of the bus window. If only his playboy nature could change. If only she could believe he'd actually wish to be a father someday, and even fall in love with Emma, as she'd fallen for him...

The double-decker bus jolted to a stop, and with an intake of breath she abruptly wiped the heart off the glass. Cesare, *love?* That was a laugh. He couldn't even stick around for breakfast, much less commit to raising a family!

Ever since she'd woken up alone in his bed that cold morning after, Emma had faithfully kept his mansion in Kensington sparkling clean in perpetual hope for his arrival. But she'd found out from one of the secretaries that he'd actually returned to London two days ago. Instead of coming home, he was staying at his suite at the flagship London Falconeri near Trafalgar Square.

His unspoken words were clear. He wanted to make sure Emma knew she meant nothing to him, any more than the stream of models and starlets who routinely paraded through his bed.

But there was one big difference. None of his other lovers had gotten pregnant.

Because unlike the rest, he'd slept with her without protection. He'd believed her when she'd whispered to him in the dark that pregnancy was impossible. Cesare, who trusted no one, had taken Emma at her word.

Her hands tightened on the handrail of the seat in front of her. Here she'd been fantasizing about homey cottages and Cesare miraculously turning into a devoted father. The truth was that when he learned their one-night stand had caused a pregnancy, he'd think she'd lied. That she'd deliberately gotten pregnant to trap him.

He'd *hate* her.

So don't tell him, a cowardly voice whispered. *Run away. Take that job in Paris. He never has to know.*

But she couldn't keep her pregnancy a secret. Even if the odds were a million to one that he'd want to be part of their baby's life, didn't even Cesare deserve that chance?

A loud burst of laughter, and the stomp of people climbing to the top deck, made Emma glance out the window. She leaped to her feet. "Wait, please!" she cried to the bus driver, who obligingly waited as she ran down the bus stairs, nearly tripping over her own feet. Out on the sidewalk, buffeted by passersby, she looked up at the elegant, imposing gray-stone Falconeri Hotel. Putting her handbag over her head to dodge the rain, Emma ran into the grand lobby. Nodding at the security guard, she shook the rain off her camel-colored mackintosh and took the elevator to the tenth floor.

Trembling, she walked down the hall to the suite of rooms Cesare occasionally used as an office and a pied-à-terre after a late evening out in Covent Garden. Cesare liked to be in the thick of things. The floor wasn't private, but shared by those guests who could afford rooms at a thousand pounds a night. Trembling, she knocked on the door.

She heard a noise on the other side, and then the door was abruptly wrenched open.

Emma looked up with an intake of breath. "Cesare..."

But it wasn't her boss. Instead a gorgeous young woman, barely covered in lingerie, stood in his doorway.

"Yes?" the woman said in a bored tone, leaning against the door as if she owned it.

A blade of ice went through Emma's heart as she recognized the woman. Olga Lukin. The famous model who had dated Cesare last year. Her body shook as she tried to say normally, "Is Mr. Falconeri here?"

"Who are you?"

"His—his housekeeper."

"Oh." The supermodel's shoulders relaxed. "He's in the shower."

"The shower," Emma repeated numbly.

"Yesss," Olga Lukin said with exaggerated slowness. "Do you want me to give him a message?"

"Um…"

"There's no point in you waiting." The blonde glanced back at the mussed bed, plainly visible in the hotel suite, and gave a catlike smile. "As soon as he's done, we're going out." Leaning forward, she confided in a stage whisper, "Right after we have another go."

Emma looked at Olga's bony shape, her cheekbones that could cut glass. She was absolutely gorgeous, a woman who'd look perfect on any billionaire's arm. *In his bed.*

While Emma—she suddenly felt like nothing. Nobody. Short, round and drab, not particularly pretty, with the big hips of someone who loved extra cookies at teatime, wearing a beige raincoat, knit dress and sensible shoes. Her long black hair, when it wasn't pulled back in a plaited chignon, hadn't seen the inside of a hairdresser's in years.

Humiliation made her ears burn. How could she have dreamed, even for an instant, that Cesare might want to marry someone like her and raise a baby in a snug little cottage?

He must have slept with her that night out of *pity*—nothing more!

"Well?"

"No." Emma shook her head, hiding her tears. "No message."

"Ta, then," she said rudely. But as she started to close the door, there was a loud bang as Cesare came out of the bathroom.

Emma's heart stopped in her chest as she saw him for the first time since he'd left her in his bed.

Cesare was nearly naked, wearing only a low-slung white towel around his hips, gripping another towel wrapped carelessly over his broad shoulders. His tanned, muscular chest was bare, his black hair still damp from the shower. He stopped, scowling at Olga.

"What are you—"

Then he saw Emma in the doorway, and his spine snapped straight. His darkly handsome face turned blank. "Miss Hayes."

Miss Hayes? He was back to calling her that—when for the past five years they'd been on a first-name basis? *Miss Hayes?*

After so long of hiding her every emotion from him, purely out of self-preservation, something cracked in her heart. She looked from him, to Olga, to the mussed bed.

"Is this your way of showing me my place?" She shook her head tearfully. "What is *wrong* with you, Cesare?"

His dark eyes widened in shock.

Staggering back, horrified at what she'd said, and brokenhearted at what she'd not been able to say, she turned and fled.

"Miss Hayes," she heard him call behind her, and then, "Emma!"

She kept going. Her throat throbbed with pain. She ran with all her heart, desperate to reach the safety of the elevator, where she could burst into tears in privacy. And start planning an immediate departure for Paris, where she'd never have to face him again—or remember her own foolish dreams.

A father for her baby. A snug home. A happy family. A man who'd love her back, who would protect her, who'd be faithful. A tear fell for each crushed dream. She wiped her eyes furiously. How could she have ever let herself get in this position—with Cesare, of all people? Why hadn't she been more careful? *Why?*

Emma heard his low, rough curse behind her, and the hard thud of his bare feet. Before she reached the elevator, he grabbed her arm, whirling her around in the hall.

"What do you want, Miss Hayes?" he demanded.

"Miss Hayes?" she bit out, struggling to get free. "Are you kidding me with that? We've seen each other naked!"

He released her, clearly surprised by her sharp tone.

"That doesn't explain what you're doing here," he said stiffly. "You've never sought me out like this before."

No, and she never would again! "Sorry I interrupted your date."

"It's not a— I have no idea what Olga is doing in my room. She must have gotten a key and snuck in."

Hot tears burned behind her eyes. "Right."

"We broke up months ago."

"Looks like you're back together."

"Not so far as I'm concerned."

"Now, that I believe," she choked out. "Because once you have sex, any relationship is pretty much over where you're concerned, isn't it?"

"We didn't just have sex." He set his jaw. "Have you ever known me to lie?"

That stopped her.

"No," she whispered. Cesare never lied. He always made his position brutally clear. No commitment, no promises, no future.

Yet, somehow many women still managed to convince themselves otherwise. To believe they were special. Until they woke alone the morning after, to find Emma serving them breakfast with their going-away present, and ended up weeping in her arms.

"I really don't care." Emma ran an unsteady hand over her forehead. "It's none of my business."

"No. It's not."

She took a deep breath. "I just came to...to tell you something."

The dim lighting of the elegant hotel hallway left hard shadows against Cesare's cheekbones, the dark scruff of his jaw, and his muscular, tanned chest. His black eyes turned grim. "Don't."

Her lips parted on an intake of breath. "What?"

"Just don't."

"You don't even know what I'm going to say."

"I can guess. You're going to tell me all about your feelings. You've always shared so little. I convinced myself you didn't have any. That I was just a job to you."

Emma almost laughed hysterically in his face. Oh, if only he knew. For years, she'd worked for him until her brain was numb and her fingers were about to fall off. Her first thought each morning when she woke—was him. Her last thought before she finally collapsed in bed each night—was him. What he needed. What he wanted. What he would need and want tomorrow. He'd always been more than a job to her.

"It kept things simple," he said. "It's why we got along so well. I liked you. Respected you. I'd started to think of us as—friends."

Friends. Against her will, Emma's gaze fell to the hard planes of his muscular, tanned chest laced with dark hair. Wearing only the low-slung white towel wrapped snugly around his hips, he was six feet three inches of powerful, hard-muscled masculinity, and he stood in the hallway of his hotel without the slightest self-consciousness, as arrogant as if he were wearing a tailored suit. A few people passed them in the hallway, openly staring. Emma swallowed. It would be hard for any woman to resist staring at Cesare. Even now she... God help her, even now...

"Now you're going to ruin it." His eyes became flinty. "You're going to tell me that you *care*. You've rushed down here to explain you still can't forget our night together. Even though we both swore it wouldn't change anything, you're going to tell me you're desperately in love with me." He scowled. "I thought you were special, but you're going to prove you're just like the rest."

The reverberations of his cruel words echoed in the empty hallway, like a bullet ricocheting against the walls before it landed square and deep in her heart.

For a moment, Emma couldn't breathe. Then she forced herself to meet his eyes.

"I would have to be stupid to love you," she said in a low voice. "I know you too well. You'll never love anyone, ever again."

He blinked. "So you're not—in love with me?"

He sounded so hopeful. She stared up at him, her heart pounding, tears burning behind her eyes. "I'd have to be the biggest idiot who ever lived."

His dark gaze softened. "I don't want to lose you, Emma. You're irreplaceable."

"I am?"

He gave a single nod. "You are the only one who knows how to properly make my bed. Who can maintain my home in perfect order. I need you."

The bullet went a little deeper into her heart.

"Oh," she whispered, and it was the sound someone makes when they've been punched in the belly. He wanted to keep her *as his employee*. She was irreplaceable in his life—*as his employee*.

Three months ago, when he'd taken her in his arms and kissed her passionately, her whole world had changed forever. But for Cesare, nothing had changed. He still expected her to be his invisible, replaceable servant who had no feelings and existed solely to serve his needs.

Tell me this won't change anything between us, he'd said in the darkness that night.

I promise, she'd breathed.

But it was a promise she couldn't keep. Not when she was pregnant with his baby. After so many years of keeping her feelings buried deep inside, she couldn't do it anymore. Maybe it was the pregnancy hormones, or maybe the anguish of hope. But emotions were suddenly bleeding out of her that she couldn't control. Grief and heartbreak and something new.

Anger.

"So that was why you ran away from me three months ago?" she said. "Because you were terrified that if I actually woke up in your arms, I'd fall desperately in love with you?"

Cesare looked irritated. "I didn't exactly run away—"

"I woke up alone," she said unsteadily. She ran her trembling hand back through the dark braids of her chignon. "You regretted sleeping with me."

He set his jaw. "If I'd known you were a virgin…" He exhaled, looking down the gilded hallway with a flare of nostril before he turned back to her. "It never should have happened. But you knew the score. I stayed away these past months to give us both some space to get past it."

"You mean, pretend it never happened."

"There's no reason to let a single reckless night ruin a solid arrangement." He folded his arms over his bare chest, over the warm skin that she'd once stroked and felt sliding against her own naked body in the dark hush of night. "You are the best housekeeper I've ever had. I want to keep it that way. That night meant nothing to either of us. You were sad, and I was trying to comfort you. That's all."

It was the final straw.

"I see," she bit out. "So I should just go back to folding your socks and keeping your home tidy, and if I remember the night you took my virginity at all, I should be grateful you were such a kind employer—comforting me in my hour of need. You are truly too good to me, Mr. Falconeri."

He frowned, sensing sarcasm. "Um…"

"Thank you for taking pity on me that night. It must have felt like quite a sacrifice, seducing me to make the crying stop. Thank you for your compassion."

Cesare glared at her, looking equal parts shocked and furious. "You've never spoken like this before. What the hell's gotten into you, Emma?"

Your baby, she wanted to say. *But you don't even care you took my virginity. You just want me back to cook and clean for you.* Anger flashed through her. "For God's sake, don't you think I have any feelings at all?"

He clenched his hands at his sides, then exhaled.

"No," he said quietly. "I hoped you didn't."

The lump in her throat felt like a razorblade now.

"Well. Sorry. I'm not a robot. No matter how inconvenient that is for you." She fought the rush of tears. "Everything has changed for me now."

"Nothing changed for me."

Emma lifted her gaze to his. "It could, if you'd just give it a chance." She hated the pleading sound of her voice. "If you'd only just listen…"

Cesare's eyes were already hardening, his sensual lips parting to argue, when they heard a gasp. Emma turned to see an elderly couple staring at them in the hotel hallway. The white-haired man looked scandalized at the sight of

Cesare wearing only a white towel, while his wife peered at him through her owlish glasses with interest.

Cesare glared at them. "Do you mind?" he said coldly. "We are trying to have a private conversation."

The man looked nonplussed. "I beg your pardon." He fled toward the elevator, pulling his wife with him, though she shot Cesare's backside one last look of appreciative regret.

He turned back to Emma with a scowl. "Nothing can change for me. Don't you understand?"

It already had. He just didn't know it. Emma swallowed. She'd never thought she'd be forced to blurt out news of her pregnancy in the middle of a public hotel hallway. She licked her lips. "Look, can't we go somewhere? Talk about this in private?"

"Why? So you can confess your undying love?" His voice was full of scorn. "So you can tell me how you'll be the woman to make me love again? How you've imagined me proposing to you? How you've dreamed of standing next to me in a white dress?"

"It's not like that," she tried, but he'd seen her flinch. It was exactly like that.

"Damn you, Emma," he said softly. "You are the one woman who should have known better. I will not change, not for you or anyone. All you've succeeded in doing with this stunt is destroying our friendship. I don't see how we can continue to maintain a working relationship after this…."

"Do you think I'll even *want* to be your housekeeper after this?"

His eyes widened, then narrowed.

"So much for promises," he bit out.

She flinched again, wondering what he would say when she told him about the far worse promise she'd unknowingly broken—the one about it being impossible for her to get pregnant.

But how could she tell him? How could she blurt out the precious news of their child, standing in a public hallway with him staring at her as if he despised her? If only they could just go back to his room—but no. His suite was already filled, with a hard-eyed blonde in skimpy lingerie.

Everything suddenly became clear.

There was no room for a baby in Cesare's life. And Emma's only place there, as far as he was concerned, was scrubbing his floor and folding his sheets.

Cesare's expression was irritated. "If things can't be like they were..."

"What? You'll fire me for caring? That's your big threat?" Looking at the darkly handsome, arrogant face that she'd loved for so long, fury overwhelmed her. Fury at her own stupidity that she'd wasted so much of her life loving a man who couldn't see a miracle when it was right in front of him. Who wouldn't want the miracle, even if he did see.

How could she have loved him? How could she have ever thought—just as he'd accused her—that she could change his playboy nature?

He exhaled, and moderated his tone in a visible effort. "What if I offered to double your salary?"

Her lips parted in shock. "You want to *pay* me for our night together?"

"No," he said coldly. "I want to pay you to forget."

Her eyes stung. Of course he would offer *money*. It was just paper to him, like confetti. One of his weapons, along with his power and masculine beauty, that he used to get his way. And Cesare Falconeri always got his way.

Emma shook her head.

"So how can we get past this? What the hell do you want from me?"

She looked up at him, her heart full of grief. What did she want? A man who loved her, who would love their child, who would be protective and loyal and show up for breakfast every morning. She whispered, "I want more than you will ever be able to give."

He knew immediately she wasn't speaking of money. That was clear by the way his handsome face turned grim, almost haunted in the dim light of the hallway. He took a step toward her. "Emma…"

"Forget it." She stepped back. Her whole body was shaking. If he touched her now, if he said anything more to remind her what a fool she'd been, she was afraid she'd collapse into sobs on the carpet and never get up again.

Her baby needed her to be strong. Starting now.

Down the hall, she heard the elevator ding. Glancing back, she saw the elderly couple hesitate in front of the elevator, obviously still watching them. She realized they'd been listening to every word. Turning back to Cesare, she choked out, "I'm done being your slave."

"You tell him, honey," the white-haired woman called approvingly.

Cesare's expression turned to cold fury, but Emma didn't wait. She just ran for the elevator. She got her arm between the doors in time to step inside, next to the elderly couple. Trembling, she turned back to face the man she'd loved for seven years. The boss whose baby she now carried, though he did not know it.

Cesare was stalking toward her, his almost-naked body muscular and magnificent in the hallway of his own billion-dollar hotel.

"Come back," he ground out, his dark eyes flashing. "I'm not done talking to you."

Now, that was funny. In a tragic, heart-wrenching, want-to-burst-into-sobs kind of way. "I tried to talk to you. You wouldn't let me. You were too terrified I'd say those three fatal words." She gave a bitter laugh. "So here are two words for you instead." Emma lifted glittering eyes to his. "I quit."

And the elevator doors closed between them.

CHAPTER TWO

I'M DONE BEING your slave.

Cesare's body was taut with fury as the elevator doors closed in front of Emma's defiant, beautiful face. He could still hear the echo of her scornful words.

I want more than you will ever be able to give.

And then she'd quit.

Cesare couldn't believe it.

It was true that in the past few months, he'd thought once or twice about firing Emma rather than face her again. But he'd promised himself he wouldn't fire her. As long as she didn't get silly or ask for a *relationship*. After all they'd been through together, he didn't want to lose her.

He'd never expected this. He was the one who left women. They didn't leave *him*. Not since...

He cut off the thought.

Turning, he stalked back down the hall, passing a wealthy hotel guest, a heavily bejeweled white-haired lady dressed in vintage Chanel, holding a small Pomeranian in her arms. An entourage of three servants trailed behind her. She glared at him.

Ah. Cesare's lip curled in a mixture of admiration and scorn. The wealthy. He hated them all sometimes. Even though he himself had somehow become one of them.

Returning to his suite, he realized he had no key. And

he was still wearing only a towel. At any moment someone would snap an embarrassing photograph, to add to the rest of his indiscretions already permanently emblazoned all over the internet. Irritated, he pounded on his own door with the flat of his hand.

Olga opened the door, still in her lingerie, holding a lit cigarette.

"There's no smoking in this hotel," he snapped, walking past her. "Put that out."

She took a long puff, then snuffed it out in the bottom of a water glass. "Problems with your housekeeping staff?" she asked sweetly.

"How did you get in here?"

"You sound as if you're not glad to see me." Pouting, Olga slinked forward, swaying her hips in a way that was no doubt supposed to be enticing. He almost wished it were. If he'd still been attracted to her, maybe he wouldn't have made such a mess of things with Emma. Because he couldn't go back to thinking of Emma Hayes just as an employee, no matter how he wished he could. Not when every time he closed his eyes, he remembered the way she'd felt beneath him in the hot breathless hush of night.

Don't worry. I can't get pregnant, she'd whispered, putting her hand over his as he'd reached for a condom in his bedside stand. *It's impossible. I promise you...*

And he'd believed her. Emma Hayes was the first, and only, woman he'd ever slept with without a condom. In his whole life.

The way it had felt—the way *she* had felt...

Cesare ground his teeth. His plan of dealing with the aftermath had not gone well. After three months apart, he'd convinced himself that surely, cool, sensible, emotionless Emma had forgotten their night together.

But she hadn't. And neither had he.

Damn it.

"You haven't been photographed with any other women for ages," Olga purred. "I knew that could only mean one thing. You've missed me, as I've missed you."

Looking up, Cesare blinked. He'd forgotten she was there.

She gave him a sultry smile. "We were good together, weren't we?"

"No." Cesare stared at her. "We weren't." Picking up the designer clothes and expensive leather boots she'd left in a neat stack by the bed, he held them out to her. "Please get out." In his current frame of mind, he was impressed with himself for managing the *please*.

Olga frowned, licking her red, bee-stung lips. "Are you kidding?"

"No."

"But—you can't send me away. I'm still in love with you!"

Cesare rolled his eyes. "Let me guess. You're having some sort of crisis because your bookings are down. You're ready to give up the difficulties of the modeling business and settle down, marry rich, have a child or two before you devote the rest of your life to shopping for jewels and furs."

Her cheeks turned red, and he knew he was right. It would have been funny, but this had happened too often for him to find it amusing anymore.

Her long lashes fluttered. "No one understands you like I do, Cesare. No one will ever love you like I do!"

Crossing the suite, he opened the door, and tossed her clothes and boots into the hallway.

"Cara," he drawled, "you're breaking my heart."

Olga's eyes changed from pleading to anger in a moment, leaving him to feel reasonably assured that her so-called love was worth exactly what the sentiment usually was: nothing, a breath of wind, once spoken, instantly lost.

"You'll be sorry!" She stomped past him, then stopped outside the doorway, wiggling her nearly-bare bottom at him. "You'll never have all *this* ever again!"

"Tragic," he said coldly, and closed the door.

His suite went quiet. Cesare stood for a moment, unmoving. He felt weary as the emotion of the past hour came crashing around him.

Emma. He'd lost her. She'd acted like all the other women, so he'd treated her like one.

The trouble was that she was different.

Maybe it's for the best, he thought. Things had gone too far between them. It had become...dangerous. Scowling, he dropped his towel and pulled a black shirt and pants from his wardrobe. The pants were slightly wrinkled, and the shirt had been oddly ironed. They didn't even have the right smell, because Emma hadn't been the one to wash, dry and fold them.

But it wasn't her laundry skills he missed most. He looked out the window. The lights of London's theater district were already twinkling in the dusk.

Cesare had always liked the environment of hotels, the way the faces of the people changed, the sameness of the rooms, the way a man could easily move out of one hotel and change to the next without anyone questioning his constancy, or thinking there was a flaw in his soul.

He'd known Emma Hayes's value since she'd first joined the housekeeping staff of his hotel on Park Avenue in New York. She'd been in charge of the penthouse floor, where he stayed while in the city, and he'd been so impressed by her work ethic and meticulous skills that she'd become assistant head housekeeper within the first year, and then head housekeeper when he'd opened the Falconeri in London. Now, she supervised the staff of his Kensington mansion. Taking care of him exclusively.

But she didn't just keep Cesare in clean socks. She kept him in line. Unlike other employees, unlike even his friends, Emma wasn't overly impressed by him. She'd become his sounding board. Almost like…family.

How could he have let himself seduce her? He needed her. He could always count on Emma. She always put his needs first. She never even asked for time off. Not until three months ago, when she'd abruptly left for a long weekend.

The Kensington house had felt strangely empty without her. He'd avoided coming home. On the third night, he'd returned from an unsatisfactory date at two in the morning, expecting to find a silent, dark house. Instead, he'd heard a noise from the kitchen and felt a flash of pleasure when he realized Emma must have returned early.

He'd found her sitting alone in the dark kitchen, holding a tequila bottle. Her black dress was wrinkled. Her eyes had dark smudges beneath them, as if she'd been crying, and her long black hair was unkempt, cascading thickly down her shoulders.

"Emma?" he'd said, hardly believing his eyes. "Are you all right?"

"I just came back from Texas," she whispered, not looking at him. "From a funeral."

He'd never seen her drink before, he realized—not so much as a glass of champagne. "I'm sorry," he said uncomfortably, edging closer. He didn't know anything about her family. "Was it someone you loved?"

She shook her head. "My stepmother." Her fingers clutched compulsively around the bottle. He saw it was still unopened. "For years, I sent money to pay her bills. But it never changed her opinion. Marion always said I was selfish, a ruiner of lives. That I'd never amount to anything." She drew in a shaking breath. "And she was right."

"What are you talking about?" he said, taking an instant dislike to this Marion person, dead though she might be.

Emma flung an unsteady arm around to indicate the immaculate, modern kitchen. "Just look."

Cesare looked around, then turned back. "It's perfect," he said quietly. "Because you're the best at what you do."

"Cleaning up other people's lives," she'd said bitterly. "Being the perfect servant. Invisible like a ghost."

He'd never heard her voice like that, angry and full of self-recrimination. "Emma…"

"I thought she'd forgive me in the end." Her voice was muffled as she sagged in the kitchen stool, covering her face with a trembling hand. "But she left me no message in her will. Not her blessing. Not her forgiveness. Nothing."

"Forgiveness—for what?"

She looked at him for a long moment, then she turned her face toward the shadows without answering. She took a deep breath. "Now I'm truly alone."

Something had twisted in Cesare's chest. An answering pain in his own scarred heart, long buried but never completely healed. Going to her, he'd taken the bottle from her hand. He'd set it on the kitchen counter. Reaching out, he'd cupped her cheek.

"You're not alone." His eyes had fallen to her trembling pink lips as he breathed, "Emma…"

And then…

He'd only meant to offer solace, but somehow, he still wasn't sure how, things had spiraled out of control. He remembered the taste of her lips when he'd first kissed her. The look in her deep, warm green eyes as he covered her naked body with his own. The shock and reverence that had gone through him when he realized he was her very first lover.

She was totally different from any woman he'd taken to his bed before. It wasn't just the alluring warmth of her makeup-free face, or her total lack of artifice, or the long, dark hair pulled back in an old-fashioned chignon. It wasn't just her body's soft plump curves, so different from the starvation regime demanded by starlets and models these days.

It was the fact that he actually respected her.

He actually—liked her.

Everything about Emma, and the way she served him without criticism or demand, was comfort. Magic. *Home.*

But if he'd known she was a virgin, he never would have—

Yes, you would, he snarled at himself, remembering the tremble of her soft, tender lips beneath his, the salt of tears on her skin that night. The way she'd felt to him that night…the way she'd made him feel…

Cesare shook his head savagely. Whatever the pleasure, the cost was too high. Waking up the next morning, he'd realized the scope of his mistake. Because there was only one way his love affairs ended. With an awkward kiss-off, a bouquet of roses and an expensive gold watch, handed over by his one indispensable person—Emma herself.

He clawed back his short dark hair, still damp from his shower. His jaw was tight as he remembered the stricken expression on her pale, lovely face when she'd seen Olga in lingerie, standing in front of a bed which had been mussed, not with lovemaking, but from his hopeless attempt at sleep after a night on the phone with the Asia office. Of course Emma wouldn't know that, but why should he be obligated to explain?

What is wrong with you, Cesare?

Nothing was wrong with him, he thought grimly. It was the rest of the world that was screwed up, with stupid promises and rose-colored illusions. With people who pretended words like *love* and *forever* were more than sentiments on a Valentine's Day card.

He'd told himself Emma had no feelings for him, that their night together had been just an escape from grief. It meant nothing. He'd told himself that again and again. Told himself that if Emma tried to call it love, he'd break in a new housekeeper—even if that meant replacing her with someone who'd have the audacity to expect tea breaks and four weeks off every August.

But he'd never expected that Emma herself would just walk away.

Cesare looked out into the deepening autumn night. She'd done him a favor, really. She couldn't be his friend *and* his lover *and* know all his household secrets. It was too much. It left him too—vulnerable.

You are truly too good to me, Mr. Falconeri.

Cesare rubbed the back of his neck. He didn't deserve that. He *had* been a good employer to Emma. Hadn't he done everything a boss could do—paying her well, respecting her opinion, giving her independence to run his home? For the past few years, as they'd grown closer, he'd resisted an inconvenient desire for her. He wasn't used to ignoring temptation, but he'd done it, at least until three months ago. And as for what had happened that night... virgin or no—the way she'd licked her full pink lips and looked up at him with those heartbreaking eyes, how could he resist that? *Christo santo,* he was only a man.

But for that momentary weakness, she was now punishing him. Abandoning him without so much as a by-your-leave.

Fine. He growled under his breath. Let her quit. He didn't give a damn. His hands tightened. He *didn't*.

Except...

He did.

Cursing himself, he started for the door.

Emma wearily climbed out of the Tube station at Kensington High Street. Making her way through crowds of early evening commuters, she wiped rain from her cheek. It had to be rain. She couldn't be crying over Cesare.

So he'd never given her a chance to tell him he was going to be a father. So she'd found him in a hotel room with his ex-girlfriend, the lingerie model. So Emma was now all alone, with a baby to raise and nothing to help her but the memory of broken dreams.

She was going to be fine.

She exhaled, shifting her aching shoulders. She'd phone Alain Bouchard and accept that job in Paris. He'd give her decent hours, along with a good paycheck. She needed to be more sensible, now that she'd soon be a single mother.

Passing a shop selling Cornish pasties, she breathed in the smell of beef and vegetables in a flaky crust, vividly reminding her of her father's barbecues in Texas when she was a child. Going to the counter, she impulsively bought one. Taking the beef pasty out of the bag, she ate it as commuters rushed past her. Tears fell down her cheeks as she closed her eyes, savoring every bite. She could almost hear her father's voice.

Let me tell you what I know, kiddo. You're going to make it. You're stronger than you think. You're going to be fine.

It did make her feel a little better. Tossing the bag into the trash, she looked out at Kensington High Street. The lights of the shops glimmered as car lights streaked by in the rain.

She barely remembered her mother, who'd died when she was four, but her dad had always been there. Teaching her to fish, telling her stories, helping with homework. When Emma had gotten ill as a teenager, he'd been by her side every day, even as he pulled extra overnight shifts at the factory to fight the drowning tide of medical bills.

Her throat ached. That was the kind of father her unborn baby deserved. Not a man like Cesare, who'd loved once, and lost, in a terrible tragedy, and was now unable to love anyone but himself.

Maybe it was for the best he would never know he was a father. She could just imagine how Cesare's careless lack of commitment would affect a child.

Why didn't Daddy come for my birthday, Mommy? Why doesn't he ever come see me? Doesn't he love me?

Emma's eyes narrowed. No more romantic illusions. No more false hopes. She'd never give Cesare the chance to break their child's heart, as he'd already broken hers.

Pulling her raincoat tighter around her body, she gripped her handbag against her shoulder and went out into the drizzly night, walking down the street and past the town hall. Her footsteps echoed loudly past the expensive townhouses on Hornton Street, in counterpoint to the splatters of rain, until she finally reached Cesare's grand three-story mansion.

It was a palace of white brick, which had cost, including renovations, twenty million pounds. For years, she'd buried herself in work here, waiting for her real life to begin. Trying to decide if she even deserved a real life.

You selfish girl. Her stepmother's hoarse voice came back to her. *It should have been you who died.*

The memory still caused a spike of pain. She pushed the thought away. Marion was the one who'd ruined her father's life. She'd made a bad choice. It wasn't Emma's fault.

Though it sometimes felt that way. She swallowed. If only her father were still alive. He always had known the right thing to do....

She walked past the gate. Her lips pursed as she remembered meeting Alain Bouchard for the first time six months ago, here in the front garden. He'd shown up drunk and wanting to start a fight with Cesare, his former brother-in-law, blaming him for his sister's death. Fortunately Cesare was away, on a business trip to Berlin; Emma knew he'd never gotten over Angélique's tragic accidental death ten years before.

Emma could have called the police. That was what the rest of the staff had wanted her to do. But looking at Alain's grief-stricken face, she'd invited him into the house for tea instead, and let him talk himself out.

The next day, Alain Bouchard had sent her flowers and a handsome note of apology for his drunken ravings. That was the proper way of showing someone appreciation, Emma thought. Not by throwing expensive jewelry at them, bought in bulk, via a paid employee.

She stalked up the shadowy steps to the mansion, punched in the security code and entered. The foyer was dark, the house empty, gloomy as a tomb. None of the other staff lived in. When Cesare was gone, which was often, she was alone. She'd spent too long in this lonely tomb.

Well, no more. Throwing down her handbag, Emma ripped off her coat and ran up the stairs, taking them two at a time. She was going to pack and leave for France immediately. Before she'd even reached her bedroom at the end of the hall, she was pulling off her knit dress, the pretty dress that hit her curves just right, that she'd bought that very day in a foolish attempt to impress Cesare. Yanking it over her head, she tossed it to the hall floor. She'd wear comfortable clothes on the train, black trousers and a plain shirt. She'd be in Paris within three hours—

A small lamp turned on by her bed. Startled, she turned.

Cesare was sitting in her antique chair with blue cushions by the marble fireplace.

She gasped, instinctively covering her lace bra and panties. "What the hell are you doing here?"

"I live here."

She straightened, and her expression hardened. "Oh, so you just remembered that, did you?"

His eyes were black in the dim light. "You left the hotel before we could discuss something important."

"How did you—" she breathed, then cut herself off. He couldn't possibly know about the baby. And she didn't intend to let him know now.

Cesare rose to his feet, uncoiling his tall, powerful body from the chair. He looked down at her.

"I've decided not to accept your resignation," he said in a low voice. "I want you here. With me."

For a moment, they stared at each other in the shadows of her bedroom. She heard a low roll of thunder outside, the deepening patter of rain. Water dripped noisily from her hair onto the glossy hardwood floor.

Her arms dropped. She was no longer trying to cover her body. Why should she? He'd already seen everything. And she meant nothing to him. Never had. Never would.

"I don't belong here," she said. "I won't stay."

"Just because we slept together?" His eyes narrowed dangerously. "Do you really have to be such a cliché?"

"You're the cliché, not me."

"One stupid night—"

"No," she cut him off. She looked at him, and said deliberately, "I'm in love with you, Cesare."

Oh, that did it. She saw him flinch. He'd taken the words like a hit. Which was fine, because she'd meant it that way.

His black eyes glinted with fury as he grabbed her shoulders. "You don't love me. It's just because I was your first experience in bed. You haven't learned the difference between sex and love."

"But you have?"

Cesare didn't answer. He didn't have to. The whole world knew his tragic story: how he'd married young, and had been desperately in love with his wife, a beautiful French heiress, before she'd died just three years later. His heart had been buried with her.

She'd known this. And she'd still let herself hope...

Pulling away from him angrily, Emma went to her closet and reached up to the top shelf for the beat-up old suitcase that had once belonged to her father. Tossing it open on the floor, she turned back to her wardrobe to reach for her clothes.

He put his hand over hers, stilling her.

"Emma. Please."

Just that one word. The word he'd never said to her before. *Please.* She swallowed, then looked at him.

"Let me go. It's better for you this way. Better for all of us."

"I can't," he said in a low voice. "There are so few people in my life I trust. So few who actually know me. But you do. That's why I know—I *know*—you can't really love me."

His words were strangely bleak. Her heart twisted. He was right about one thing. She, of all people, did know him. She knew he was not the emotionless man the world believed him to be.

Emma ached to reach up and stroke the roughness of his cheek, to whisper words of comfort. Her hand trembled.

Shadows from the closed window blinds left lines across his dark, handsome face. His eyes burned through her.

But even more: her secret burned inside her, with every beat of her heart. She was pregnant with his child. Her silence in this moment was the biggest lie any woman could tell any man.

"Why ever did you think you couldn't get pregnant, Mrs. Hayes?" her physician had asked, looking shocked. "Childhood cancer, especially ovarian cancer, can occasionally cause difficulties, yes. But in your case it worked out just fine. I see it's a surprise, but this baby is wanted, yes?"

"Of course this baby is wanted," she'd answered. Oh, yes. Emma had believed for so long that she'd never be a mother. That it wasn't even a possibility. Fighting the same deadly, silent disease years before, her mother had never been able to have another child. Caroline Hayes had ultimately died when Emma was only four, at the age of twenty-nine. Barely older than Emma was now.

"Cara." Cesare's handsome face was almost pleading as he gave an awkward laugh. "How many times did we joke about it? That I wasn't worthy of any good woman's love?"

She blinked hard. "Many times."

"So you must see. What you think you feel—it's not love. Just sex."

Hot tears burned at the backs of her eyes and she feared at any moment tears would spill over her lashes. "For *you.*"

"For both of us. You just aren't experienced enough to realize it yet," he said gently. "But someday soon, you will…"

Emma stiffened. Was he already picturing her moving on, finding sex or love with another man? Cesare could imagine this, without it ripping out his heart?

Not Emma. It had nearly killed her to find him with

Olga. And even if he hadn't slept with her—that time—she knew there had been other women. Many, many others. And there would always be.

She ripped her hand away. She didn't have to live like this. Not anymore. She'd never have to spend another lonely night staring at her ceiling, listening to the noise down the hall while he had yet another vigorous one-night stand with yet another woman he'd soon forget. She was done.

It was like a burst of sunlight and fresh air after years of imprisonment.

"I don't want to love you anymore," she whispered.

He tried to smile. "See—"

"Do you realize that I've never taken a single vacation in seven years? No personal days, no time off, except for my stepmother's funeral?"

"I just thought you were devoted to your work, like I am."

"I wasn't devoted to my work. I was devoted to *you*." She shook her head. "I've lived in London for years and still only seen Trafalgar Square from the bus. I've never been inside the museums—or even had a picture of myself taken in front of Big Ben."

He stared at her incredulously. "I'll call my driver, take you down to Trafalgar Square and take your picture myself, if that's what it takes. I'll lower your schedule to thirty hours a week and give you two months off every year." He tried to give his old charming smile. "Forget our night together, and I'll forgive your infatuation. So long as it ends now."

She shook her head. "I'm done working for you."

"And there's nothing I can do to change your mind?"

The deep, sexy timbre of his voice caused a shudder to

pass through her body, all the way to her fingertips. She forced herself to ignore it.

"I can't change your nature," she choked out. "And you can't change mine. There is nothing either of us can do." She looked away. "Please ask Arthur to cut my last paycheck. I'll pick it up on the way to St. Pancras."

"St. Pancras?"

"I'm taking the train to Paris." She licked her lips. "For a new job."

He stared at her.

"You're not even giving me two weeks' notice?"

"Sorry," she mumbled.

Silence fell between them. In the distance, she heard the sounds of a police siren, with its European sound, so different from New York's.

"It seems I've been an awful boss to you these past years." Something in Cesare's tone made her look up. From where he stood on the other side of the bed, his handsome face was half-hidden in shadow. "Let me save you the trouble of a trip to the office. I'll pay you now."

"It's not necessary."

"But it is," he said coldly. In his long-sleeved black shirt and trousers, he looked sophisticated, like the international tycoon he was. But the power of his muscled shoulders and cold fury in his black eyes were anything but civilized. "Here."

Pulling a handful of fifty-pound bills out of his wallet, he tossed them toward her. Wide-eyed, Emma watched them float like feathers to the bed.

"Your paycheck," he said grimly. Reaching back into his wallet, he threw out American money next. "The vacation time you refused to take." He tossed out Euro notes. "Your Christmas bonus." Then Japanese yen. "Overtime."

Dirhams and Russian rubles flew next. "The raise I should have given you."

Shocked, Emma watched the blizzard of money fall like snowflakes onto the bed, a flurry of money from all over the world, pesos and reals and kroner, dollars from Canada and Australia.

Frowning, Cesare suddenly looked into his wallet. Empty. It seemed even billionaires had a limit to ready cash. Pulling the platinum watch off his tanned wrist, he dumped it on the bed, on top of the Matterhorn of money.

"There," he said coldly. "Will that compensate you for all the anguish you suffered working for me? Are we done?"

She swallowed. Even now, in his generosity, he was being cruel—using his wealth as a weapon against her. Making her feel small.

"Yes," she choked out. "We're done."

"So you're no longer my employee. As of this moment."

Head held high, Emma walked toward the money on the bed. *Just take it,* she told herself. She had earned that money—all of it and more! The money he'd tossed at her so carelessly was nothing to him, barely more than he might spend impulsively on an amusing night out, buying thousand-pound bottles of scotch for all his rich friends.

But still. There was something truly awful about reaching for a pile of money left on her bed. Something sordid.

She tried to force herself forward, then stiffened. She exhaled, pulling back her hand.

"What's wrong now?"

"I can't take it," she said. "Not like this."

He slowly walked around the bed toward her. "It's yours. You earned it."

"Earned it how?" she whispered.

"For God's sake, Emma!"

She whirled back to him. "I can't take it off the *bed*. As if I were your…"

She couldn't say the word, but he did.

"My whore?" Cesare came toward her, his dark eyes like fire. "You are driving me insane," he ground out. "If you do not want the money, then leave it. If you are so determined to go, then go. I don't give a damn what you do."

"You've made that painfully clear," she said hoarsely.

"And you," he snarled, "have made it clear that there is no way I can win. You think I'm a selfish bastard, you hate me, you hate yourself for your so-called *love* for me. You're sick of the sight of me and you're using our night together as an excuse to quit."

She sucked in her breath.

"An *excuse?*" It was humiliating how her voice squeaked on the word.

"Yes." Cesare was close to her now, very close. She was suddenly very aware that she was wearing almost nothing and they were alone in her dark bedroom. Her nipples were hard beneath her white lace bra. Her own breathing seemed loud in her ears. His powerful body towered over hers, and she could feel the warmth emanating off his skin. The heat in his gaze scared her—almost as much as the answering heat in her own body. He said in a low voice, "You're running away from me like a coward."

She gasped, "Are you kidding? *I'm* running like a coward?"

Cesare's hand reached out to touch her cheek, and as she felt his fingertips against her skin, it was all she could do not to turn her face into the warmth of his caress, even now. "You mean nothing to me, Emma," he growled. His dark eyes burned through her. "You never have. You never will."

"Good," she choked out. "Because I can hardly wait

to leave you. I'm so happy that after tonight I'll never see you again…."

His hand trailed down her cheek, to her neck, to her bare shoulder. She barely heard his harsh intake of breath over the pounding of her own heart. She trembled, knowing she was on the knife's edge.

Cesare roughly seized her in his arms, and crushed her lips with his own.

CHAPTER THREE

CESARE'S KISS WAS angry and searing. His lips plundered hers, and all her anger and grief and pain seemed to explode beneath the fire of his touch, into an inferno.

He wrapped a strong arm around her waist, holding her tight against him, and his other hand ran along her bare arm, up her shoulder, down her naked back. She felt his body, hard against hers, and against her will a soft moan came from the back of her throat. Her skin felt scorched everywhere he touched. She was desperate to have him closer.

Now.

Her hand cupped the rough edge of his jawline, then moved back to tangle in his dark hair, pulling his mouth harder and deeper into hers.

She heard his hoarse intake of breath as he cupped her full, aching breasts over the lace of her bra. She was overflowing the cups now, and her belly was starting to get fuller as well. Would he notice? Would he guess? Would Cesare be able to see how he'd permanently branded her body as his, always and forever, without her saying a single word?

"All this time, I've been hating myself for a lack of self-control," he said in a low voice. "Now I can hardly believe I had such restraint." He lifted his gaze to hers, even as one of his hands slowly stroked her nearly naked body, over her white lace, causing her to tremble with need. "I can't believe I waited so long." His sensual lips curved as he cupped her face, tilting back her head. "No other woman has even interested me since that night...."

Her lips parted. No. Surely he couldn't mean what she thought he meant....

With their bodies so close, standing together beside her bed, she felt his warmth and strength. She breathed in the bare hint of masculine cologne. She felt the electricity of his words, of his touch—the overwhelming sensual force of his complete attention. And Emma's only defense, anger, crumbled.

He kissed her softly, briefly, butterfly kisses to each of her cheeks, tantalizingly close to the corners of her mouth. But hope, like a fragile spring bud unfolding in the snow, began to build inside her. She could hardly believe his shocking confession.

He'd been faithful....

"There's really been no other woman for you since our night?" she breathed.

He shook his head, his eyes dark. "Has there been someone for you?"

The question made her choke out a laugh. "How could there be?"

"Does that mean no?"

"Of course not!"

"Good."

His sudden masculine smugness irritated her. "You admit something, too," she said sharply.

"What?"

"You didn't seduce me three months ago just because I was crying. You weren't just trying to comfort me."

He stared at her, then said quietly, "No."

Her soul thrilled at the concession. She gloried in it. "You wanted me, too."

He spoke a single grudging word, as if it were pulled from deep inside him. "Yes."

"For how long?"

"Years," he bit out.

"Why didn't you tell me?" she whispered.

"I was afraid you'd do exactly what you did today." His hands undid the plaits of her braids, causing her long dark hair to fall down her back. She trembled as his hands stroked her long, tumbling waves of hair. "You'd get some crazy delusion of loving me, and then I'd have to fire you."

"I am in love with you."

He snorted. "If you really loved me, wouldn't you be begging me to stay?"

"Because begging works so well with you."

Slowly he lowered his head until his mouth was inches from hers.

"It's just lust, *cara*," he whispered, his lips almost brushing hers. "Not love...."

And holding her against his hard body in the shadowy bedroom, he kissed her, clutching her as if he were a drowning man and only she could save him. His lips plundered hers, teasing, gentling, searing.

As they stood together, he slowly kissed down her throat, his fingertips roaming softly over her naked skin. She felt the warmth of his hands cupping her breasts, stroking tight, aching nipples that peeked through white lace.

Leaning back in his arms, she gasped with pleasure and need. Until she lost her balance, and fell back against the bed, his arms still around her, their bodies entangled in their embrace.

The bed felt made of feathers beneath her. Still in her bra and panties, Emma slid against the duvet cover, and felt something sharp and cold beneath her thigh. She pulled it out and looked at the shining platinum face with confusion. "Your watch."

"Forget it." Taking it from her hand, he tossed the expensive watch across the room, causing it to scatter noisily across the hardwood floor before it hit the wall with a soft thunk.

She realized what the "feathers" she'd felt beneath her body actually had to be. Twisting, she tried to look beneath her. She was lying almost naked beneath him *on a bed of money.* "Everything's still on the bed—"

"I don't care," he said roughly, and kissed her, until she forgot about the money, and wouldn't have cared if she did.

Pulling away, he pulled off his shirt in an abrupt movement. Emma's throat constricted as she reached out to touch the intoxicating vision of his naked chest, muscular and hard, with tanned skin that felt like silk over steel. She stroked down to the flat six-pack of his belly, laced with a scattering of dark hair. He was flesh and blood, this man she'd wanted so hopelessly, and loved for so long.

Covering her body with his own, Cesare kissed her. She felt his weight crushing her breasts, felt the slide of his warm bare skin against her own. He released the clasp of her bra and pulled off the slip of white lace, tossing it aside. He pulled her panties slowly past her hips, over her thighs, down her legs.

She was naked beneath him. Lying on a pile of money. She shouldn't be doing this, she thought. Then he pulled off his pants and silk boxers, and rational thought left her entirely.

She gasped as she saw how large he was, how huge and hard. Slowly, he kissed down her body, licking and suckling her breasts. He caressed down the curve of her belly, then kissed her lips in a long, deep embrace that

seemed to last forever, until she forgot where she ended
and he began. Their bodies fused together in heat, skin to
skin, slick and salty and sweet. Moving down her body, he
pushed her legs apart with his knee, spreading them wide
with his hands. Lowering his head, he nuzzled between
her thighs. She felt his hot breath.

She gasped as, holding her hips firmly against the bed,
he spread her wide and tasted her.

She twisted, rocking beneath him. The pleasure was too
sharp, too explosive. Beneath the ruthless insistence of his
tongue, she trembled and shook, gasping on the bed. Every
time she moved, money went flying into the air. Durhams
and dollars, pounds and pesos flew violently, then fell back
softly like snow, sliding down the naked bodies clutched
together on the bed.

The money felt whisper-soft, brushing against Emma's
face or shoulder or breast while she felt the hard, bristly
roughness of his masculine body between her legs.

"Lust," Cesare said in a low voice.

Their eyes locked over the curves of her naked body.
She shook her head.

"Love…"

With a low growl, he lowered his head back between
her legs. She felt the heat of his breath on her tender skin,
and his tongue took another wide taste of her, then another.
Slowly he caressed her, licking her in delicate swirls until
her breathing came in gasps and her hands were gripping
the bedsheets beneath her, along with fistfuls of yen and
euros.

"Lust," he whispered against her skin.

"No," she choked out.

He thrust his tongue an inch inside her. She gave a
shocked gasp in a voice she hardly recognized as her

own. His hands roamed possessively over her, cupping her breasts, her waist, her hips. Reaching beneath her, he pressed her bottom upward, lifting her more firmly against his mouth, and impaled her more deeply with his tongue. His lips and soft wet tongue suckled the aching center of her need as he moved two thick fingertips inside her, where his tongue had been. She cried out, overwhelmed by the intensity of pleasure.

Her back arched from the feel of his fingers inside her and his tongue swirling over her and she gripped his shoulders as waves of ecstasy started to pull reality beneath her feet, crashing over her. She exploded, and as if from a distance, she heard herself scream—

Rolling beside her, he pulled her into the warm haven of his arms. Emma looked up at him with tears in her eyes.

It wasn't just lust between them. It *wasn't*.

If he'd only just give her a chance. If only he'd say something that would make her think she could tell him about the baby...

Leaning up, Emma put her hand on his cheek and kissed him in a deep, lingering embrace that left her chin and cheeks tingling from the rough bristles of his jaw. She could still feel his body straining against her. As he kissed her back, holding her tight, breathless hope ripped through her. She could show him he had nothing to fear. That their relationship could be so much more than lust. She knew the man he really was, yes. But she also knew the man he could be....

"Love," she whispered silently against his lips.

Emma abruptly rolled him beneath her on the bed. He looked up at her, surprised. She smiled, her soul welling up with sudden certain joy. If he wouldn't let her speak words of love...

She would show him.

* * *

Cesare stared up at the woman who'd just rolled him beneath her on the bed. He felt Emma's hands stroke down his chest, as her legs straddled his hips.

She was so impossibly beautiful, he thought, dazzled by the pink flush of her creamy skin, the emerald gleam of her eyes. She looked down at him fiercely, like an ancient warrior queen who commanded an army of thousands eager to die in her name. Power emanated from her proud, curvaceous body like light. Power he'd never seen in her before.

"Emma," he breathed. "What's gotten into you?"

"Haven't you figured it out?" Her full red lips curved into a smile as she lowered her head. She whispered against his mouth, "You have."

She kissed him, and he felt that something had changed in her. Something he didn't understand. She seemed—different. New. Beneath her touch, sparks flew up and down his body, a fire that burned him to blood and bone.

He'd wanted her for months. Years. But never like this. His body shook with need. She'd never, ever made the first move before.

He could hardly believe he'd once thought of Emma as having no feelings. This was who she really was: a seductive sex goddess, innocent and wanton, powerful and glorious…

As her lips caressed his, her long dark hair tumbled over his body, sliding over his overheated skin. Her full breasts brushed against his chest. With a moan, he cupped them with his hands. Breaking off their kiss, he wrenched his head to suckle a taut, pink nipple, licking it, pulling it into his mouth. His hand tangled in her hair, stroking down her naked back. He heard her moan. Felt her thighs tighten around his hips. He felt the soft, wet core of her brush the tip of his hardest edge as she swayed in innocently tantalizing torture.

Twisting away with a choked gasp, he started to reach for the wallet in his jacket hanging on a nearby chair, intending to retrieve a condom, but she stopped him.

"It's not necessary." She hesitated, then said slowly, "This time because I'm actually—"

"You're still on the Pill?" He exhaled. "Thank God." She stiffened, and he wondered if he'd said something rude, though he couldn't imagine what. Women could be sensitive, and even though Emma was the most rational woman he knew, she was still undeniably a woman. Oh, yes. Running his hand down the curve of her bare breast—even fuller than he remembered—he looked up at her with heavy-lidded eyes. "I love that you are always prepared, Miss Hayes."

She leaned forward, allowing her long dark hair to trail sensuously across his bare chest as she said pointedly, "Emma."

"Emma," he groaned as her fingertips trailed down his body. "Oh, God—Emma—"

Reaching up, he kissed her, and as she leaned down to kiss him back, he could wait no longer. Pulling her down on him with his hands, he simultaneously thrust up with his hips, pushing inside her, and heard her gasp as he filled her soft, wet body.

God. He'd never felt anything like this. He rammed inside her, filling her hard and deep. She slid over his hips, riding him, and his whole body started to tighten. No. No, it was too soon. The intensity of pleasure was too much. But being inside her without a condom…skin to skin…

He gripped her shoulders. "I'm not sure how long I can last," he said hoarsely. "Give me… Give me a minute to…"

But it seemed Emma's days of obedience were over. She

continued to slide against him. He looked up, intending to protest. He stopped when he saw how her eyes were closed, her beautiful face rapt and shining in ecstasy.

No! He squeezed his eyes shut. He couldn't see her like that! Not when at any moment he could... He could... But even with his eyes closed, he could still see her shining face, see her full breasts swaying above him as she moved. He felt tighter—tighter—about to explode...

"You feel so good," she whispered. "So—good..."

"Oh, my God," he said in a strangled voice. "Stop!"

Gripping his shoulders, she leaned forward, so close he could feel the brush of her lips against his earlobe, and whispered, "Love."

It was the one thing that made him cold.

"Lust," he growled back, and flung his body over hers, lying her beneath him on the bed. He ran his hands down her body, licking and sucking every inch of her skin. Sitting back against the pillows, he pulled her into his lap, wrapping his arms around her.

Tangling his hands in her hair, he tilted back her head and kissed her deeply. Lifting up her body, he lowered her hips heavily against him, thrusting slowly inside her. He rocked against her, controlling the rhythm and speed, slowing down when he came too close to exploding. Face-to-face, breath to breath, their eyes locked, their arms wrapped around each other, as close as two lovers could possibly be. He made love to her for what felt like hours until finally she gasped against him one more time, closing her eyes with a cry.

Cesare could hold back no longer. Kissing her shoulder, he sucked hard against her skin, and let himself go. He thrust inside her four times, so deep and hard that he exploded, so close to heaven that he saw only stars.

He saw only *her.*

Exhaling, he collapsed, still holding her tight.

It took long moments for Cesare to fall back to earth. He slowly became aware of the ticking of the old antique clock on the mantel. Blinking in the darkness, he saw he was in Emma's bed, in her suite of rooms on the second floor of his Kensington house. Moonlight was creeping in through the edges of the window shades as he still cradled her in his arms. He felt her cheek against his chest. Against his heart.

He shifted, cuddling her in the crook of his arm, her naked body against his own. He saw a small mark on her shoulder, where he'd sucked a little too hard in a love bite. That would leave a bruise, he thought. He'd marked her as his own. And for some reason he didn't want to examine, he was glad.

Emma blinked, smiling up at him sleepily before she glanced down at the bed. "What a mess we've made."

He looked down. The duvet and sheets were twisted at their feet and there were banknotes *everywhere*.

Cesare prided himself on discipline. He'd tried to do the sensible thing with Emma, to make them both forget their intoxicating night and return to their employer-employee relationship.

He'd failed. Massively.

And he was glad.

Now they could both have what they actually wanted. Yes, his home might fall apart without her in charge. At the moment he didn't give a damn. Who cared about milk in the fridge or having his bed made perfectly? Who cared about it being made at all, so long as he had her in it?

Emma yawned, her eyes closing as she settled deeper into his arms. Leaning forward, he kissed her softly on the temple. His own eyelids were heavy.

As she drowsed in his arms, he still shuddered with aftershocks of pleasure from their lovemaking. Making love without a condom, to a woman he liked and trusted, was a wholly new experience.

He'd certainly never had it with his wife.

Cesare looked down at Emma's face, half-hidden in shadow as she slept in his arms. She looked like a slumbering angel, her black eyelashes stark against her pale skin, and masses of her long, glossy dark hair tumbling over the pillow.

He felt exhausted, utterly spent. But as he closed his eyes, he smiled. He'd proved his point, and he was suddenly glad Emma had quit her job with him. That meant she'd be available for full-time pleasure. Their relationship might last for weeks, even months, now she understood there was no love involved. There would be no arguments, no goals of marriage or children to fight over. They could just enjoy each other's company for as long as the pleasure lasted.... He fell asleep, smiling and warm.

When he woke, the shadows of the room had changed to the soft gray light of dawn. Emma was stirring in his arms. He saw she was looking up at him with big, limpid eyes.

"Good morning," she said shyly.

Cesare stroked her cheek with amusement. "Good morning."

She bit her lip. "Um. If you want to go sleep in your own room, I'll understand...."

He placed a finger to her lips, gently stopping her. "I don't."

Her expression suddenly glowed. "You don't?"

He didn't blame her for being surprised. He was somewhat surprised himself. Usually he couldn't wait to get out of a woman's bed the morning after. He usually left long before morning, in fact.

But he felt oddly comfortable with Emma. He didn't

need to pretend with her, or play games, or be polite. It was strange, but he felt like he could just be himself, without trying to hide his flaws. How could he hide them? She knew them all.

"I'm hungry," Emma confessed, sitting up. "I can't stop thinking about fried eggs and bacon and oranges…"

Cesare kissed her bare shoulder. He was not thinking about food. "We could go down to the kitchen." He let his fingertips trail over her breast. "Or we could have a little breakfast in bed first…."

"Yes," she whispered, lifting her lips toward his. He stroked back her wildly tousled black hair.

"I'm so glad you came to your senses," he murmured as he kissed her.

She drew back with a frown. "My senses?"

He smiled, twisting a long black tendril of her hair around his finger. "You are going to be a very enjoyable bit of carry-on baggage."

"Oh, so now I'm baggage, am I?"

"I've decided you were right."

Her green eyes suddenly shone. "You did?"

"I'm glad you quit," he said lazily, running the pad of his thumb over her nipple, for the masculine pleasure of watching it instantly pebble beneath his touch. "I need to be in Asia tomorrow, Berlin on Friday."

Lifting a dark eyebrow, she said lightly, "And I need to take that job in Paris."

"You're thinking about your job?" He snorted. "I want you to come with me."

"Give up my career to do what—just hang out in your bed?"

"Can you think of a better idea?"

"I like my career." Her voice had a new edge to it. "I'm good at it."

"Of course you are. The best," he said soothingly. He hadn't meant to insult her. "But I'll cover your expenses while you're with me. We can just both enjoy ourselves. For however long this lasts."

"Are you joking?" She sounded almost angry.

Cesare was still waiting for her burst of excited joy and arms to be thrown around him at the brilliance of his plan. Her joy didn't seem to be forthcoming. "Don't you understand what I'm offering you, Emma?"

"I must not," she said. "Because it sounds like you expect me to drop everything for you, when all you want is sex."

"Sex with *you*," he pointed out. He would have thought that would be obvious. "And friendship," he added as an afterthought. "It'll be…fun."

"Fun?" she said in a strangled voice.

"What's wrong with that?"

"Nothing. Wow. It's the answer to all my childhood dreams. *Fun.*"

He was starting to grow irritated "You can throw away your mop and broom. No more twenty-four-hour days with a jerk for a boss." He tried to laugh, but she didn't join him at the joke. He continued weakly, "You'll travel with me—see the world…"

Pulling away from him entirely, she looked at him in the gray dawn.

"For how long?" she said quietly.

"How should I know?" Sitting up straighter against the headboard, he folded his arms grumpily. "For as long as we're enjoying ourselves."

"And you'll kindly pay me for my time."

He ground his jaw. "You're twisting this all around, making it sound like I'm trying to insult you. Why aren't you happy? You should be happy—I've never offered any woman so much!"

She rebelliously lifted her eyes. "We both know that's not true."

A cold chill went down his spine. "You're talking about my wife."

She didn't answer. She didn't have to.

"Christo." Cesare clawed back his hair. This couldn't be happening. "We've been together only two nights, I've barely asked you to be my mistress, and you're already pressuring me to marry you?"

"I didn't say that!"

"You don't have to." He could see it in her face: that terrible repressed hope. The same expression he'd seen in so many women's faces. The desire to pin him down, to hold him against his will, in a place he didn't want to be. To make iron chains of duty and honor replace delight or even pleasure.

"You did get married once. You must have had a reason."

Anger rushed through him. The memory of Alain Bouchard's hateful voice. *You married my sister for her money and then made her life a living hell. Is it any wonder she took the pills? You might as well have poured them down her throat.*

Cesare's lips parted to lash out. Then he forced himself to focus on Emma's lovely, wistful face. It wasn't her fault. He choked back furious, hateful words.

"I married for love once," he said flatly. "I'll never do it again."

"Because you still love her," she whispered. "Your wife."

Cesare could see what Emma believed. That he'd loved Angélique so much that even a decade hadn't been enough to get over the grief of losing her. He let it pass, as he always did. The beautiful, simple lie was so much better than the truth.

He set his jaw, facing her across the bed, not touching. Just moments before, they'd been so close. Now an ocean divided them.

"I thought I made myself clear. But it wasn't enough. So hear this." He looked at her. "I will never love you, Emma. I will never marry you. I will never want to have a child with you. Ever."

In the rising pink dawn, every ounce of color drained from Emma's beautiful, plump-cheeked face, causing the powerful light of joy to disappear, as if it had never existed.

It was hard to watch. Cesare took a steadying breath. He had to be cruel to be kind. If they were to be together, even for just a few weeks, she had to accept these things from the beginning.

"My feelings in this matter will never change," he said quietly. "I thought you understood. I thought you felt the same." He reached for her hand, trembling where it rested on the bed. "Lust."

In a flash of anguish, her luminous eyes lifted to his. She shook her head. His eyes narrowed.

"You must accept this," he said, "for us to have any future."

A low, bitter laugh bubbled to her lips—the most bitter thing he'd ever heard from her. She ripped her hand away. "Future? No love, no marriage, no child. What kind of future is that?"

His jaw tightened. "The kind that is real. No promises to be broken. No pretense. No fakery. We just take it day by day, enjoying each other's company, taking pleasure for as long as it lasts."

"And then what?"

"We part as friends." He looked at her. "I don't want to lose your friendship."

"My friendship?" Her lip curled. "Or my services?"

"Emma!"

"You want to stop paying me as your housekeeper, and hire me straight out as your whore. No, I get it." Holding up her hand, she said coldly, "I'm sorry, this is awkward for you, isn't it? Usually I'm the one who handles this, who puts out your trash the morning after." She looked past the tangled mess of bedcovers at the foot of the bed, still surrounded by an explosion of money, to his platinum watch lying on the floor. "You even gave me a watch. Just like all the rest."

His own personal watch was even more expensive than the Cartier ones, but he sensed telling her that wouldn't impress her. "Emma, you're being idiotic...."

"I really am just like the rest." She threw the sheets aside and stood up from the bed. "I'll just collect my things and buy myself some roses on the high street, shall I?"

But as she started to walk away from the bed, Cesare grabbed her wrist.

"Don't do this," he said in a low voice.

"Do what?"

"This." He looked up at her, his eyes glittering. "I want you in my bed. For now. For as long as it's fun for both of us. Can't that be enough? Why do you need false promises of more? Why can't you just accept what I freely offer you?"

Their eyes locked. He could see the pain in her gaze.

"I want more. I want it all," she whispered. "Love. Marriage." She swallowed, looking up at him. "I want a baby. Our baby."

The air around him suddenly felt thin. He shrank back from her words. Literally. "Emma..."

"I don't need a wedding proposal. Or for you to say you're ready to be a father." Her eyes met his. "I just need to know you might want those things someday." She blinked fast. "That you might be open to the possibility… if something ever…"

"No," Cesare choked out. Still naked, he scrambled back on the bed, putting his hand to his neck, feeling as if he had something tight around his throat. He took a deep breath, forcing his hands down, trying to calm down, to breathe. "Either this is a fun diversion, a friendship with benefits, or it's nothing. You decide."

She stared at him for a long moment, her face as pale as marble. Then, violently, she grabbed her white bra and panties off the floor and yanked them on her body. Walking to her closet, she pulled out big armfuls of clothes. "What was I thinking—" she kicked open her old suitcase "—to believe—" she tossed the clothes inside "—in miracles!"

Cesare rose to his feet. Still naked, he padded across the hardwood floor. Without her warmth next to him, the bedroom felt chilly in the autumn morning. He heard traffic noise from the street outside. Soon, the house's day staff would arrive. He desperately wanted this settled before they were interrupted. He felt Emma was slipping away from him. He didn't understand why. With a deep breath, he tried once more.

"Why are you throwing everything away for the sake of some distant future? Think about today." Wrapping his arms around her waist from behind, he nuzzled the side of her neck and said in a low voice, "Let tomorrow take care of itself.…"

Her skin was cold to the touch. She pulled away. Her beautiful face looked more than forlorn now—she looked frozen.

He sucked in his breath. He searched her face. "You're still going to leave, aren't you," he breathed. "You're still going to throw everything away for dreams of love, marriage and children. For a *delusion*. I can't believe you'd be such a…"

Emma's eyes were stony. She looked as if her soul had been shattered.

"…fool?" she finished.

He gave a single stiff nod.

She shook her head, wiping her eyes. "You're right. I have been a fool. A stupid romantic fool who believed a man like you could ever change."

Kneeling down, she gathered all the piles of money off the floor and dumped it into her suitcase. Picking up the platinum watch, she tossed it inside, then closed the suitcase with a bang. She looked down.

"Thank you for your offer," she said in a low voice. "I'm sure some other woman will take you up on it." She looked up, her eyes luminous with tears. "But I'm going to have a baby, and a home. And a man who loves us both."

Her words, spoken with such finality, hit him like a blow. He'd just offered Emma more than he'd offered any woman in ten years. And this was his reward for letting himself be vulnerable. Though he stood in front of Emma right now in flesh and blood, she was still rejecting him for some ridiculous fantasy of love and a child.

Something Cesare hadn't felt in a long, long time— something he'd thought he would never feel again—sliced through his heart.

Hurt.

His arms dropped. He stepped back.

"Bene," he said stiffly. "Go."

She pulled on jeans and a T-shirt. She picked up a few errant fifty-dollar banknotes off the floor and tucked them securely in her pocket, then lifted her chin. "Don't worry. I won't bother you again. I'll leave you alone to live the life you want. I give you my word." She held out her hand as if they were strangers. "Goodbye, Cesare."

His lips tightened, but he shook her hand.

"*Arrivederci,* Signorina Hayes. I hope you find what you're looking for."

Her green eyes shimmered, and she turned away without a word. Gathering her suitcase, her coat and her bag, Emma left the tidy bedroom. Cesare listened to her suitcase *thump, thump, thump* down his stairs. He listened to the front door open—and then latch closed.

She'd really gone. He couldn't believe it.

Going to the window, he looked down and watched her walk away, down the sidewalk toward Kensington High Street, in the drizzling rain of London's gray morning. He watched her small, forlorn figure with an old suitcase and a beige mackintosh, and felt a strange twist in his chest.

It's better this way, he told himself fiercely. Better for her to go, before the small hole in his heart had a chance to grow any larger. He watched her get smaller and smaller.

"Go," Cesare said aloud in the empty room. "You mean nothing to me."

But still, his hands tightened at his sides. *She'll be back,* he thought suddenly. No woman he wanted had ever been able to resist for long. And the sex had been too good between them. Emma wouldn't be able to stay away.

She'd soon be back, begging to negotiate the terms of her surrender. He exhaled, his shoulders relaxing. He allowed himself a smile. She'd be back. He knew it.

Within the week, if not the day.

CHAPTER FOUR

Ten months later

CESARE LOOKED OUT the window as his driver pulled the Rolls-Royce smoothly through the traffic of the Quai Branly, past the Pont de l'Alma. The September sun was sparkling like diamonds on the Seine.

Paris was not Cesare's favorite city. Yes, the city was justly famous for its beauty, but it was also aloof and proud. Like a coquette. Like a cold, distant star. Like his late wife, Angélique, who was born here—and took her lover here, a scant year after their marriage.

Sì. He had reason to dislike Paris. Since his wife's death over a decade before, he'd avoided the city. But now he was building a Falconeri Hotel here, upon the demand of his shareholders.

But Paris had changed since his last visit, he realized. The city felt…different.

Cesare looked up at the elegant classical architecture of cream-colored buildings. Through the vivid yellows and reds of the trees, the golden sun was bright in the blue sky. The city had a new warmth and charm he'd never felt before.

Because we finished the business deal, he told himself. After months of mind-numbing negotiations, his team had finally completed the purchase of an old, family-run hotel on the Avenue Montaigne, which—after it was exhaustively remodeled—would become the first Falconeri Hotel in France. *I'm just pleased about the deal.*

But he shifted in his leather seat. Even he didn't buy that.

Closing his eyes, he felt the sun on his skin. Against his will, he thought of her, and his body flashed with heat that had nothing to do with sunlight.

Emma lived in Paris.

You don't know that, he told himself fiercely. It had been almost a year since she'd left him in London that dreary November morning. For all he knew, she'd moved on to another job, another city. For all he knew, she'd changed her mind and never taken a job in Paris at all. For all he knew, she'd found another lover, a man who would love and marry her and be willing to have a child with her, just as she'd wanted.

For all he knew, she was already his wife. Pregnant with his child.

Cesare's hands tightened involuntarily.

For ten months, he'd made a point of not knowing where Emma was or whom she was with. He'd told himself he didn't care. At first, he'd been sure she'd soon return. It had taken him months to finally accept she wasn't coming back. Cesare knew she'd wanted him, as he wanted her. He'd been surprised to discover she'd wanted her dreams even more.

He'd been furious, hurt; and yet he'd respected her the more for it. She was the one who'd gotten away. The one he couldn't have. But she'd made the right choice. They wanted different things in life. Emma wanted a love, a home, a husband and a family of her own.

Cesare wanted—

What was it he wanted?

He tapped his fingers on the leather armrest as he stared out at the sparkling river. More, he supposed. More money. More hotels. More success for his company. More, more, more of the same, same, same.

His PR firm would soon announce how absolutely ecstatic the Falconeri Group was to finally have a hotel in this spectacular French city. His lips twisted. Well, Cesare would be ecstatic to leave it. This magical city seemed to have a strange power to steal any woman he actually tried to keep for longer than a night.

He wondered suddenly if Emma's dreams had been haunted, as his had been. Or if all she felt for him now was indifference. If she'd forgotten him entirely. If he alone was cursed with the inability to forget.

His driver stopped at a red light. Resentfully Cesare watched smiling tourists cross the street, walking from the popular *bateaux* of the Seine to the nearby Eiffel Tower. He still saw Emma in his dreams at night. Still felt her breath against his skin. Still heard her voice. Even by the light of day—hell, even now—his feverish imagination...

Cesare's eyes widened as he saw a woman crossing the street. She passed by quickly, before he could see her face. But he saw the black, glossy hair tumbling down her shoulders, saw the way her hips swayed and the luscious curve of her petite frame as she walked away from him. No. It couldn't be her. This woman was pushing a baby stroller. No, he was imagining things. Paris was a city of over two million people. There was no way that...

Cesare gripped the headrest of the seat in front of him.

"Stop the car," he said softly.

The chauffeur frowned, looking at Cesare in the rearview mirror. "Monsieur?" he said, sounding puzzled.

When the light turned green, he drove the Rolls-Royce forward with traffic.

Cesare watched the woman continue walking away. It couldn't be Emma for a million reasons, the most obvious being the stroller.

Unless she'd really meant what she said about finding a man who would give her a child, and she'd done it in a hurry.

I'm going to have a baby. And a home. And a man who loves us both.

Watching her disappear down the street, he remembered the cold, gray morning last November, when he'd watched Emma walk down Hornton Street. He'd been so sure she'd come back. She never had. Not a message. Not a word.

He watched this woman go, with one last sway of her hips, one last shimmering beam of sunlight on her long, glossy black hair, before she turned toward the Champ de Mars. Disappearing…again…

Cesare twisted his head savagely toward the driver. "Damn you!" he exploded. "I said stop!"

Looking a little frightened, the driver immediately plunged through traffic to the side of the road. The Rolls-Royce hadn't even completely stopped before Cesare opened the door and flung himself on the sidewalk, causing several pedestrians to scatter. People stared at Cesare like he was crazy.

He felt crazy. He turned his head right and left as he started to run, getting honked at angrily by a tour bus as he crossed the street.

Where was the dark-haired woman? Had he lost her? Had it been Emma? He clawed his dark hair back, looking around frantically.

"Attention—monsieur!"

He moved just in time to avoid getting run over by a

baby carriage pushed by a gray-haired woman dressed in Gucci. *"Excusez-moi, madame,"* he murmured. She shook her head in irritation, huffing. Even Parisian grandmothers, even the *nannies,* wore designer clothes in this arrondissement.

He ran down the Avenue de la Bourdonnais, where he'd last seen her, and followed the crowds into the nearby park, the Champ de Mars, looking right and left, turning himself in circles. He walked beneath the shadow of the Eiffel Tower, past long queues of people. He walked down the paths of the park, past cheery couples and families having picnic lunches on this beautiful autumn day. Wearing his suit and tie, Cesare felt unbearably hot, running all over Paris in pursuit of a phantom from his past.

Cesare stopped.

He heard the soft whir of the wind through the trees, and looked up at the blue sky, through leaves that were a million different shades of green, yellow, orange. He heard the crunch of gravel beneath his feet. He heard children's laughter and music. In the distance, he saw a small outdoor snack stand, and beyond that, a playground with a merry-go-round.

What the hell was he doing?

Cesare clawed back his hair. *Basta.* Enough. Scowling, he walked to the snack stand and bought himself a coffee, then did something no true Parisian would ever do in a million years—he drank it as he walked. The black, scalding-hot coffee burned his tongue. He drank it all down, then tossed the empty cup in the trash. Grimly he reached into his pocket for his cell phone, to call his driver and get back on schedule, back to sanity, and return to the private airport on the east of the city where his jet waited. Walking, he lifted the cell phone to his ear. "Olivier, you can come get me at…"

He heard a woman gasp.

"Cesare?"

He froze.

Emma's voice. Her sweet voice.

"Sir?" his driver said at the other end of the line.

But Cesare's arm had already gone limp, the phone dropping to his side. Even now, he was telling himself that it wasn't her, it couldn't possibly be.

He turned.

"Emma," he whispered.

She was standing in front of a park bench, the stroller beside her. Her green eyes were wide and it seemed to Cesare in this moment like every bit of sunlight had fled the sky to caress her pink blouse, her brown slacks, her long black hair with a halo of brilliant golden light. The rest of the park faded from sight. There was only *her,* shining like a star, ripping through his cold soul like fire.

"It is you," she breathed. She blinked, looking back uneasily at the stroller before she turned back, biting her lip. "What are you...doing here?"

"I'm here..." His voice was rough. He cleared his throat. "On business."

"But you hate this city. I've heard you say so."

"I bought an old hotel on the Avenue Montaigne. Just this morning."

He'd somehow walked all the way to her without realizing it. His eyes drank her in hungrily. Her cheeks were fuller, her pale skin pink as roses. Her dark hair fell in tumbling soft waves over her shoulders. She'd put on a little weight, he saw, and it suited her well. The womanly softness made her even more beautiful, something he wouldn't have thought possible.

"It's—a surprise to see you," she faltered.

"Yes." His eyes fell on a dark-haired, fat-cheeked baby

sleeping in the stroller. Who was this baby? Perhaps the child of her employer? Or could it possibly be...hers? His gaze quickly fell to her left hand. No wedding ring.

So the baby couldn't be hers, then. She'd been very specific about what she'd said she wanted. *A husband, a home, a baby.* She surely wouldn't have settled for less—not after she'd left him for the sake of those dreams.

The pink in Emma's cheeks deepened. "You didn't come searching for me?"

His pride wanted him to say it was pure coincidence he'd stumbled upon her in the park. But he couldn't.

"I came to Paris for the deal," he said quietly. "But on my way out of town, I thought I saw you cross the street. And I couldn't leave without knowing if it was you."

They stood facing each other in the sunlit park, just inches away, not touching. He dimly heard birds sing in the trees above, the distant traffic of tour buses at the Eiffel Tower, the laughter of children at the merry-go-round.

"I was so sure you would return to me," he heard himself say in a low voice. "But you never did."

Her green eyes scorched through his heart. Then, in a voice almost too quiet to hear, she said, "I...couldn't."

"I know." Before he even realized what he was doing, he'd reached out a hand to her cheek.

Her skin was even softer than he remembered. He felt her shiver beneath his touch, and his body ignited. He wanted to take her in his arms, against his body, to kiss her hard and never let go.

Just moments before, he'd felt admiration about how she'd sacrificed the pleasure they might have had together, in order to pursue her true dreams. But in this instant, all those rational considerations were swept aside. He searched her gaze. "Did you ever wonder what we could have had?"

A shadow crossed her face.

"Of course I did."

He barely heard the noises around them, the soft coo of the baby, the chatter around them in a multitude of languages as tourists strolled by.

He'd missed her.

Not just her housekeeping skills. Nor even her sensual body.

Emma Hayes was the only woman he'd ever trusted. The only one he'd ever let himself care about, since the nightmare of his marriage so long ago.

Standing with Emma in this park in the center of Paris, Cesare would have given a million euros to see her smile at him the way she used to. To hear her voice gently mocking him, teasing him, putting him politely but firmly in his place. They'd had their own private language, he saw that now, and he suddenly realized how unusual that was. How special and rare.

No one called him on his arrogance anymore. No one else could challenge him with a single dimpled smile. No one kept him on his toes. Kept him breathless with longing.

He'd found a different housekeeper to keep his kitchen stocked and do his laundry. Perhaps, someday, he'd find a woman equally alluring to fill his bed. But who could fill the void that Emma had left in his life?

She'd been more than his housekeeper. More than his lover. She'd been his friend.

His hand moved down her neck to her shoulder. He felt her warmth through the soft pink fabric of her blouse.

"Come back to London with me," he said suddenly.

She blinked, then, glancing at her baby, she licked her lips. Her voice seemed hoarse as she asked, "Why?"

Cesare hesitated. If there was one thing he'd learned in life, it was that a man should never show weakness. Not even with a woman. *Especially* not with a woman. "The housekeeper I hired to replace you has been unsatisfactory."

"Oh." With a sigh, she looked down. "Sorry. I am working for someone else now. He's been good to me. I have no desire to leave him."

I have no desire to leave him. Cesare didn't like the sound of those words. He had a sudden surge of irrational jealousy for this unknown employer. He glanced back at the stroller. And who was this baby?

He said only, "I'll pay double what you're paid now."

Emma's eyes hardened. "We've already had this conversation, haven't we? I won't work for you at any price. It's not a question of money. We want different things. And we always will. You made that painfully clear to me in London."

The dark-haired baby gave an unhappy whimper from the stroller. Going down on one knee, she grabbed a pacifier from a big canvas bag and gave it to the baby, who instantly cheered up. She looked at the plump-cheeked, dark-eyed baby, then slowly rose to her feet, facing Cesare.

"Don't come looking for me again. Because nothing is going to change. And all you will bring us—all of us—is unhappiness."

Who was this baby? The question pounded in his heart. Her employer's? Emma's? But he couldn't ask. To ask the question would imply that he cared.

She stared at him for a moment, then turned away.

"I don't want you as my housekeeper," he said in a low voice. "The truth is...I miss you."

She looked back at him with an intake of breath, her lovely face stricken. She glanced at the baby in the stroller, who was simultaneously sucking like crazy on the pacifier, and trying to reach for his own feet. "I have other responsibilities now."

Cesare followed her gaze. The baby looked familiar somehow....

"I need a man I can trust. One I can count on to be permanent in my life. An equal partner. A father...for my baby."

For a moment, Cesare stared at her. Then as the meaning of her words sunk in, he literally staggered back. "*Your* baby?"

Emma nodded. Her eyes looked troubled, her expression filled with worry.

He could understand why.

"So much for all your big dreams," he ground out. "You left me for the wedding ring and the white picket fence." He couldn't control the bitterness in his voice as he flung his arm toward her bare left hand. "Where is your ring?"

"My baby's father didn't want to marry me," she said quietly.

"So you gave yourself away to some playboy? Someone who couldn't even give what I offered?" Jealousy raced through him. Once again, the woman he'd wanted, the one he'd chosen—had thrown herself away on another man. His hands curled into fists and he took a deep breath, regaining control. "I thought better of you." He lifted his chin. "So who is the father? Let me guess. Your new boss?"

"No," she said in a low voice. Slowly she lifted her eyes to his. "My old one."

He snorted. "Your old—"

Cesare gave an intake of breath as he looked down at the chubby black-haired baby.

I don't need a wedding proposal. He heard the echo of her trembling voice from long ago. *Or for you to say you're ready to be a father. I just need to know you might want those things someday. That you might be open to the possibility...if something ever...*

And he'd told her no. Flat-out. *Either this is a fun diversion, a friendship with benefits, or it's nothing.*

I'm going to have a baby, she'd said then. He'd thought she was trying to pin down his future. He hadn't realized she'd been talking about the present.

Cesare stared down at the baby's familiar black eyes—the same eyes he looked at every day in the mirror—and his knees nearly gave way beneath him.

"It's me," he breathed. "I'm the father."

CHAPTER FIVE

EMMA'S HEART POUNDED as she waited for Cesare's reaction.

She couldn't believe this was happening. For the past ten months, she'd dreamed of this. She'd thought of him constantly as their baby grew inside her. The day Sam was born. And every day since.

But now, she was afraid.

Alain Bouchard had been a wonderful boss to Emma, looking out for her almost like a brother through the months of her pregnancy and the sleepless nights beyond. But Alain hated Cesare, his former brother-in-law, blaming him for his sister Angélique's death. For ten months, Emma had waited for this day to come, for Cesare to find out about the baby—and the identity of her employer.

Over the past year, as she walked through the streets of Paris doing Alain's errands, shopping for fresh fruit and meats in the outdoor market on the Rue Cler, whenever she'd seen a tall, broad-shouldered, dark-haired man, she held her breath. But it was never Cesare. He hated Paris. It was partly why she'd chosen this job.

So today, when she'd seen a tall, dark-haired man pacing across the park, looking around with a strange desperation, she'd forced herself to ignore her instincts, because they were always wrong. She'd simply sat on the bench as her baby dozed in his stroller, and felt the warmth of the

September sun on her skin. It had been almost a year since she'd last seen Cesare's face, since she'd last felt his touch. So much had happened. Their baby was no longer a tiny newborn. Sam had grown into a roly-poly four-month-old who could sleep seven hours at a stretch and loved to smile and laugh. Already, she could see his Italian heritage in his black eyes, the Falconeri blood.

But still, as Emma sat in the park, she hadn't been able to look away from the dark-haired man in a tailored suit, who seemed out of place as he stomped down the path, gulping down a coffee. She'd told herself her imagination was working overtime. It absolutely *was not* Cesare.

Then he'd walked past her, barking into his cell phone. She saw his face, heard his voice. And time stood still.

Then, without thought, she'd reacted, leaping to her feet, calling his name.

Now, as she looked up at him, the world seemed to spin, the tourists and trees and dark outline of the Eiffel Tower a blur against the sky. There was Cesare. Only Cesare.

For so long, she'd craved him, heart and soul. Cried for him at night, for the awful choice she'd had to make. He'd told her outright he didn't want a child, but she'd still struggled with whether she'd made an unforgivable mistake, not telling him. Twice she'd even picked up the phone.

Now he was just inches away from her, close enough to touch. All throughout their conversation, she'd glanced at their baby out of the corner of her eye. How could he not instantly see the resemblance? How could he not see little Sam in the stroller, and *know?*

Well, Cesare knew now.

"I'm the father," he breathed, looking from Sam to her.

"Yes." Emma felt a thrill in her heart even as a chill of fear went down her spine. "He's yours."

Cesare's dark eyes were shocked, his voice hoarse. "Why didn't you tell me?"

"I…"

"How could you not tell me?" Pacing back two steps, he clawed back his dark hair. Whirling back to face her, he accused, "You knew you were pregnant when you left London."

She nodded. His dark eyes were filled with fury.

"You lied to me."

"I didn't exactly lie. I said I was going to have a baby…."

He sucked in his breath, then glared at her. "I thought you meant *someday*. And you let me believe that. So *you lied*."

She licked her lips. "I wanted to tell you…"

"You were never on the Pill."

"I never said I was!"

His eyes narrowed. "You said—"

"I said I couldn't get pregnant," she cut him off. "I didn't think I could. When I was a teenager, I was—very sick—and my doctor said future pregnancy might be difficult, if not impossible. I never thought I could…" She lifted her gaze to his and whispered, "It's a miracle. Can't you see that? Our baby is a miracle."

"A miracle." Cesare glowered at her. "And you never thought you should share the miracle with me?"

"I wanted to. More than you can imagine." Emma set her jaw. "But you made it absolutely clear you didn't want a family."

"Did you get pregnant on purpose?" he demanded. "To force me to marry you?"

Emma couldn't help herself. She laughed in his face.

"Why are you laughing?" he said dangerously.

"Oh, I'm sorry. I thought you were making a joke."

"This isn't a joke!"

"No. It isn't. But *you* are!" she snapped, losing patience.

He blinked as his mouth fell open.

She took a deep calming breath, blowing a tendril of hair off her hot forehead. "I've gone out of my way not to trap you. I'm raising this baby completely on my own. I wouldn't marry you even if you asked me!"

"Really?"

She stiffened, remembering that she had indeed once yearned to marry him—even hinted at it aloud! Her cheeks burned with humiliation. She lifted her chin. "Maybe once I was stupid enough to want that, but I've long since realized you'd make a horrible husband. No sane woman would want to marry a man like you."

"A man like me," he repeated. He looked irritated. "So you'd rather be a housekeeper, slaving for wages, instead of a billionaire's wife?" He snorted. "Do you really expect me to believe that?"

She glared back at him. "And do *you* really believe I'd want to sell myself to some man who doesn't love me, when I can support myself and my child through honest work?"

"He's not just your child."

"You don't want him. You said so in London. Right to my face."

"That was different. You made it sound like a choice. You didn't tell me the decision was already made." He folded his arms, six feet three inches of broad-shouldered masculine stubbornness. "I want him tested. To have DNA evidence he's my child."

She ground her teeth. "You don't believe me?"

"The woman who swore she couldn't get pregnant? No."

Ooh. She stamped her foot. "I'm not having Sam pricked with a needle for some dumb DNA test. If you don't believe me, if you think I might have been sleeping around and now I'm lying just for kicks, then forget about us. Just leave. We'll do fine without you."

He clenched his hands at his sides. "You should have told me!"

"I tried to, but when I started hinting at the idea of a child, you nearly fainted with fear!"

"I absolutely did *not* faint—" he began furiously.

"You did! From the moment I found out I was pregnant, I wanted to tell you. Of course I wanted to tell you. What do you take me for? My parents were married straight out of high school and loved each other until my mom died. That's what people do in my hometown. Get married and stay married. Buy a home and raise a family. Do you honestly think—" Emma's voice grew louder, causing nearby people in the park to look at them "—that I wanted to be a single mother? That this is something I *chose?*"

Cesare looked astonished, his sensual lips slightly parted, his own tirade forgotten. Then he scowled.

"Don't even try to—"

"Even now," she interrupted, feeling the tears well up, "when I've just told you you're a father, what are you doing? You're yelling at me, when any other man on earth would be interested in—I don't know—meeting his new *son!*"

He stopped again, staring at her, his mouth still open. Then he snapped it shut. He glared at her. "Fine."

"Fine!"

Cesare turned to the baby. He knelt by the stroller. He looked into Sam's chubby face. As Emma watched, his eyes slowly traced over the baby's dark eyes; exactly like his own. At the same dark hair, already starting to curl.

"Um," he said, awkwardly holding out a hand toward the baby. "Hi."

The baby continued to suck the pacifier, but flung an

unsteady hand toward his father. One little pudgy hand caught his finger. Cesare's eyes widened and his expression changed. He moved closer to Sam, then gently stroked his hair, his plump cheek. His voice was different as he said more softly, "Hi."

Seeing the two of them together, Emma's heart twisted.

"You named him Sam?" he asked a moment later.

"After my dad."

"He looks just like me," Cesare muttered. Pulling away from the baby, he rose to his feet. "Just tell me one thing. If I hadn't come to Paris, if I hadn't seen you today—would you ever have told me?"

She swallowed.

"You really are unbelievable," he ground out.

"You don't want a family." Her voice trembled. "All you could have given him was money."

"And a *name*," he flung out.

"He already has both." She looked at him steadily. "I've given him a name—Samuel Hayes. And I earn enough money. Not for mansions and private jets, but enough for a comfortable home. We don't need you. We don't want you."

Cesare ground his teeth. "You're depriving him of his birthright."

She snorted. "Birthright? You mean you'd have insisted on sending him to a fancy school and buying him something extravagant and useless at Christmas, like a pony, before you ignored him the rest of the year?" She shook her head. "And that's the best-case scenario! Because let's not pretend you actually want to be in the picture!"

"I might..." he protested.

"Oh, please." Her eyes narrowed. "All you could have offered was money and heartbreak. Better no father at all than a father like you. My child will never feel like an ignored, unwanted burden." She straightened her shoulders, lifting her chin. "And neither will I."

Cesare stared at her. Then his mouth snapped shut.

"So that's what you think of me," he muttered. "That I'm a selfish bastard with nothing but money to offer."

She stared at him for a long moment, then relented with a sigh. "You are who you are. I realized last year that I could not change you. So I'm not going to try."

His handsome face looked suddenly haggard. In spite of everything, her traitorous heart went out to him. Living with him for seven years, learning his every habit, she'd seen glimpses of the vulnerability that drove Cesare to a relentless pursuit of money and women he neither needed nor truly wanted. When he came home late at night, when he paced the hallways in sleepless hours, she'd seen flashes of emptiness beneath his mask, and the despair beneath his careless charm. There could never be enough money or cheap affairs to fill the emptiness in his heart, but he kept trying. And Emma knew why.

He'd lost the woman he'd loved, and he'd never be able to love anyone again.

Even through her anger, she felt almost sorry for him. Because without love, what could there be—but emptiness?

"It's not your fault," she said slowly. "I understand why you can't let anyone into your heart again. You loved her so much—and then you lost her…" At his expression, she reached her hand to his rough cheek. Her voice trembled as she whispered, "Your heart was buried with your wife."

Cesare seemed to shudder beneath her touch. "Emma…"

"It's all right." Dropping her hand, she stepped back and tried to smile. "We're fine. Truly. Your son is happy and well. I have a good job. My boss is a very kindhearted man. He looks out for us."

Something in her voice made him look up sharply.

"Who is he? This new boss?"

She licked her lips. "You don't know?"

He shook his head. "After you left, I tried my best to forget you ever existed."

It shouldn't have hurt her, but it did. Emma put her hands on the handlebar of the stroller. "That is what you should do now, Cesare. Forget us...."

But he grabbed the handlebar, his hand over hers. "No. This time, I'm not letting you go. Not with my son."

She swallowed, looking up at his fierce gaze.

"You only want us because you think you can't have us. *No* is a novelty, it's distracting and shiny. But I know, if I ever let myself...count on you, you'd leave. I won't let anyone hurt Sam. Not even you."

She tried to pull away. He tightened his grip.

"He's my son."

"Let us go," she whispered. "Please. Somewhere, there's a man who will love us with all his heart. A man who can actually be a loving father to Sam." She shook her head. "We both know you're not that man."

The anger in Cesare's face slid away, replaced by an expression that seemed hurt, even bewildered.

"Emma," he breathed. "You think so little of me—"

"You heard her," a man growled behind them. "Let her go, damn you."

Alain Bouchard stood behind them with two body-guards.

Cesare's eyes widened in shock. "Bouchard...?"

Alain was a powerful man, handsome in his way. In his mid-forties, he was a decade older than Cesare. His salt-and-pepper hair was closely clipped, his clothing well-tailored. His perfect posture bespoke the pride of a man who was CEO of a luxury goods firm that had been run by the Bouchard family for generations. But the red hatred in the Frenchman's eyes was for Cesare alone.

"Let her go," Alain repeated, and Emma saw his two burly bodyguards, Gustave and Marcel, take a step forward in clear but unspoken threat.

For an instant, Cesare's grasp tightened on her hand. His eyes narrowed and she was suddenly afraid of what he might do—that a brutal, juvenile fistfight between two wealthy tycoons might break out in the Champ de Mars.

Desperate to calm the situation down, she said, "Let me go, Cesare. Please."

He turned to her, his black eyes flints of betrayed fury. "What is he doing here?"

"He's my boss," she admitted.

"You work for Angélique's brother?"

She flinched. Strictly speaking, that might seem vengeful on her part. "He offered me a job when I needed one. That's all."

"You're raising my son in the house of a man who hates me?"

"I never let him speak a word against you. Not in front of Sam."

"That's big of you," he said coldly.

She saw Gustave and Marcel draw closer across the green grass. "Please," she whispered, "you have to let me go...."

Cesare abruptly withdrew his hand. There was a lump in Emma's throat as she turned away, quickly pushing the baby stroller toward Alain.

"Are you all right, Emma?" Alain said. "He didn't hurt you?"

Out of the corner of her eye, she saw Cesare stiffen.

"Of course I'm all right. We were just talking." She glanced behind her. "But now we're done."

"This isn't over," Cesare said.

His handsome face looked dark as a shadow crossed the sun. She took a deep breath. "I know," she said miserably.

"Allons-y," Alain said, putting a hand on the stroller handle, just where Cesare's had been a moment before. They walked together down the path and out of the park, and at every step, she felt Cesare's gaze on the back of her neck. She didn't properly breathe until they were out of the Champ de Mars and back on the sidewalk by the street.

"Are you really all right?" Alain asked again.

"Fine," she said. But she wasn't. A war was coming. A custody war with her precious baby at the center. She could feel it like the dark clouds of a rising storm. Trying to push aside her fear, she asked, "What were you doing at the park? How did you know we were there?"

"Gustave called me."

Her brow furrowed. "How did Gustave know?"

Alain's cheeks colored slightly. "I sometimes have my bodyguards watch you, at a distance. Paris can be a dangerous city..."

His voice trailed off as they were passed by two elegant women dripping diamonds and head-to-toe Hermès.

"This neighborhood?" Emma said in disbelief.

He gave a graceful Gallic shrug. *"On ne sait jamais."* His expression darkened. "And it seems I was right to have you followed, with that bastard Falconeri showing up. He's Sam's father, isn't he?"

She was sure he meant to be protective, but her privacy felt invaded. "Yes," she admitted. "But I don't blame him for being upset. I never told him I was pregnant."

"You obviously had reason. Is he going to try to take the baby?"

"I don't know," she said in a small voice.

"I won't let him." He stopped, looking down at her with

his thin face and soulful eyes. "I'd do anything to protect you, Emma. You must know that."

She looked at her boss uneasily. "I know." In spite of all his kindness, she'd found herself wondering lately if he might be more interested in her than was strictly proper for an employer. She'd told herself she was imagining things. But still... She shook her head. "We'll be fine. I can take care of us."

Ahead, she saw Alain's black limited-edition Range Rover parked illegally on the Avenue de la Bourdonnais, with his chauffeur running the engine.

"After what he did to my sister, I won't let any woman be hurt by Cesare Falconeri, ever again," Alain vowed. Emma stiffened.

"Cesare didn't do anything to her. It was a tragic accident. He loved her."

"Ah, but you think the best of everyone." His expression changed from rage to gentleness as he looked down at her. His jaw tightened. "Even him. But that bastard doesn't deserve you. He'll get what he deserves. Someday."

Looking at him, Emma's heart trembled at what she might have unthinkingly done by accepting a job with Alain. He was convinced that his sister's death had been something more than a tragic accidental overdose. But Cesare was innocent. He'd never been charged with any crime. And Emma, of all people, knew how he'd loved his wife. She took a deep breath and changed the subject.

"Sam and I will be fine," she said brightly. "Cesare doesn't want a family to tie him down. He'll soon return to London and forget all about us."

But as dark clouds crossed the bright sun, Emma thought of the tender expression on Cesare's face when he'd first caressed his baby son's cheek. And she was afraid.

* * *

"To the airport, sir?"

Cesare leaned back heavily in the backseat of the Rolls-Royce. For a moment he didn't answer the driver. He pressed his hands against his forehead, still trembling with shock and fury from what he'd learned.

He had a child.

A son.

A baby born in secret, to the woman who'd left him last November without a word. And gone to work for his enemy.

Closing his eyes, he pressed his fingertips against the lids. He didn't believe Emma had gotten pregnant on purpose. No. She'd been right to laugh at his knee-jerk reaction earlier. She was clearly no gold digger. But leaving him in London, without a word, taking his child away, taking his *decision* away...

He took a deep breath. She'd done it all as if Cesare didn't even matter. As if he didn't even *exist*.

"Sir?"

"Yes," he bit out. "The airport."

The limousine pulled smoothly back into the Paris traffic. Cesare's throat was tight. He struggled to be fair, to be calm, when what he wanted to do was punch the seat in front of him and scream.

His baby was being raised in the house of Alain Bouchard, a man who unfairly blamed him for his sister's death. Bouchard didn't know the truth, and knowing how the man had loved his sister, Cesare had kept it that way.

But now, he pictured Bouchard's angry face, the way he'd stepped protectively in front of Emma.

Was it possible that over the past year, while Cesare had been celibate as a monk hungering for her, Emma had become Bouchard's lover?

No, his heart said. Impossible. But his brain disagreed. After all, the two of them were living in the same house. Perhaps she'd been lonely and heartsick. Perhaps he'd found her crying in the kitchen, as Cesare once had, and she'd fallen into the other man's bed, as she'd once fallen into his.

He hopelessly put his hands over his ears, as if that could keep his own imagination away. Anger built inside Cesare, rising like bile in his soul.

As the car turned west, heading toward the private airport outside the city, he looked out the window. He could see the top of the Eiffel Tower above the charming buildings, over two young lovers kissing at a sidewalk café.

He ground his teeth. He'd be glad to leave this damn city. He hated Paris and everything it stood for. The romance. The *love.*

Whether Emma was Bouchard's mistress or not, she had no love for Cesare anymore. She'd made her low opinion of him, as a potential father or even as a human being, very clear. She didn't want a thing from him. Not even his money. The thought made him feel low.

It would be simple to take the easy out she offered. Leave Paris. Go back to London. Forget the child they'd unintentionally created.

His child.

He could still see the baby's face. His soft black hair. Those dark eyes, exactly like his own.

He had a son.

A child.

He closed his eyes. Over the memory of the baby's sweet babble, he heard Emma's voice: *We don't need you. We don't want you.*

Cesare's fist hit the window with a bang.

"Sir?" His driver quivered, looking at him in the rear-view mirror.

Cesare's eyes slowly opened. Perhaps he wasn't ready to be a father. But that no longer mattered.

Because he was one.

"Go back."

"Back?"

"To my hotel." Cesare rubbed at the base of his skull. "I'm not leaving Paris. Take me back now."

Pulling his phone from his pocket, he dialed a number in New York City. Mortimer Ainsley had been his uncle's attorney, twenty years ago, and presided over his will when he'd died and Cesare gained possession of his aging, heavily mortgaged hotel. Later, Mortimer Ainsley had looked over the prenuptial agreement given to Cesare by Angélique Bouchard, the wealthy older French heiress who had proposed after just six weeks.

Morty, who'd appeared old to Cesare's eyes even then, had harrumphed over the terms of Angélique's prenup. "If you leave this Bouchard woman, you get nothing," he'd said. "If she dies, you get everything. Not much of a deal for you. She's only ten years older so it may be some time before she dies!"

Cesare had been horrified. "I don't want her to die. I love her."

"Love, huh?" Morty had snorted. "Good luck with that."

Remembering how young and naive he'd been, Cesare waited for Morty to answer the phone. He knew the old man would answer, no matter what time it was in New York right now. Morty would know the right attorney in Paris to handle a custody case.

Better no father at all than a father like you.

Cesare's jaw tightened. Emma would realize the penalty for what she'd done. She'd see that Cesare Falconeri would not be ignored, or denied access—or even knowledge!—of his own child.

"Ainsley." Morty's greeting was gruff, as if he'd just woken from sleep.

"Morty. I have a problem...." Without preamble, Cesare grimly outlined the facts.

"So you have a son," Morty said. "Congratulations."

"I told you. I don't have a son," Cesare said tightly. "*She* has him."

"Of course you can go to war over this. You might even win." Morty cleared his throat. "But you know the expression, *Pyrrhic victory?* Unless the woman's an unfit mother..."

Cesare remembered Emma's loving care of the baby as she pushed him in the stroller through the park. "No," he said grudgingly.

"Then you have to decide who you're willing to hurt, and how badly. 'Cause in a custody war, it's never just the other parent who takes it in the neck. Nine times out of ten, it's the kid who suffers most." Morty paused. "I can give you the number of a barracuda lawyer who will cause the sky to rain fire on this woman. But is that what you really want?"

As his Rolls-Royce crossed the Seine and traveled up the Avenue George V, Cesare's grip on his phone slowly loosened. By the time he ended the call a few minutes later, as the car pulled in front of the expensive five-star hotel where he'd stayed through the business negotiations, Cesare's expression had changed entirely.

The valet opened his door. "Welcome back, monsieur."

Looking up, Cesare didn't see the imposing architecture of the hotel as he got out. Instead he saw Emma's troubled expression when they'd parted in the Champ de Mars.

She was expecting him to start a war over this. *Christo*

santo, she knew him well. Now that he knew about Sam, she expected him to fight for custody, to destroy their peace and rip their comfortable life into shreds. And then after that, after he'd made a mess of their lives for the sake of his pride, she expected Cesare to grow bored and quickly abandon them both.

That was why she hadn't told him about the baby. That was why she thought Sam was better off with no father at all. She truly believed Cesare was that selfish. That he'd put his own ego over the well-being of his child.

His lips pressed into a thin line. He might have done it, too, if Morty hadn't made him think twice.

You have to decide who you're willing to hurt, and how badly. 'Cause in a custody war, it's never just the other parent who takes it in the neck. Nine times out of ten, it's the kid who suffers most.

Before his own parents died, Cesare'd had a happy, almost bohemian childhood in a threadbare villa on Lake Como, filled with art and light and surrounded by beautiful gardens. His parents, both artists, had loved each other, and they'd adored their only child. The three of them had been inseparable. Until, when he was twelve, his mother had gotten sick, and her illness had poisoned their lives, drop by drop.

His father's death had been quicker. After his wife's funeral, he'd gone boating on the lake in the middle of the night, after he'd drunk three bottles of wine. Calling his death by drowning an *accident,* Cesare thought, had been generous of the coroner.

Now his hands tightened. If he didn't go to war for custody, how else could he fulfill his obligation to his son? He couldn't leave Sam to be raised by another man—especially not Alain Bouchard. Sam would grow up believing Cesare was a monster who'd callously abandoned him.

Cesare exhaled.

How could he bend Emma to his will? What was the fulcrum he could use to gain possession of his child? What was her weakness?

Then—*he knew*.

And if some part of him shivered at the thought, he stomped on it as an irrational fear. This was no time to be afraid. This time, he wouldn't be selling his soul. There would be no delusional *love* involved. He would do this strictly for his child's sake. *In name only*.

He had a sudden image of Emma in his bed, luscious and warm, naked in his arms....

No! He would keep her in his home, but at a distance. *In name only,* he repeated to himself. He would never open his heart to her again. Not even a tiny corner of it.

From this moment forward, his heart was only for his son.

Grabbing the car door as it started to pull away, he wrenched it open and flung himself back into the Rolls-Royce.

"Monsieur?"

"I changed my mind."

"Of course, sir," replied the driver, who was well accustomed in dealing with the inexplicable whims of the rich. "Where may I take you?"

Emma expected a battle. He would give her one. But not in the way she expected. He would take her completely off guard—and sweep her completely into his power, in a revenge far sweeter, and more explosive, than any mere *rain of fire*.

"Around the corner," Cesare replied coldly. "To a little jewelry shop on the Avenue Montaigne."

CHAPTER SIX

EMMA JUMPED WHEN her phone rang.

All afternoon, since she'd left Cesare in the park, she'd been pacing the halls of Alain's seventeenth-century *hôtel particulier* in the seventh arrondissement. She'd been on edge, looking out the windows, past the courtyard gate onto the Avenue Rapp. Waiting for Cesare to strike. Waiting for a lawyer to call. Or the police. Or... She didn't know what, but she'd been torturing herself trying to imagine.

When her cell phone finally rang, she saw his private number and braced herself.

"I won't let you bully me," she whispered aloud to the empty air. Then she answered the phone with, "What do you want?"

"I want to see you." It shocked her how calm Cesare's voice was. How pleasant. "I'd like to discuss our baby."

"I'm busy." Standing in the mansion's lavish salon with its fifteen-foot-high ceilings, she looked from the broom she hadn't touched in twenty minutes to Sam, lying nearby on a cushioned blanket on the floor, happily batting at soft toys dangling above him in a baby play gym. She set her jaw. "I'm working."

"As mother of my heir, you don't need to work, you

know." He sounded almost amused. "You won't worry about money ever again."

He was trying to lull her into letting down her guard, she thought.

"I don't worry about money *now*," she retorted. As a single mother, she'd been even more careful, tucking nearly all her paycheck into the bank against a rainy day. "I have a good salary, we live rent-free in Alain's house and I have a nice nest egg thanks to you. I sold your watch to a collector, by the way. I couldn't believe how much I got for it. What kind of idiot would spend so much on a— Oh. Sorry. But seriously. How could you spend so much on a watch?"

But Cesare didn't sound insulted. "How much did you get for it?"

"A hundred thousand euros," she said, still a little horrified. But also pleased.

He snorted. "The collector got a good deal."

"That's what Alain said. He was irritated I didn't offer the watch to him first. He said he would have paid me three times that…." She stopped uneasily.

"Bouchard takes good care of you."

Cesare's good humor had fled. She gritted her teeth. What was the deal between those two? She wished they'd leave her out of it. "Of course Alain takes care of me. He's an excellent employer."

"You can't raise Sam in his house, Emma. I won't allow it."

"You won't allow it?" She exhaled with a flare of nostril. "Look, I told you that Sam's your child because it was the right thing to do…"

"You mean because I gave you no choice."

"…but you can't give orders anymore. In case you haven't noticed, you're no longer my boss."

His voice took on an edge. "I'm Sam's father."

"Oh, you're suddenly sure about that now, are you?"

"Emma—"

"I can't believe you asked me for a paternity test! When you know perfectly well you're the only man I've ever slept with in my whole life!"

"Even now?"

His voice was a little tense. Cesare was worried she'd slept with other men over the past year? She was astonished. "You think I was madly dating while I was pregnant as a whale? Or maybe—" she gave a low laugh "—right after Sam was born, I rushed to invite men to my bed, hoping they'd ignore the dark hollows under my eyes and baby spit-up on my shoulder." She snorted. "I'm touched, really, that you think I'm so irresistible. But if I have a spare evening I collapse into bed. For sleeping, not orgies, in case that was your next question."

For a moment, there was silence. When next he spoke, his tone was definitely warmer. "Leave Sam at home with a babysitter. Come out with me tonight."

"Why?" She scowled. "What do you have planned—the guillotine? Pistols at dawn? Or let me guess. Some lawyer is going to serve me a subpoena?"

"I just want to talk."

"Talk," she said doubtfully.

"Perhaps I was a little rough with you in the park…."

"You think?"

He gave a low laugh. "I don't blame you for believing the worst of me. But I'm sure you'll forgive my bad manners, when you think of what a shock it was for me to learn I have a son, and that you'd hidden that fact from me for quite some time."

He sounded reasonable. Damn him.

"What's your angle?" she asked suspiciously.

"I just want us to share dinner," he said, "and discuss

our child's future. Surely there is nothing so strange in that."

Uh-oh. When Cesare sounded innocent, she *knew* he was up to something. "I'm not giving up custody. So if that's what you want to discuss, we should let our lawyers handle it." She tried to sound confident, like she even *had* a lawyer.

"Oh, *lawyers*." He gave a mournful sigh. "They make things so messy. Let's just meet, you and me. Like civilized people."

She gripped the phone tighter, pacing across the gleaming hardwood floors. "If you're thinking of luring me out of the house so your bodyguards can try to kidnap Sam, Alain's house is like a fortress...."

"If you're going to jump to the worst possible conclusion of everything I say, this conversation is going to take a long time. And I wouldn't mind a glass of wine," he said pointedly.

She watched her baby gurgle with triumph when he caught the end of his sock. Falconeri men were such determined creatures. "You're not going to try to pull anything?"

"Like what?" When she didn't answer, he gave an exaggerated sigh. "I'll even take you someplace crowded, with plenty of strangers to chaperone us. How about the restaurant at the top of the Eiffel Tower?"

She pictured the long circling queues of tourists. Surely even Cesare couldn't be up to much, amid such a crowd. "Well..."

"You left London without a word. You kept your pregnancy secret and went to work for Bouchard behind my back. I don't think a single dinner to work out Sam's custody is too much to ask."

Emma was about to agree when her whole body went on alert at the word *custody*. "What do you mean, custody?"

"I'm willing to accept your pregnancy was an accident. You didn't intentionally lie. You're not a gold digger."

"Gee, thanks."

"But now I know I have a son, I can't just walk away. We're going to have to come to an arrangement."

"What arrangement?"

"If you want to know, you'll have to join me tonight."

"Or else—what?"

"Or else," Cesare said quietly. "Let's just leave it at that."

"You don't want to be a father," she said desperately. "You couldn't be a decent one, even if you tried—not that you would try for long!"

For a moment, the phone fell silent.

"You think you know me," he said in a low voice.

"Am I wrong?"

"I'll pick you up at nine." There was a dangerous sensuality in his voice that caused a shiver down Emma's body. She suddenly remembered that Cesare had ways of making her agree to almost anything.

"Make it seven," she said nervously. "I don't want to be out too late."

"Have a curfew, do you?" he drawled. "He keeps tight hold on you."

"Alain doesn't have anything to do with—"

"And Emma? Wear something nice."

The line went dead.

The sun was setting over Paris, washing soft pink and orange light over the white classical facades of the buildings as Emma stood alone on the sidewalk of the Avenue Rapp.

It was three minutes before seven. She'd dressed carefully, as requested, in a pink knit dress and a black coat.

She'd considered showing up in a T-shirt and jeans, just to spite him. Instead she spent more time this afternoon primping than she'd spent in a year. For reasons she didn't like to think about. For feelings she was trying to convince herself she didn't feel.

Emma had stopped wearing the severe chignon when she'd come to Paris. Now her black hair had been brushed until it shone, and fell tumbling down her shoulders. Her lipstick was the same raspberry shade as her dress. She was even wearing mascara to make her green eyes pop. She hoped.

No. She ground her teeth. She *didn't* hope. She absolutely didn't care what Cesare thought she looked like. She *didn't*.

It was only for Sam's sake she was meeting Cesare tonight. Where her own romantic dreams were concerned, she'd given up on him that cold, heartbreaking morning in London when he'd informed her he would never ever: 1. love her, 2. marry her or 3. have a child with her. He'd said it outright. What could you do with a man like that?

What indeed...

Emma shivered in her thin black wool coat, tucking her pink scarf more firmly around her neck. Pulling her phone out of her pocket, she glanced at the time: six fifty-eight.

She sighed, wondering why she'd bothered to be on time. Cesare would likely be half an hour late, as usual, and in the meantime she was standing out here looking like a fool as taxi drivers gawked at her standing on the sidewalk. She would have gone back to wait inside, except the bad blood between Alain and Cesare made her reluctant to allow the two men to meet.

She'd already tucked her baby son into bed, leaving him

with Irene Taylor, the extremely capable young woman who until recently had been an au pair for the Bulgarian ambassador. Irene was bright, idealistic and very young. Emma had never been that young.

Her eye was caught by a flash of light. Looking up over the buildings, she could see the tip of the Eiffel Tower suddenly illuminated with brilliant sparkling lights. That meant it was seven o'clock. Her lips turned down. And just as she'd thought, Cesare was late. He'd never change....

"Buona sera, bella."

With an intake of breath, Emma turned to see Cesare on the sidewalk, looking devastatingly handsome in a long black coat.

"You're on time," she stammered.

"Of course."

"You're never on time."

"I am always on time when it matters to me."

Her cheeks turned hot. Feeling awkward, she looked right and left. "Where's your car?"

Cesare came closer. "It's a beautiful night. I gave my driver the night off." He tilted his head. "Why are you waiting on the sidewalk? I would have come to get you."

"I didn't want to start World War III."

He snorted. "I don't hold any grudge against Bouchard."

She looked at him steadily. "He holds one against you. The things he has said..."

His eyes narrowed. "On second thought, perhaps you are right to separate us. I am starting to resent the way he's taken possession of something that should belong only to me."

Emma trembled at the anger in his dark eyes. He meant Sam. He had to mean Sam.

"You look beautiful tonight," he said huskily.

"Oh. Thanks," she said, suddenly shy. Cesare looked

even more handsome than she remembered, and cripes, was that a tuxedo beneath his black coat? "So do you." Her cheeks flamed. "Er, handsome, I mean. Not that it matters," she added hastily, "because we're just going out to talk about our son...."

She stopped talking as he took her hand in his own. She felt the warmth of his palm against hers. He glanced at her high-heeled shoes. "Do you mind walking a few blocks?"

In this moment, it was hard for Emma to remember what pain felt like. Wordlessly she shook her head.

He smiled, an impossibly devastating smile, and her heart twisted in her chest. "Too bad. I would have offered to carry you."

Carry her? Against his chest? Her mouth went dry. She tried to think of a snappy comeback but her brain suddenly wasn't working quite right. His smile increased.

Still holding her hand, he led her across the street and up the narrow, charming rue de Monttessuy. The Eiffel Tower loomed large, directly ahead of them. But it wasn't that world-famous sight that consumed her.

She glanced down at Cesare's hand as they walked up the quiet street, past the brasseries and shops. He held her hand as if she were precious and he never wanted to let her go.

"Is something wrong, *cara?*"

Emma realized she'd stopped on the sidewalk right in front of the boulangerie. "Um..."

He pulled her closer, looking down at her with dark intense eyes as his lips curved. "Perhaps you want me to carry you, after all?"

She swallowed.

Yes.

No.

She took a deep breath of air, scented with warm, buttery croissants and crusty baguettes, and reminded herself she wasn't in London anymore. She didn't love Cesare. She'd left that love behind her. He had no power over her here. None.

"Absolutely none," she whispered aloud.

Moving closer, he stroked her cheek. "None?"

She pulled away from him, trembling. "Why are you acting like this?"

"Like what?"

"Like you care."

"I do."

She shook her head, fighting tears. "I don't know what you're planning, but you—"

"Just dinner, Emma," he said quietly. "And a discussion."

"Nothing more?"

He gave her a lopsided grin that tugged at her heart. "Would I lie?"

"No," she sighed.

He pulled her across the Avenue de la Bourdonnais, which was still busy with early-evening traffic. They walked down the charming tree-lined street into the Champ de Mars, to the base of the Eiffel Tower. She exhaled when she saw the long lines of tourists. In spite of all his promises, she still almost feared Cesare might try something. Not seduce her, surely?

No, why would he?

Unless it was a cold-blooded calculation on his part. Unless he thought he could overwhelm her with sensuality until she was so crazy she agreed to give up custody of Sam. Her hands tightened at her sides. He wouldn't even get a single kiss out of her if he tried. And the next time he contacted her, she really would have a lawyer....

"Elevator or stairs?" he asked, smiling.

Tilting her head back to look up the length of the tower, Emma had a sudden image of tripping on the stairs in her high heels, and Cesare sweeping her up into his arms. She could almost imagine how it would feel to cling to him, her arms around his body, her cheek against his chest.

"Elevator," she said quickly.

They went to a private elevator at the south pillar of the Eiffel Tower. There was no queue here. *Strange,* she thought. She'd heard this restaurant was really popular.

She was even more shocked when the elevator opened with a ding on the second platform of the Eiffel Tower, and they walked into a beautiful restaurant...

And found it empty.

Emma stopped cold. With an intake of breath, she looked at Cesare accusingly. "Where is everyone?"

He shrugged, managing to look guilty and innocent at the same time. "What do you mean?"

She looked over all the empty tables and chairs of the modern restaurant, with its spectacular views of Paris from all sides. "No one is here!"

Coming behind her, he put his hands on her shoulders. "*We* are here."

Slowly he pulled off her coat, then handed it to a host who discreetly appeared. Cesare's eyes never left hers as he removed his own coat, revealing his well-cut tuxedo. Emma shivered beneath his gaze for reasons that had nothing to do with being cold. As he led her to a table by the window, the one with the best view, she felt suddenly hot, as if she'd been lying beneath the sun. No, worse. As if she'd been *standing* on it.

They sat down, and a waiter brought them a bottle of wine. Emma glanced at the tables behind them and saw they were all covered with vases of long-stemmed roses.

"Roses?" she said. Her lips curled humorlessly. "To go

along with the watch you gave me? The finishing touch on the parting-gift extravaganza for one-night stands?"

"I should think it's obvious," he drawled, pouring wine into her glass, "you're not a one-night stand."

"A two-night stand, then."

He looked at her without speaking. Her cheeks burned.

"I won't let you talk me into signing custody away," she said hoarsely. "Or seduce me into it, either."

He gave a low laugh. "Ah, you really do think I'm a coldhearted bastard." He held out her glass, filled with wine a deeper red than roses. "That's not what I want."

"Then, what?"

He just looked at her with his dark eyes. Emma's heart started pounding.

Her hand shook as she reached out for the glass. She realized she was in trouble. Really, really big trouble.

He held up his own wine. "A toast."

"To what?"

"To you, *cara*," he murmured.

He clinked her glass and then drank deeply. She looked down at the glass and muttered, "Should I wonder if this is poisoned?"

He gave a low laugh. "No poison, I promise."

"Then, what?" she whispered.

Cesare's dark eyebrow quirked. "How many times must I say it? I want to have *dinner*. And *talk*." He picked up the menu. "What looks good?"

"I'm not hungry."

"Not hungry? With a menu like this? There's steak— lobster…"

"Will you just stop torturing me with all this romantic nonsense and tell me why you've brought me here?"

He tilted his head, looking at her across the table, before he gave a low laugh. "It's the roses, isn't it? Too much?"

"I'm not one of your foolish little starlets getting tossed out after breakfast, sobbing to stay." She narrowed her eyes. "You never try this hard. You never have to. So it must be leading up to something. Tell me what it is."

Cesare leaned forward across the candlelit table, his dark eyes intense. Her whole body was taut as she leaned toward him, straining to hear. He parted his sensual lips.

"Later," he whispered, then relaxed back in his chair as if he had not a care in the world. He took another sip of wine and looked out the huge wall of windows overlooking the lights of Paris, twinkling in the twilight.

Emma glared in helpless fury. He clearly was determined to take his own sweet time, to make her squirm. Fine. Grabbing her glass, she took a big gulp of the wine. Since she'd moved to Paris, she'd grown to appreciate wine more. This was a red, full-bodied Merlot that was equal parts delicious and expensive. Setting down her glass, she looked around them.

"This restaurant is kind of famous. It's hard to even get reservations here. How on earth did you manage to get the whole place?"

He gave a low laugh. "I pulled some strings."

"Strings?"

"It wasn't easy."

"For you," she said darkly, "everything is easy."

"Not everything." He looked at her across the table. His eyes seemed black as a midnight sea. Then he looked past her. Turning around, she saw the waiter approaching their table.

"Monsieur?" the man asked respectfully. "May I take your order?"

"Yes. To start, I'd like…" Cesare rattled off a list that included endives, foie gras, black truffle sauce, venison and some kind of strange rose-flavored gelatin. It all sounded very fancy to Emma, and not terribly appetizing.

"And for madame?"

Both men looked at her expectantly.

Emma sighed. "I'm afraid I don't much care for French food."

The waiter did a double take. So did Cesare. The scandalized looks on both male faces was almost funny. Emma stifled a laugh.

"Of course you like French food," Cesare said. "Everyone does. Even people who hate Paris love the food."

"I love Paris," she said. "Just not the food."

"I can give madame some suggestions from the menu…" the waiter tried.

She shook her head. "Sorry. I've lived here for almost a year. Trust me, I've tried everything." She looked at him. "What I would really like is a cheeseburger. With French fries. *Frites,*" she amended quickly, as if that would make her order sound more gourmet, which of course it didn't.

The waiter continued to stare at her with a mix of consternation and bewilderment. In for a penny, in for a pound….

"And ketchup." She handed him the menu with a sweet smile. "Lots and lots of ketchup. *Merci.*"

The waiter left, shaking his head and muttering to himself.

But Cesare gave a low laugh. "Nice."

"Shouldn't I order what I want?" she said defensively.

"Of course you should. Of course a nice American girl, on a romantic night out at the Eiffel Tower, would order a cheeseburger with ketchup."

"Romantic night?" she said with a surge of panic. He gave her an inscrutable smile. To hide her confusion, she looked out the window. "I can still enjoy the view."

"Me, too," he said quietly, and he wasn't looking at the window. A tingle of awareness went up and down Emma's body.

"This is my first time inside the Eiffel Tower," she said, trying to fill the space between them. She gave an awkward laugh. "I could never be bothered to wait in the lines."

"Doesn't Bouchard ever give you time off?"

She glanced at him with a snicker. "You're one to talk."

He had the grace to look discomfited. "I was a difficult boss."

"That," she said succinctly, "is an understatement."

"I must have been an awful employer."

"A monster," she agreed.

"You never even got to see inside the British Museum." He had a hangdog look, like a puppy expecting to be kicked. "Or take a picture of Big Ben."

She squelched an involuntary laugh, covering it with a cough. Then sighed.

"Perhaps you weren't entirely to blame," she admitted.

He brightened. "I wasn't?"

"I blamed you for not having time to tour London. I swore Paris would be different. But even though Alain has bent over backward to be the most amazing employer I could possibly imagine..."

Cesare's expression darkened.

"...I still haven't seen much of the city. At first, I was overwhelmed by a new job in a new city. Then I had the baby, and, well...if I have extra time, I don't tour a museum any more than I go on a date. I collapse in a stupor on the couch." She sighed, spreading her arms. "So it seems I'm full of excuses. I could have climbed the Eiffel Tower before now, and brought Sam with me, if I'd made it a priority. Instead I haven't been willing to wait in line or pay the money."

"What if I promised you'd never have to do either, see-ing the sights of London?"

She tried to laugh it off. "What, there's no line to see the Crown Jewels anymore?" she said lightly. "It's a free ride for all on the London Eye?"

He took another sip of his wine, then put it back down on the table. His dark eyes met hers. "I want you both to come back to London with me."

She set her jaw. She'd been afraid he'd say that. "There's no way I'm leaving my job to move back to London with you. Your interest in Sam will never last."

"You have to know I can't abandon him, now I know. Especially not in Bouchard's house."

"I thought you said you didn't bear Alain any grudge."

"I don't. But that doesn't mean I'll let him raise my son." The votive candle on the table left flickering shad-ows on the hard lines of his handsome face. He said qui-etly, "Bouchard wants you for himself, Emma."

"Don't be ridiculous," she said uncomfortably, then re-called her own recent concerns on that front. "And any-way, I don't see him that way."

"He wants you. And he already knows that taking care of Sam is the way to your heart." His voice was low. Be-hind him, she could see the sparkling lights of Paris in the night. "As you yourself said—Sam deserves a father."

"Yes, he does," she said over the lump in her throat. "An actual father who'll love him and kiss his bruises and tuck him in at night. A father he can count on." Looking up at him, she whispered, "We both know you're not that man."

"How do you know?"

The raw emotion in Cesare's voice made her eyes widen. She shook her head.

"You said yourself you don't want a child. You have no idea what it means to be a parent...."

"You're wrong. I do know. Even though I'm new at being a father, I was once a son." He looked away. "We had no money, just an old house falling down around us. But we were happy. My parents loved each other. And they loved me."

She swallowed. "I've never heard you talk about them before."

"There's not much to tell." His lips twisted down at the edge. "When I was twelve, my mother got sick. My father had to watch her slowly die. He couldn't face life without her, so after her funeral, he went drinking alone on the lake at night. The empty boat floated to shore. His body was found the next day."

"I'm sorry," she choked out, her heart in her throat. "How could he do that—leave you?"

"I got over it." He shrugged, his only sign of emotion the slight tightening of his jaw. "I was sent to a great-uncle in New York. He was strict, but tried his best to raise me. I learned English. Learned about the hotel business. Learned I liked hard numbers, profit and loss. Numbers made sense. They could be added, subtracted, controlled. Unlike love, which disappears like mist as soon as you think it's in your arms."

His wife. He was still brokenhearted over his loss of her. Emma fought back tears as she said, "Love makes life worth living."

His lips twisted sardonically. "You say that, even after you wasted so many years trying to get love from your stepmother, like blood from a stone? All those years trying and failing, with nothing but grief to show for it."

Pain caught at her heart.

"I'm sorry," Cesare said, looking at her. "I shouldn't have said that."

"No. You're right." Blinking back tears, she shook her

head. "But others have loved me. My parents. My mother died when I was four, even younger than you were. Ovarian cancer. Just like…" She stopped herself. *Just like I almost did,* she'd almost said.

"I'm sorry," he said.

"It's all right. It was a long time ago. And my father was an amazing man. After my mom died, it was just the two of us. He gave me my work ethic, my sense of honor, everything." She pressed her lips together. "Then he fell in love with a coworker at his factory.…"

"Cruel stepmother, huh?"

"She was never cruel." She sobered. "At least not at first. I was glad to see my father happy, but I started to feel like I was in their way. An outsider interrupting their honeymoon." She glanced up at the waiter, who'd just brought their meals. He set the cheeseburger and fries before her with the same flourish he used on Cesare's venison and risotto with black truffle sauce. It must have been hard for him, she thought, so she gave him a grateful smile. *"Merci."*

"So you left home?" Cesare prompted after the waiter left.

"Well." She dipped a fry into a ramekin of ketchup, then chewed it thoughtfully. It was hot and salty and delicious. She licked her lips, then her fingers. "At sixteen, I fell head over heels for a boy."

Cesare seemed uninterested in his own food as he listened with his complete attention. "A boy."

"The captain of the high school football team." She gave a smile. "Which in Texas can be a big deal. I was flattered by his attention. I fell hard. A few kisses, and I was convinced it was love. He talked me into going all the way."

"But you didn't." Taking a bite of his food, he grinned at her. "I know you didn't."

"No." She swirled another fry through the ketchup. "But I went to the doctor to get birth control pills." With a deep breath, she looked him in the eye. "That's how I found out I had cancer."

His jaw dropped. "Cancer?"

"Ovarian, the same as my mom had had." She kept stirring the fry in the ketchup, waiting for him to freak out, for him to look at her as if she still had one foot in the grave. "I was on chemotherapy for a long time. By the time I was in remission, Mark had long since dumped me for a cheerleader."

Cesare muttered something in Italian that sounded very unkind. She gave a grateful smile.

"He did me a huge favor. I'd had no symptoms. If I hadn't gone to the doctor then, I never would have known I was sick until it was too late. So in a funny way—that broken heart was the price that saved my life." She ate a bite of French fry, then made a face when she realized the bite was almost entirely ketchup. She set it down on her plate. "Though for a long time I wished I *had* died."

"Why?"

"My illness took everything. My childhood. My dreams of having a family someday. The medical bills even took our house." Her throat ached, but she forced herself to tell the worst. "And it killed my father."

Reaching across the table, he grabbed her hand. "Emma…"

She took a deep breath. "It was my fault. My father wasn't the kind of man who could declare bankruptcy and walk away from debt. So to pay all the bills, he took a night job. Between his jobs and taking care of me, he started to neglect my stepmother. They started fighting all the time. But the day my doctor announced I was in remission, I convinced my father to take me home early. It was Valentine's Day. I talked him into stopping at the florist to buy flowers. As a surprise." She paused. "Marion was surprised, all right. We found her at home, in bed, with the foreman from their factory."

Cesare sucked in his breath. "And?"

"My father had a heart attack," she whispered. She ran her hand over her eyes. "He was already so run-down from taking care of me. From working two jobs. Marion blamed me for everything." Her voice caught as she covered her face with her hands. "She was right."

His voice was gentle as he pulled back her hands. "It wasn't your fault."

"You're wrong." Emma looked at him across the table, and tears ran unchecked down her face. "If I hadn't fought so hard to live, I'd never have been such a burden. My father wouldn't have had to work two jobs, my stepmother wouldn't have felt lonely and neglected, and they'd still be together. It's my fault. I ruined their lives."

"Your stepmother said that?"

She nodded miserably. "After the funeral, she kicked me out of the house. I was eighteen. She had no legal obligation to take care of me. A friend let me stay until I graduated high school, then I left Texas for New York. I wanted to make something of myself, to prove Marion wrong." She blinked fast. "But nothing I ever did, not all the money I sent her, ever made her forgive what I did."

Rising to his feet, Cesare came around the table. Gently pulling Emma from the chair, he wrapped her in his arms. "So that's why you looked so stricken," he murmured. "The night we first... The night you came back from her funeral."

"Yes. Plus..." She swallowed. It was time to tell him the worst. To tell him everything. She thought of all her lonely years, loving him, devoting herself only to him. She looked up, barely seeing his face through her tears. "When

I told you I loved you last year, you tried to convince me it was just lust. But there's a reason I knew all along that it wasn't." She took a deep breath and said, "I've loved you for years, Cesare."

His hands, which had been caressing her back, abruptly stopped. He looked down at her. "Years?"

"You never knew?"

Wide-eyed, he shook his head.

"I loved you from almost the first day we met," she said quietly. She gave a choked laugh. "I think it was the moment you said you were glad to have me, because I looked smart, and the previous housekeeper on the penthouse floor had just been fired for being idiot enough to fall for you."

He looked bewildered. "That made you love me?"

She gave a low laugh. "I guess you were wrong when you said I looked smart."

"I thought you had no feelings. I never knew…"

"I hid it even better than I thought." Her lips quirked. "I knew you would fire me if you ever guessed."

"But why? Why would you love me in silence for years? I ran roughshod over you. Bossed you around. Expected you to be at my beck and call."

"But I saw the rest, too," she said over the lump in her throat. "The vulnerability that drove you to succeed, as if the devil himself were chasing you. The way you were kind to children when you thought no one was looking. Giving money to charity, helping struggling families stay in their homes—anonymously. So no one would know."

He abruptly released her, pacing back a step in his tuxedo. His handsome face looked pale.

"But now." He took a deep breath, then licked his cruel, sensual lips. "But now, surely you don't…love me."

She saw the fear in his eyes.

"Don't worry," she said softly. "I got over loving you the day I left London. I knew we'd never have a future. I had to leave my broken heart behind me, to start a new life with my child."

For a moment he didn't reply. Then he pressed his lips together. "*Our* child."

"Yes." She sighed. She looked straight into his eyes, her heart aching as she said, "But not for long."

"What do you mean?"

"You won't last."

He stepped toward her. "You really think I would abandon him? After everything I've said?"

She matched him toe to toe. "I won't be a burden, or let Sam feel like one, either, wondering what's wrong with him that his own father can't be bothered to spend time with him." She lifted her chin, but as their eyes locked, she faltered. "You're not a bad person, Cesare. But trying to raise him separately, together, it's just not going to work."

"So you can find some other man to raise my son."

Her eyes shone with tears as she whispered, "You can't promise forever. You know you can't. So if you have any mercy in your heart—if you truly do care for Sam—please, let us go."

His expression changed. He took a long, dragging breath.

"Everything you're saying," he said slowly, "is bull."

Her lips parted in a gasp.

Cesare glared at her. "You didn't keep the baby a secret because you were trying to protect me from this choice. You didn't do it to protect Sam, either. You did it for one person and one person only. Yourself."

"How can you say that?" she demanded.

"Are you honestly telling me that it's better for Sam to believe his own father abandoned him? Yes, I'm selfish. Yes, I work too much. Yes, it's possible I might buy him a pony. Maybe I wouldn't be a perfect father. But you wouldn't—won't—even give me a chance. It isn't Sam that you fear will be a burden." He looked at her. "*It's you. You're afraid I will take charge of him, and you'll be left behind. You're afraid for yourself. Only yourself.*"

Emma stared at him, her lips parted in shock. The accusation was like a knife in her heart.

Was he right? Could he be?

She shook her head fiercely.

"*No.* You're wrong!"

"You don't want to lose him," he growled. "Neither do I. From this moment, his needs must come first." He paused. "I did think of suing you for full custody…"

Those words were an ice pick in Emma's heart. She made a little whimpering sound. "No…"

"But a custody battle would only hurt my son. I'm not going to leave him in Bouchard's care, either. Or abandon him, whatever you say. I'm not going to shuttle a small child between continents, between two different lives. That leaves only one clear path. At least it's clear to me." Pulling a small jewelry box from his tuxedo pocket, he opened the box, revealing an enormous diamond ring.

"Emma Hayes," he said grimly, "will you marry me?"

CHAPTER SEVEN

CESARE STOOD BEFORE her, waiting for her answer. He hadn't even thought of bending down on one knee. His legs were shaking too badly. He was relieved his voice hadn't trembled at the question. The words felt like marbles in his mouth.

Hearing a soft gasp, he glanced behind him. Five members of the restaurant's staff were peeking from the kitchen door, smiling at this moment, waiting for Emma's answer, in that universal interest in the drama of a wedding proposal.

Will you marry me?

Four simple words. A promise that was easy to say, though not so easy to fulfill.

Cesare had the sudden memory of his father's bleak face after his beloved wife had died in his arms. The same look of stark despair on Angélique's face when Cesare had come home and found her dead, an empty bottle of sleeping pills on the floor beside her.

No. He wouldn't let himself remember. This was different. *Different.*

Cesare held the black jewelry box up a little higher, to disguise how his hand was shaking.

"Marry you?" Emma's eyes were shocked. Even horrified. She gave an awkward laugh. "Is this a joke?"

"You think I would joke about this?"

Biting her lip, she looked at the ring. "But you don't want to get married. Everyone on earth knows that, and from the day I've known you, every woman has tried to marry you anyway. We used to laugh about it."

"I'm not laughing now," he said quietly. "I'm standing in front of you with a twenty-carat ring. I don't know how much more serious I can be."

Her beautiful face looked stricken. "But you don't love me."

"It's not a question of love—at least not between us. It's a question of providing the best life for our son."

Her gaze shuttered, her green eyes filling with shadows in the flickering candlelight of the restaurant. She backed up one step—physically backed away—wrapping her arms across her body, as if for protection.

Nothing prepared him for what came next.

"I'm sorry, Cesare," she said quietly. "My answer is no."

He was so shocked, his hand tightened on the jewelry box, closing it with a snap. He'd assumed she would say yes. Instantly and gratefully.

He heard gasps behind him and whirled to face the restaurant staff hanging about the kitchen doorway.

"Leave us," he growled, and they ran back into the kitchen. He turned to face Emma, his jaw taut. "Might I ask—why?"

She swallowed. He saw her face was pale. This was hard on her, too, he realized. "I told you. I won't be a burden."

"Burden. You keep using that word. What does it mean?"

His dangerous tone would have frightened most. But standing her ground, she lifted her chin.

"You know what it means."

"No, I don't. I know you've lied to me for months, that you stole my son away without a word. But instead of trying to take him away from you, instead of seeking revenge, I'm trying to do the right thing—a new experience for me, I might add—while you keep whining words like *love* and *burden*."

Her shoulders drooped as, biting her lip, she looked down. For a long moment, she didn't answer, and he looked at her in the darkness of the restaurant. She looked so beautiful in the flickering candlelight, with all of the lights of Paris at her feet.

Cesare's throat tightened.

He thought of the night he'd found her in the dark kitchen, after her stepmother's funeral. He'd taken one look at her tearstained face, at the anguish in eyes which had never shown emotion before, and his own long-buried grief had risen in his own soul, exploding through his defenses. He'd thought he was offering her solace, but the truth was that he'd been seeking it himself. Against his will, in that moment, Emma had made him *feel* again....

Now he heard her take a deep breath.

"Whatever you think now, this desire to commit won't last. You don't want the burden of a wife and child. We both know it. You don't know what marriage means."

"We both know I do," he said quietly.

Her eyes were anguished as tears sparkled—unheeded, unfought—down her cheeks like diamonds. "But you don't love me," she whispered again.

"And you don't love me," he said evenly. "Do you?"

Wordlessly she shook her head. He exhaled. "This marriage has nothing to do with romance."

She gave a half-hysterical laugh, swooping her arm to indicate the roses, the view of Paris, the twenty-carat diamond ring. "What do you call that?"

He gave her a crooked half grin. "I call it...strategic negotiation."

Emma gave another laugh, then her smile fell. "A marriage without love?"

"Without complications," he pointed out. "We will both love our son. But between us—the marriage will be in name only."

"In name only?" He'd shocked her with this. He saw it in her face. "So you wouldn't expect us to…"

He shook his head. "Sex complicates things." Not to mention made it hard to keep the walls around his heart intact. At least where she was concerned. He hesitated. "Better that we keep this relationship…"

"Professional?"

"Cordial, I was going to say."

She took a deep breath.

"Why would I agree to give up any chance at love?"

"For something you want more than love," he said quietly. "For a family. For Sam."

"Sam…"

"I will love him. I'll be there with him every step of the way. Every single day. Isn't that better than trying to shuttle him between two separate lives, where he never knows where he belongs?"

Raw yearning filled her soft green eyes. Blinking fast, she turned away, to the dark, sparkling view of Paris. "I've worried about what would happen to Sam, if anything ever happened to me…" Looking up at him, she swallowed. "I've been in remission a long time, but there are no guarantees. If the cancer ever came back…" She looked up at him. "I've been selfish," she whispered. "Maybe you're right. Maybe even a flawed father is better than none."

"I will be the best father I can be."

"Would you?" she said in a small voice. Her beautiful face was tortured, her pink lips trembling, long dark lashes sweeping against pale cheeks. "Or, if I were crazy enough to accept, would you panic within a month and run off with some lingerie model?"

Coming toward her, he took both her hands in his own. "I swear to you, on my life," he said softly. "Everything your father was for you—I will be for him."

He felt her hands tremble in his.

"I won't let you break his heart," she whispered.

"I don't lie, and I don't make promises. You know that."

Her voice was barely audible. "Yes."

"I don't make promises because I consider myself bound by them." Gently he placed the black jewelry box with the silver Harry Winston logo into her palm. "I'm making you a promise now."

Her anguished eyes lifted to his. "Please..."

"You are the mother of my child. Be my wife." Brushing back long tendrils of black hair from her shoulder, he lowered his head to her ear. He took a deep breath, inhaling the scent of her. She smelled like vanilla and sunlight, like wildflowers and clean linen and everything good he'd once had but had lost so long ago. He felt a shudder of desire, but pushed it aside. He wouldn't let sex complicate this relationship. He couldn't. Pulling back, he said softly, "Be my wife, Emma."

Were her hands still trembling? Or were his?

"Cesare...." He saw how close she was to falling off the precipice. She tried, "We don't have to marry. We can live apart, but still raise Sam together...."

"In separate houses? In separate cities? Sending a small child with a little suitcase back and forth between two lives? You already said that wouldn't work. And I agree." Slowly, so slowly it almost killed him, he pulled her into the circle of his embrace, encircling her like a skittish thoroughbred into an enclosure. His gaze searched hers. "Marry me now. Take my name, and let my son be a Falconeri. I swear to you. On my life. That I will be the father you dreamed he could have."

She swallowed. "You swore you'd never get married again," she breathed. "We both know—" their eyes met "—you're still in love with your lost wife, and always will be."

He didn't deny this. It was easier not to.

"But we won't be lovers," he said. "We'll be equal partners." His fingers stroked her black hair, tumbling in glossy waves down her back. "And together—we'll raise our son."

She exhaled, visibly trying to steady herself. "For how long?"

"For always," he said in a low voice. "I will be married to you...until death do us part."

Her skin felt almost cold to the touch. He could almost feel her heart pounding through her ribs. "It would be a disaster."

"The only disaster would be to let any selfish dreams—yours or mine—destroy our son's chance for a home." Stroking down her cheek, he cupped her face. "Say you'll be my wife, Emma," he said huskily. "Say it."

Tears suddenly fell off her black lashes, trailing haphazardly down her pale cheeks.

"I can't fight you," she choked out. "Not when you're using my own heart against me. My baby deserves a father. It's all I've wanted since the day I found out I was pregnant." Her beautiful eyes were luminous with emotion, her body tense, as she stood in his arms in the rose-strewn restaurant of the Eiffel Tower, all the lights of Paris beneath them. "You win," she said. "I'll marry you, Cesare."

"Do you want me to come up with you?"

For answer, Emma shook her head, though she didn't

let go of Cesare's hand. She hadn't let it go for the whole walk home from the Eiffel Tower. Her knees still felt weak. Now, as they stood outside Alain's gated courtyard, she was trembling. Possibly from the weight of the enormous diamond on her left hand.

Either that, or from the knowledge that she'd just thrown all her own dreams away, her precious dreams of being loved, for someone she loved more than herself: her son.

"Are you sure? Bouchard might not be pleased at the news."

"It will be fine." She still couldn't believe she'd agreed to Cesare's marriage proposal. He'd loved only one woman—his long-dead wife—and would never love another. Knowing that, how could she have said yes?

But how could she not? He'd offered her everything she'd ever wanted for Sam. A home. A family. A real father, like she'd had. How could she not have made the sacrifice of something so small and inconsequential as her own heart?

At least she didn't need to worry about falling in love with Cesare again. She'd burned that from her soul. She *had*...

"You won't change your mind the instant I let you out of my sight?" he said lightly.

She shook her head.

"I think I'd better stay close, just to be safe." Cesare's voice was husky as he carefully tucked her jaunty pink scarf around her black coat. "Bouchard might try to talk you out of marrying me."

Even though she didn't love him anymore—*at all*— having Cesare so close did strange things to her insides. Emma took a deep breath. But she couldn't let herself feel anything. Not love. Not even lust. Not this time.

She was going to be his wife. In name only. She'd have to keep her distance, while living in the same house.

"Seriously, don't come," she said. She looked past the gate at Alain Bouchard's mansion. "I'd better give Alain this happy news on my own."

Cesare gave her a lopsided grin that made her heart go thump, thump in her chest. "I'll get the car, then. Meet you back here in ten minutes?"

"Ten?" she said incredulously.

"Twenty?"

"Better make it an hour. It's amazing how long it takes to pack up a baby."

"Really? He seems small."

"*He* is, but he has a lot of stuff." At his bemused expression, she snorted. "You'll learn."

"Can't wait." Pulling her close, Cesare looked down into her eyes. Cupping her face, he looked down at her one last time as they stood on the street with the lights of Paris twinkling around them. "Thank you for saying yes. You won't regret it."

"I regret it already," she mumbled, then gave a small laugh to show she was joking, holding up her left hand. "This diamond ring weighs, like, a thousand pounds. See you in an hour."

Turning, she went through the gate, past the security guard into Alain's courtyard. One of his personal bodyguards was waiting by the mansion door.

"Monsieur Bouchard is not happy with you, mademoiselle," Gustave said flatly.

She stopped. "Were you—following me?"

The man jutted his chin upward, toward the house. "He's waiting for you."

Emma had meant to tell Alain her news in the most gentle way possible. Instead it seemed he already had a good guess what was coming. Well, fine. She narrowed her eyes. He shouldn't have had her followed.

Going upstairs, she walked right past Alain's office, but not before she saw him scowling at his desk. First, she went to check on her baby, and found him sleeping in his crib. For a moment, she listened to his soft breath in the darkness. Tenderness and joy caught at her heart. Smiling to herself, she whispered aloud, "You're going to have a family, Sam. You're going to have a real dad."

Creeping out, she closed the door, and went to the next-door sitting room, where she found Irene Taylor reading tranquilly in an armchair.

"How was everything?" Emma asked.

"Oh, he was perfect. An angel." Smiling, Irene tucked her book, a romantic novel by Susan Mallery, carefully into her handbag. "Did you have a nice evening?"

Wordlessly Emma held out her left hand. Irene gasped, snatching up her hand and staring at the ring.

"Are you *kidding?*" She made a big show of rubbing her eyes. "Ah! It's blinding me!" She looked up at Emma with a big grin. "You sly girl, I didn't even know you were dating someone."

"Well—I wasn't. But Sam's father came for a visit, and one thing led to another…"

"Oh, how wonderful," Irene sighed. "True love prevails."

"Um. Right." Emma's cheeks went hot. She couldn't tell Irene that love had nothing to do with it, that she'd kept her pregnancy a secret and now they were only getting married for Sam's sake. "Well. I'm leaving for London with him right now. Would you mind helping me pack Sam's things?"

"I'd love to. All his cute, tiny baby things. And now you're off to London, swept away to be wed like a princess in a story." Irene looked wistful. "I hope I find a love like that someday, too."

Her friend's idealistic notion of love, the same dreams she'd once had for herself, cast a pall over Emma's heart. How could she tell Irene that she had nothing to be envious about—that Emma was settling for a loveless marriage so her baby would have a father?

Sam deserves it, she told herself again. She tried to remember the calmness she'd had about her decision just a moment before, when she'd stood in her baby's room, listening to him sleep. She turned away. "I'll be back."

Squaring her shoulders, Emma went down the hall to Alain's office. She took a deep breath and went in.

Her employer was sitting at his desk. He didn't look up. When he spoke, his voice was sour. "Have a good time at the *Tour Eiffel?*"

She was glad he was taking that tone with her. It made this so much easier. "Yes, I had a wonderful evening," she said sweetly. "Thank you."

Alain glared at her. "I don't appreciate you staying out so late. I was worried."

"I don't appreciate you having me followed."

"I wanted to keep you safe."

"Safe," she said.

"I don't trust Falconeri. You shouldn't, either."

"Right. Well. I'm sorry to tell you, but I have to turn in my notice."

Alain's eyes widened. He slowly rose to his feet. "What?"

"And by *notice,* I mean I'm leaving right now." Her cheeks flamed. "I am actually sorry to do it to you, Alain. It's not very professional. In fact it's completely rude. But Cesare and I are going back to London with the baby...."

"He's stringing you along, Emma, toying with you! I

can't believe you would fall for his lines. He'll leave you high and dry when..."

"We're getting married," she said flatly.

Alain's mouth literally fell open.

"What?"

Emma held up her engagement ring, then let her hand drop back to her side. "You've been good to me, Alain. I know you deserve better than me leaving you like this." She swallowed. "But I have to take this chance, for Sam's sake. I'm sorry. I'll never forget your kindness and generosity over the past year...."

"I'm sorry, too," Alain said shortly. "Because you're making a mistake. He ruined Angélique's life."

"Your sister's death was a terrible tragedy, but the coroner ruled the overdose an accident...."

"Accident," he said bitterly. "Falconeri drove my sister to her death. Just as surely as if he'd poured the sleeping pills down her throat."

"You're wrong." Steadying herself, she faced him in his office, clenching her hands at her sides. "He loved her. I know that all too well. He loves her still," she said quietly.

"She gave him everything," Alain continued as if he hadn't heard. "He lured her into marrying him. She loved him. Trusted him." His eyes were wild. "But from the moment they were wed, he neglected her. So much so that she told me she meant to divorce him—then she mysteriously died before she could."

Emma blinked at his implication. "You can't think—"

"If she'd divorced him, he would have gotten nothing. A few hundred thousand dollars. Instead he got her entire fortune. He used that money to turn his shabby little hotel in New York into a multibillion-dollar international hotel conglomerate. You know he's ruthless."

"But not ruthless like that," she whispered. She reminded herself that Alain's words were spoken in anger, that he was a grief-stricken brother. Going toward him, she put her hand gently on his shoulder. "I'm sorry about Angélique. I truly, truly am. But you have to stop blaming Cesare. Her death wasn't his fault. He loved her. He never would have hurt her."

Alain slowly put his hand over her own. "Someday you'll see the man he really is. And you'll come back to me. I'll give you your old job back…or better yet…" His eyes met hers. "I'll give you exactly what Falconeri is offering you now."

Marriage. He meant marriage. Emma swallowed, then pulled her hand away. "I'm sorry, Alain. I care about you deeply, but not in that way." She stepped back from him and said with her heart in her throat, "I wish you all the best. Please take care of yourself." She turned away. "Goodbye."

"Wait."

She turned back at the door. Alain's jaw was tight as he looked at her.

"My sister shone like a star," he said. "She was so beautiful, the life of every party. But even Angélique couldn't keep his attention for long. Don't think you will, either." He faced her across the shadows. "Loving him destroyed her, Emma. Don't let it destroy you."

CHAPTER EIGHT

WHAT A RIDICULOUS warning. Emma still couldn't believe it. It was laughable.

Yes, laughable. Emma felt pleased at the word. She hardly knew which was more ridiculous: the idea that Cesare would have caused his wife, the only woman he'd ever loved, to kill herself with sleeping pills, or that Emma would still be stupid enough to love him, knowing he'd never love her back.

Because she wouldn't.

Love him.

At all.

Ever again.

Even though Cesare had been so wonderful since they'd arrived in London two weeks ago. He'd taken days off from work just to spend time with them, walking across the city, seeing the sights, pushing Sam together in his baby buggy, strolling like all the other happy families along the Thames. But what did Emma care about that?

She certainly wouldn't fall in love with him just because they'd shared champagne while riding the huge Ferris wheel of the London Eye. Or because he'd agreed to a lunch of fish and chips at the Sherlock Holmes pub, when he'd wanted sushi, purely because she'd begged. She didn't care that they'd gone to Trafalgar Square to show Sam the stone lions, and Cesare had taken about a thousand pictures, and let her take some of him making funny faces as he pretended to fall from the stone pedestal. Those memories didn't matter. Her heart was made of stone.

Stone.

They'd visited the National Gallery. The British Museum. They'd gotten a tour of the new Globe Theatre, then bought fresh bread and cheese at the outdoor Borough Market. But her heart was completely safe. Cesare wasn't doing this for her. He was just following through on his promise to be an amazing father to Sam. That was all.

But he was keeping that promise beyond her wildest dreams.

Just yesterday, he'd insisted on going to Hamleys on Regent Street, where he'd bought so many toys that they'd needed to order an extra car to bring all the bags back to the Kensington house.

"When exactly are you expecting Sam to be interested in this?" Emma had asked with a laugh, looking from their sleeping five-month-old baby to the cricket bat and ball on the top of the toy pile.

"He is already fascinated with cricket. Can't you tell?" Cesare had leaned the foam cricket bat across Sam's lap, placing it in the baby's tiny hand as he slept on with a soft baby snore in the stroller. He stepped back. "Look. He's clearly a prodigy."

Holding a foam ball, Cesare elaborately wound his arm, then gently tossed the ball underhand. It bounced off the plastic edge of the stroller and rolled across the floor.

"Prodigy, huh?" she said.

He picked the ball up with a grin. "It might take a bit of practice."

"For him or you?"

"Mostly me. He already seems to have the knack."

"You're just a big kid yourself," she'd teased. "Admit it."

They'd looked at each other, smiling—then the air between them suddenly changed, sizzled with electricity.

Cesare had looked away, muttering something about going to the cashier to pay. And Emma's hands had gripped the stroller handle, as in her mind she repeated the words *In name only* about a thousand times.

Now she shivered as she went up the stairs of the Kensington house. He'd shown her every bit of attention he'd promised, and more. And as promised, he hadn't once tried to kiss her. Not even once.

But that was starting to be a problem. Because in her heart of hearts, she was starting to realize that she wanted him to…

She veered past his bedroom, and continued to her own bedroom, down the hall, where Sam was currently sleeping.

Emma told herself she was being stupid. They weren't even married yet, and she wanted to give him her body? Stupid, stupid. Because how much harder would it be not to give him her heart in the bargain?

We won't be lovers, he'd said in Paris. *We'll be equal partners.*

Her brain had accepted this as the best possible course when she'd agreed to his proposal. And yet…

She was supposed to be planning the wedding right now. But every time she started, something stopped her. Something that had nothing to do with choosing the cake or venue or church.

She was sacrificing her heart. For her son. She could accept that. There was one thing she was trying not to think about.

A marriage in name only would inevitably mean that Cesare would take lovers on the side.

What else could it mean—that Cesare would do as she planned to do, and go without sex for the rest of her life? No. For a red-blooded man like him, that would be impossible.

She was trying not to think about it. Trying and failing.

Emma leaned heavily back against her own bedroom door, closing it behind her. She didn't want to be jealous. She didn't want to be afraid.

But the day they'd returned to Kensington, Emma had fired the housekeeper. Miss Maddie Allen was an attractive young blonde, and Emma had instantly felt she hadn't wanted her within a million miles of Cesare. He'd said he was glad to see her go, that she was the worst housekeeper imaginable and had regularly left iron marks on his shirts. But Emma had given her a year's salary as severance, out of guilt for the real reason she'd fired the beautiful Miss Allen—out of pure, raw fear.

She didn't want to feel this way. With a sigh, Emma walked across her bedroom. A garment bag from a designer shop on Sloane Street was laid carefully upon her bed. Zipping open the bag, she looked down at the gown she would wear tonight at their official engagement party.

For a moment, she just stood there looking at it. Then she reached out and stroked the slinky silver fabric. Pulling off her clothes, she put on a black lace bra and panties and black garter she'd gotten from a French lingerie shop. She didn't dare look at herself in the full-length mirror as she put them on, for fear she'd lose her nerve.

Tonight, she would be introduced to Cesare's friends, and London society in general, not as his housekeeper, but as his future wife, and the mother of his child. She didn't want to embarrass him.

And if, by some miracle, he thought she looked pretty, maybe their marriage could become real. Maybe he'd take her in his bed, and she'd never have to feel insecure again....

Even Angélique couldn't keep his attention for long. Don't think you will, either.

She pushed away the memory of Alain's words. She had to stop this ugly insecurity! After all her jealousy, she'd found out Cesare hadn't slept with Maddie Allen anyway. Emma knew this because—her blush deepened—she'd blurted out that question immediately after the house-keeper had departed. His reply had been curt.

"No. I did not sleep with her." His jaw had been tight as he looked at the fire in the fireplace, leaving flickering red-and-gold light across the spines of the leatherbound books. He'd parted his lips, drawing in breath as if he meant to say something more, then stopped.

Nearly jumping out of her own skin, she'd said, "But did you ever..."

"No more questions. I won't have you torture us both by asking for a list of my lovers. You of all people know the list is long." Putting his hands on her shoulders, he'd looked down and said softly, "This home is yours now, Emma." He'd cupped her face. "I will never disrespect you here."

His words had thrilled her. *Then.* Later, she'd parsed his words. *This home is yours. I will never disrespect you here.* Meaning—he'd disrespect her elsewhere? At a hotel?

Now, reaching down for the silver dress, long and glamorous like the gown of a 1930s film star, she let the whisper of fabric caress her skin as she pulled it up her body. She didn't want to be jealous. She didn't want to worry.

She wanted him to want—*her.*

Emma's throat tightened. Sitting in the chair at the vanity desk, she began brushing her dark hair with long, hard strokes. She looked at herself in the antique gilt mirror. She was nothing special. Just a regular girl, with round cheeks and big, vulnerable green eyes, who looked scared out of her mind.

How could she marry him, even for Sam's sake, knowing that Cesare would never uphold the promise of their wedding vows? How could she allow Sam to grow up watching his father repeatedly cheat on his mother—and her explicitly allowing him to do it? What kind of sick ideas would that teach her precious boy about love, marriage, trust and family?

If only Cesare would want her. Her hand slowed with the brush. If only they could truly be lovers, in the same bed, maybe he'd stay true to their wedding vows, and they could be a real family....

"Not ready yet?"

She twisted in the chair to see Cesare in the doorway. He was wearing a tuxedo a little different than the one in Paris—less classic, more cutting edge. But with his dark hair and chiseled good looks, he melted her, whatever he might be wearing. Even wearing nothing.

Especially wearing nothing.

She gulped, turning away. She couldn't stop thinking about the two hot nights he'd made love to her. So long ago now. Almost a year since he'd touched her...

"You look beautiful," he said huskily, coming into her bedroom.

"Oh," she said. "Thank you." Their eyes met in the mirror. Her cheeks turned pink.

"You're just missing one final touch." Coming up behind her, he pulled a sparkling diamond necklace from his pocket and placed it around her neck. Emma's lips parted as she saw it in the mirror, huge diamonds dripping past her collarbone. Involuntarily she put her hand against the necklace, hardly able to believe it was real.

"Almost worthy of the woman wearing it," he murmured.

"You...you shouldn't have." Nervously she rose to her feet, facing him. Realizing her fingertips were still resting against the sparkling stones, she put her hand down.

"It's nothing. A mere trinket." His black eyes caressed her. Leaning forward, he brushed long tendrils of glossy black hair from her bare shoulders, back from the necklace, and whispered, "Nothing is too good for my future wife."

Emma felt the warmth of his breath against her bare skin. She shuddered with a sudden pang of need. Of desire.

She couldn't let herself want him like this. Couldn't. It left her too vulnerable. And the one thing she knew about Cesare was that he detested needy women. She wouldn't, couldn't, be one.

And yet...

Turning away, she went back to the mirror and put on her bright red lipstick with a shaking hand. She tried to ignore his gaze as she ran the red tube carefully over her lips. Sitting back on the bed, she reached for her high-heeled shoes, gorgeous Charlotte Olympia pumps with bamboo on the platform sole and pink cherry blossoms crisscrossing the straps. Emma had seen them in a shop on Sloane Street and in spite of her best efforts—since they were quite expensive—had fallen instantly in love with the 1930s Shanghai glamour.

"Mr. Falconeri said you're to have whatever you wish, madame," the salesgirl had insisted, and Emma, with baby Sam in his stroller next to Cesare's personal bodyguard, had quickly succumbed. It was so wrong to buy shoes that were so expensive. Wrong to want something so forbidden. So clearly out of reach. Emma looked at Cesare.

Or was it?

She rose to her feet, her long black hair tumbling over

the low cowl neck of her gown, which melted like liquid silver against her body. She felt transformed—like a glamorous, mysterious starlet from a black-and-white film. She'd never felt so beautiful, or less like the plain, sensible person she'd always been. She took a deep breath, and looked at Cesare.

"I'm ready," she said softly.

He stared at her. She saw his hands tighten at his sides as his gaze slowly went down the length of her dress. And when he spoke, was it her imagination or was his voice a little strained?

"You look…fine." Clearing his throat, he held out his arm. "Ready to meet the firing squad?"

"That's how you refer to your friends?"

He gave her a wicked grin, quirking his dark eyebrow. "You should hear how they refer to me."

"I already know." As she took his arm, Emma's smile fell. "You're the playboy who will never be caught by any woman."

He winked at her, a gesture so silly and unexpected that it caused her heart to twist in her chest. "They'll understand when they meet you."

Their eyes locked, and the squeeze on her heart suddenly became unbearable.

I love you. The words pushed through her soul, through her heart. *I love you, Cesare.*

It was a realization so horrible, Emma sucked in her breath in a gasp so rough and abrupt that it made her double over, coughing.

He rubbed her back, his voice filled with concern. "Are you all right?"

She held up her hand as she regained her breath. Downstairs, she could hear the rising noise of guests arriving at the Kensington mansion for the engagement party. All of his snooty rich friends, and their beautiful girlfriends—half of whom Cesare had probably slept with over the years. Half? Probably more.

"Cara?"

She finally straightened, her eyes watery. "I'm fine," she said, wiping her eyes. It was a lie.

She loved him.

Almost a year ago, she'd left him in despair, believing they had no chance for a future. But now, after just two weeks of wearing his engagement ring on her hand, an awful, desperate hope had pushed itself into her soul. Against her will.

She was in love with him. The truth was she'd never stopped loving him. She was utterly and completely in love with her former boss, the father of her baby.

A man who was going to marry her out of pure *obligation*. Who didn't even want to touch her. Who wanted their marriage to be *in name only*. For their son's sake. A shell. A sham...

"Emma?"

She couldn't let him see her face. Couldn't let him guess what she felt inside. Pretending not to see his outstretched arm, she walked swiftly ahead.

"Wait," he said sharply.

Emma stopped. She took a deep breath, and looked back at him in the hallway.

Smiling down at her in a way that caused his eyes to crinkle, he took her arm and wrapped it around his own. "It's an engagement party. We should enter the ballroom together."

Together. How she wished they could truly be together.

"Are you cold?" He frowned. "You're trembling."

"No... Yes... Um." She twisted her ankle deliberately. "It's the shoes."

He snorted, looking at the four-inch heels. "No wonder."

As they walked down the stairs, she clutched his arm as if her beautiful shoes were really the problem, trying to convince herself everything would be just fine. All right, so she was in love with Cesare and he'd never love her back. All right, so her whole body yearned for him to touch her, but he insisted on separate bedrooms and was likely planning to hook up with the next gorgeous actress who struck his fancy.

But they had a child together. Their marriage would be like a business partnership. That counted for something, didn't it?

Didn't it?

Her throat tightened.

As they approached the mansion's ballroom, she saw his friends—tycoons, actresses, diplomats and royalty. The women were thin and young and beautiful, in chic, tight clothes with no stretch marks from pregnancy. They all turned to look at her speculatively. She could see their sly assumption: that Emma had gotten pregnant on purpose. That was how a gold-digging housekeeper trapped an uncatchable playboy.

Their expressions changed as they looked from her to Cesare. And she realized that being in love with him just made Emma exactly the same as every other woman in the room. They all wanted him. They all broke their hearts over him.

She swallowed, glancing up at him through her lashes, suddenly desperate for reassurance, unable to fight this green demon eating her alive from the inside out.

Cesare abruptly stopped at the bottom of the stairs, in front of the open ballroom doors. "Time to face the music."

His voice was strangely flat. All the emotion had fled from his expression. Meeting her eyes, he gave her a forced smile, as if he already regretted his unbreakable, binding promise to marry her. "Let's get this over with, shall we?"

She suddenly wanted to ask him if those were the words he'd say to himself on their wedding day, too. She looked down at her diamond necklace. At her enormous engagement ring.

I can do this, she told herself. *For Sam.*

Cesare led her into the ballroom, and as she walked across the same marble floor she'd once scrubbed on her hands and knees, she pasted a bright smile on her face as she was formally introduced to London society: the housekeeper who'd been lucky and conniving enough to trap a billionaire playboy into marriage.

"So the great Cesare Falconeri is caught at last," Sheikh Sharif bin Nazih al Aktoum, the emir of Makhtar, said behind him. His voice was amused.

"Caught?" Cesare turned. "I haven't been caught."

The sheikh took a sip of champagne and waved his hand airily. "Ah, but it happens to all of us sooner or later."

Cesare scowled. The two men were not close; he'd invited the sheikh as a courtesy, as his company sought to get permission to build a new resort hotel on one of his Persian Gulf beaches. He'd never thought the man might actually come, but he'd showed up at the Kensington mansion in a black town car with diplomatic flags flying, in full white robes and trailing six bodyguards.

Six. Cesare had to stop himself from rolling his eyes. Bringing two bodyguards was sensible, six was just showing off. He bared a smile at his guest. "I'm the luckiest man on earth to be engaged to Emma. It took me a year to convince her to marry me." Which was true in its way.

The sheikh gave a faint smile. "Some men are just the marrying kind, I suppose."

Cesare raised his eyebrows. "You think *I'm* the marrying kind?"

He shrugged. "Clearly. You've experienced it once and choose willingly to return to it." The dark eyes looked at him curiously, as if Cesare were an exhibit in a zoo. "As for myself, I'm in no rush to be trapped with one woman, subject to her whims, forced to listen to her complain day and night—" He cut himself off with a cough, as if he'd just realized that saying such things at an engagement party might be poor form. "Well. Perhaps marriage is different from the cage I picture it to be."

A cage. Cesare felt the sudden irrational stirrings of buried panic. He could hear the harsh rasp of Angélique's exhausted voice, a decade before.

If you ever loved me, if you ever cared at all, let me go.

But Angélique, you are still my wife. We both gave a promise before God....

Then He will forgive, for He knows how I hate you.

We can go to marriage counseling. He'd reached for her, desperate. *We can get past this.*

Her lip had curled. *What will it take for you to let me go?* She narrowed her eyes maliciously. *Would you like to hear how long and hard Raoul loves me every time we meet, here and in Paris, all this past year, while you've been busy at your pathetic little hotel, trying to make something of yourself? Raoul loves me as you never will.*

Cesare had tried to cover his ears, but she'd told him, until he could bear it no longer and went back on everything he'd ever believed in. *Fine,* he told her grimly. *I'll give you your divorce.*

Twenty-four hours later, Angélique had returned from Buenos Aires and swallowed an entire bottle of pills. Cesare had been the one to find her. He'd found out later that Raoul Menendez was already long married. That he'd laughed in Angélique's face when she'd shown up on his doorstep.

So much for love.

So much for marriage.

Oh, my God. A cold sweat broke out on Cesare's forehead as he remembered that panicked sense of failure and helplessness. The sheikh was right. A cage was exactly what marriage was.

"Your bride is beautiful, of course," the man murmured. "She would tempt any man."

Cesare looked up to see Emma floating by on the dance floor in the arms of Leonidas, his old friend and former wingman at London's best nightclubs. The famous Greek playboy had a reputation even worse than Cesare's. Emma's beautiful face was laughing, lifted to the Greek's admiring eyes. Cesare felt a surge of jealousy.

Emma was his woman. *His.*

"Ah. So lovely. Her long dark hair. Her creamy skin. And that figure…" The sheikh's voice trailed off.

"Don't even think about it," Cesare said dangerously.

He held up his hands with a low laugh. "Of course. I sought merely to praise your taste in a wife. I would not think of attempting to sample her charms myself."

"Good," he growled. "Then I won't have to think of attempting to knock your head off your body."

The man eyed him, then shook his head with a rueful snort. "You have it badly, my friend."

"It?"

"You're in love with her."

"She's the mother of my son," Cesare replied sharply, as if that explained everything.

"Naturally," the other man said soothingly. But his black eyes danced, as if to say: *you poor fool, you don't even see how deeply your neck is in the noose.*

Reaching up his hand in an involuntary movement, Cesare loosened the tuxedo tie around his neck. Then he grabbed a glass from a passing waiter and gulped down an entire glass of Dom Perignon in one swallow before he said, "Excuse me."

"Of course."

Going to the other side of the dance floor, Cesare watched Emma dance. He saw the way her face glowed. *Sì*. Think of her. Beautiful. So strong and tender. It wouldn't be so awful, would it, having her in his house?

As long as they didn't get too close.

As long as he didn't try to seduce her.

That was the only way this convenient marriage would ever work. If they kept their distance, so she didn't get any crazy ideas back about loving him. And he didn't start thinking he needed her, or let his walls down.

Vulnerability was weakness.

Love was pain.

Cesare's face went hot as he remembered how he'd felt last year when she'd left him staring after her in the window like a fool. He'd been so sure she'd be back. That she wouldn't be able to resist him.

But she had. Very well.

While he hadn't even slept with another woman since their last night together, almost a year ago.

How the world would laugh if they knew *that* little truth about Cesare Falconeri, the famous playboy. They would laugh—*sì*—they would, because it was pathetic. Fortunately he had no intention of sharing it with anyone. Not even Emma.

He almost had, the first day they'd arrived here, when she'd been so strangely jealous of the silly blonde housekeeper. He'd almost told Emma the truth, but it had caught in his throat. He couldn't let her know that secret. He would never allow himself to be that vulnerable to anyone ever again.

You love her, the sheikh had accused. Cesare snorted. Love? Ridiculous. Love was a concept for idealistic young souls, the ones who thought *lust* was not a big enough word to describe their desire. He'd been that way once. He'd married his wife when he was young and stupid. He'd thought sex meant love. He'd learned his lesson well.

Now his eyes narrowed as he watched Emma smile up encouragingly at Leonidas.

Before he realized what he was doing, he was on the dance floor, breaking up their little duo. "I'd like to dance with my fiancée, if you don't mind."

Emma had been in the middle of laughing but she looked at Cesare in surprise, as if, he thought grimly, she'd already forgotten his existence. As if she already suspected her power over him, and knew his weakness.

Leonidas looked tempted to make some sarcastic remark, but at Cesare's scowl, thought better of it. "Alas, my dear," he sighed to Emma. "I must hand you over to this brute. You belong to him now."

She gave another low laugh, and it was all Cesare could do not to give the Greek shipping tycoon a good kick on the backside to help speed him off the dance floor. With narrowed eyes, he took Emma in his arms.

"Having fun?" he growled as he felt her soft body against his, in her slinky gown of silver.

"It's been dreadful." She peeked up at him. "I'm glad to see you. I know he's your friend, but I didn't think I could take much more. Thank you for saving me!"

"Are you sure?" he said through gritted teeth. "The two of you seemed so cozy."

She blinked. "I was being nice to your friend."

"Not much nicer, I hope," he ground out, "or I might

have found the two of you making use of a guest bedroom!"

"What's gotten into you? You're acting almost—"

"Don't say it," he warned.

She tossed her head. "Jealous!"

Cesare set his jaw. "Tell me, what exactly was Leonidas saying that you found so charming?"

Sparks were starting to illuminate her green eyes. "I'm
not going to tell you."

He glared at her. "So you admit that you were flirting."

"I admit nothing. You are the one who said we shouldn't
ask each other questions!"

"About the past, not the present!"

"That's fine for you, because as you well know, *you* are
my only past, while *your* past could fill every bedroom in
this mansion. And probably has!"

Her voice caught, and for the first time he heard the
ragged edge of repressed tears. He frowned down at her.
When he spoke again, his voice was low, barely audible
over the music. "What's wrong?"

"Other than you accusing *me* of flirting, while I torture
myself with questions every time I meet one of your beautiful guests—wondering which ones you've slept with in
the past? And suspecting—all of them!"

Her voice broke. Her green eyes were luminous with
unshed tears. He glanced around uneasily at the women
around them. Emma was right. He'd slept with more than
one of them. No wonder she was upset. He'd nearly exploded with irrational jealousy, just seeing Leonidas talking to her.

Pulling her tighter in his arms, he swayed them to the
music, continuing to dance as he spoke to her in a low
voice.

"They were one-night stands, Emma. Meaningless."

"You called our first night together *meaningless,* too. The night we conceived our baby."

He flinched. Then emotion surged through him. He glared at her.

"This is why I wanted our marriage to be in name only. To avoid these arguments and stupid jealousies."

"You mean the way you practically hit your good friend in the face for the crime of dancing with me and making me laugh?"

For a moment, he scowled at her. Then, getting hold of himself, he took a deep breath.

"Sorry," he muttered. "I never meant...to make you cry."

Emma looked away, blinking fast. "That's not why I was crying."

"What is it, then?"

"It's stupid."

"Tell me."

She swallowed.

"They all think I'm a sly gold digger. All your friends." She wiped her eyes. "A few women actually *congratulated* me on tricking you into marriage. Some of them could hardly believe a woman as—well, fat—as me could do it. Others just wanted tips for how to trick billionaire husbands of their own. They wanted to know if I poked holes in the condom wrapper with a needle or what."

Cesare's hands tightened on her back. He stared down at her, vibrating with rage as they swayed to the music. "I will take a horsewhip to all of them."

She gave a small laugh, even as tears spilled down her cheeks. "It doesn't matter," she said softly, but he could feel how much that wasn't true. To her, the simple question of honor and a good name did matter. Her pride had been hurt.

He fiercely wiped a tear off her cheek with her thumb. "You and I, we know the truth."

"Yes. We do. But I still wish," she whispered, "we were a million miles from here."

"From London?"

"As long as we're in London, I'll always be your gold-digging housekeeper. And you'll be the playboy who's slept with every woman in the city." She looked up at him with tearful eyes. "I wish we could just go. Move away. Some-where I'll never have to wonder, every time I see another woman, if she's ever been in your bed." She shuddered. "I hate what my imagination is doing to me—"

"Since the first night we slept together, I haven't touched another woman."

Her lips parted. "What?"

Cesare was almost as surprised as she was that he'd said it. But damn it—how could he not tell her? He couldn't see her pain and do nothing. "It's true."

"But—why?"

He stopped on the dance floor.

"I haven't wanted to," he said quietly.

"I don't understand." Emma shook her head. "If that's the case, why would you say you wanted a marriage in name only?"

Reaching out, he brushed back some dark hair from the soft skin of her bare shoulder above her gown. "Because all my love affairs have ended badly."

She swallowed. "Mine, too."

"Our marriage is too important. I cannot let it end in fights and tears and recriminations. The only way to make sure our relationship never ends...is never to start it in the first place."

"It won't work. Listen to us! We're still fighting any-way."

"Not like we would if—" He cut himself off, then shook his head. "You know lovers are a dime a dozen to me. But you... You are special." Reaching up, he stroked her cheek. "I need you as a partner. As my friend." He set his jaw. "Sex would ruin everything. It always does."

Swallowing, she exhaled, looking away.

"All right," she said finally. "Friends." There was a shadow of worry behind her eyes as they lifted to his. "You really haven't slept with any other women?" she said in wonder. "Since the night we conceived Sam?"

He gave her an unsteady grin. "Don't tell anyone. It would ruin my reputation."

"Your secret is safe with me." She smiled up at him, even as her eyes still shone with tears. "And you might as well know—your friend Leonidas is a very clumsy dancer. That's why I was laughing at his dumb jokes. To try to disguise yelps of pain every time he stomped on my foot."

A hard pressure in Cesare's chest suddenly released. For a moment, they just looked at each other, and though they were in the middle of a dance floor surrounded by a hundred guests, it was as if it were just the two of them in the world.

He never should have brought her back to London, Cesare thought suddenly. Of course not. How could he have expected Emma to return as a wife to the house where she'd once been his employee, and sleep in the same lonely bedroom down the hall from the bed where he'd seduced other women, again and again? The house where he'd once expected her, as a matter of course, to make breakfast for his one-night-stands and escort them out with gifts and a shoulder to cry on?

"We don't have to stay here," he said slowly. "There's someplace else we can go. A place where we can be married and start fresh, just the three of us. As a family."

"Where?"

His heart twisted to remember it. But he forced himself to meet her gaze. To smile.

"Home," he said simply.

CHAPTER NINE

THE TWO-HUNDRED-year-old villa on the shores of Lake Como stood like an ancient castle, caught in the shadows between the gray water and lowering clouds of dusk.

Emma took a deep breath, savoring the cool air against her cheeks and crunch of gravel beneath her feet as she walked along the forest path around the lake toward home. From the cushioned front pack on her chest, Sam let out another low cry, waving his plump arms. She sighed, looking down at her baby, then rubbed his soft downy hair.

"I thought for sure that a walk would do it," she said mournfully. He was irritable because he hadn't gone down for a nap all day, not for lack of her trying. "Ah, well. Let's see what we can rustle up for dinner, shall we?"

Her own stomach was growling after their long walk. She had spent hours trying to coax him to sleep, but as tired as Sam was, as soon as he started to nod off, he kept jerking himself awake. Now, she was finally forced to admit failure. The darkening October sky was drawing her back home.

That, and knowing Cesare was waiting for them...

Emma smiled to herself as she walked the lake path back toward the villa, which had been in the Falconeri family for hundreds of years. They'd been living here a month now, and it was starting to feel like home, though their first day, when he'd shown her around, she'd been shocked. "You grew up in this palace?" she'd blurted out, thinking of her two-bedroom bungalow on the Texas prairie.

He'd snorted. "It didn't always look like this. When I was a child, we barely had indoor plumbing. Our family ran out of money long before I was born. And that was even before my parents decided to devote their lives to art." His lips quirked. "Five years ago, I decided I wouldn't let it fall apart." His voice turned grim. "Although I was tempted."

"I remember you talking about the remodel." Emma had walked through room after room, all of them with ceilings fifteen feet high, with gilded details on the walls and even a fresco in the foyer. "I never imagined I might someday live here as your wife."

She could see why the remodel of this house, which she remembered him grumbling about, had required so much money and time. Every detail of the past had been preserved, while made modern with brand-new fixtures, windows, heated floors and two separate kitchens.

She'd been amazed when she saw a beautiful oil painting of Cesare as a young boy of maybe three or four, with chubby cheeks and bright innocence in his eyes—along with a determined set to his jaw. His clothes were ragged and covered with mud. She'd pointed at it with a laugh. "That was you?"

"My mother painted me perfectly. I was always outside in the garden, growing something or other."

"You liked to garden?" It astonished Emma. She couldn't reconcile the image of the happy, grimy boy in the painting with the sophisticated tycoon who now stood before her.

He rolled his eyes. "We were that kind of family. If I wanted fruit, I had to grow it myself. My parents' idea of childcare was to give me a stick and send me outside to play in the dirt." He fell silent. "But for all that, we were happy. We loved each other."

"I'm sorry," she'd whispered, seeing the pain in his eyes. She'd put her arms around him. "But we're here now."

For a moment, Cesare had allowed her to hold him, to offer comfort. Then he'd pulled away. "It all worked out," he said gruffly. "If I hadn't had my little tragedy and been sent to New York, I might never have started Falconeri International." His lips curved. "Who knows. I might still have been living here in a ruin, growing oranges and flowers, digging in the garden."

Now, as Emma walked along the lake's edge with her baby in her front pack, she stared at that overgrown garden. Alone of everything on the estate, the villa's garden had not been touched. It had been left untended and wild, choked with weeds. It was as if, she thought, Cesare could neither bear to have it destroyed, nor have it returned to its former glory.

A white mist was settling across the lake, thick and wet. Emma shivered as she pushed open the tall, heavy oak door that led into the Villa Falconeri. The scrape of the door echoed against the checkered marble floor and high ceiling with its two-hundred-year-old fresco above, showing pastoral scenes of the countryside.

"Cesare?" she called.

There was no answer. Emma heard a soft snore from her front pack and looked down. After hours of trying, Sam had finally dropped to sleep. His dark eyelashes fluttered downward over his plump cheeks. Smiling to herself, she went upstairs to tuck him into his crib.

She was sharing her beautiful bedroom with her baby. There was plenty of room for his crib and changing table. The room was enormous, in powder-blue, with a canopy bed and a huge window with a balcony overlooking the lake. Gently lifting her sleeping baby out of the carrier, she tucked him into his bed.

Alone in the room, without her baby's warmth against her, she felt a shiver of cold air in the deepening twilight. Even here, in this beautiful place, she slept alone.

You are special. I need you as a partner. As my friend. Sex would ruin everything.

Emma took a deep breath.

Tomorrow, their three-day wedding celebration would begin, first with a church ceremony, followed by a civil service the next day. Private celebrations with just a few friends: a white dress. A cake. Vows that could not be unspoken.

How she wished it all could be real. She longed to be his real wife. She looked at her empty bed. She wanted to sleep in his arms, to feel his lips on hers, to feel his hard, naked body cover hers at night. A flash of heat went through her and she touched her lips with her fingers. She could remember him there...

She shivered, closing her eyes.

As much as her brain told her that marriage was the rational solution, as much as her heart longed to be permanently bound to the man she loved, her body was tense and fighting the wedding every step of the way.

Marry a man who would never touch her?

A man who was still in love with his long-dead wife?

A man who would satisfy his sexual needs elsewhere, discreetly, leaving Emma to grow old and gray and die in a lonely, solitary bed?

Emma had been shocked when Cesare had told her in London that he hadn't slept with another woman since their first night together. But as amazing as that was, she knew it wouldn't last. It couldn't. Cesare wasn't the kind of man to tolerate an empty bed for the rest of his life. There were too many women in the world who would eagerly join him, married or no.

Cesare didn't equate sex with love the way she did, either. To Cesare, satisfying a sexual need was no different than satiating a hunger for food or sleep. It was just physical. Not emotional.

Lovers are a dime a dozen to me.

Emma swallowed, crossing her arms over her body.

She could ask him outright if he planned to be unfaithful to her. But she was afraid, because if she asked, he would tell her the truth. And she didn't think her heart could take it.

No, it was easier to live in denial, in the pretty lie of marriage vows, and to try not to think about the ugly truth beneath....

"There you are, *cara*."

Whirling around to see Cesare in the doorway, she put a finger to her lips. "Shh. Sam is finally asleep," she whispered, barely loud enough to hear. "I just got him down."

His handsome face looked relieved. *"Grazie a dio."* He silently backed away, and she followed him out of the room. She closed the door behind them, and they both exhaled.

"What made him sleep? Was it your walk?"

"No," she said softly. "I think it was coming home."

For a long moment, they looked at each other.

"I'm glad you are thinking of it as home, *cara*." He smiled. "And starting tomorrow, we will be husband and wife."

A lump rose in her throat. She tried to stay silent, but her fear came out in blurted words. "Are you still sure it's what you want?"

The smile slid from his face. "Why wouldn't I be?"

"A lifetime without love—without…" She gulped, then forced herself to meet his gaze. "Without sex…"

"The decision has already been made." His voice had turned cold. "I've made you dinner. Come."

She was very hungry after her walk, but she hesitated, glancing behind her. "I can't just leave Sam up here. Not until the baby monitor arrives. This house is so big and the old walls are thick. Downstairs in the dining room, we'd never hear him if he cried…."

"I thought you might feel that way." Cesare tilted his head, looking suddenly pleased with himself. "We're not going far."

Placing his hand in the small of her back, he pushed her gently down the hall. A sizzle of electricity went up her body at even that courteous, commanding touch. Biting her lip, she allowed him to lead her…

…a mere ten steps, to his own bedroom next door.

"We're having dinner in your room?" she said, a little sheepish that he'd guessed her feelings about the baby so well.

He nodded. "A private dinner for two on my balcony."

"Lovely," she said. "Um…any particular reason?"

"I just thought before our guests arrive in the morning, it would be nice to have a quiet dinner. To talk."

"Oh." That sounded ominous. The last time they'd had a private dinner and a talk she'd walked out engaged, with her whole life changed forever. She was afraid what might come out of it this time. The questions she might ask. The answers he might give. All words that could never be unheard or forgotten.

She licked her lips and tried to smile as she repeated, "Lovely."

Cesare led her into his enormous en suite bedroom, with a fireplace and a huge bed that she tried not to look at as they walked past it. He led her out to the balcony, where she found a charming table for two, lit by candle-light, and two silver plates covered by lids. Beyond the table, the dark sweep of Lake Como trailed moonlight in a pattern of gold.

Emma looked at Cesare, noticing for the first time how he had carefully dressed in a crisp black shirt and pants. With his dark hair, black eyes and chiseled jawline, he looked devastatingly handsome. He was the man every woman wanted. While she... Well.

Emma touched her hair, which was tumbling over her shoulders, messy from Sam tugging on it, and from the wind of their walk. She looked down at her simple pink blouse and slim-fit jeans. "I'm not dressed for this." For all she knew, she might have baby spit-up on her shoulder. She tried to look, but she couldn't see. "Um. I should go change..."

"Go back to your bedroom and risk waking up our son? Don't you dare. Besides." He looked over her body with a heavily lidded gaze. "You are perfect just as you are." He held out her chair with a sensual smile. *Signorina, per favore.*

Nervously Emma sat down. He sat down across from her, poured them each a glass of wine, then lifted off the silver lids of the plates. She took a deep breath of fettuccine primavera, with breaded chicken, salad and fresh bread. Placing the linen napkin in her lap, she picked up her heavy fork, also made of solid silver. "This looks delicious."

"It is an old family recipe."

"You cooked it yourself?"

"Not the bread, but the pasta, yes. I had to do something to be useful while you were fighting the war to put Sam to sleep." He paused. "I had Maria pick up the vegetables from town, but I made the sauce as well."

"I had no idea you knew how to cook."

He gave a low laugh. "When I was a boy, I helped with everything. Milked our cow. Made cheese and grew vegetables in the garden."

"Your life is very different now." She sipped red wine. She wasn't going to ask him if he planned to be faithful after their marriage. She *wasn't*. Placing a trembling hand over her throat to keep the question from popping out, she asked in a strained tone, "So why have you let the garden grow so wild and unloved? I could cut back the weeds, and bring it back to its former glory...."

His hand tightened on his wineglass, even as he said politely, "It's not necessary."

"I wouldn't mind. After all, it's my home, too, now...."

The candlelight flickered in the soft, invisible breeze. "No."

His short, cold word echoed across the table. As their eyes locked, Emma's heart cried out. For all the things they both weren't saying.

Was this to be their marriage? Courtesy, without connection? Proximity without words?

Would this beautiful villa become, like the Kensington mansion had been, her empty, lonely tomb?

Taking another gulp of wine, she blinked fast, looking out at the dark, quiet night. Lights of distant villas sparkled like stars across the lake. She heard the cry of unseen night birds, and the soft sigh of wind rattling the trees.

"How did you first meet her?" she asked softly. "Your wife?"

"Why do you want to know?" He sounded guarded.

"I'm going to be your wife tomorrow. Is it so strange that I'd want to hear the story of the first Mrs. Falconeri? Unless—" she bit her lip and faltered "—you still can't bear to speak of her..."

For a moment, she thought he wasn't going to answer. Then he exhaled. "I was twenty-three." He paused. "I'd inherited my uncle's hotel. Not the hotel you worked at on Park Avenue, but an old, rickety fleabag on Mulberry Street. I struggled to keep it afloat, working each day until I dropped, doing everything from carrying luggage to bookkeeping to making breakfast." He paused. "Angélique stumbled into the lobby one evening, taking cover from a rainstorm."

He fell silent. He cut a piece of chicken, took a bite. Set his fork and knife down. Emma leaned forward over the table, on edge for what he would say next, barely aware of the cool night breeze against her overheated skin.

Cesare looked out at the dark, moonswept lake, haunted with October mist. "For me," he said softly, "it was love at first sight."

Emma's heart lurched in her chest.

"She was so glamorous, ten years older, sexually experienced and—well, French…"

Everything she was not. Emma felt the pain twist more deeply beneath her ribs.

"We were married just six weeks after we met."

"That's fast," Emma mumbled. He'd known her for almost eight *years*.

"I was dazzled by her. It seemed like a miracle that she wanted to marry me. After we wed, I was more determined than ever to make the hotel a success. No one would ever accuse me of living off my wife."

"No," she whispered over the lump in her throat. She took another gulp of wine, finishing off her glass.

"She was unique," Cesare said in a low voice. "My first."

He couldn't mean what she thought he meant. "Your—first?"

"Yes," he said quietly.

"But—you were *twenty-three*."

"Amusing, yes?" His lips curved. "The famous playboy, a virgin at twenty-three. My uncle was strict, and after he died, I was too focused on the hotel. I had no money, nothing to offer any potential wife."

It was a good thing she hadn't been drinking wine or she would have spit it out in shock. "You were trying to save yourself—for marriage?"

"I was idealistic," he said quietly. "I thought love was supposed to be part of it." He glanced behind him at the villa, then at the dark water, scattered with gold and silver moonlight like diamonds on citrine. "Then it all died."

Yes. She'd died. His one and only love.

"You still love her, don't you?" Emma choked out. "And you always will."

Cesare's dark eyes abruptly focused on her. He put his hands over hers and said softly, "It doesn't matter."

She felt the warmth of his hands over hers, beneath the dizzying stars in the wide black-and-violet sky. Her heart beat frantically in her chest. She wanted to throw herself at his feet. To beg him to be faithful. To beg him to forget his long-dead wife and love her, instead.

"Of course it matters," she said hoarsely. "My father used to say love is all that matters. It's the only thing we leave behind."

His expression hardened. "We both love Sam."

"But is that truly enough for you to be happy?"

"Marriage isn't about happiness," he said. "It's about keeping a promise. Until death do us part. And the truth is, you and I are already bound together. By our child."

Bound, Emma thought unhappily. Bound like a rope around his wrists. Like a shackle. Like a chain.

She rose unsteadily to her feet. "I can't do this."

"What?"

"Marry you." She shook her head tearfully. "I can't let this beautiful villa be turned into a tomb, like your house was for me in Kensington, with nothing but silence and shadows to fill my bed…. I can't spend the rest of my life alone. Trapped with a man who doesn't even want me."

"You think I don't want you?" His voice was dangerous.

"You say that I am special," she said bitterly. "Your partner. Your *friend*. But we both know, once we are wed, you'll take lovers. But I won't. Because—I…" *I love you,* she almost said, but her throat closed when she saw Cesare's face.

"Not *want* you. My God." There was fury in his black eyes as he stood in the moonlight. "I told you I haven't touched another woman in over a year, and you think I don't want you?"

Her mouth suddenly went dry. "You—"

"You have no idea how hard it's been not to touch you." Reaching out, he slowly stroked down her neck, then leaned forward and whispered, "I've yearned to have you in my bed. Every night. I've thought of nothing else—but you."

Sparks flew up and down her body everywhere he touched.

"But I was trying to do the right thing for once in my damned life," he ground out. "In sickness and in health. For richer or for poorer. I was trying to do the right thing for our son. But the truth is all I've been able to think about, every single night, is having you naked beneath me."

Emma couldn't breathe.

Cesare's gaze dropped to her lips. "And this is my reward for my sacrifice. You mean nothing more to me now than the housekeeper you were. You think—"

His voice ended with a growl as he ripped her into his

arms. Holding her against his chest in the moonlight, he lowered his head, then stopped, his mouth an inch from hers.

Emma trembled at the warmth of his breath. She could almost taste his lips. Electricity seared through her veins.

"Please," she whispered, hardly knowing what she was asking for. She licked her lips, felt her tongue almost brush against his skin. She shuddered with blinding need, from her body to her heart. *He doesn't love me. His heart is buried with his wife.* "Lust," she breathed aloud, staring at his lips. "It's just lust."

She heard his harsh intake of breath. In sudden movement, he pushed her against the wall, and lowered his mouth to hers in a savage, hungry kiss.

Sparks sizzled down her skin as she felt his body, hard against hers. His hand roamed down her neck, ruthlessly reaching beneath the neckline of her blouse, to cup her breast beneath her bra. She gasped as she felt his hand brush her aching nipple. As her lips parted in the gasp, he deepened the kiss, twining and flicking his tongue against hers. He took her mouth roughly, in a way that left no doubt who was master.

A soft moan came unbidden from deep inside her. Her arms rose of their own accord to wrap around his shoulders. His tall, muscular body pressed against hers, hip to hip, and she felt lost in his passionate embrace. She clutched his back, feeling the steel of his muscles beneath his shirt. His hips swayed, grinding against her.

Cesare kissed her, his tongue twisting hot and hard in her mouth, tangling, giving and taking. And Emma knew that whatever her brain told her she should want, that in her body and heart she'd wanted this, only this, for the past year. For years before that.

The truth was that she'd waited for it all her life.

But this wasn't just lust for her. No matter how she'd tried to convince him otherwise. The truth was trembling inside her. *I love you. I never stopped loving you.*

Her hands reached up, tangling in his short black hair. She pulled him closer, clutching his shoulders, lifting on her tiptoes to kiss him with all the anguished love in her heart. He gripped her hard against the rough stone wall.

They kissed on the balcony, with the moonswept lake at their feet, and if a cool October wind blew against Emma's overheated skin, she no longer felt it. Cesare's hands moved over her body, sliding down her thin blouse, up her arms. Her breasts were crushed against his hard chest, and every inch of her was on fire.

His kiss possessed her with an intensity and force she'd never felt before. It was as if she alone could save him from destruction, as if he were taking her very breath to live.

When he drew back, he looked down at her, his eyes wide. Tilting back her head, he gently ran his thumbs over her full, swollen lips.

"Tell me to stop," he said with a shuddering breath. "For God's sake. Tell me now…"

But she couldn't. She could no more tell him to stop than she could tell herself to stop breathing, or the stars to stop shining. She loved him, and for one more night, the pathetic truth was that she was willing to do anything, pay any price.

With a low groan, he lifted her up into his arms as if she weighed nothing at all and carried her through the balcony door into his bedroom. He set her down gently on the enormous bed.

Still dressed, he covered her body with his own, pressing her back against the softness of the white pillows and thick white comforter as he kissed her. She felt the roughness of his chin against her skin, felt the heat and strength of his body. His hands trailed down her throat, to the hollow of her collarbone, then along the sides of her body, over her blouse. Her breasts felt full and heavy, her nipples tight.

She felt him unbuttoning her blouse. Never breaking their kiss, he slowly pulled it off her body, in a whisper of fabric skimming against her skin. Her hands trembled as she did the same with his black shirt, overwhelmed with desire to feel his heat. Her fingertips ran down the muscles of his back, and she tossed his shirt to the floor.

Looking up at him in the moonlight, she saw the stark shadows beneath the lines of his hard chest, the trail of dark hair down his taut belly. Her fingers traced down his velvety-smooth skin, over the powerful muscles of his body.

With a low growl, he kissed and stroked down her skin, nibbling her chin, down her neck to the valley between her breasts. Undoing the front clasp of the bra with a well-practiced movement, he cupped her full breasts with his large hands. She shivered at the sensation, but he continued down her body, flicking his tongue in her belly button, grasping her hips. Unbuttoning her jeans, he slowly pulled them down her legs, along with her panties, before tossing them to the floor.

She felt his shoulders between her bare legs, the heat of his breath on the sensitive, tender skin between her thighs. She gripped his shoulders in agonizing anticipation, then felt his tongue slide between her legs to her deepest, most secret place. He brushed his tongue against her, pushing two fingertips inside her—slowly, so slowly—until her body was so tight that she gripped his shoulders, holding her breath.

"Wait…" she gasped.

He refused to obey. He ruthlessly pushed her to the limit, and beyond, until with a soft scream she exploded beneath the unrelenting pleasure of his tongue between her legs. The moment she cried out, gripping her finger-nails into his flesh, he ripped off the rest of his clothes. He shoved himself roughly inside her, ramming to the hilt in a single deep thrust.

The sensation of him filling her, just seconds after her ecstasy, caused a shocking new wave of pleasure to build inside her. He thrust again, and she gasped with the sensation of a new wave of desire, taking off from the level it had been a moment before, climbing higher and higher, tighter and tighter. She began to rock back and forth, trembling with almost unbearable pleasure.

He rode her harder, faster, panting for breath, as their sweaty bodies clung together in the dark, hot night. A cool breeze whipped in from the Italian lake, banging back the balcony doors. But neither of them noticed as he was deep, pounding inside her, splitting her apart. She gasped, clutching his taut backside, feeling his muscles grow hard as stone beneath her hands. With a shuddering intake of breath, he slammed inside her one last time, and they both let go, flying, falling, collapsing into thin air.

Cesare landed on top of her, then, as if he feared he would hurt her with his weight, immediately rolled on one side of her. He pulled her against him on the bed, nuzzling her forehead, both of them so close, so close. Both of them the same.

Emma closed her eyes. She suddenly felt like weeping.

A moment before, all she'd wanted was this, only this. But now, she'd barely had what she wanted and already wanted more. Not just sex. She was greedy beyond all imagining. She wanted his love.

In this moment of glory, heartache filled her. She pulled away from him, moving into the shadows of the bed.

"What is it, *cara?*" he asked in a low voice, as his hand

gently stroked her bare back. She knew she shouldn't answer. She should just leave it.

But the words came out of her throat against her will.

"Will you be faithful to me?" she whispered. "Can you be?"

For a moment, he didn't answer. She couldn't see his face. And she knew she'd made a horrible mistake. She turned to face him on the bed.

"Is fidelity so important to you?" he said in a low voice.

The lump in her throat suddenly felt like a razorblade.

"No," she whispered. Really, what use was fidelity without love? What was it but cold pretense, the form of love without the heart of it?

"Tomorrow we wed." Sleepily he pulled her into his arms and kissed her forehead. "So many nights I dreamed of you, *cara,* did you know that? And now you are in my bed. Our wedding night before we are wed…"

"Yes." She ran her fingertips along the warmth of his bare chest. She would marry him tomorrow. She'd given her word. She would raise his child and sleep in his bed, and be at his command for the rest of her life. And Cesare, the onetime playboy who notoriously enjoyed such a variety of women, would do his best to accomplish his obligation of fidelity—at least for a month, or possibly a year…

Holding her in his arms, he closed his eyes. A few moments later, his breathing became even and deep.

But Emma didn't have the same peace.

She leaned against his naked body, so warm and powerful and protective around her own. She looked through the open balcony door, past the moonlight to the distant bright star, the first star of morning. In a few hours, the dark violet sky would change to red, then pink, then a glorious Italian blue as the sun would rise on her wedding day.

The first and only wedding day she'd ever know. She'd be married to the man she loved. The father of her baby.

Cesare would marry her. For Sam's sake.

But what happiness could they know, in a marriage where only one partner loved, and was faithful?

The truth was that, wedding or not, Emma was no better than any of the other women Cesare might take to his bed.

His real wife was, and always would be, Angélique.

Loving him destroyed her, Emma. Don't let it destroy you.

Emma shuddered this time as she remembered Alain's words. He knew how wildly his sister had loved Cesare. What he hadn't known was the fierce love Cesare had for her in return. Angélique hadn't been destroyed by loving him.

But Emma would be.

She looked at Cesare's handsome sleeping face in the shadowy bedroom. She listened to the sound of his breath. Could she really marry him? Knowing she'd be nothing more than the mother of his child, the keeper of his home, or at best—a warm body in the night?

Could Emma accept an eternity of knowing she was the other woman—that if given the choice, her husband would have traded her life in an instant for Angélique's?

You're stronger than you know, kiddo. She heard her father's words. *You'll get through this, and have a life more amazing than you can even imagine. Filled with sunshine and flowers and above all, love. All the things you deserve, Emma. I love you, sweetheart.*

Blinking fast, Emma stared out at the dark lake. The last streak of silvery moonlight stretched out before her like a path, like a single forlorn tear, leading to an unseen future.

* * *

Cesare held her hand tightly, unable to look away from her beautiful face.

Emma was wearing a beautiful wedding dress, holding a bouquet of pink roses. But somehow, as they left the chapel, her fingers slipped from his grasp. She ran ahead of him. He called her name, and she glanced back, laughing as she disappeared in the mist. He saw her plummet down the chapel steps, down, down, down, her bouquet exploding into a million pale pink petals falling thickly like snow.

His feet were heavy as concrete as he tried to reach her. It seemed an eternity before he found her, on a soft bed of grass. But something had changed. Emma's beautiful face had turned hollow-cheeked like his mother's, her eyes blank with despair like Angélique's. Emma was dying, and he knew it was his fault. Desperate, he jumped on a boat and took off across the lake to find a doctor. But halfway across, the boat's engine died, leaving him stranded and alone, surrounded by dark water, and he suddenly knew he was too late to save her. He looked down at water like black glass in the moonlight. There was only one thing to do now...only one way to end the pain...

With a shuddering gasp, Cesare sat up straight in bed.

Still panting for breath, he looked out the window. The sky was blue. The sun was shining. He heard birds singing. It was a dream, he told himself. All a dream. But his body was covered with cold sweat.

Today was his wedding day.

He looked down at the bed where he'd made love to her last night. Empty. He put out his hand. The sheets were long cold.

Cesare suddenly wondered if he might have woken her with his nightmare, tossing and turning or worse, crying out. He clawed back his hair, exhaling with a flare of nostril. The thought of being so vulnerable was horrifying.

But not as much as what he was about to do today.

Naked, he got up from the bed, and his legs seemed to shake beneath him. Downstairs, he could already hear guests arriving. Some twenty people, friends and acquaintances from London, Rome and around the world, would be staying at the villa for the next three days. Today, there would be a long prewedding lunch, followed by a ceremonial church wedding at twilight in the small, ancient chapel on his estate. Tomorrow they'd have the civil service in town.

The next three days would be nothing but one party after another, and the thought suddenly made him grit his teeth. He'd chosen this. Shouldn't he feel satisfaction, or failing that, at least some kind of resigned peace?

Instead his body shook with a single primal emotion—fear.

I can do it for Sam.

Closing his eyes, he pictured his sweet baby's face. Then the woman holding his son in her arms.

Emma. Her beauty. Her kindness. She was the perfect mother to Sam. The perfect homemaker. The perfect lover. He thought of the ecstasy he'd experienced last night in her arms. But reflecting on all the ways he valued Emma didn't calm the frantic beat of his heart. To the contrary. It just made him feel more panicked.

He'd sworn he'd never have a child. Then he'd found out about Sam.

He'd sworn he'd never marry again. Then he'd proposed to Emma.

He'd sworn their marriage would be in name only. Then he'd swept her straight into bed last night.

What was next? What fresh vow would he break?

There was only one left, and it was a line that he could not, would not cross. Because if he did, if he ever let himself love her, he'd be utterly annihilated. Just like before...

With an intake of breath, he paced across the bedroom, the same grand room which, decades before, had belonged to his parents. So in love, before everything came crashing down.

Whether by death, or divorce, love always ended. And ended in pain.

Cesare couldn't let himself love Emma. It would be the final bomb exploding his life into pieces. Any time he tried to love someone, to depend on them, they left—as far and fast as they possibly could. Through death.

He couldn't survive it again.

His heart pounded frantically. He looked out the window, past the overgrown garden, toward the lake. He should never have brought Emma here. Never should have let himself see the bright laughter in her eyes as she held their baby yesterday, carrying him through that garden. *This is a lemon tree, and this is verbena...*

Just as his own mother had once done. He could still remember his mother's warm embrace, back when he was very young and happy and thought the sunshine would last forever. He could hear his father's deep, tender voice. *Ti amo, tesoro mio.*

Cesare shuddered, blinking fast. He'd thought if he was careful not to love anyone, never to care, that he would be safe. Instead he'd accidentally created a child.

Or had it been an accident? Some part of him must have been willing to take that risk—since he'd never slept with any woman without protection before. Not even Angélique. But then, she'd been too selfish to want a child. All she'd wanted was a man to worship her, and when Cesare had gotten too busy with work, she'd found another man to offer her the worship she desperately craved.

Emma was nothing like Angélique. If the Frenchwoman had been cold and mysterious as moonlight, Emma was sunlight on a summer's day. Warmth. Life.

But he couldn't let himself love her. She could leave him. She could die. Her cancer could return, and leave Cesare, like his father, bereft at midnight on an endless black lake.

Looking out at Lake Como, he had the sudden impulse to throw on his clothes and run away from this house. From this wedding. Far, far away, where grief and pain and need could never find him again.

Stop it. Cesare took a deep breath, clenching his hands at his sides. *Get ahold of yourself.* He couldn't fall to pieces. He had to marry her. He'd promised. His child deserved a real home, like he'd once had. Before his parents had abruptly left, stripping his happiness away without warning…

Closing his eyes, he took a deep breath. He ruthlessly forced down his feelings. Shut down his heart.

Jaw tight, he opened his eyes. He would marry Emma today. Whatever he felt now, he'd given his word. He would marry her and never, ever love her.

And no irrational nightmare, no mere *terror,* would stop him from fulfilling his promise.

CHAPTER TEN

"OH, EMMA," IRENE whispered. Her eyes sparkled with tears. "You make such a beautiful bride."

Looking at herself in the gilded full-length mirror, Emma hardly recognized herself. The sensible house-keeper had been magically transformed into a princess bride from a nineteenth-century portrait. Her beautiful cream-colored silk dress had been handmade in Milan, with long sleeves and elaborate beadwork. Her black hair was pulled up in a chignon, tucked beneath a long veil that stretched all the way to the floor.

The green eyes looking back at her in the mirror were the only thing that seemed out of place. They weren't tran-quil. They were tortured.

Just last night, passion had curled her toes and made her cry out with pleasure. That morning, she'd risen from the warmth of their bed early to feed Sam. She had drowsed off while rocking the baby back to sleep, and when she returned later, Cesare was gone.

But something had changed in him. All day, as they welcomed their newly arriving guests—who, with the ex-ception of Irene, were all Cesare's friends, not hers—he'd barely looked at her. She'd told herself he was just busy, trying to be a good host. But the truth was that in the tiny corner of her heart, she feared it was more than that. No. She *knew* it was more than that.

This marriage was a mistake.

Emma looked at herself again in the mirror, at the beautiful wedding gown. She smoothed the creamy silk beneath her hands. *The decision is already made,* she told herself, but her hands were trembling.

Since she'd left his bed that morning, the day had flown by, in a succession of celebrations leading up to tonight's first wedding ceremony, at twilight in the chapel. Emma had been genuinely thrilled to see Irene, who'd been flown in from Paris courtesy of Cesare. But as she'd shown the younger woman around her new home, Irene's idealistic joy had soon become grating.

"It's all like a dream," she'd breathed, seeing her beautifully appointed guest room, with its Louis XV furniture and accents of deep rose and pale pink. She'd whirled to face Emma, her rosy face shining. "You deserve this. You worked so hard, you put your baby first, and now you've been rewarded with a wedding to a man who loves you with all his heart. It's just like a fairy tale."

Feeling like a fraud, Emma had muttered some reply, she couldn't even remember what. Later, as she was congratulated by his friends, even a sheikh of some sort with long white robes who, in perfect British English, wished her well, the feeling only worsened.

Out of everyone at the villa, only one person didn't speak to her. He didn't even look at her. Not since he'd made love to her last night.

How could he turn so fast from passion to coldness?

The answer was clear.

Cesare didn't want to marry her.

It was only his promise that was forcing him to do it. Emma's gaze fell on baby Sam, who was currently lying on her soft bed, proudly chewing the tip of his own sock, which was stretched out from his foot.

"Here's your bouquet," Irene said now, smiling as she wiped her own happy tears away. She handed her a small, simple bouquet of small red roses. "Perfect. This is all so romantic...."

Emma looked down at the flowers, feeling cold. How could she destroy Irene's dreams, and tell her that *romantic* was the last thing this wedding would be? She exhaled.

"I just wish my father were here," Emma whispered. With his steady hand and good advice, he'd know just what to do.

Irene's face instantly sobered. "It must be so hard not to have him here, to walk you down the aisle. But he's with you in spirit. I know he is. Looking down on you today and smiling."

Emma swallowed. That thought made it even worse. Because today, marrying Cesare, she was doing something her heart told her was wrong. Doing something that her heart told her could only ultimately end in disaster, no matter how good their intentions might be for their son.

It's too late to back out, she told herself. *There's nothing I can do now.*

Irene looked at the watch on her slender wrist.

"It's time," she said cheerfully. She picked up Sam, who was wearing a baby tuxedo in his strictly honorary capacity of ring bearer. "We'll be sitting in the front row. Cheering for you both. And probably crying buckets." She waved a linen handkerchief. "But I came prepared!" She tucked it in her chiffon sash. "See you in the chapel."

"Wait." Emma swallowed, feeling suddenly panicky. She held out her arms. "I need Sam with me."

Irene looked bemused. "You want to walk up the aisle holding a baby?"

"Yes. Because—" she grasped at straws "—we're a family."

"But your hands are full…."

Emma instantly dropped the bouquet on the floor in a splash of petals, and stretched out her hands desperately. She needed to feel her baby in her arms. She needed to remind herself what she was doing this for—marrying a man who was forever in love with his dead wife. His *real* wife. She needed to feel that she was sacrificing her life for a good reason. "Give him to me."

"Aw, your poor flowers," Irene sighed, looking at the bouquet on the floor. Then, looking up, she slowly nodded. "But maybe you're right. Maybe this is better. Here you go."

Emma took Sam in her arms. She felt the warmth of his small body and inhaled his sweet baby smell, and nearly cried.

Turning away, Irene paused at the door of Emma's bedroom. "The three of you are already a family," she said softly, "but today makes it official. Thanks for inviting me. Seeing what's possible…it makes me more happy than you'll ever know."

And her young friend left, leaving Emma holding her baby against her beaded silk dress, her throat aching as she fought back tears that had nothing to do with joy.

"All right, Sam. I guess we can't be late." She looked out the window, at the vast sky above the lake, already turning red in the twilight. "I only wish I had a sign," she murmured over the lump in her throat. "I wish I knew whether I'm making the right choice—or ruining all our lives."

Sam, of course, didn't answer, at least not in words she could understand. Holding her baby close, she walked out of her bedroom as an unmarried woman for the last time.

When next she returned, she would be the mistress of this villa. From now on, her place would be in Cesare's bed.

Until he grew tired of her. And started sleeping elsewhere. She pushed the thought aside.

Emma's white satin shoes trembled as she walked down the sweeping stairs. The villa was strangely silent. Everyone had gone to the chapel, even the household staff. She heard the echoing footsteps of her shoes against the marble floor before she pushed open the enormous oak door and went outside.

Holding her baby close, she walked down the path carved into the hillside, along the edge of the lake. "This marriage is for you, Sam," she whispered. "I can live without your father loving me. I can live without him being faithful to me. For you, I can live the rest of my life with a numb, lonely heart...."

Emma stopped in front of the medieval chapel, which was lit by torchlight on the edge of the lake. Such a romantic setting. And every drop of romance a lie.

Trembling, she walked toward it, nestling her baby against her hip as the veil trailed behind them.

The twelfth-century chapel had been carefully and lovingly restored to its Romanesque glory. The medieval walls were thick, with just a few tiny windows. The arched door was open.

Heart pounding, she stepped inside.

The dark chapel was illuminated by candlelight, its tall brass candlesticks placed along the aisle. She heard the soft music of a lute, accompanied by guitar. As she appeared in the doorway, there was an audible gasp as the people packed into the tiny chairs rose to their feet.

Emma's legs felt like jelly. She felt a tug on her translucent silk veil and saw Sam had grabbed it in his pudgy fist, and was now attempting to chew it. She smiled through her tears, then took a deep breath as the music changed to the traditional wedding march.

Looking at all the faces of the guests, she didn't recognize any of them as she slowly walked forward, feeling more dizzy with every step. She tried to focus on Cesare at the end of the aisle. She took another step, then another. She was six steps from the altar.

And then she saw his face.

Cesare looked green, sick with fear—as if only sheer will kept him from rushing straight past her in a panic. He tried to give her a smile.

Her footsteps stopped.

"Stop! Don't do it! Don't ruin your life!"

The man's voice was a low roar, as if from the deepest reaches of the earth, coming up through the stone floor. For an instant, Emma couldn't breathe. Her father's voice from beyond the grave...? Then she saw Cesare glare at someone behind her.

Whirling around, she saw Alain.

The slim salt-and-pepper-haired Frenchman took another step into the chapel. "Don't do this," he pleaded. "Falconeri has already caused the death of one woman I loved. I won't let him take another."

There was a gasp and growl across the crowd. Cesare gave a low hiss of fury. He was going to come down and smash Alain's face for doing this, she realized.

For stopping a wedding that Emma never should have agreed to in the first place.

"Don't marry him." Alain held out a trembling hand to her. "Come with me now."

She'd wanted a sign?

With tortured eyes, she turned back to Cesare.

"I can't do this," she choked out. "I'm sorry."

Cradling her baby, she picked up the hem of her cream-colored silk gown with one hand, and followed Alain out of the chapel. She ran from Cesare as if the happiness of her whole life—and not just hers, but Sam's and Cesare's—depended on it.

Which she finally knew—*it did.*

As a thirteen-year-old, coming home in a strange big city, Cesare had once been mugged for the five dollars in his pocket. He'd been kicked in the gut with steel-toed boots.

This felt worse.

As if in a dream, Cesare had watched Emma walk up the aisle of the chapel, a bride more beautiful than he'd ever imagined, with their child in her arms. Then, like a sudden deadly storm, Alain Bouchard had appeared like an avenging angel. Emma had looked between the two men.

Cesare had been confident in her loyalty. He'd known she would spurn Bouchard, and marry him as she'd promised.

Instead she'd turned on him.

She'd *abandoned* him.

For a moment, as the chapel door banged closed behind her, Cesare couldn't breathe. The pain was so intense he staggered from it.

The chapel was suddenly so quiet that he could hear the soft wind blow across the lake. The deepening shadows of the candlelit chapel seemed relentlessly dark as endless eyes focused on him, in varying degrees of shock, sympathy and worst of all—pity.

The priest, who'd met with them several times over the past weeks, spoke to him in Italian, in a low, shocked voice. He could barely hear.

Cesare's tuxedo tie was suddenly too tight around his throat. He couldn't let himself show his feelings. He couldn't even let himself *feel* them.

Emma had left him.

At the altar.

With Bouchard.

And taken their child with her.

He looked at the faces of his friends and business acquaintances, including the white-robed, hard-eyed sheikh of Makhtar in the back row, who alone had no expression of sympathy on his face. Cesare parted his lips to speak, but his throat was too tight. After all, what was there to say?

Emma had betrayed him.

Ripping off his black tie, he tossed it on the stone floor and strode grimly out of the chapel in pursuit of her.

So much for mercy. So much for the high road.

He never should have listened to old Morty Ainsley. Cesare's throat was burning, and so were his eyes. He should have sued Emma for full custody from the moment he learned of Sam's existence. He should have gotten his revenge. Gotten his war.

Instead he'd offered her everything. His throat hurt. His name. His fortune. His fidelity. Hadn't he made it clear that if she wished it, he would remain true to her? Hadn't he proven it with more than words—with his absolute faithfulness over the past year? How much more clear could he be?

And Emma had spurned all of it. In the most humiliating way possible. He'd never thought she could be so cruel. Making love to him last night—today, leaving him for another man.

He pushed through a grove of lemon trees. He would make her pay. He would make her regret. He would make her...

His heart was breaking.

He loved her.

The realization struck him like a blow, and he stopped. He loved her? He'd tried not to. Told himself he wouldn't. But all this time, he'd been lying to himself. To both of them. He'd been in love with her for a long time, possibly as long as she'd loved him.

He'd certainly been in love with her the night they'd conceived Sam. It wouldn't have made sense for him to have taken such a risk otherwise.

His body had already known what his brain and heart refused to see: he loved her. For reasons that had nothing to do with her housekeeping skills, or even now her skills as a mother, or her skills in bed. He didn't love her for any skills at all, but for the woman she was inside: loving, warm, with a heart of sunlight and fire.

And now, all that light and fire had abruptly been ripped out of his life, the moment he'd started to count on her. He wasn't even surprised. He'd known this would happen. Known the moment he let himself love again, she would disappear.

He had only himself to blame....

"Thank God you saw sense." Hearing the low rasp of Alain Bouchard's voice, Cesare ducked behind a thicket of orange trees. Peering through the branches, he saw two figures standing on the shore, frosted silver by moonlight. "Here." Bouchard's accented voice was exultant. "Get in my boat. You've made the right choice. I won't let him hurt you now."

Clenching his fists, Cesare took a step toward them. Then he saw Emma wasn't making a move to get in the boat. She had turned away, and was trying to calm the baby, who had started to whimper in her arms. Her long white veil trailed her like a ghost in moonlight.

"He didn't hurt your sister, Alain," she said in a low voice. "He would never hurt her. He loved her. In fact, he's still in love with her. That's why I…why I couldn't go through with it."

Cesare stopped, his eyes wide, and a branch broke loudly beneath his feet. Bouchard twisted his head blindly, then turned back to Emma. "Hurry. He might come at any moment."

"I'm not getting in the boat."

The Frenchman laughed. "Of course you are."

"No." Emma didn't move. "You have to accept it. Cesare is always brutally honest, even when it causes pain. Her death was a tragic accident. He's never gotten over it. Cesare is a good man. Honorable to his core."

Bouchard took a step closer to her on the moonlit shore.

"If you really believe that," he said, "what are you doing out here?"

Cesare strained to hear, not daring to breathe. He saw Emma tilt up her head.

"I love him. That's why I couldn't marry him."

Cesare stifled a gasp. She loved him?

Bouchard stared at her, then shook his head. "That doesn't make any sense, *chérie.*"

She gave a low laugh. "It actually does." She wiped her eyes. "He'll never love anyone but Angélique. Heaven help me, I might have married him anyway, except…except I saw his face in the chapel," she whispered. "And I couldn't do it."

Cesare took a deep breath and stepped out of the thicket of trees. Both figures looked back at him, startled.

"What did you see?" he asked quietly.

"Falconeri!" Bouchard stepped between them. "You might have fooled Emma, with her innocent heart. But we both know my sister's death was no accident."

"No."

"So you admit it!"

"It's time you knew the truth," Cesare said in a low voice. "I've kept it from you for too long."

"To hide your guilty conscience—"

"To protect you."

Bouchard snorted derisively. "*Protect* me."

"When she married me, she didn't want a partner. She wanted a lapdog." Cesare set his jaw. "When I threw myself into work, trying to be worthy of her, she hated the loss of attention. She hated it even more when I started to succeed. Once I no longer spent my days at her feet, worshipping her every moment, Angélique was restless. She cheated on me. Not just once, but many times. And I put up with it."

"What?" Emma gasped.

Bouchard shook his head with a snarl. "I don't believe you!"

"Her last lover was an Argentinean man she met while visiting Paris, who frequently traveled to New York on business. She decided Menendez was the answer to the emptiness in her heart."

Bouchard started. "Menendez? Raoul Menendez?"

"You know him?"

"I met him once, as he was having a late dinner in a hotel in Paris with my sister," he said uneasily. "She swore they were just old friends."

Cesare's lips curved. "Their affair lasted a year."

He frowned. "That's why she wanted a divorce?" For the first time, he sounded uncertain. "Not because you cheated on her?"

"I never could have done that," he said wearily. "I thought marriage meant forever. I thought we were in love." He turned to Emma and whispered, "Back then, I didn't know the difference between lust and love."

Emma caught her breath, her eyes luminous in the moonlight.

Bouchard stood between them, his thin face drawn. "She called me, the night before she died—sobbing that her only love had betrayed her, abandoning her like trash, that he'd been sleeping with someone else all the while. I thought she meant you. I never thought…"

Cesare shook his head. "She wore me down over that year, demanding a divorce so she could marry Menendez. She hated me, accusing me of being her jailor—of wanting our marriage to last longer just so I'd get more of her fortune. Do you know what it's like? To live with someone who despises you, who blames you for destroying her only happiness?"

"Yes," Emma whispered, and he remembered her stepmother. His heart twisted at the pain in her beautiful face. He wanted to take her in his arms and tell her she'd never feel that kind of grief again. Trembling, he took a step toward her.

"So you let her go," Bouchard said.

"I finally set her free so she could marry him," Cesare said. "She ran off to Argentina, only to discover Menendez already had a wife there. She came back to New York broken. I'm still not sure if she was trying to kill herself—or if she was just trying to make herself go to sleep to forget the heartbreak…."

Bouchard paced, then stopped, clawing back his hair. He looked at Cesare. "If this is true, why did you never tell me? Why did you let me go on believing you were at fault—that you were to blame?"

"Because you loved your sister," he said quietly. "I didn't want you to know the truth. That kind of blind love and faith is too rare in this world."

"I insulted you, practically accused you of…" He

stopped. "How could you not have thrown the truth in my face?"

Cesare shook his head. "I thought I loved her once. And I had my faults, too. Perhaps if I hadn't worked so much…"

"Are you kidding?" Emma demanded incredulously, juggling their baby against the hip of her wedding gown. He smiled.

"I'm telling you now because you both deserve to know the truth." He looked at Emma. "I didn't want anyone to know my weakness, or the real reason I never wanted to marry again. I thought love was just delusion, that led to pain." He paused. "Until I fell in love with you…"

Emma's lips parted in a soft gasp.

The Frenchman tilted his head, looking thoughtfully between them. "I think it's time for me to go." Stepping forward, he held out his hand. "*Merci,* Cesare. I have changed my mind about you. You are—not so bad. You must not be, for a woman like Emma to love you." Turning back, he kissed her softly on the cheek and gave her one final look. "*Adieu, ma chérie.* Be happy."

Climbing into his small boat, Alain Bouchard turned on the engine and drove back across the lake.

Cesare turned to face Emma. As he looked down at her beautiful stricken face, so haunted and young beneath the long white veil as she held his child, her eyes were green and shadowed as the forest around them. His heart was pounding.

"You left me at the altar," he said.

She swallowed. "Yes. I guess I did."

"You said you saw something in my face that drove you away," he said in a low voice. "What did you see?"

Moonlight caressed her beautiful face. She took a deep breath.

"Dread," she whispered. "I saw dread." Her voice caught.

"I couldn't marry a man with a face like that. No matter how much I was in love with you. I couldn't trap you into a loveless marriage for the rest of your life. And pretend not to notice as you—cheated on me, again and again."

"Cheated on you?" he demanded.

The baby started to whimper. Comforting him, she nodded miserably. "I assumed—"

"No." Going to her, he grabbed her shoulders and looked down at her. "Now you know the story, you have to know I would never betray you."

"I thought you still loved your wife," she whispered. "That I had no chance of holding your heart—"

"I was too proud to tell you the truth. I never wanted to appear vulnerable, or feel weak like that ever again. I did love her. I loved my parents, too. And all I learned was that when you love anyone—they leave."

"Oh, Cesare." Her eyes glimmered in the moonlight as she shook her head. "I'm so sorry…"

"I swore I'd never let anyone that close to me again." His lips lifted at the edges as he looked down at her. "Then I met you. And it was like coming home."

"You never said…"

"I told myself you meant nothing to me. That I'd only brought you from the hotel to be my housekeeper. But I think it was for you that I bought that house. Even then, some part of me wanted to settle down with you. With you, I lowered my guard as I never did with anyone else. And when I found you crying that night in the kitchen, it broke through me," he said hoarsely. "When I finally took you in my arms, I took everything I'd ever wanted and more…." He looked at Sam, then back at her fiercely. "Do you think it was an accident that I took such a risk? I've long since realized that my body and my heart must have known what my brain spent years trying to deny."

"What?" she whispered.

He looked down at her. "That you are for me. My true love. My only love."

She was crying openly now. "I never stopped loving you—"

He stopped her with a finger to her lips.

"I nearly died when I saw you leave with him," he said in a low voice. "It was like all my worst fears coming true."

"I'm sorry," she choked out. "When he broke into our wedding, I thought it was a sign, the only way to save us both from a life of misery—"

"Won't you shut up, even for a minute?" Since his finger wasn't working, he lowered his head and covered her mouth with his own. He felt her intake of breath, felt her surprise. He kissed her in the moonlight, embracing her with deep tenderness and adoration. Her lips were sweet and soft like heaven. When he finally pulled away, his voice was hoarse.

"All this time, I was afraid of loving anyone again. Because I didn't think I could handle the devastation of losing them. But I think I've always been in love with you, Emma." Reaching out, he cupped her face. "From the day we first met. And I told you that you looked smart. And that I was glad you came into my life."

A little squeak came out of her lips.

"Do you think I really came to Paris for some deal over a hotel? No." He searched her gaze. "I was looking for you. When I found out about the baby, I asked you to marry me. Then I slept with you. I did all the things I swore I'd never do. I kept breaking my own rules again and again. Over you."

"What are you saying?" she whispered.

He looked down at her in the moonlight, caressing her cheeks, running the pads of his thumbs over her pink full lips.

"Where you are concerned, from now on there is only one rule." He smiled, and her image seemed to shimmer as he said hoarsely, "I'm going to love you for the rest of my life."

"You—you really love me," she breathed.

He saw the incredulity in her eyes, the desperate hope. He thought of her years of devotion going far beyond that of any paid employee. Thought of how she'd always been by his side. How she'd always had the strength and dignity to stand up for what was right. Even today.

Especially today.

"You've shown me what love can be," he whispered. "Love isn't delusion, it isn't trying to avoid grief and pain, but holding your hand right through it, while you hold mine." He took her hand, cradling it in his own. "All this time," he said in a low voice, running his other hand along her pale translucent veil, "I was afraid of loving someone and losing them. I turned it into a self-fulfilling prophecy."

She swallowed, shifting Sam's weight against her shoulder. "It still could happen. I could get sick again. I could get hit by a bus."

"Or you could stop loving me. You could leave me for another man."

"Never," she cried, then suddenly blushed, looking down at her wedding gown. "Er, except for just now, I mean. And I didn't leave you for Alain, I never thought of him that way."

"I know."

"I couldn't marry a man who didn't love me. Because I've realized it's love that makes a family. Not promises."

Slowly Cesare lowered himself to one knee, as he should have done from the beginning. "Then let me love you for the rest of our lives. However long or short those lives might be." Taking her hands in his own, he fervently kissed each palm, then pressed them against his tuxedo jacket, over his chest. "Marry me, Emma. And whatever your answer might be, know that you hold my heart. For the rest of my life."

"As you hold mine," she said as tears ran down her face. Moving her hands, she cupped his face. And nodded.

"Yes?" he breathed, searching her gaze. "You'll marry me?"

"Yes," she said, smiling through her tears.

"Now," he demanded.

She snorted. "So bossy," she said with a laugh. "Some things never change." Her expression grew serious. "But some things do. I want to marry the man I love. The man who loves me." Her eyes grew suddenly shadowed as she shook her head. "And if anything ever happens to us..."

"We're all going to die someday." Cesare's eyes were suspiciously blurry as he looked down at her. Beneath her veil, several pins had fallen out of her chignon, causing her lustrous hair to tumble wildly down her shoulders. He pulled out the rest, tangling his fingers in her hair. "The only real question is if we're ever going to live. And from now on, my darling," he whispered as he lowered his lips to hers, "we are."

"Emma!"

"We're over here!" she called, but she knew Cesare wouldn't be able to see her in the villa's garden. It was August, and everything was in bloom, the fruit trees, the vegetables, even the corn. She tried to stand up, but being over eight months pregnant, it wasn't easy. She had to push herself up off the ground with her hands, and then bend around in a way that made Sam, now fifteen months old and digging in the dirt beside her with his little spade, giggle as he watched her flop around.

"Mama," he laughed, yanking a flower out of the ground.

"Fine, go ahead and laugh," she said affectionately, smiling down at him. "I did this for you, too, you know."

"Fow-a." With dark, serious eyes, he handed her the flower. Every day, he looked more like Cesare, she thought. But he'd also started to remind her of her own father, Sam's namesake. She saw that in the toddler's loving eyes, in his sweetly encouraging spirit.

"Emma!" Cesare called again, more desperately.

"Over here!" She waved her hands over the bushes, trying to make him see her. "By the orange grove!"

The garden had been transformed. Just like her life. The gold-digging supermodels of London would have been shocked and dismayed to learn that, as a billionaire's wife, Emma now spent most of her days right here, with a dirty child, growing fruits and vegetables for their kitchen and beautiful flowers to fill the vases of their home. Except, of course, when they had to fly down to the coast and go yachting along the Mediterranean, or take the private jet to see friends in London or New York. It was nice to do such things. But nicer still, she thought, to come back to their home.

The wedding had been even better than she'd imagined. After their breathless declaration and kiss by the lake, she and Cesare had gone back to the chapel arm in arm—only to discover their guests had already given up on them and started to mill back to the villa to gossip about them over some well-deserved limoncello. Even Irene looked as if she'd almost given up hope.

They'd called them all back to the chapel, and with some small, blushing explanation, the wedding had gone forward as planned. Right up to their first married kiss, which had been so passionate that it made all the guests burst into applause, and made Emma's toes curl as she'd thought she heard angels sing. The priest had been forced to clear his throat and gently remind them the honeymoon hadn't quite started yet.

She exhaled. They were a family now. They were happy. Cesare still had his international empire, but he'd cut back on travel a bit. Especially since they'd found out she was pregnant again.

"Cara." Cesare came into the clearing of the garden and took her in his arms for a long, delicious kiss. Then he knelt by their son, who was still playing in the dirt, and tousled his dark hair. "And did you have a good day, *piccino?"*

Watching the two of them, father and son, tears rose in Emma's eyes. Slowly she looked over the beauty of the garden. The summer trees were thick and green, and she could see the roof of the Falconeri villa against the bright blue Italian sky. How happy her parents would be if they could see how her life had turned out. Cesare's parents, too. She could feel their love, every time she looked at Cesare. Every time she looked at their son.

And soon, their daughter would join them. Emma's hand ran over her huge belly. In just a few weeks, their precious daughter would be born. They had already picked her name: Elena Margaret, after her two grandmothers.

Emma felt the baby kick inside her, and smiled, putting both hands over her belly now. "You like that, do you?" she murmured, then turned her face back to the sun.

"What happened while I was gone today?" Cesare rose to his feet, a frown on his handsome face. "You are crying."

Smiling, she shook her head, even as she felt tears streak down her cheeks.

Reaching out, he rubbed them away. "What is it?" he said anxiously. "Not some problem with the baby? With you?"

"No." The pregnancy had been easy. She'd been healthy all the way through, in spite of Cesare's worry. All her checkups had put her in the clear. She was safely in remission, had been for over a decade, and all her life was ahead of her. "I can't explain. I'm just so—happy."

"I'm happy, too," he whispered, putting his arms around her. He gave a sudden wicked grin. "And I'll be even happier, after Sam is tucked in bed…"

She saw what he was thinking about, in the sly seduction of his smile, and smacked him playfully on the bottom. "I'm eight months pregnant!"

"You've never been more beautiful."

"Right," she said doubtfully.

"Cara." He cupped her face. "It's true."

He kissed her until she believed him, until she felt dazed, dazzled in this garden of flowers and joy. She knew they would live here for the rest of their lives. If they were lucky, they'd someday be surrounded by a half-dozen noisy children, all splashing in the lake, sliding up and down the marble hallways in their socks, screaming and laughing like banshees. She and Cesare would be the calm center of the storm. The heart of their home.

He pulled her against him, and they stood silently in the garden, watching their son play. She heard the wind through the leaves. She exhaled.

She'd gotten everything she'd ever wanted. A man who loved her, whom she loved in return. Marriage. A snug little villa. As she felt the warmth of the sun, and listened to the cheerful chatter of their son, she leaned into her husband's embrace and thought about all the love that had existed for the generations before them. Their parents. Their parents' parents. And the love that would now exist for generations to come.

We're all going to die someday, her husband had once said. Emma realized he was wrong.

As long as love continued, life continued. Love had made them what they were. It had created Emma, and created Cesare. It had created Sam, and soon, their daughter. Love was what lasted. Love triumphed over death.

And anyone who truly loved, and was loved in return, would always live on—in this endlessly beautiful world.

* * * * *

BOUND BY A BABY

KATE HARDY

*For Gerard, Chris and Chloe – the best
research team ever – with all my love.*

Kate Hardy always loved books and could read
before she went to school. She discovered Mills &
Boon books when she was twelve and decided this
was what she wanted to do. When she isn't writing
Kate enjoys reading, cinema, ballroom dancing
and the gym. You can contact her via her website:
www.katehardy.com.

CHAPTER ONE

'I ASSUME YOU know why you're both here,' the solicitor said, looking at Emmy and then at Dylan.

Of course Emmy knew. Ally and Pete had asked her to be their son Tyler's guardian, if the unthinkable should ever happen.

If. She swallowed hard. That was the whole point of her being here. Because the unthinkable *had* happened. And Emmy still couldn't quite believe that she'd never see her best friend again.

She lifted her chin. Obviously today was about making things all official legally. And as for Dylan Harper—the only man she'd ever met who could make wearing a T-shirt and jeans feel as if they were a formal business suit—he was obviously here because he was Pete's best friend and Pete and Ally had asked him to be the executor of their will. 'Yes,' she said.

'Yes,' Dylan echoed.

'Good.' The solicitor tapped his pen against his blotter. 'So, Miss Jacobs, Mr Harper, can you confirm that you're both prepared to be Tyler's guardians?'

Emmy froze for a moment. *Both?* What was the man talking about? No way would Ally and Pete have asked them both to be Tyler's guardian. There had to be some mistake.

She glanced at Dylan, to find him looking straight back at her. And his expression was just as stunned as her own must be.

Or maybe they'd misheard. Misunderstood. 'Both of us, Tyler's guardians?' she asked.

For the first time, the solicitor's face showed an expression other than smooth neutrality. 'Did you not know they'd named you as Tyler's guardian in the will, Ms Jacobs?'

Emmy blew out a breath. 'Well, yes. Ally asked me before she and Pete revised their wills.' And she'd assumed that Ally had meant *just* her.

'Pete asked me,' Dylan said.

Which almost made Emmy wonder if Ally and Pete hadn't spoken to each other about it. Though obviously they must've done. They'd both signed the will, so they'd clearly known that both of their best friends had agreed to be there for Tyler. They just hadn't shared that particular piece of information with either Dylan or herself, by the looks of things.

'Is there a problem?' the solicitor asked.

Apart from the fact that she and Dylan disliked each other intensely and usually avoided each other? Or the fact that Dylan was married—and Emmy was pretty sure that his wife couldn't be too pleased that her husband had been named co-guardian with another woman, one who was single? 'No,' she said quickly, and looked at Dylan. This was his cue to explain that no, he couldn't do it.

'No problem,' Dylan confirmed, to her shock.

'Good.'

Good? No, it just made everything much more complicated, Emmy thought. Or maybe it meant he intended to fight her for custody of the baby: family man versus single mum, so it was obvious who'd win. But she didn't have a chance to protest because the solicitor went on with the reading of the will. 'Now, obviously Ally and Pete left financial provisions for Tyler. I have all the details here.'

'I'll deal with it,' Dylan said.

Immediately assuming that a flaky, air-headed jewellery designer wouldn't have a clue what to do? Emmy knew that was how Dylan saw her—she'd overheard him say it to Pete, on more than one occasion—and it rankled. She'd been her own boss for ten years. She was perfectly capable of dealing with things. Whereas he was so uptight and stuffy, she couldn't even begin to imagine him looking after a baby or a toddler. Given that Ally had always been diplomatic about Dylan's wife, merely saying that she worked with Pete, Emmy was pretty sure that Nadine Harper was from the same mould as Dylan. A cold workaholic who wouldn't know what fun was if it jumped out in front of him and yelled, 'Boo!' And not the sort that Ally would've wanted caring for her son.

But the solicitor was off again, going through the details of the arrangements made in the will. Emmy had to ignore her feelings and listen to what the man was telling her before she got completely lost. This was *important*.

And then at last it was all over.

Leaving her and Dylan to pick up the pieces. Together. Unthinkably.

She gave the solicitor a polite smile, shook his hand, and walked out of the office. On the doorstep of the building, she came to a halt and faced Dylan.

'I think,' she said, 'we need to talk. Like *now*.'

He nodded. 'And I could do with some coffee.'

There were shadows under his cornflower-blue eyes, and lines at the corners betraying that he hadn't slept properly since the crash; for the first time ever, Dylan actually looked vulnerable—and as if he hurt as much as she did, right now. It stopped her from uttering the kind of snippy remarks they usually made to each other.

'Make that two of us,' she said. On the sleep front, as well as the need for coffee. Vulnerability, no way would she admit to. Especially not to Dylan Harper. No way was she giving him an excuse to take Tyler from her. He and Nadine were *not* taking her place.

'Where's Tyler?' Dylan asked.

'With my mum. She'll ring me if there's a problem.' She lifted one shoulder, daring him to criticise her. 'I didn't think the solicitor's office would be the best place for him.'

'It isn't.'

Another first: he was actually agreeing with her. Maybe, she thought, they might be able to work something out between them? Maybe he'd be reasonable? A baby wouldn't fit into his busy, workaholic lifestyle. It'd be tough for Emmy, too, but at least she'd spent time with her godson and would have some clue about looking after him.

'Shall we?' she asked, indicating the café across the road.

'Fine.'

At the counter in the café, Emmy ordered a latte. 'What would you like?'

'I'll get these,' Dylan said immediately.

She gave a small but determined shake of her head. No way was she going to let him take charge. 'I offered first.'

'Then thank you—an espresso would be great.'

'Do you want anything to eat?'

He grimaced. 'Thank you for the offer, but right now I really can't face anything.'

She, too, hadn't been able to choke much down since she'd heard the news. It seemed that the situation had shaken him as much as it had shaken her. In a way, that was a good thing. Maybe they could find some common ground.

'If you go and find us a table, I'll bring our coffee over,' she said.

And she was glad of that small space between them. Just so she could marshal her thoughts. Right now, she didn't want to fight with Dylan. She just wanted her best friend back. For everything to be the same as it had been, three days ago. For Pete to have taken Ally on a surprise anniversary trip to Venice, for them to be happy and for Ally to be texting her to let her know they were on their way back and couldn't wait to see their little boy and tell her all about the trip. For them to be *alive*.

Emmy paid for the coffees, and carried them over to the quiet table Dylan had found for them in the corner.

'So you had no idea Pete had asked me to be Tyler's guardian?' Dylan asked.

Typical Dylan: straight in there. No pussyfooting around. Though, for once, she agreed with him. They needed to cut to the chase. 'No. And you had no idea that Ally had asked me?'

'No.' He spread his hands. 'Of course I said yes when he asked me—just as you obviously did when Ally asked you.' He sighed. 'I know you shouldn't speak ill of the dead—and Pete was my best friend, the closest I had to a brother—but what the *hell* were they thinking when they decided this?'

'They're both—*were* both,' she corrected herself, wincing, 'only children. Pete's dad is nearly eighty and Ally's mum isn't well. How could Pete and Ally's parents be expected to cope with looking after a baby full-time? And it isn't going to get any easier for them over the next twenty years. Of course Pete and Ally would ask someone nearer their own age to be Tyler's guardian.'

Dylan gave a pained sigh. 'I didn't mean *that*. It's obvious. I mean, why *us*?'

Why ask two people who really didn't get on to take care of the most precious thing in their lives? Good question. Though that wasn't the one uppermost in her mind. 'Why you and me instead of you and your wife?' she asked pointedly.

He blew out a breath. 'That isn't an issue.'

'If I was married and my husband's best friend asked him to be the baby's guardian if the worst happened, I'd be pretty upset if another woman was named as the co-guardian instead of me,' Emmy said.

'It isn't an issue,' Dylan repeated.

Patronising, pompous idiot. Emmy kept a rein on her temper. Just. 'Don't you think this discussion ought to include her?'

'You're the one who said we needed to talk.'

'We do.' She switched into superpolite mode, the one she used for difficult clients, before she was tempted to strangle him. 'Could you perhaps phone her and see when's a good time for her to join us?'

'No,' he said tightly.

Superpolite mode off. 'Either she really, *really* trusts you,' Emmy said, 'or you're even more of a control freak than I thought.'

'It isn't an issue,' Dylan said, 'because we're separated.' He glared at her. 'Happy, now?'

What? Since when had Dylan split up with his wife? And why? But Emmy damped the questions down. It wasn't any of her business. Whereas Tyler's welfare—that was most definitely her business.

'I guess it makes this issue a bit less complicated,' she said. Especially given what the social worker had suggested to her yesterday—something Emmy had baulked at, but which might turn out to be a sensible solution now.

She took a sip of coffee. 'Maybe,' she said slowly, 'Pete and Ally thought that between us we could give Tyler what he needs.'

He narrowed his eyes at her. 'How do you mean?'

'We have different strengths.' And different weaknesses, but she wasn't going to point that out. They were going to need to work together on this, and now wasn't the time for a fight. 'We can bring different things to his life.'

He folded his arms. 'So I do the serious stuff and you do all the fun and glitter?'

Emmy had been prepared to compromise, but this was too much. And this was exactly why she'd disliked Dylan from practically the moment they'd met. Because he was judgemental, arrogant, and had the social skills of a rhino. Either he genuinely didn't realise what he'd just said or he really didn't care—and she wasn't sure which. She lifted her chin. 'You mean, because I work with pretty, shiny things, they distract my poor little female brain from being able to focus on anything real?' she asked, her voice like cut glass.

His wince told her that he hadn't actually meant to insult her. 'Put that way, it sounds bad.'

'It *is* bad, Dylan. Look, you know I have my own business. If I was an airhead, unable to do a basic set of yearly accounts and work out my profit margins, then I'd be starving and in debt up to my eyeballs. Just to clarify the situation for you, that's not the case. My bank account's in the black and my business is doing just fine, thank you. Or will you be requiring a letter from my bank manager to prove that?'

He held her gaze. 'OK. I apologise. I shouldn't have said that.'

'Good. Apology accepted.' And maybe she should cut him some slack. He'd said that Pete was as close to him as a brother, so right now he was obviously hurting as much as she was. Especially as he was having to deal with a relationship break-up as well. And Dylan Harper was the most formal, uptight man Emmy had ever met, which meant he probably wasn't so good at emotional stuff. No doubt lashing out and making snippy remarks was his way of dealing with things. Letting it go—this time—didn't mean that she was going to let him walk all over her in the future.

'OK, so we don't get on; but this isn't actually about us. It's about a little boy who has nobody, and giving him a stable home where he can grow up knowing he's loved and valued.' And this wasn't the first time she and Dylan had had to put their differences aside. They'd managed it for Pete and Ally's wedding. When, come to think of it, Dylan's wife had been away on business and hadn't been able to attend, despite the fact that she worked with the groom and was married to the best man.

Emmy and Dylan had put their differences aside again two months ago, in the same ancient little church where Ally and Pete had got married, when they'd stood by the font and made their promises as godparents. Dylan's wife had been absent then, too. So maybe the marriage had been in trouble for a while, and Pete knew what was going on in Dylan's life. Which would make a bit more sense of the decision to ask both Dylan and Emmy to be Tyler's guardian.

She looked Dylan straight in the eye. 'I meant every word I said in church on my godson's christening day. I intend to be there for him.'

Was Emmy implying that he wasn't? Dylan felt himself bristling. 'I meant every word I said, too.'

'Right.'

But he couldn't discern an edge in her voice—at least, not like the one that had been there when he'd as good as called her an airhead. And that mollified him slightly. Maybe they could work together on this. Maybe she'd put the baby first instead of being the overemotional, needy mess she'd been when he'd first met her. Emmy wasn't serious and focused, like Nadine. She was unstructured and flaky. Something Dylan refused to put up with; he'd already had to deal with enough of that kind of behaviour in his life. No more.

'Look, Ally and Pete wanted us to take care of their baby, if anything happened to them.' She swallowed hard. 'And the worst *has* happened.'

Dylan could see the sheen of tears in her grey eyes, and her lower lip actually started to wobble. Oh, no. Please don't let her cry. He wasn't good with tears. And he'd seen enough of them in those last few weeks with Nadine to last him a lifetime. If Emmy started crying, he'd have to walk out of the café. Because right now he couldn't cope with any more emotional pressure. As it was, he felt as if the world had slipped and he were slowly sliding backwards, unable to stop himself and with nothing to hang on to.

She dragged in a breath. 'We're going to have to work together on this and put our personal feelings aside.'

'Fair point.' They didn't have a lot of choice in the matter. And at least she was managing to hold the tears back. That was something. 'We'll work together.' Dylan was still slightly surprised at how businesslike she was being. This wasn't Emmy-like behaviour. She'd been late the first three times they'd met, and given the most feeble of excuses. And he'd lost count of the times he'd been over at Ally and Pete's and Ally had had to rush off to pick up the pieces when yet another of Emmy's disastrous relationships had ended. It was way, way too close to the way his mother behaved, and Dylan had no patience for that kind of selfishness.

And his comment about the glitter hadn't been totally unfounded. He was pretty sure she'd choose to do the fun things with Tyler and leave him to do all the serious stuff. Emmy was all about fun. Which wasn't enough: sometimes you had to put the fun aside and do what needed to be done rather than what you wanted to do. 'So you've been looking after Tyler?'

'Since they left.' She shrugged. 'Babysitting.'

Except now it wasn't babysitting anymore. There wasn't anyone to hand Tyler back to.

She blew out a breath. 'The social worker came to see me last night. She said that Tyler needs familiarity and a routine. So I guess the first thing we need to do is to set up a routine, something as near as possible to what he's used to.'

Considering the chaos that usually surrounded Emmy Jacobs, Dylan couldn't imagine her setting up any kind of routine. But he bit his tongue. He'd already annoyed her today. Right now he needed to be conciliatory. For his godson's sake. 'Right.'

'And, as the solicitor said, we're sharing custody.'

'Meaning that one week you have him, the next week I do?' Dylan suggested. 'Fine. That works for me.'

'It doesn't work at all.'

He frowned at her, not understanding. 'Why not?'

'Just as Tyler gets settled in with me, I have to bring him to you; and just as he gets settled with you, you have to bring him to me?' She shook her head. 'That's not fair on him.'

'So what are you suggesting?'

'The social worker,' she said, not meeting his gaze,

'suggested that Tyler stays in his own home. She says that whoever cares for him needs to, um, live there, too.'

He blinked. 'You're planning to move into Ally and Pete's house?'

She coughed. 'Not just me.'

What she was saying finally sank in. 'You're suggesting *we live together*?' The idea was so shocking, he almost dropped his coffee.

'No.' She lifted her chin, looking affronted. 'The social worker suggests that we share a house and share Tyler's care. Believe you me, it's not what I want to do—but it's the most sensible solution for Tyler. It saves us having to traipse a tired and hungry baby all over London at times that don't suit him. We'll be fitting round him, not the other way round.'

'Share a house. That sounds like living together, to me.' Something Dylan knew he wasn't good at. Hadn't he failed spectacularly with Nadine? His marriage had broken up because he hadn't wanted a family and the wife he'd loved had given him an ultimatum. A choice he couldn't accept. And now Emmy Jacobs—a woman who embodied everything he didn't like—seriously expected him to make a family with *her*?

'It isn't living together. It's just sharing a house.' Her mouth tightened, and she gave him a look as if to say that he was the last person on earth she'd choose to live with.

He needed to be upfront about this. 'I don't want to share a house with you,' he said.

'It's not my idea of fun, either, but what else—?' She paused. 'Actually, no, there *is* an easy solution to this. You can agree to me having full-time care of Tyler.'

'That isn't what Pete and Ally wanted.' And he didn't think Emmy was stable enough to look after Tyler, not permanently. Then again, Dylan couldn't imagine himself taking care of Tyler, either. He knew practically nothing about babies. He'd never even babysat his godson. Pete and Ally had never asked him, knowing that his personal life was in chaos and his head wasn't in the right place. And Dylan was guiltily aware that he'd jumped at the excuse rather than face up to the fact that he wasn't a very good godfather.

He'd agreed to be Tyler's guardian. Of course he had. For the same reason that Emmy had agreed, probably, wanting to support his best friend. But he'd never thought it would actually happen. He'd considered himself to be a safety net that would never need to be used.

And now…

Lack of sleep. That was why his head was all over the place. There was a black hole where his best friend had once been. And now there were all these new demands on him and he wasn't sure he could meet them. He'd promised to be there for Tyler, and he hated himself for the fact that, now he actually had to make good on that promise, he didn't want to do it. He resented the way that a baby could wreak such havoc on his life and turn everything upside down; and then he felt guilty all over again for resenting someone so tiny and defenceless, because it wasn't the baby's fault and—well, he was being *selfish*.

Emmy was offering him a get-out. It would be, oh, so easy to take it. And yet Dylan knew that he'd never respect himself again if he took it—if he did what his mother had done, and dumped all his responsibilities on someone else. If he ignored a child who needed him.

'I know it isn't what Pete and Ally wanted,' Emmy said, clearly oblivious to the turmoil in Dylan's head. 'But it's not fair to keep uprooting Tyler, just to suit ourselves.'

'He's a baby. He's not even going to notice his surroundings,' Dylan said.

'Actually, he is. And if we did alternate weeks he'd have to get used to two different sets of rules, two different atmospheres. That's too much to expect.'

'And you're an expert on childcare?' he asked, knowing how nasty it sounded but unable to stop himself, because it was easier to fight with her than to admit how mixed up and miserable he felt right now.

'No. But I've read up on it. I've spent time with him. And I know how Ally wanted him brought up.'

'Fair point,' he muttered, feeling even more guilty. He hadn't done any of those things.

'You don't want to live with him, but you don't want to let me have full-time care of him, either.' She sighed. 'So what *do* you want, Dylan?'

'Pete and Ally back. Life as it was supposed to be.' The words came out before he could stop them.

'Well, unless you can turn into a superhero and spin the world round the other way to reverse time, and then stop the accident happening...' She looked away. 'Life isn't like the movies. I wish it could be. That I could wave a magic wand and everything would be OK again. But I can't. I'm a normal godmother, not a fairy godmother. And we have to do what's right for Tyler. To make his world as good as it can be, now his parents are gone and he has only us.'

She was right. Which made Dylan feel even more guilty. He was acting like a spoiled brat, crying for the moon and stars. And it was *wrong*. 'So what do you suggest?'

'The way I see it, we have two choices. Either we do what Pete and Ally wanted, and we find some way to be civil to each other while we bring up their child, or you let me bring him up on my own.'

'Or I could bring him up on my own,' Dylan suggested, nettled that she hadn't listed it as a third option.

She scoffed. 'So, what? You get a live-in nanny and

dump his care on her, and see him for two seconds when you get home from work?'

'That's unfair.'

'Is it?' she asked pointedly.

He'd rather have all his teeth pulled out without anaesthetic than admit it to her, but it was probably accurate. 'I don't want to live with you.' He didn't want to live with anyone.

'Newsflash. I don't want to live with you, either. But I'm prepared to put Tyler's needs before mine. Just as I know Ally would've done for me, if our positions were reversed.'

And just as Pete would've done for him. Disgust at himself flared through Dylan's body. At heart, he really was a chip off the old block, as selfish as his mother. And that didn't sit well with him. He didn't want to be like her. 'Caring for a baby on your own is a hell of a commitment.'

'I know. But I'm prepared to do it.'

'Pete and Ally knew it was too much to ask one person to do. It's why they asked us both.'

'And you've had second thoughts.' She shrugged. 'Look, it's fine. I'll manage. I can always ask my mum for help.'

Which was a lot more than Dylan could do. And how pathetic was he to resent that?

'I need some time to think about this,' he said. Time where he could work things out, without anyone crowding his head. Where he could do what he always did when he made a business decision: work out all the scenarios, decide which one had the most benefits and least risks. Plan things without any emotions getting in the way and messing things up. 'How long is it until you need to get back to Tyler?'

'Mum said she could babysit for as long as I needed. I had no idea how long things would take at the solicitor's.'

He made a snap decision. 'OK. We'll meet again in an hour. When we've both had time to get our heads round it.'

'I don't need t—' she began, then shut up. 'You're right. I've had time to think about what the social worker said. You haven't. And it's a big deal. Of course you need time to think about it. Is an hour enough?'

He'd make sure it was. 'An hour's fine. I'll see you back here then.'

CHAPTER TWO

FRESH AIR. THAT would help, for starters. Dylan found the nearest park and walked, ignoring the noise from tourists and families.

Pros and cons. He didn't want to live with anyone. He was still licking his wounds from the end of his marriage—ironic, considering that he'd been the one to end it. And even more ironic that, if Nadine had waited six more months before issuing that ultimatum, she would've had her dream.

But it was too late, now. He couldn't go back. He didn't love her anymore, and he knew she was seeing someone else. Someone who was prepared to give her what he wouldn't. What hurt most now was that he'd failed at being a husband.

That left him with a slightly less complicated situation; though it didn't make his decision any easier. If he did have to live with someone else, an emotional, flaky woman and a tiny baby would be right at the bottom of his list. He had a business to run—something that took up as much of his energy as he could give. He didn't have *time* for a baby.

But...

If he backed out, if he let Emmy shoulder all the responsibilities and look after the baby, he'd only be able to block out the guilt for a short time. It would eat away at him, to the point where it would affect his business decisions and therefore the livelihoods of everyone who worked for him. Besides, how could he live with himself if he abandoned the child his best friend had loved so dearly?

Given how often he'd been dumped as a child, how could he do the same thing to this baby?

He couldn't let Tyler down. Couldn't break a promise he'd made.

Which meant he had to find a way of coexisting with Emmy.

She'd said earlier that they wouldn't be living together, just sharing a house. They could lead completely separate lives. All they'd need to do was to set up a rota for childcare and then brief each other at a handover. He could do that. OK, so he'd have to delegate more at work, to carve out that extra time, but it was doable. His flat was on a short-term lease, so that wasn't a problem. And he had no intention of getting involved with anyone romantically, so that wouldn't be a problem in the future, either.

So the decision was easy, after all.

He walked back to the café, and was slightly surprised to find that Emmy was already there. Or maybe she'd never left. Whatever.

'Coffee?' he asked. 'You paid last time, so this one's on me.'

'Thank you.'

He ordered coffee then joined her at the table. 'If we're going to share a house and Tyler's care, then we need to sort out some ground rules. Set up a rota.'

She rolled her eyes. 'Obviously. Childcare and housework.'

'Not housework. We'll get a housekeeper.'

She shook her head. 'I can't afford to pay a housekeeper.'

'I can. So that's settled.'

'No. This is shared equally. Time and bills.'

Did she have to be so stubborn about this? It was a practical decision. The idea was to look at how they could make this work, with the least pain to both of them. Why do something he didn't have time for and didn't enjoy, when he could pay someone to do it? 'Look, I'm going to have a hard enough time fitting a baby into my work schedule, without adding in extra stuff. And I'm sure it's the same for you. It makes sense to pay someone to clean the house and take some of the pressure off us.'

'I can probably stretch to paying someone to clean for a couple of hours a week,' she said, 'but that's as far as it goes.'

'So you're saying we both have to cook?'

'Well, obviously. It's a bit stupid, both of us cooking separately. It makes sense to share.' She stared at him. 'Are you telling me you can't cook?'

He shrugged. 'I shared a house with Pete at university.' And Emmy must know how hopeless Pete was—had been, Dylan corrected himself with a jolt—in the kitchen. 'So it was starve, eat nothing but junk, or learn to cook.'

'And what did you opt for?'

Did she *really* have to ask? He narrowed his eyes at her, just to make the point that she was being overpicky. 'I learned to cook. I only do basic stuff—don't expect Michelin-star standard—but it'll be edible and you won't get food poisoning.' He paused as a nasty thought struck him. 'Does that mean *you* don't cook?'

'I can do the basics,' she said. 'I shared a house with Ally at university.'

And Ally was an excellent cook. Dylan had never turned down the offer of a meal at his best friend's; he was pretty sure it must've been the same for Emmy. 'And she did all the cooking?' he asked.

'Our deal was that she cooked and I cleaned.' Emmy shrugged. 'Though I picked up a few tips from her along the way.'

But she wasn't claiming to be a superchef. Which made two of them. Basic food it would have to be. Which wasn't much change from the way he'd been living, the last six months. 'Right. So we'll pay a cleaner, and have a rota for childcare and cooking.'

He took a sip of his coffee, though it didn't do much to clear his head. Three days ago, he'd been just an ordinary workaholic. No commitments—well, *almost* no commitments, he amended mentally. No commitments once his divorce papers came through and he signed them.

Today, it was a different world. His best friend had died; and it looked as if he'd be sharing the care of his godson with a woman who'd always managed to rub him up the wrong way. Not the life he'd planned or wanted. But he was just going to have to make the best of it.

'So who looks after Tyler when we're at work?' he asked.

'We take turns.'

'I'm not with you.'

'Ally wasn't planning to go back to work until after his second birthday. She wanted to be a stay-at-home mum and look after her own baby.' Emmy looked awkward. 'I don't think she would've wanted us to put him in day care or get a nanny.'

'We're not Ally and Pete, so we're going to have to make a decision that works for both of us,' Dylan pointed out. 'We both have a business to run. Taking time off work isn't going to happen. Not if we want to keep our businesses running.'

'Unless,' Emmy suggested, 'we work flexible hours. Delegate, if we have to.'

'Delegate?' He frowned. 'I thought you were a sole trader?'

'I am, but you're not.'

He almost asked her if she was using the royal 'we', and stopped himself just in time. That wasn't fair. She was trying. And he bit back the snippy comment that she was trying in more than one sense of the word.

'Are you a morning or an evening person?' she asked.

He usually worked both. That had been another of Nadine's complaints: Dylan was a workaholic who was always in the office or in his study. 'Either.'

'I prefer working in the evenings. So, if you're not bothered, how about you go in early and I'll take care of Tyler; and then you take over from me at, say, half-three, so I can get on with my work?'

'And what if I need to have a late meeting?'

'We can be flexible,' she said. 'But if you're late back one day, then you'll have to be home much earlier, the next day, to give me that time back.' She shrugged. 'There might be times when I have meetings and need you to take over from me. So I guess we're going to have to be flexible, work as a team, and cover for each other when we need to.'

Work as a team with a woman he'd always disliked. A woman who reminded him of the worst aspects of his mother—the sort who'd dump her responsibilities on someone else with no notice so she could drift off somewhere to 'find herself'.

Dylan pinched himself, just to check that this wasn't some peculiar nightmare. But it hurt. So there was no waking up from this situation.

'OK. We'll sort out a rota between us.' He paused. 'I still don't want to live with you, but I guess the only option is to share the house.' It didn't mean they had to share any time together outside the handover slots.

'So when do we move in to Pete and Ally's?' she asked

'I have to sort out the lease on my flat,' he said.

'And I'll need to talk to the bank about subletting my flat, to make sure it doesn't affect the mortgage.'

Dylan was surprised. He hadn't thought Emmy would be together enough to buy her own place.

'And they might be able to put me in touch with a good letting agency,' she finished.

She'd obviously thought this through. Then again, she'd had time to think about it. The social worker had talked to her about it already.

'So we could move in tomorrow.'

He'd rather not move in at all, but he had no choice. Not if he was going to carry out his duty. 'Tomorrow.' He paused. 'Look—we really need to put Tyler first. We don't like each other, but we've agreed to make an effort for his sake. What happens if we really can't get on?'

'I don't know.'

'In a business, if you hire someone in a senior role, you'd have a trial period to make sure you suited each other. Then you'd review it and decide on the best way forward.'

'This isn't a job, Dylan.'

'I know, but I think a trial period might be the fairest way for all of us. Give it three months. See if we can make it work.'

She nodded. 'And, if we can't, then you'll agree that I'll have sole care of Tyler?'

He wasn't ready to agree to that. 'We'll review it,' he said. 'See what the viable options are.'

'OK. Three months.' She paused. 'But if anything big

comes up, we discuss it before the situation gets out of hand.'

That worked for him. 'Agreed.'

'So that's settled.' She lifted her chin. 'Before we go any further, I need to know something. Is there anyone who'd be upset about us sharing a house?'

He frowned. 'I've already told you, I'm separated from Nadine. It won't be a problem.'

'What about the woman you had an affair with?'

He stared at her in disbelief. 'What woman?'

'Oh, come on. It's the main reason why marriages break down. Someone has an affair. Usually the man.'

Was she really that cynical?

Had that happened to her?

He couldn't remember Pete or Ally ever talking about going to Emmy's wedding, but at the end of the day a marriage certificate was just a piece of paper. Maybe Emmy had been living with someone who'd let her down in that way. 'Not that it's any of your business why my marriage broke up, but for the record neither of us had an affair,' he said tightly.

Colour stained her cheeks, 'I apologise.'

Which was something, he supposed. 'There's nobody who would be affected by us sharing a house,' he said quietly.

Or was there another reason why she'd asked? A way to introduce the subject, maybe, because there was someone in her life who'd be upset? 'If it's a problem for you, I'm happy to—'

'There's nobody,' she cut in.

Was it his imagination, or did she suddenly look tired and miserable and lonely?

No. He was just reflecting how he felt on her. Tired and miserable, because he'd barely slept since the news of the crash; and lonely, because the one person Dylan could've talked to about this—well, he'd been *in* that crash and he wasn't here anymore.

'Though I could do without a string of dates being paraded through the house,' she added.

He raised an eyebrow. 'I'm not quite divorced yet. Do you really think I'm dating?' Despite the fact that he knew his almost-ex wife was, he wasn't.

She grimaced. 'Sorry. I take that back. It's not your fault I have a rubbish taste in men. I shouldn't tar you with the same brush as them.'

He'd been right, then. Someone had let her down. More than one, he'd guess.

Dylan had never noticed before, probably because he'd been more preoccupied with being annoyed by her, but Emmy Jacobs was actually pretty. Slender, with a fine bone structure highlighted by her gamine haircut. Her hair was defiantly plum: not a natural shade, but it suited her, bringing out the depths in her huge grey eyes.

Though what on earth was he doing, thinking about Emmy in those sorts of terms?

Better put it down to the shock of bereavement. He and Emmy might be about to share a house and the care of a baby, but that was as far as it would go. They'd be lucky to keep things civil between them. And he definitely wasn't in the market for any kind of relationship. Been there, done that, and failed spectacularly. It had taught him to steer clear, in future. He was better off on his own. It meant there was nobody to disappoint. Nobody to walk away, the way his mother had and Nadine had.

'I assume you have a set of keys to Pete and Ally's house?' he asked.

She nodded. 'You, too?'

'So I could keep an eye on the place while they're not

there. For emergencies. Which I always thought would be a burst pipe or something like that. Not...' His throat closed, and he couldn't get the words out. For the first time in years, he was totally speechless.

To his surprise, Emmy reached across the table to take his hand and squeezed it briefly. With sympathy, not pity. 'Me, too. I keep thinking I'm going to wake up and discover that this is all just some incredibly realistic nightmare and everything's just fine. Except I've woken up too many times already and found out that it's not.'

Whatever her faults—and Dylan knew there were a lot of them—Emmy's feelings for Ally and Pete were in no doubt. Surprising himself further, he returned the squeeze. 'And we've still got the funeral to go through.'

She sighed and withdrew her hand. 'I guess their parents will want to arrange it.'

'You said yourself, Pete's dad is elderly and Ally's mum isn't well. They'll need support. I was going to offer to sort it out for them. If they tell me what they want, I can arrange it.'

'That's good of you to take the burden off their shoulders.' She took a deep breath. 'Count me in on the support front. Anything you need me to do, tell me and I'll do it.'

She wasn't being polite, Dylan knew. The tears were shimmering in her eyes again. And he wanted to get out of here as fast as he could, before she actually started crying. 'Thanks. I guess we'd better exchange phone numbers. Home, work, whatever.'

She nodded, and took her mobile phone from her handbag. It was a matter of seconds to give each other the details. 'And we'll meet at the house after work tomorrow to sort out the rota.'

'OK. I'll call you when I'm on my way.'

'Thanks.' She drained her cup. 'I'd better get back to Tyler. See you later.'

He watched her walk out of the café. The woman who annoyed him more than anyone he'd ever met. The woman he was going to move in with tomorrow.

Yeah, life was really throwing him a curveball. And he was just going to have to deal with it. Somehow.

The next morning, Emmy unlocked the door to Pete and Ally's three-storey Georgian house in Islington, pressed in the code for the alarm, and put her small suitcase down in the hallway.

'It's just you and me for now, Ty,' she said softly to the baby, who was securely strapped into his sling and cradled against her heart. 'We're home. Except—' her breath caught '—it's going to be with me and Dylan looking after you, from now on, instead of your mum and dad.'

It still felt wrong. But over the course of the day she managed to make a list of the rest of the things she needed to bring from her flat, feed Tyler, give him a bath and put him to bed in his cot, and make a basic spaghetti sauce for dinner so that all she'd have to do was heat it through and cook some pasta when Dylan turned up after he'd finished work.

Home.

Would she ever come to think of this place as home? Emmy thought with longing of her own flat in Camden. It was small, but full of light; and it was *hers*. From next week, a stranger would be living there and enjoying the views over the local park. And she would be living here in a much more spacious house—the sort she would never have been able to afford on her own—with Dylan and Tyler.

Almost like a family.

Just what she'd always wanted.

Well, she didn't want *Dylan*, she amended. But Emmy had envied part of her best friend's life: having a husband who loved her and a gorgeous baby. Something Emmy had wanted, herself. A real family.

'But I didn't want to have it *this* way, Ally,' she said softly. 'I wanted someone of my own. Someone who wouldn't let me down.' Someone that maybe somebody else should've picked for her, given how bad her own choices of life partner had been in the past.

And that family she was fantasising about was just that: a fantasy. The baby wasn't really hers, and neither was the house. And she was sharing the house with Dylan Harper, as a co-guardian. She couldn't think of anyone less likely to be the love of her life, just as she knew that she was the exact opposite of the kind of women Dylan liked. Chalk and cheese wasn't the half of it.

But then again, Tyler might not be her flesh and blood, but he was her responsibility now. Her godson. A baby she'd known for every single day of his little life. A baby she'd cradled in her arms when he was only a few hours old, sitting on the side of her best friend's hospital bed and feeling the same surge of love she'd felt for the woman who'd been as close as a sister to her.

She drew her knees up to her chin and wrapped her arms round her legs, blinking away the tears. 'I promise you I'll love Tyler as if he was my own, Ally,' she said softly into the empty room. 'I'll do my best by him.'

She just hoped that her best would be good enough. Though this was one thing she really couldn't afford to fail at. There wasn't a plan B.

The lights on the baby listener glowed steadily, and Emmy couldn't hear a thing; Tyler was obviously sound asleep. She glanced at her watch. Hopefully Dylan wouldn't be too much longer. In the meantime, she had a job to do.

She uncurled and headed back to the kitchen, where she took a large piece of card and marked it out into a two-week rota for childcare and chores. She worked steadily, putting in different coloured sticky notes to show which were her slots and which were Dylan's.

All the way through, she kept glancing at her watch. There was still no sign of Dylan, and it was getting on to half-past seven.

This was ridiculous. Had he forgotten that he was meant to be here, sorting things out with her? Or was he just in denial?

And to think he'd pegged himself as the sensible, organised one.

Yeah, right.

Irritated, she picked up her mobile phone and rang him.

He answered within two rings. 'Dylan Harper.' Though he sounded absent, as if his attention was elsewhere.

'It's Emmy,' she said crisply. 'Emmy Jacobs.' Just in case he was trying to block that out, too.

There was a pause. 'Oh.'

'Are you not supposed to be somewhere right now?' She made her voice supersaccharine.

'You suggested we meefairt at the house today after work.'

'Mmm-hmm. Which is where I am now. So are you expecting me to stay up until midnight or whenever you can be bothered to turn up and sort things through?'

He sighed. 'Don't nag.'

Nag? If he'd been fair about this, she wouldn't have to nag. 'This is meant to be about teamwork, Dylan. There's no "I" in team,' she reminded him.

'Oh, spare me the clichés, Emmy,' he drawled.

Her patience finally gave out. 'Just get your backside over here so we can sort things out,' she said, and hung up.

CHAPTER THREE

IT WAS ANOTHER hour before Emmy heard the front door
open, and by that point she was ready to climb the walls
with frustration.

Be conciliatory, she reminded herself. Do this for Pete
and Ally. And Tyler. Even though you want to smack the
man over the head with a wok, you have to be nice. At least
for now. Make things work. It's only for three months, and
then he'll realise that it'd be best if you looked after Tyler
on your own. Come on, Emmy. You can do this. *Smile.*

'Good evening. Is pasta OK with you for dinner?' she
asked when he walked into the kitchen.

He looked surprised. 'You cooked dinner for me?'

'As I was here, yes. By the way, that means it's your
turn to cook for us tomorrow.'

'Uh-huh.' He looked wary.

'One thing you need to know. If I get hungry, I get
grumpy.' She gave him a level stare. 'Don't make me wait
in future. You *really* won't like me then.' Which was a bit
ironic. He didn't like her now, and he hadn't even seen her
on a really bad day.

'You could've eaten without me,' he said. 'I wouldn't
have minded just reheating something in the microwave.'

'I had no idea how long you were going to be, and I
would've felt bad if you'd turned up while I was halfway

through eating my dinner.' She paused. 'Do you really work an hour's commute away from here?'

'No. I work in Docklands. About half an hour away.' At least he had the grace to look embarrassed. 'I had to finish something, first.'

She blew out a breath. 'OK. Take the lecture as read. We're sharing Tyler's care so, in future, you're either going to have to learn to delegate, or you'll have to work from home when the baby's napping.'

Hearing his godson's name seemed to galvanise Dylan. 'Where is he?'

'Asleep in his cot.' She gestured to the kitchen table. 'Sit down. I've made a start on the rota, given what we discussed yesterday morning. Perhaps you can review it while I finish cooking dinner, and move any of the sticky notes if you need to.'

'Sticky notes?' He looked puzzled.

'Because it's a provisional rota. Sticky notes mean it's easy to move things around without the rota getting messy. Once we've agreed our slots, I'll write it in properly. I'll get it laminated. And then we can use sticky notes day by day to make any changes to the rota—that way it'll be an obvious change so we'll both remember it.'

'OK.' He looked at her. 'Sorry.'

Dylan Harper had apologised to her? That was a first. Actually, no, it was the second time he'd said sorry to her in as many days. And, even though Emmy thought that he more than owed her that apology just now, she decided to be gracious about it. Be the bigger person. 'It's a bit of a radical lifestyle change for both of us. I think it'll take us a while to get used to it.'

He nodded. 'True.'

She concentrated on cooking the pasta and heating the sauce, then served up their meal at the kitchen table.

He put the card to one side. 'The rota looks fine to me. I notice it's a two-week one.'

'I thought that would be fair, giving each other alternate weekends off.'

'Yes, that's fair,' he agreed. He ate a mouthful of the pasta. 'And this is good. Thank you. I wasn't expecting dinner. I was going to make myself a sandwich or something.'

She knew exactly where he was coming from. 'I do that too often. It doesn't feel worth cooking for one, does it?'

'Especially if cooking isn't your thing.' He blew out a breath. 'I never expected to be living with—well, *you*.'

He'd made that perfectly clear. He really didn't have to harp on about it. 'We'll just have to make the best of it, for Tyler's sake,' she said dryly.

'Agreed. How did you get on with the mortgage and the letting agency?' he asked.

'It's all sorted. I'm letting my flat in Camden from Monday. You?'

'It's a short-term lease. Nadine has the house.'

His wife. 'Have you told her about this?'

His expression said very clearly, *that's none of your business*, and she shut up. No, it wasn't her business. And he'd already said that nobody would be upset by him sharing a house and Tyler's care with her.

'I'll go back to my place tonight to pick up the basics, and move the rest in over the next few days.' He looked at her. 'I assume you've done the same?'

'Yes to the basics today, but I haven't chosen a room yet. I was waiting for you.' She grimaced. 'I'm really glad Ally and Pete have two spare bedrooms as well as the nursery. I don't think I could face using their room.'

'Me, neither.' He shrugged. 'Which of the spare rooms I have doesn't bother me. Pick whichever one you like.'

'Thanks.' Though it wasn't the bedroom that concerned her most. 'Can I use Pete's study? I work from home,' she explained, 'and I need somewhere to set up my equipment. And that means a room with decent lighting.'

She was glad she'd been conciliatory when he said, 'That's fine by me. I can work anywhere with a laptop and a briefcase. So you have, what, some kind of workbench?'

It was the first time he'd ever shown any interest in her work, and it unnerved her slightly. She wasn't used to Dylan being anything other than abrupt to her. 'Yes, and I have a desk where I sketch the pieces before I make them. And before Tyler gets mobile I'll need to get a baby gate fixed on the doorway. I don't want him anywhere near my tools because they're sharp and dangerous.' She looked at him. 'Are you any good at DIY?'

'No. I'd rather pay someone to do it,' he said.

That was refreshing. The men she'd dated in the past had all taken the attitude that having a Y chromosome meant that they'd automatically be good at DIY, and they weren't prepared to admit when they were hopeless and couldn't even put a shelf on straight. Then again, she wasn't actually dating Dylan. He might be easy on the eye—she had to admit that he was good-looking—but he was the last man she'd ever want to date. He was way too uptight. 'OK. I know the number of a good handyman. I'll get it sorted.'

He looked at their empty plates. 'I haven't organised a cleaner yet.'

'And I wouldn't expect a cleaner to do dirty dishes,' Emmy said crisply. 'Especially as Ally and Pete have a dishwasher.'

'Point taken. I'll stack the dishwasher, then go and pick up my stuff.'

She chose her room while he was out, opting for the room she'd stayed in several times as a guest. It was strange to think that—unless things changed dramatically during their three-month trial—she'd be living here until Tyler had grown up. And even stranger to think she'd be sharing the house with Dylan Harper. Even if it might only be for a short time.

Still, she'd made a promise to Ally. She wouldn't back out.

She unpacked the small case she'd brought with her, then checked on Tyler. He was still sound asleep. Unable to resist, she reached down to touch his cheek. Such soft, soft skin. And he was so vulnerable. She and Dylan really couldn't let him down, whatever their doubts about each other. 'Sleep tight, baby,' she whispered, and went downstairs to the kitchen to wait for Dylan. She'd left the baby listener on; she glanced at it to make sure the lights were working, then put a cello concerto on low and began to sketch some ideas for the commission she'd been working on before the whole world had turned upside down.

When Dylan came back to the house, he was surprised to discover that Emmy was still up. He hadn't expected her to wait up for him. Or was she checking up on him or trying to score some weird kind of point?

'Is Tyler OK?' he asked.

She nodded. 'He's fast asleep.'

'Whose turn is it on the rota for night duty?' Then he grimaced. 'Forget I asked that. You've been looking after him since Ally and Pete went to Venice, so I'll go tonight if he wakes. Do I need to sleep on the floor in his room?'

'No. There's a portable baby listener.' She indicated the device with lights that was plugged in next to the kettle. 'Plug it in near your bed, and you'll hear him if he wakes. The lights change when there's a noise—the louder the noise, the more lights come on. So that might wake you, too.'

'Is he, um, likely to wake?' He didn't have a clue about how long babies slept or what their routines were. Pete had never talked about it, and Dylan hadn't really had much to do with babies in the past. His mother was an only child, so there had been no babies in his family while he'd been growing up; and Pete was the first of his friends to have a child. Babies just hadn't featured in his life.

Although he'd accused Emmy of leaving him to do the serious stuff, he was guiltily aware that he'd never babysat his godson or anything like that, and she clearly had. She'd been a better godparent than he had, by far—much more hands-on. He'd just been selfish and avoided it.

'He'd just started to sleep through, a couple of weeks back; but I guess he's picked up on the tension over the last few days because he's woken every night since the accident.' Emmy sighed. 'He might need a nappy change or some milk, or he might just want a cuddle.'

'How do you know what he needs?' Babies were too little to tell you. They just screamed.

'The nappy, you'll definitely know,' she said dryly. 'Just sniff him.'

'*Sniff* him?' Had she really said that?

She smiled. 'Trust me, you'll know if he has a dirty nappy. If he's hungry, he'll keep bumping his face against you and nuzzling for milk. And if he just wants a cuddle, hold him close and he'll settle and go to sleep. Eventually.'

'Poor little mite.' Dylan felt a muscle clench in his cheek. 'I hate that Pete's never going to get to know his son. He's not going to see him grow up. He's not going to teach him to ride a bike or swim. He's not going to…' He blew out a breath. 'I just hate all this.'

'Me, too,' she said softly. 'I hate that Ally's going to miss all the firsts. The first tooth, the first word, the first

steps. All the things she was so looking forward to. She
was keeping a baby book with every single detail.'

'I never thought I'd ever be a dad. It wasn't in my life
plan.' Dylan grimaced. 'And I haven't exactly been a
hands-on godparent, so far. Not the way you've been. I'm
ashamed to say it, but I don't have a clue where I should
even start right now.'

'Most men aren't that interested in babies until they
have their own,' she said. 'Don't beat yourself up about
it too much.'

'I've never even changed a nappy before,' he confessed.
There really hadn't been the need or the opportunity.

'Are you trying to get out of doing night duty?'

Was she teasing him or was she going to throw a hissy
fit? He really wasn't sure. He couldn't read her at all.
Emmy was almost a stranger, and now she was going to
be a huge part of his life, at least for the next three months.
Unwanted, unlooked for. A woman who'd always managed
to rub him up the wrong way. And he was going to have
to be nice to her, to keep the peace for Tyler's sake. 'No,'
he said, 'I'm not trying to get out of it. But you know what
you're doing—you've looked after Tyler for the last few
days on your own. And I was just thinking, it might be an
idea if you teach me what I need to do.'

She blinked at him. 'You want *me* to teach *you*?' She
tested the words as if she didn't believe he'd just said them.

'If I don't have a business skill I need, I take a course
to learn it. This is the same sort of thing. It might save
us both a lot of hassle,' he said dryly. 'And I think it'd be
better if you show me in daylight rather than tell me now.
You know the old stuff about teaching someone—I hear
and I forget, I see and remember, I do and I understand.'

She nodded. 'Fair enough. I'll keep the baby listener

with me tonight. But, tomorrow, please make sure you're back early so I can teach you the basics—how to change a nappy, make up a bottle of formula, and do a bath. By early, I mean before five o'clock.'

When was the last time he'd left the office before seven? He couldn't remember. Tough. Tomorrow, he'd just have to make the effort. 'Deal,' he said.

'OK. See you tomorrow.'

He realised that she'd been working when she closed a folder and picked up a handful of pencils. But then again, hadn't she said something about preferring to work in the evening? So he squashed the growing feeling of guilt. She was self-employed. A sole trader who didn't need to keep to traditional business hours. She obviously worked the hours that suited her.

'See you tomorrow,' he said. 'Which room did you pick?'

'The one opposite Tyler's.'

Which left the one next to Pete and Ally's room for him. 'OK. Thanks.' And then he realised he hadn't brought any bedding with him.

'The bed's already made up,' she said. 'I used linen from Ally and Pete's airing cupboard. I don't think they'd mind and it'd be a waste not to use it.'

He pushed a hand through his hair. 'Sorry. I didn't realise I'd said that aloud.'

'It's a lot to take in. A lot of change.' She shrugged. 'We'll muddle through.'

'Yeah. Sleep well.' Which was a stupid thing to say; of course she wouldn't, because Tyler would wake up.

But she didn't look annoyed. Her eyes actually crinkled at the corners. Again, Dylan was struck by the fact that Emmy Jacobs was pretty. And again it tipped him off balance. He couldn't even begin to think about Emmy in that way; it would make things far too complicated.

'Sleep well, Dylan,' she said, and strolled out of the kitchen.

Given how late Dylan had been the previous night, and the fact that Emmy had asked him to be back before five, he thought he'd better take the afternoon off to deal with the baby-care issues. He walked in to the house to find Emmy playing with the baby and singing to him, while the baby gurgled and smiled at her.

This felt distinctly weird. He'd never been that interested in babies and he'd never wanted a family of his own—which was most of the reason why he'd married Nadine, because she'd been just as dedicated to her career as he was and didn't pose any kind of emotional risk. Or so he'd thought. He hadn't expected her to change her mind and give him an ultimatum: give me a baby or give me a divorce. He didn't want a baby, so the choice was obvious.

And now he was here. Instead of being in his minimalist Docklands bachelor flat, he was living in a family home. Sharing the care of a tiny, defenceless baby. And he didn't have the least idea about what he was doing.

Emmy looked up at him. 'Hey, Ty, look, it's Uncle Dylan.' She smiled. 'You're back early.'

It was the first time Dylan could ever remember Emmy smiling spontaneously at him, as if she were genuinely pleased to see him, and he was shocked that it made him feel warm inside.

Was he going crazy, reacting like this to her?

No, of course not. It was just because he'd been knocked off balance by Pete and Ally's death. Grief made him want to hold someone, that was all; to feel connected to the world, still. He was *not* becoming attracted to Emmy Jacobs. Even though he was beginning to think that maybe she wasn't quite who he'd always thought she was.

'We agreed you were going to teach me about nappies and baths,' he said. 'And you asked me to come back early. Here I am.' He spread his hands. 'So let's get it sorted.'

She blew a raspberry on Tyler's tummy, making the baby giggle. 'He's clean at the moment, so we might as well hold off on that side until he really needs a nappy change. But he's wide awake, so you can play with him.'

'Play with him?' Dylan repeated. He knew it was ridiculous—he was the head of a very successful computer consultancy and could sort out tricky business problems quickly and effectively. But he didn't have a clue about how to play with a baby. He'd never done it. Never needed to do it.

She rolled her eyes. 'Dylan, you can't just sit and work on your laptop when you're in charge and Ty's awake. You need to play with him. Read to him. Talk to him.'

Dylan frowned. 'Isn't he a bit young for books?'

'No. Pete used to read to him,' she said softly. 'Ally read up about it and she wanted Tyler to have a good male role model. So Pete always did the bedtime story.'

OK. Reading to a baby couldn't be that hard. Talking, too. But playing...where did you start? He didn't know any baby games. Any nursery rhymes.

As if the panic showed on his face, she smiled at him. 'Come and give him a cuddle.'

And this was where Dylan got nervous. Where things could go terribly wrong. Because he didn't have a clue what he was doing. And he hated the fact that he had to take advice from someone as flaky as Emmy, because she clearly knew more about babies than he did. 'Do I have to hold his head or something?'

'No. He's four months old, not a newborn, so he can

support his head just fine. He can't sit up on his own yet, but that'll happen in a few weeks.' She looked at him. 'OK. You might want to change.'

'Why?'

'Unless you don't mind your suit getting creased and needing to go to the cleaner's more often.'

The question must've been written all over his face, because she added, 'You're going to be on the floor with him a lot.'

She had a point. 'I'll be down in a minute.' Dylan took the stairs two at a time to his room, then changed into jeans and T-shirt.

When he came downstairs, she gave him an approving look. 'Righty. He's all yours.'

Panic seeped through Dylan. What was he meant to do now?

She kissed the baby. 'See you later, sweetie. Have fun with Uncle Dylan.' And then she went to hand the baby to him.

He could muddle through this.

But it was important to get it *right*.

'Uh—Emmy.' He really hated this, but what choice did he have? It was ask, or mess it up. 'I don't know what to do.'

She rolled her eyes. 'We've already discussed this. Play with him. It's not rocket science.'

She wasn't going to make this easy for him, was she? 'I haven't had anything to do with babies before.'

She scoffed. 'He's four months old and he's your god-son. Of course you've spent time with him.'

'He's always been asleep or Ally was feeding him. Pete and I didn't do baby stuff together, not like you and Ally.'

She looked at him and nodded. 'It must really stick in your craw to have to ask *me* for help. And if I was a different kind of woman, I'd just walk away and let you get on with it. But Tyler's needs come first, so I'll help you.'

'For his sake, not mine. I get it. But thank you anyway.'

'So how come you're so clueless? Pete always said you were the brightest person he knew—Ally, too. And you're the same age as the rest of us. I don't understand how, at thirty-five years old, you can know absolutely nothing about babies.'

Although he knew there was a compliment in there, of sorts, at the same time her words were damning. And he was surprised to find himself explaining. 'I'm an only child. No cousins, no close family.' At least, not since his grandmother died. His mother had never been close to him. 'Pete and Ally were the first of my friends to have children, and I…' He sighed. 'I guess I've been a bit pre-occupied, the last few months.'

'Relationship break-ups tend to do that to you.' She looked rueful. 'And yes, I know that from way too much experience. OK. I never thought I'd need to show you any of this, but these are the kinds of things he likes to do with me.' She sat on the floor and balanced Tyler on her knees. 'Humpty Dumpty sat on the wall. Humpty Dumpty had a great…' She paused, and the baby clearly knew what was coming because he was beaming his head off. 'Fall,' she said, lowering her knees as she straightened her legs, and managing to keep the baby upright at the same time.

Her reward was a rich chuckle from the baby.

Something else that made him feel odd. 'And you always do the pause?' he asked, to take his focus off his feelings. This was about learning to care for a baby, not how he felt.

'I do. He's learned to anticipate it. He loved doing this with Ally. She used to string it out for ages.' She blew a raspberry on the baby's tummy, making him laugh, and handed him to Dylan. 'Your turn.'

'Humpty Dumpty sat on the wall,' Dylan intoned, feeling absolutely ridiculous and wishing he were a hundred miles away. Or, better still, back at his desk—where at least he knew what he was doing. 'Humpty Dumpty had a great...' He glanced at Emmy, who nodded. 'Fall,' he finished, and straightened his legs, letting the baby whoosh downwards but supporting him so he didn't fall.

Tyler laughed.

And something around Dylan's heart felt as if it had cracked.

There was a look of sheer wonder on Dylan's face as Tyler laughed up at him. He really hadn't been exaggerating about being a hands-off godfather, and this was obviously the first time he'd actually sat down with the baby and played with him. Emmy had the feeling that Dylan Harper, the stuffiest man in the world, kept everyone at arm's length. Well, you couldn't do that when you lived with a baby. So this was really going to change Dylan. It might make him human, instead of being a judgemental, formal machine.

When he did the Humpty Dumpty game for the third time, and laughed at the same time as the baby, she knew he was *definitely* changing. Tyler was about to turn Dylan Harper's life upside down again—but this time, in a good way.

'OK for me to go to work?' she asked.

'Sure. And, um, thanks for the lesson.' He still looked awkward and embarrassed, but at least they'd managed to be civil to each other.

Hopefully they could keep it up.

'No problem,' she said. 'I'll be in Pete's study if you get stuck with anything.'

CHAPTER FOUR

DYLAN WAS SURPRISED to discover how much he enjoyed playing with the baby. How good it was to hear that rich chuckle and know that he'd given Tyler a moment of pure happiness. If anyone had told him three weeks ago that he'd be having fun waving a toy duck around and quacking loudly, he would've dismissed it as utter insanity. But, this afternoon, it was a revelation.

He was actually disappointed when Tyler fell asleep.

Though it wasn't for long. The baby woke again and started crying, and Dylan picked him up almost on instinct. Then he wrinkled his nose. Revolting. It looked as if he needed another lesson from Emmy. He went to find her in Pete's study.

'Problem?' she asked.

'He needs a nappy change. Can you show me how to do it?'

'Ah, no. You're the one who said, "I do and I understand" is the best. I'll talk you through it.'

When they went upstairs to the nursery, Emmy did at least help Dylan get the baby out of his little all-in-one suit, for which he was grateful. But then she stood back and talked him through the actual process of nappy-changing.

How could someone so small produce something so—so *stinky*? he wondered.

He used wipe after wipe to clean the baby.

And it was only when he realised Emmy was grinning that he thought there might've been another way of doing it—one that maybe didn't use half a box of wipes at a time. 'So you're perfect at this, are you?' he asked, slightly put out.

'No—it usually takes me three or four wipes. Though Ally used to be able to do it in one.' Her smile faded, and she helped him put Tyler back in his Babygro.

'I'm going to do some work,' she said. 'Call me when Tyler needs a bath. His routine's on the board in the kitchen, so you'll know when he's due for a feed. If he's grizzly before then, try him with a drink. There's some cooled boiled water in sterilised bottles in the fridge.'

Again, Dylan was surprised by Emmy's efficiency. Maybe he'd misjudged her really badly, or he'd just seen her on bad days in the past—a *lot* of bad days—and taken her the wrong way.

'Oh, and you need to wind him after a feed,' she added. 'Hold him upright against your shoulder, rub his back, and he'll burp for you.'

'Got it.'

'Are you sure you can do this?'

No. He wasn't sure at all. But he didn't want Emmy to think that he was bailing out already. 'Sure,' he lied.

He carried Tyler downstairs and checked the routine board in the kitchen—which Emmy had somehow managed to get written up properly and laminated while he'd been at work. Apparently the baby needed a nap for about an hour; then he'd need a bath and then finally a feed.

And it was also his turn to make dinner.

He hadn't even thought about buying food. He'd only focused on the fact that he'd needed to get everything done and leave the office ridiculously early. He opened the fridge door, and was relieved to discover that there were ingredients for a stir-fry. And there were noodles and soy sauce in the cupboard. OK. He could work with that.

Now, how did you get a baby to sleep?

He sat down, settling Tyler against his arm. Sure, he'd given his godson a brief cuddle before, but Ally had understood that he wasn't used to babies and wasn't much good at this, so she hadn't given him a hard time about it. But it also meant she hadn't talked to him about baby stuff. And Emmy had just left him to it.

'I have no idea what to do now,' he said to the baby.

Tyler just gave him a gummy smile.

'Emmy seems to know what to do with you. But I don't.' OK, so he'd enjoyed playing with the baby, but was that all you were supposed to do?

'She's abandoned us,' he said, and then grimaced. 'And that's not very fair of me. If she'd stayed, I would've assumed she didn't trust me to do a good enough job with you and was being a control freak. So she can't win, whatever she does.'

Maybe he needed a new approach to Emmy. And she had given up some of her work time to show him how to care for Tyler. As she'd pointed out, she could've left him to muddle through and fall flat on his face, then gloated when he'd made a mess of things. But she hadn't. She'd played nice.

Maybe she was nice. Maybe he hadn't really given her a chance, before.

'I don't know any nursery rhymes,' he told the baby. Except for "Humpty Dumpty". He made a mental note to buy a book and learn some. 'I could tell you about computer programming.'

Another gummy smile.

'Binary code. Fibonacci sequence. Debugging.' He could talk for hours about that. 'Algorhythms.'

Well, the baby wasn't crying. That was a good thing, right? Dylan carried on talking softly to Tyler, until eventually the baby's eyes closed.

Now what? Did he just sit here until the baby woke up again? Or did he put the baby to sleep in his cot? He wished he'd thought to ask Emmy earlier. It wouldn't be fair to disturb her now. She needed time to get on with her work. And he could really do with checking his emails. OK. He'd put the baby down.

Gingerly, he managed to move out of the chair and placed the baby on his playmat. The mat was nice and soft, and Tyler would be safe there. Did he need a blanket? But his little hands felt warm. Maybe not, then.

While Tyler slept, Dylan caught up with some work on his laptop.

Not that it was easy to concentrate. He kept glancing over at the baby to check that everything was all right.

Eventually Tyler woke, and Dylan saved the file before closing the laptop and picking the baby up. 'Bath time. We need to go and find Emmy.'

He carried the baby through to Pete's study. The door was open, and soft classical music was playing. Another surprise; he'd pegged Emmy as someone who would listen to very girly pop music, the kind of stuff that was in the charts and that he loathed. Although he'd gone into the office earlier, he hadn't really taken any notice. He'd never seen her in a professional environment before, and there was a different air about her. Total focus and concentration as she worked on something that looked very intricate.

If he interrupted her now, would it make her jump and wreck what she was doing?

He waited, jiggling the baby as he'd seen her do, until

her hands moved away, and then he knocked on the open door. 'You said to come and get you when Tyler woke up and it was bath time.'

She looked up from her workbench, smiled, and put her tools down. 'Sure.'

He caught a glimpse of the work on her bench; it looked like delicate silver filigree. Again, it wasn't what he'd expected from her; he'd thought that she'd make in-your-face ethnic-style jewellery, or lots of clinking bangles.

'All righty. We need a bottle of boiled cooled water from the fridge.' She collected it on the way up to the bathroom.

'What's that for?' he asked.

'Washing his face—it's how Ally did it. She has what she calls a "top and tail" bowl.'

'A what?'

'To give him a quick wash instead of a bath. But you still use it for his face when you give him a bath.'

'Right.'

In the bathroom, she put the baby bath into the main bath. 'It's easier to use this than to put him in a big bath, because he can't sit up all on his own yet.'

'When will he do that?'

'When he's about six months old.'

Dylan looked at her, not sure whether to be impressed at her knowledge or annoyed by the one-upmanship. 'How come you know so much about babies?' Had she wanted a child of her own? he wondered. Were all women like Nadine, and just woke up one morning desperate for a baby?

'My bedtime reading,' she said lightly. 'I'll lend you the book, if you like—you'll probably find it useful.'

She undressed the baby, though Dylan noticed that she left Tyler's nappy on, and wrapped him in a towel. 'This is just to keep him warm while we're filling the bath. It needs to be lukewarm, and you need to put the cold water in first—it's better for it to be too cool, and for you to add a bit more warm water, than the other way round.' She demonstrated.

'How do you know when it's the right temperature?'

'You check the temperature of the water with your elbow.' She dipped her elbow into the water. 'If it feels too warm, it'll be too hot for the baby.'

'Why don't you use that thermometer thing?' He gestured to the gadget on the side of the bath.

She laughed. 'That was one of Pete's ideas. You know how he loves gadgets.' Her smile faded. 'Loved,' she corrected herself softly.

Awkwardly, Dylan patted her shoulder. 'Yeah.'

She shook herself. 'OK—now you pour the cooled water into the bowl, dip a cotton wool pad into it and squeeze it out, so it's damp enough not to drag his skin but not so wet that water's going to run into his eyes, then wipe his eyes. You need to use a separate one for each eye; apparently that's to avoid infection.'

'Right.' He followed her instructions—which were surprisingly clear and focused—and then worried that he was being too clumsy, but the baby didn't seem to mind.

'Now you wash his face and the creases round his neck with a different cotton wool pad.'

When he'd finished doing that, she said, 'And finally it's bath time.' She eyed his clothes. 'Sorry, I should've told you. Tyler likes to splash his hands in the bath, so you might get a bit wet.'

Dylan shrugged. 'It doesn't matter. This stuff will wash.'

She gave him an approving smile. It should've annoyed him that she was taking a position of superiority, but instead it made him feel warm inside. Which was weird. Emmy shouldn't make him feel warm inside. At all. He stuffed that into the box marked 'do not open' in his head, and concentrated on the task in hand.

'What about his hair?' he asked, looking at Tyler's soft fluffy curls.

'Do that before you put him in the bath,' she said. 'Keep him in the towel so he's warm, support his head with your hand and support him with your forearm—then you can scoop a little bit of water onto his hair and do the baby shampoo.'

Dylan felt really nervous, holding the baby—what if he dropped Tyler?—but Emmy seemed to have confidence in him and encouraged him as he gave Tyler a hair-wash for the very first time.

'Now you pat his hair dry. Be gentle and careful over the fontanelles.'

'Fontanelles?' he asked.

'Soft spots. The bones in his skull haven't completely fused, yet.'

That made Dylan feel even more nervous. Could he inadvertently hurt the baby? He knew he was making a bit of a mess of it, but she didn't comment.

'OK, now check the bath water again with your elbow.'

He dipped his elbow in. 'It feels fine.'

'Good. Now the nappy comes off, and he goes into the bath—support him like you did with the Humpty Dumpty thing.'

So far, so easy. Tyler seemed to enjoy the bath; as Emmy had warned him, there was a bit of splashing and chuckling.

Emmy stayed while he got the baby out of the bath and wrapped him in a towel with a hood to keep his head warm, then waited while Tyler did the nappy and dressed Dylan in a clean vest and Babygro.

She smiled at him. 'See, you're an expert now.'

Dylan didn't feel like it; but he was starting to feel a lot more comfortable around Tyler, thanks to her. 'I'm trying, anyway.'

'I know you are—and that's all Tyler would ask for,' she said softly.

Dylan remembered how he'd thought she was trying in more than one sense; yet she wasn't judging him that way. He felt a bit guilty. 'I looked in the fridge. Is chicken stir-fry all right for dinner?'

'That'd be lovely, thanks.'

'Good. I'll call you when it's ready.'

'Are you OK about feeding him?' she asked. The doubts must have shown on his face, because she added, 'Just put the bottle of milk in a jug of hot water for a couple of minutes to warm up, then test it on the inside of your wrist to make sure it's warm but not hot.'

'How do you mean, test it on the inside of my wrist?'

'Just hold the bottle upside down and shake it over your wrist. A couple of drops will come out. If it feels hot then the milk's too hot.' She looked slightly anxious. 'Don't take this the wrong way—I'm not meaning to be patronising—but when you feed him you need to make sure the teat's full of milk, or he'll just suck in air.'

'Right.'

'And when you put him in his cot at bedtime, his feet need to be at the bottom of the cot so he doesn't end up wriggling totally under the covers and getting too hot.'

'OK,' he said, hoping he sounded more confident than he felt.

'Call me if you get stuck,' she said.

Which would be a cop-out. He could do this. It wasn't that hard to feed a baby, surely?

He managed to warm the milk, then sat down and settled the baby in the crook of his arm. Remembering what she'd said about the air, he made sure he tilted the bottle. The baby was very focused on drinking his milk, and Dylan couldn't help smiling at him. There was something really satisfying about feeding a baby, and he wished he'd been more involved earlier in the baby's life instead of backing off, fearing the extra intimacy.

This was what Nadine had wanted from him. What he hadn't been able to give, although now he was doing it for his best friend's child because he simply had no other choice. Except to walk away, which he couldn't bring himself to do.

He couldn't imagine Nadine doing this, even though he knew she'd wanted a baby of her own. She wouldn't have been comfortable exchanging her sharp business suits and designer dresses for jeans and a T-shirt. Dylan simply couldn't see her on the floor playing with a baby, or singing songs.

Unlike Emmy. Emmy, who'd been all soft and warm and cute...

He shook himself. He hadn't wanted children with Nadine. So her ultimatum of baby or divorce had given him an obvious choice. And he didn't want to think about his relationship with Emmy. Because, strictly speaking, it wasn't actually a relationship; it was a co-guardianship. They were here for Tyler, not for each other.

'Emotions and relationships,' he said softly to the baby, 'are very much overrated.'

When the baby had finished feeding, Dylan burped him in accordance with Emmy's instructions, then carried him up to the nursery and put him in his cot. There was a stack of books by the cot; Dylan found one in rhyme and read it through, keeping his voice soft and low. Tyler's eyelids seemed to be growing heavy; encouraged, Dylan read the next two books. And then finally Tyler's eyes closed.

Asleep.

Good. He'd managed it.

He touched the baby's soft little cheek. 'Sleep well,' he whispered.

Then he headed for the study and knocked on the open door.

Emmy looked up. 'How did you get on?'

'Fine. He's asleep. Dinner in ten minutes?'

'That'll be great. I'll just finish up here.'

She joined him in the kitchen just as he was serving up.

'OK if we eat in here, tonight?' Dylan asked.

'That's fine.' She took her first mouthful. 'This is very nice, thank you.'

He flapped a dismissive hand. 'It wasn't exactly hard—just stir-fry chicken, noodles, vegetables and soy sauce.'

'But it's edible and, more importantly, I didn't have to cook it. It's appreciated.'

There was an awkward silence for a few moments.

Work, Dylan thought. Work was always a safe topic. 'I saw that necklace you were making. I had no idea you made delicate stuff like that.'

'You mean you thought I just stuck some chunky beads on a string and that was it?' she asked.

He felt his face colour with embarrassment. 'Well, yes.'

She shrugged. 'There's nothing wrong with a string of chunky beads.'

He thought of his mother, and wanted to disagree.

'But no, I do mainly silverwork—and I also work with jet. I carve animals.'

'Like those ones on the shelf in Tyler's room?'

She nodded. 'Ally wanted a Noah's ark sort of thing, so I'd planned to do her one a month.'

'They're very good.'

'Thank you.' Emmy inclined her head at his compliment

but he noticed that she accepted it easily. She clearly knew she was good at what she did. Just as he was good at what he did. Something they had in common, then.

'Why jet?' he asked.

'We always used to go to my great-aunt Syb's in the school summer holidays, up in Whitby.'

'Dracula country,' he said.

She smiled. 'Well, it's known for that nowadays, but it's also the Jurassic coastline, full of fossils—that's why there's lots of jet and amber in the cliffs there.'

'Amber being fossilised tree resin, right?'

She nodded. 'And jet's fossilised monkey puzzle tree. They used to use it a lot in Victorian times for mourning jewellery, but it's been used as jewellery for much longer than that. There are some Roman jewellery workshop remains in York, and archaeologists have found gorgeous jet pendants carved as Medusa's head.'

Dylan noticed how her eyes glittered; this was clearly something she felt really passionate about. For a second, it made him wonder what her face would look like in the throes of passion, but he pushed the thought away. It was way too inappropriate. He needed to keep his focus on work, not on how lush Emmy Jacobs' mouth was. 'And that's when you got interested in making jewellery, at your great-aunt's?'

She nodded. 'We used to go beachcombing for jet and amber because Great-Aunt Syb's best friend Jamie was a jeweller and worked with it. I was fascinated at how these dull-looking, lightweight pebbles could suddenly become these amazingly shiny beads and flowers. Jamie taught me how to work with jet. It's a bit specialised.' She grimaced. 'I'd better warn you, it does tend to make quite a bit of dust, the really thick and heavy sort, but I always clean up after I've worked.'

If she'd said that a week ago, he would've scoffed; from what he'd seen, Emmy Jacobs was as chaotic as his mother. But now, having shared a house with her for a day and discovered that she ruled her life with lists and charts, he could believe it. She might appear chaotic, but she knew exactly what she was doing. 'How do you sell your jewellery? Do you have a shop?' He hadn't thought to ask before.

'No. I sell mainly through galleries—I pay them a commission when they sell a piece. Plus there's my website.'

'So what's the plan—to have a shop of your own?'

She shook her head. 'If I had a shop, I'd need to increase production to cover all the extra expenses—rent, utilities and taxes, not to mention staffing costs. And I'd have to spend a lot of time serving customers instead of doing the bit of my job that I like doing most, creating jewellery. And then there's the worry about who'd cover the shop when an assistant was on holiday or off sick...' She grimaced. 'No, I'd rather keep it this way.'

She'd clearly thought it all through, taking a professional view of the situation, Dylan thought. He would never have expected that from her. And it shook him to realise how badly he'd misjudged her. He'd always thought himself such a good judge of character. How wrong he'd been.

'So what actually do you do?' she asked. 'I mean, Pete said you're a computer guru, but I assume you don't actually build computers or websites?'

He smiled. 'I can, and sometimes that's part of a project, but what I do is software development—bespoke stuff for businesses. So I talk to them about their requirements, draw up a specification, then do the architecture.'

'Architecture?' She looked puzzled.

'I write the code,' he said, 'so the computer program does what they want it to do. Once the code's written, you set up the system, test it, debug it, and agree a maintenance programme with the client.'

'So businesses can't just buy a software package—say like you do with word-processing, spreadsheets and accounting programs?'

'Obviously those ones they can, but what my clients tend to want is database management, something very specific to their business. So if they had a chain of shops, for example, they need to have the tills linked with the stock system, so every time they sell something it updates and they can see their stock levels. Once they get down to a certain stock level, it triggers a reorder report, based on how long it takes to get the stock from the supplier,' Dylan explained. 'It's also helpful if the till staff take the customer's details, because then they can build up a profile for the customer based on past purchases, and can use that knowledge to target their marketing more specifically.'

'Very impressive,' she said.

He shrugged. 'It's basic data management—and it's only as good as the data you feed in. That's why the requirements and spec side is important. What the client thinks they want might not be what they actually want, so you have to grill them.'

'I can see you'd be good at that,' she said, then winced. 'Sorry, that was rude. I'm not trying hard enough.'

He should've been annoyed and wanting to snipe back; but he liked the fact that she was being honest. Plus he was beginning to suspect that she had quite a sharp wit, something he appreciated. 'It's OK. We've never really got on before, so we're not exactly going to be best friends, are we?'

'No, but we don't have to be rude to each other, either.'

'I guess not.' He paused. 'So do you use a computer system?'

'Sort of. I do my accounts on a spreadsheet because I'm a sole trader and don't need anything more complicated, but I did have my website designed so I could showcase my work and people could buy what they wanted online from me direct. It shows whether the piece they want is in stock or if they need to order it and how long it'll take—but, yes, I have to update that manually.'

Dylan made a mental note to look up her website. Maybe there was something he could add to it to make her life easier. Which didn't mean he was going soft; making things run smoothly for her meant that he wouldn't have to prop up their roster for more than his fair share of effort.

'So what's your big plan?' she asked. 'Expansion?'

'Pretty much keep doing what I do now,' he said. 'I have a good team. They're reliable and they're prepared to put in the hours to get the projects in on time.'

'And you like your job?'

'It's like breathing, for me,' he said honestly. Something that Nadine had never really quite understood. His job was who he was.

'Same here,' she said, surprising him. It was something else they had in common.

When they'd finished the meal, she said, 'It's my turn to do the dishes, and I'm not weaselling out of it—but there's something I need to share with you. Back in a tick.'

She returned with a book and handed it to him.

He read the title. '*The Baby Bible.* What's this?'

'You asked me how come I know so much about babies. It's because of this. I bought it when Ty was born, so I'd know what to do when Ally asked me to babysit. It tells you everything you need to know—how to do things, what all the milestones are.' She spread her hands. 'And if that doesn't work then I'll bring in my other secret weapon.'

'Which is?'

She looked slightly shame-faced. 'Ring my mum and ask her advice.'

He thought about what would happen if he rang his mother and asked for help with a baby. No, it wasn't going to happen. He was pretty sure his mother hadn't been able to cope with having a baby or a child, which was why she'd dumped him on her parents so many times. The only person he could've asked about babies was his grandmother, but she'd died a year ago now. After he'd married Nadine, but before the final split. And, although she'd never judged, never actually said anything about it, Dylan knew his grandmother had thought the wedding was a huge mistake.

How right she'd been.

What would she think about this set-up?

What would she have thought about Emmy?

He shook himself. 'Do you need it back soon?'

'I've read it through cover-to-cover once. But if you could leave it in Tyler's room or the kitchen when it's my shift, so I can refer to it if I need to, that'd be really helpful.' She glanced at her watch. 'Do you mind if I go back to work now and do the washing up later?'

'Sure—and I'm on nights tonight.'

'I would say sleep well, but…' She shrugged. 'That's entirely up to Tyler.'

'Yes.' And Dylan wasn't so sure he'd sleep well anyway. He still had to get his head round a lot of things. New responsibilities, having to share his space with someone else when he'd just got used to his bachelor lifestyle, and having a totally new routine for starters. Not to mention that getting to know Emmy was unsettling, because all his preconceptions about her were starting to look wrong. 'Sleep well,' he said, and went to settle down with his new reading material.

CHAPTER FIVE

THE BABY WOKE at half past three, and the wails coming through the baby listener seemed incredibly loud.

Dylan surfaced from some weird dream, switched off the baby listener and staggered out into Tyler's nursery.

According to what Emmy had told him—and what he'd read last night—screaming meant the baby was dirty, hungry, tired or wanted a cuddle. He picked the baby up and sniffed him. Nothing like yesterday's appalling whiff, so Tyler didn't need a nappy change. It was the middle of the night, so he could be tired—but then again, he wouldn't have woken if he was tired. So was he hungry, or did he just want a cuddle?

He probably wanted his mum. Though, Tyler was way too little to understand that Ally couldn't be there for him anymore. Not like Dylan's mother, who hadn't been there because she hadn't wanted to; Tyler had been very much loved by both his parents. And it was wrong, wrong, *wrong* that they'd died so young.

The baby nuzzled him.

Hadn't Emmy said that was a sign of hunger?

'OK, Ty, food it is,' he whispered. He took the baby down to the kitchen, managed to switch on the kettle and get the milk out of the fridge, and walked up and down with the baby, stroking his back to sooth him and jiggling him.

Dear God, why had nobody told him that babies were so *loud*? If Tyler carried on much longer, Emmy was bound to wake. And that wasn't fair because this was his shift, not hers, and he should be able to deal with this.

It seemed to take forever to heat the milk, and Tyler's wails grew louder and louder. Eventually Dylan managed it and tested the milk against his wrist. It wasn't as warm as yesterday, but hopefully it would be warm enough to keep the baby happy.

He sat in the dark while the baby guzzled his milk.

'Better now?' he asked softly. Not that he was going to get an answer.

Then he remembered about the burping thing. The last thing he wanted was for the baby to wake again, crying because his tummy hurt. Dylan felt like a zombie as it was. He held Tyler on his shoulder and rubbed the baby's back, then nearly dropped the baby when he heard a loud burp and felt an immediate gush of liquid over his bare shoulder. What? Why hadn't Emmy warned him about this? It hadn't happened last time. Had he done something wrong?

The baby began to cry again. Oh, hell—the burped-up milk had probably soaked his clothes, too, and he'd be cold. He needed a change of clothes; Dylan couldn't possibly put him back into his cot in this state.

Luckily the overhead light in the nursery was on a dimmer switch. Dylan kept it as low as possible, and hunted for clean clothes. Tyler seemed to have grown four extra arms and six extra legs, all of which were invisible, but eventually Dylan managed to get him out of the Babygro.

The nappy felt heavy; clearly that needed changing, too, before Dylan put clean clothes on the baby. But when he settled Tyler on the changing unit and opened the nappy, the baby promptly peed over him. Dylan jumped back in shock, then dashed forward in horror. This was his first night in charge and he was making a total mess of it. The baby could've rolled over and fallen off the changing station and been badly hurt.

His heart was hammering. Please, no. He'd already lost Pete and Ally; he couldn't bear the idea of anything happening to Tyler. Even though the baby had disrupted his life, even though it panicked him that he didn't know what he was doing, he was beginning to feel other emotions than just resentment towards Tyler.

He tried to make light of it, even though he was in a cold sweat. 'Help me out here, Ty,' he muttered. 'I'm new at all this.'

But finally the baby had a clean nappy and clean clothes. Dylan put him in the cot and made sure the covers were tucked in properly; within seconds Tyler had fallen back to sleep in his usual position with his arms up over his head, looking like a little frog.

Dylan went back to his room feeling almost hung-over. It was way too late to have a shower; the noise from the water tank would wake Emmy. So he simply sponged off the worst of the milk at the sink in his en-suite, and fell into bed. How did parents of newborns cope with even less sleep than this? he wondered as he sank back into sleep. How had Pete not been a total zombie?

The next morning, his alarm shrilled at the usual time. Normally Dylan woke before his alarm, whereas today he felt groggy from lack of sleep. He staggered out of bed and showered; he didn't feel much better afterwards, though at least he didn't smell of burped-up milk anymore.

He went to the nursery to look in on Tyler. The baby was asleep in his cot, looking angelic. 'It's all right for some,' Dylan said wryly. 'I could do with a nap. So have an extra one for me.'

He dragged himself downstairs. Was it his imagination, or could he smell coffee?

Emmy was in the kitchen, sitting at the table with a mug of coffee. She raised an eyebrow when she saw him. 'Rough night?' she asked.

'Apart from Ty throwing up half the milk over me and then peeing over me...'

She burst out laughing and he glared at her. 'It's not funny.'

'Yes, it is.'

'You could've *warned* me he'd do that.'

She spread her hands. 'To be fair, he hasn't actually done that to me. But Ally told me he once did it to Pete.'

'Just don't tell me it's a male bonding thing,' he grumbled.

'And I thought you were supposed to be a morning person.' She laughed, and poured him a mug of coffee. 'Here. This might help.'

'Thanks. I think.' He took a sip. 'I was useless last night. I nearly let him fall off the changing station.'

She flapped a dismissive hand. 'I'm sure you didn't.'

'I jumped back from him when he peed on me.'

'Which is a natural reaction, and you would've been there to stop him if he'd started to roll.'

It still made him go cold, how close it had been. '*Can* he roll over?'

'Yes.' She rolled her eyes. 'Stop panicking, Dylan. You know what to expect now. You won't let him fall.'

How could she have so much confidence in him, when he had absolutely none in himself? And what had happened to her, anyway? The Emmy Jacobs he knew would've sniped about him not being good enough. This Emmy was surprisingly supportive. Which made him feel even more adrift. He was used to being in charge and knowing exactly what he was doing. Right now, he was winging it, and he hated feeling so useless.

He covered up his feelings by saying, 'I could do with some toast. Do we have bread?'

'Not much. But it's my turn for the supermarket run today, so I'll get some.'

'Right.'

'Any food allergies, or anything you hate eating?'

'No to the first, offal to the second.'

She smiled. 'That makes two of us. I'll pick up dinner while I'm out.'

He thought about it. Really, this was much like sharing a student house. Except it wasn't with his friends, it was with a near stranger. And he had the added responsibility of a baby. 'We need to sort out a kitty.'

'Sure. We can do that later.'

'And we need a rota for doing the shopping. Or maybe we could get the shopping delivered.' He frowned. 'Do you have a car?'

'Yes. And I know how to fit Ty's baby seat in it.' She paused. 'What about you?'

'Yes to having a car. I don't have a clue about a baby seat.'

'We only have one baby seat between us. I think we're going to need one for your car as well as mine.'

He frowned. 'So I need to take another afternoon off?'

She shrugged. 'Or we could go at the weekend.'

Her weekend on, his weekend off—and he was going to have to spend it doing baby stuff instead of catching up with work. Great. Yet more disruption. And then the guilt surged through him again. It wasn't Tyler's fault that he needed to be looked after—or that Dylan had agreed to do it. 'OK. We'll go at the weekend,' he said.

Saturday morning saw them in the nursery department of a department store in the city.

'Your baby's gorgeous,' the assistant said, cooing over Tyler.

Dylan was about to correct her when Emmy said, 'Yes, we think so.' She shot him a look, daring him to contradict her.

He thought about it. Strictly speaking, Tyler *was* their baby. Just not a baby they'd actually made together.

Then he wished he hadn't thought about making babies with Emmy. How soft her skin would be against his. How she smelled of some spicy, floral scent he couldn't quite place. How it made him want to touch her, taste her...

Oh, hell. He really couldn't have the hots for *Emmy*. He hadn't even looked at another woman since he'd split up with Nadine. Abstinence: that had to be what was wrong with him. That, or the fact that he'd done the night shift, the previous night, and Tyler had woken three times, so lack of sleep had fried his brain.

He shut up and let Emmy do the talking.

And then Emmy spied a cot toy, something that apparently beamed pictures of stars and a moon on the ceiling and played a soft tinkling lullaby.

'Can we get this as well? I think he'd love it.'

'You mean, *you* love it.' Emmy seemed to like simple, childlike things. And Dylan hadn't quite worked out yet whether he found that more endearing or annoying. He certainly didn't loathe her as much as he once had. She was good with the baby, too.

Her eyes crinkled at the corners. 'OK, then, let's ask him.' She picked up the cot toy, crouched down beside the pram, switched it on and let Tyler see the lights and hear the lullaby.

Tyler's eyes went wide, then he laughed and held his hands out towards it.

Emmy looked up at him and smiled. 'I think that's a yes.'

Again a surge of attraction hit him. Was he crazy? This was Emmy Jacobs, who sparred with him and sniped at him and was his co-guardian. She was the last person he wanted to get involved with. But at the same time he had to acknowledge that there was something about her that really got under his skin. Something that made him want to know more about her. Get closer.

And that in itself was weird. He didn't do close. Never had. He didn't trust anyone to let them near enough—even, if he was honest with himself, Nadine.

The rest of the weekend turned out to be Dylan's first weekend of being a dad. Although it was officially Emmy's weekend on duty, he somehow ended up going to the park with her to take Tyler out for some fresh air. He noticed that she talked to Tyler all the time, even though there was no way a baby could possibly understand everything she said. She pointed out flowers and named the colours for him; she pointed out dogs and birds and squirrels.

She was clearly taking her duties as godmother and guardian really seriously, and Dylan was beginning to wonder just why he'd ever disliked her so much. Then again, this new Emmy didn't have a smart-aleck mouth. She didn't snipe, and she wasn't cynical and hard-bitten like the Emmy Jacobs he was used to.

Which one was the real Emmy? he wondered. Was she letting her guard down and letting him see the real her? Or was this just some kind of mirage and Spiky Emmy would return to drive him crazy?

They stopped at the café in the park, and Emmy asked for a jug of hot water to heat Tyler's milk. While she found them a table, he bought the coffees. He'd seen her looking longingly at the cinnamon pastries, so he bought her one of those as well.

'That's really kind of you,' she said when he brought the tray over to their table.

But her eyes were full of anguish. What was going on here? 'What's wrong?' he asked.

She sighed. 'I struggle with my weight. And no, that isn't your cue to tell me that I'm fine as I am. My job's pretty sedentary, so I only manage to keep my weight under control because I go to an exercise class three times a week. But things have changed, now, and I'm not going to have time for classes anymore. I haven't been since the week before Ally and Pete went to Venice.'

'You miss your classes?'

She shrugged. 'I'll manage.'

'That's not what I asked. You miss them?'

'Yes,' she admitted. 'It's ridiculously soon. But yes, I miss them. I spend too much time sitting at my desk—I really lose track of time when I'm working—and the classes used to help me get the knots out and stretch my muscles.'

'When are they?'

'Mornings. Straight after the school run.' She shrugged. 'So when Ty's at school, in four years' time or so, I can go back to them.'

'Maybe,' he said, 'we can change our rota. I'll go in to the office a bit later, on the mornings when you have a class—though obviously that means I'll be back later on those days to make up the time.'

'You'd do that for me?' She looked startled, almost shocked; and then she gave him a heart-stopping smile. It was his turn to be shocked then, by how much her smile affected him. How it made him feel as if the room had just lit up. 'Thank you, Dylan. What about you—do you do anything you've had to give up and miss already?'

'The gym,' he admitted. 'It's my thinking time. And I kind of like the endorphin hit at the end.'

'Let me know when your sessions are, and we'll switch the rota round.' She looked at the pastry, then at him, and gave him another smile. 'Thank you, Dylan. That's so nice.'

'Pleasure,' he responded automatically. And he stifled the thought that actually, it was a pleasure, seeing her made happy by such a little thing.

He'd surprised himself, offering to change the rota so she could do her weekly classes. And she'd surprised him by immediately offering to do the same for him. Why had he ever thought her selfish, when she so obviously believed in fairness? Had he just read her wrong in the past, and it had snowballed to the point where it was easier to dislike her than to wonder if he'd got it wrong? Not wanting to think about his burgeoning feelings, he said, 'I've been talking to Pete's parents about the funeral. They'd like it to be in the same church where Pete and Ally got married.'

She nodded. 'Ally's parents said the same.'

'Good. It makes it easier that they agree.' He paused. 'But Pete's parents also said they want the wake at the house rather than in a hall somewhere.'

'So we'll have to cater it, you mean?'

He nodded.

She blew out a breath. 'Then I vote we get the local deli to do as much of it as possible, so all we have to do is lay stuff out on serving platters on the dining room table. And I'll rope my mum in to help. Between us we can manage the drinks.'

There was no point in asking his mother to help. Dylan

couldn't remember whether she was in India or Bali, but he knew she was on retreat somewhere, and he also knew from experience that she wouldn't allow anything to interrupt that. Even if her only child really needed her help. He'd learned that one at a pretty early age. 'Right,' he said shortly.

She narrowed her eyes. 'Is everything OK, Dylan?'

'Yes.' He raked a hand through his hair. 'Just this whole thing...I still can't quite get my head around it. I still keep thinking Pete's going to walk through the door and ask us if we missed him.'

'Me, too,' she said. 'Ally's the first person really close to me I've lost. I guess it's a normal reaction, but I wonder when I'm going to stop missing her.'

'You don't stop missing her. You just get better at dealing with it.'

She said nothing, just looked at him. Those wide grey eyes were full of empathy rather than pity, so he found himself unexpectedly telling her the rest. 'My grandmother. She died last year. It's little things that catch you—a bit of music that reminds me of her, or walking past someone who's wearing the same perfume. Or seeing something in the shop that I know she'd love, and suddenly remembering that she's not going to be here for her birthday or Christmas so there's no point in buying it.'

She reached over and squeezed his hand. Just long enough to let him know that she understood and sympathised, but not long enough to be cloying. Weird. He hadn't expected to actually start *liking* Emmy.

He gave her the smallest, smallest smile. 'I'll talk to the vicar and sort that side of it out. The funeral directors just want a decision on the casket. Can I ask you to sort the food and drink?'

'Sure. Does anything else need doing?'

'I'm doing a eulogy for Pete. Do you want to do one for Ally?'

She shook her head. 'I don't think I could stand up there and do it. I would...' She paused, clearly swallowing back a sob. 'Well, I don't want to let her down by crying through it. She deserves more than that.'

He'd done enough presentations in his time to be able to get through it. 'I'll do it for you, if you like. Just tell me what you want to say and I'll read it out.'

She swallowed hard. 'Thank you.'

'No problem.'

'I could do a wall, though,' she said. 'I could scan in some of the photographs from when they were small, as well as the digital ones I've got from more recent years. We could talk to their parents and get their favourite memories as well.'

'That's a good idea. I'll talk to Pete's again while you talk to Ally's?'

'That works for me.'

'I think they'd like to stay at the house, that night,' Dylan said. 'I was thinking, it wouldn't be fair for either couple to stay in Pete and Ally's room.'

'You're right,' she agreed. 'It's my night on call, so I can use a sleeping bag in Tyler's room.'

'And I'll take the sofa,' he said.

Funny how their minds were in tune on this one.

Would they be in tune in other ways, too? The thought crept insidiously into his head and lodged there, and even though he tried to block it out he couldn't help being aware of just how attractive Emmy actually was.

She leaned down to touch the sleeping baby's cheek. 'You'll definitely know your mum and dad, Ty. Dylan and I, we have photographs and memories, all sorts of things we can share with you when you're older. Your mum did a "This Is Your Life" book for me when I was thirty, and I can do something like that for you of her.'

'I'll chip in with stuff about your dad,' he said, touching Tyler's other cheek.

They shared a glance and Dylan wondered—did it have to take the death of our best friends for us to get along? It was odd how easily they'd fallen into teamwork—since they'd moved into the house, he hadn't sniped once and neither had she—and he was shocked to realise that he actually liked her. A lot. Emmy was funny, clever, good company. How had he never noticed that before?

Emmy just about managed to get through the funeral, though she couldn't help bawling her eyes out during 'Abide With Me'. The bit about where was Death's sting always got to her. 'Amazing Grace' put a lump in her throat as well, and when the church echoed to Eva Cassidy singing 'Somewhere Over the Rainbow' there wasn't a dry eye anywhere.

Though she was glad that everyone was wearing bright colours rather than black, to celebrate Ally and Pete's life and the precious memories. It was important to share the good stuff as well as mourn them. To give them a decent send-off.

Tyler was an angel.

And Dylan was amazing.

He was sitting in the front row, next to her; when he stood up to do the eulogies from the pulpit, she couldn't take her eyes off him. Even though the tears were spilling down her cheeks as he spoke the words she'd written about her best friend.

She hugged him when he returned to his seat. 'You did a fantastic job,' she whispered. 'Just perfect.'

* * *

Dylan returned the hug, even though bits of him worried that he quite liked the feel of Emmy in his arms. He dismissed it simply as grief coming out. He *wasn't* attracted to Emmy Jacobs.

Ha—who was he trying to kid? Of course he was.

But he couldn't act on that attraction, for Tyler's sake. Getting involved with Emmy would make everything way too complicated. It would be better to keep his distance, the way he always did.

Friends neither he nor Emmy had seen since university days had come to the funeral. Back at the house, everyone was talking about the room divider Emmy had made with the photographs, sharing memories and the house echoed with as much laughter as tears.

The food was working out, too. Emmy was bustling around, sorting out the drinks and topping up the empty plates. Her mum had helped out and done way, way more than his own mother would've done if she'd been there. Between the three of them, they'd managed to handle this.

Finally everyone went and the clearing up started.

'You look really tired,' Emmy said gently to Ally's and Pete's parents. 'Why don't you go and lie down for a bit? Dylan and I can sort all this out.'

'We can't leave you to do all this, love,' Ally's dad said.

'Yes, you can. It's been a really tough day for us all, and I can't even begin to imagine how hard it's been for you. You need some rest. I'll bring you up a cup of tea in a minute.'

'Thank you, love,' Pete's mum said.

Again, Dylan found himself marvelling. Pete and Ally's parents clearly knew Emmy well and liked her. He was beginning to think that he was the one who was totally out of step. She'd been brilliant today. He made a mental note to cut her more slack in future.

Emmy's mum stayed to help, then kissed Emmy good-bye and, to Dylan's surprise, gave him a hug. 'Take care of yourself and call me if you need me, OK? That goes for both of you. Any time.'

He found himself envying Emmy's closeness to her mum. If only his own mother had been like that, maybe things would've been different. Maybe he would've known how to really love someone and not made such a mess of his marriage. Though he appreciated the way Emmy's mother had included him. How would Emmy have got on with his family? He had a feeling that Emmy would've liked his gran, and his gran would've liked Emmy.

And this was dangerous territory. He couldn't let himself think about this.

Emmy put Tyler to bed while he finished moving all the furniture back. Then she took a tray up to Pete and Ally's parents with tea and sandwiches.

When she came back down, Dylan noticed that she looked upset.

'Are you OK?' he asked.

She nodded. 'They're not coming down again today. I think it's exhausted all of them.' She bit her lip. 'It's so wrong, having to bury your child. It isn't the natural order of things. I really feel for them. Today they all seemed to age ten years in a matter of seconds. Did you see Ally's dad walking into church? He had to hold on to the side of the pew until he composed himself. It's not that long ago he was walking down that aisle with Ally on his arm in that gorgeous fishtail dress, and you and Pete were waiting at the altar.'

'Yeah, I remember,' Dylan said softly. 'And you're right. Burying a parent must be hard, but it's more the natural order. Burying your child must be the worst feeling in the world.'

'And there's nothing we can do to make it better.' Her voice cracked and she looked anguished.

'I know, but I think we did Pete and Ally proud,' he said. 'Everyone was here celebrating them.'

She nodded. 'You're right. I think it's what they would've wanted.'

He wandered over to look at the photos on the divider, and saw the one of Emmy and Ally together as students.

'Your hair looks absolutely terrible. Whatever made you dye it blue?'

She came to join him and shrugged. 'I was a design student. We all did that sort of thing back then.'

'It looks nice now. Obviously it's not your natural colour but it suits you. It brings out your eyes.' He reached out to brush a lock of hair from her face.

'Careful, Dylan. Anyone might think we were on the way to being friends, with you paying me compliments like that.'

He raised an eyebrow. 'Maybe we are.'

She dragged in a breath. 'I wish it hadn't taken Ally and Pete to die before we started to see—well, what *they* saw in us.'

'Me, too.' He gave her a crooked smile. 'We can't change the past. But, for what it's worth, I'm sorry I misjudged you. You're not the needy, flaky mess I thought you were.'

Her eyes filled with tears. 'I'm sorry I misjudged you, too. You're still a bit judgemental, and you open your mouth before you think about what's going to come out of it. You might have the social skills of a rhino, but you do have a heart.'

Did he? Sometimes he wasn't so sure. He'd built so many walls around it that it was lost.

She rubbed her eyes with the back of her hand. 'Now I'm being wet. Ignore me.'

'It's OK. I'm not that far off crying, myself,' he admitted. He looked at her. 'Do you want a glass of wine?

She nodded.

'Me, too. Come on.'

He poured them each a glass of wine and then put some soft piano music on before curling up on the opposite end of the sofa to her. Her toes touched his ankle, but it didn't make him want to pull away. Weirdly, he felt more comfortable with her now, on one of the saddest days of his life, than he ever had before.

'I like this. What is it?' she asked.

'Einaudi. You work to classical music, don't you?'

'Vivaldi—not "the Four Seasons", because that's been overplayed to the point where I find it almost impossible to listen to it, but I like his cello concerti. They're calming and regular, good to work to.'

'I was looking at your website,' he said. 'You're very talented.'

She looked surprised, but inclined her head in acknowledgement of the compliment. 'Thank you.'

'But you could really do with a proper stock management program. I've written one and tested it for you. Let me know your admin password, and I'll install it for you.'

Her eyes widened. 'You've written me a program?'

'It's only a simple one.' He flapped a dismissive hand. 'It's pretty intuitive, so it won't take you five minutes to get to grips with it.'

'You've actually written me a program.' Tears glittered in her eyes.

He shrugged, feeling awkward. 'It's no big deal, Emmy. It wasn't that time-consuming.'

'But you still made the time to do it. Which is amazing, especially as we've both got all these new responsibilities and we're adjusting to all the changes in our lives.' She dragged in a breath. 'Thank you, Dylan.'

'It was entirely selfish of me,' he said. 'If it makes your life easier, then our rota will run more smoothly.'

She gave him a look that told him she didn't believe a word of it. That she knew he'd done it partly because he'd wanted to do something nice for her, even though there was no way he'd ever admit that out loud. 'Even so. Thank you.' She bit her lip. 'I just wish it hadn't taken—well, *this*, to get us in any kind of accord.'

'Me, too. But we've cracked the first week and a half. We're both there for Tyler. We'll make this work,' he said. And he meant every single word.

CHAPTER SIX

OVER THE NEXT few weeks, Emmy and Dylan settled in to their new routine. They shared Tyler's care during the week; Emmy had found a Pilates class nearby, which was scheduled at a similar time to her old class, and Dylan had found a gym nearby, too. And Emmy was surprised at how quickly she'd got used to the routine of working and family life.

'You know, Ty, I never thought it would end up being like this,' she said, jiggling the baby on her lap. 'I thought he'd be a nightmare to share a house with. Fussy and demanding and annoying. But he's actually OK, when you get to know him. He still has the social skills of a rhino, but I think that's because nobody taught him, not because he's too arrogant to care.'

Tyler cooed at her.

She laughed. 'He's better with you, too. I've heard him reading to you. Funny, he said he never wanted to be a dad, but he's managing just fine with you.' Her smile faded. 'I can't quite work him out. Why was he so adamant that he didn't want kids? And why did his marriage break up?'

She jiggled Tyler still further. 'Before we became your guardians, I would've said that Dylan was the problem. Nobody could put up with someone who's that formal and stuffy.' She frowned. 'Except that's not what he's really like. Now we've managed to reach a truce, I think I actually like him. He's got a dry sense of humour, and that smile...'

No. She wasn't going to allow herself to think about his smile and how it made her feel. She needed to keep her head where Dylan Harper was concerned, and keep this strictly—well, not business, exactly, but co-guardianship meant being professional and letting her head rule her heart. Total common sense.

She couldn't ask Dylan why he didn't want kids or why his marriage had fallen apart, because she knew it would annoy him. Dylan didn't like emotional stuff. Even if she did manage to push past that particular boundary, he was intensely private and she knew he'd give little away.

'I guess I'm going to have to learn not to ask,' she said, and Tyler gave her a solemn look as if he agreed.

The baby had started sleeping through the night again; clearly he was beginning to settle after the huge upheaval in his life. But when he began to wake two or three times in the night again, Emmy was at her wits' end.

'Lavender oil?' Dylan asked when she suggested it as a solution.

'A couple of drops on a hankie in his room. Apparently it's relaxing.'

'That's so flaky,' Dylan said. 'There's no scientific proof that it works.'

'I don't care. It's worth a try.' When he continued to look sceptical, she said, 'We have to do *something*, Dylan. I mean, I know we're taking alternate nights to go in to him—but when he wakes up, he's yelling loudly enough to wake whoever's not on duty.'

'I guess so.'

'I don't know about you, but I feel like a zombie.' She couldn't help yawning.

'Me, too,' he admitted. 'OK. Try the lavender oil.'

But it didn't work.

The next day, Emmy made an appointment with the health visitor. 'We might have a solution,' she told Dylan when he came home. 'Ally's health visitor says either he's starting to cut teeth, or he's ready to start solid food.'

'So what do we do now? Buy jars of stuff?' Dylan asked.

Emmy shook her head. 'We start with baby rice and mix it with his milk—so then the taste is quite near what he's used to.' She produced a packet of organic baby rice she'd bought at the supermarket on the way home from seeing the health visitor. 'So let's do this.'

Dylan read out the instructions from the back of the packet, and Emmy followed them.

'It doesn't look much,' Dylan said doubtfully. 'Are you sure you measured out the right amount?'

'I did what you read out,' she said, and sat down with Tyler. She put a tiny amount of the rice on the end of the spoon. 'Come on, sweetie, just one little mouthful,' she coaxed, and put the spoon into Tyler's open mouth.

The result was baby rice spattered all over her.

Dylan smothered a laugh. 'Sorry. But...'

'I look ridiculous. I know.'

'Let me see if I can persuade him to try it,' Dylan suggested.

But he got nowhere, either.

He looked at Emmy. 'So, Ally didn't do any of this with him?'

Emmy thought about it. 'She did talk about weaning him. She said she was planning to start—' she gulped '—when she got back from Venice.'

But that moment was never to happen.

Dylan patted her shoulder briefly in sympathy, then

grabbed a paper towel, wetted it under the tap, and wiped the spattered baby rice from her face.

She gave him a wry smile. 'I'm glad you used water on that paper towel before you wiped my face.'

'A dry towel wouldn't have got it off.'

'That's not what I meant.'

He frowned. 'I'm not with you.'

'I mean, I'm glad that you used water and not spit.'

She saw the second the penny dropped. 'That's really *gross*!' But he laughed.

'It's what my mum used to do,' she said with a grin. 'Didn't yours?'

'No.' His tone was short and his smile faded.

What was Dylan's issue with his mum? Emmy wondered. Was he not close to her? Was that why he kept people at a distance?

He switched the subject by tasting the rice. 'I think I know why he's spitting it out.'

'Why?'

'Try it.'

She did. 'It's tasteless. Bland.' She grimaced. 'But I guess it's about getting him used to texture rather than taste.'

'So we'll have to keep going.'

They muddled through the next few days, and finally Emmy cheered. 'Yay! He's actually eating it.'

She put up a hand to high-five Dylan. He paused—but then he surprised her by high-fiving her. 'Result.'

'*The Baby Bible* says we should introduce one new food at a time, leaving three or four days in between, so we can spot any food allergies,' Emmy said later that evening. 'They say it's good to start with carrots—so I'll steam some and purée them for him tomorrow night.'

The carrots went down as badly as the baby rice had the previous week.

'It's a new taste. It took a couple of days with the baby rice, so we'll have to just persevere,' Dylan said. He scooped Tyler out of his high chair. 'And I will clean up this little one while you, um…' His eyes crinkled at the corners. 'While you de-carrot yourself.'

'I am *so* wearing an apron, next time I try and get him to eat solids,' Emmy said. 'Thanks. I need to change.'

But when she came out of the bedroom, she saw Dylan coming out of the bathroom wearing just his jeans and no shirt, with the baby cradled in his arms.

'Did you get splashed?' she asked.

'Just a bit.' He grinned at her.

Oh, help. Her mouth had gone dry. She knew he went to the gym regularly, but she'd had no idea how perfect his musculature was. That he had a six-pack and well-shaped arms.

And she really hadn't expected to feel this surge of attraction to a man who'd always been prickly and standoffish with her, and sometimes downright rude.

Then again, she had a rubbish choice in men. She'd picked loser after loser who'd let her down and made her feel like the most unattractive woman in the universe. OK, Dylan wasn't a loser, and he wasn't the stuffy killjoy she'd also thought him; but he was the last person she could get into a relationship with. Her relationships never lasted, and Tyler would be the one who paid the price when it all went wrong. She couldn't do that to the baby, especially as he'd already lost so much. So instead she made a light, anodyne comment, let Dylan put Tyler to bed, and fled to the safety of her workbench. Working on an intricate piece would take all of her mental energy, and she wouldn't have enough space left to think about Dylan. To dream about something that just couldn't happen.

The next night, Tyler woke an hour after she put him to bed, and started crying.

She groaned. 'I'm rubbish at this parenting business. He's never going to sleep again.'

Dylan followed her up to his room. 'The book said babies cry because they need a nappy change, they're hungry, they're tired, they're bored, or they want a cuddle.'

'I've fed him, and he's had more solids today, so I don't think he's hungry. He's clean and dry, so it's not that. I don't think he's bored. But this isn't the same cry as when he's tired or wants a cuddle.' She bit her lip. 'I think I might need to call Mum.'

'Wait a second. Do you think he's teething?' Dylan asked. 'Didn't the health visitor say something about that?'

Emmy frowned. 'His face is red, so he might be. Give him a cuddle for a second, will you, while I wash my hands? Then I can check his mouth.'

Dylan held the baby until she came back with clean hands. She put her finger into Tyler's mouth and rubbed it gently over his gums. 'I can't feel anything—but, ow, his jaws are strong.'

Tyler was still crying.

'What are we going to do, Dylan?'

He grimaced. 'I was reading something the other day about you have to let them lie there and cry so they get used to falling asleep on their own.'

She shook her head. 'I hate that idea. He's upset about something or he wouldn't be crying.'

'Let me try something.' Dylan rocked the baby and seemed to be talking to him, but his voice was so soft that Emmy couldn't quite catch what Dylan was saying. But the amazing thing was that the baby actually settled and went back to sleep.

Dylan put him down gently in the cot, and Tyler started crying again.

'What did you do before?' Emmy asked.

He flushed. 'I sang to him.'

Emmy was surprised; she hadn't thought Dylan was the type to sing. 'Do it again—but don't pick him up, because maybe it was putting him back down that woke him.'

Dylan shrugged, and sang 'Summertime' in a rich baritone.

And she was mesmerised. OK, so she'd heard him sing in church at the funeral, but she'd been preoccupied then. She'd had no idea he could sing like this. Like melted chocolate, rich and smooth and incredibly...

She stopped herself. Not sexy. It would be a bad move to think of that word in conjunction with Dylan Harper.

The baby yawned, and finally his hands flopped down and his eyes closed.

Dylan stopped singing and leaned over the edge of the cot. 'How can they sleep like that? He looks a bit like a frog—and I'm sure that can't be comfortable.'

'It's probably a lot more comfortable than it looks, or he'd lie in a different position,' she pointed out. 'I think he looks cute.' She shared a glance with Dylan. 'You have a good voice, Dylan.'

He raised an eyebrow. 'Was that grudging or surprised?'

'Surprised,' she admitted. 'I didn't think you'd—well, be a singer. Or know a song like that.'

'My grandmother used to sing it to me when I was little.'

She smiled. 'It's a beautiful song.'

'Yes.' And it was weird how much that compliment from her had warmed him. Nobody had ever commented on his singing before. Then again, he'd never really sung in front of anyone, except in church at a wedding or christening. His throat tightened: *or at a funeral*. 'We'd better leave him to sleep,' he said gruffly, and left the room abruptly before he did anything stupid, like asking Emmy to spend time with him. They were co-guardians, and that was all.

A couple of days later, Dylan came home early to find Emmy in tears. His stomach clenched. What was wrong?

'Is something wrong with Tyler?' he asked.

She shook her head. 'I would've called you if there was a problem.'

'What's the matter?'

'I just—' she gulped '—I just miss Ally. Tyler…She's missing out on all his firsts. He's getting his first tooth—you can actually see a little bit of white on the edge of his gums now.'

'That must be why he was crying the other night.'

She nodded. 'And he said "dada" today.' She dragged in a breath. 'Ally would've called me to talk about all this. And I'm the one seeing it, when it should be her, and I can't even talk to her about it. This is all so *wrong*.'

Tears would normally send Dylan running a mile. He'd hated it when Nadine cried. He'd always found an excuse to back away. But he couldn't just walk away and leave Emmy distressed like this.

'I miss them, too,' he said, and wrapped his arms round her.

Big mistake.

She was warm and soft in his arms. Her hair smelled of spring flowers, and felt like silk against his cheek, smooth and soft and shiny.

Emmy froze. This was bad. Dylan was holding her. And she was holding him right back.

Comfort. This was all this was, she told herself.

But then she pulled back and looked up at him.

His eyes were a dark, stormy blue.

And his mouth—since when had Dylan had such a lush mouth? She wasn't sure whether she wanted to stroke it first, or kiss it, or what. Just that she wanted him.

She glanced back up to his eyes and realised he was staring at her mouth, too.

No. *No.* This was a seriously bad idea.

But her mouth was already parting, her head tipping back slightly in offering.

His mouth was parting, too.

And slowly—oh, so slowly—he lowered his head to hers. His mouth skimmed against hers, the touch as light as a butterfly's wing. It wasn't enough. It wasn't anywhere near enough. She wanted more. Needed more.

Even though her common sense was screaming at her to stop, her libido was doing the equivalent of sticking fingers in ears and saying, 'La, la, la, I can't hear you.' And she found herself reaching up on tiptoe to kiss him back, her lips brushing against his. It was like some kind of exquisite torture; close, yet not close enough.

His arms tightened round her, and then he was really kissing her. His mouth moved against hers, tentative and unsure at first, then more demanding. And she was kissing him all the way back, matching him touch for touch.

She'd never, ever felt like this before. Even the guy she'd once thought she'd end up marrying hadn't made her feel like this when he kissed her. What on earth was going on?

Dylan untucked her shirt from the waistband of her jeans and slid his fingers underneath the cotton, splaying his palms against her back. He moved his fingertips in tiny circles against her skin; his touch aroused her still more, near to fever pitch.

If he asked her, she knew she'd go to bed with him right now and to hell with the consequences. She wanted Dylan more than she'd ever wanted anyone in her entire life.

She made a tiny sound of longing, and he stopped.

He looked utterly shocked. His mouth was reddened and swollen, and she was pretty sure hers was in the same state.

This was bad. Really bad.

'Emmy, we—I—' He looked dazed.

'I know. We shouldn't have done this,' she said quickly, and pulled away from him. She needed to do some serious damage limitation, and fast. 'Let's pretend this didn't happen. I was upset and you were comforting me, and you're missing Ally and Pete as much as I am, and it just got a bit out of hand.'

His face was suddenly inscrutable. 'Yes, you're right. It didn't happen.'

'I—um—I'd better start making dinner. I'm running a bit late. Sorry, I know you hate it when things aren't on time.' Flustered, she rushed out to the kitchen before he could say anything else. She really didn't want to humiliate herself any further.

Dylan watched her go, not stopping her. Oh, help. He really shouldn't have kissed her like that. Now he knew what Emmy tasted like, it was going to haunt his dreams.

But he knew she was right. They couldn't do this. It would make things way too complicated because of Tyler.

They'd just have to be firmer with themselves in future. A lot firmer.

CHAPTER SEVEN

EMMY PUT THE phone down, beaming and hugging herself. She wanted to leap up and cheer and do a mad dance all through the house, but she knew she couldn't or else she'd wake the baby.

This was the best promotional opportunity she'd ever been offered. It could lead to a real expansion of her business; and it could be the making of her name.

Her smile faded as she thought about it. The deadline was tight. She was going to have to work crazy hours to get the pieces made on time. Which meant that she was going to have to ask Dylan to help her out.

And things had been awkward between them since—well, since she'd wept all over him and he'd held her and they'd ended up kissing. He'd kept out of her way as much as possible, and they only stayed in each other's company for as long as it took to update each other about Tyler or to eat dinner. And dinner meant no talking, because Dylan had retreated into reading journals at the table. It was horribly rude and she knew he knew it; but it was an excuse to avoid her, and there was nothing she could do about it.

They'd agreed early on that they'd work as a team and support each other when they needed it. But had their kiss cancelled out that agreement?

Maybe if she made something really special for dinner,

it would knock Dylan off balance and he'd talk to her. And then she could ask him.

She browsed through Ally's cookery books and found a fabulous recipe for monkfish wrapped in parma ham. It seemed pretty simple to cook but it looked really swish. That would have to do the trick, surely? She made a list of what she needed and took Tyler out in his pram to the parade of shops round the corner. After the fishmonger's, she went to the deli, the baker's and the greengrocer's.

She chatted to the baby on the way. 'This could be my big career break. Clap your hands and wish Aunty Emmy good luck, Ty.'

Tyler clapped his hands and giggled. She laughed back at him. 'You're just gorgeous—you know that?'

So was Dylan.

And she wasn't supposed to be thinking about that.

She played with the baby when they got home; both of them thoroughly enjoyed the bubble-blowing. Tyler was grabbing toys now and rattling them. It was amazing how a little one could take over your life like this. Emmy could see entirely why Ally hadn't wanted to go back to the job she'd once loved, not once Tyler was around.

Then her phone beeped. She checked it to find a text message from Dylan. *Sorry, emergency project meeting. Will be late home. Let me know if problem.*

Normally, Emmy would've been a bit cross at the late notice of a rota change; but today she was relieved, as it would mean that Dylan would come home feeling slightly in her debt and he might be more amenable to what she wanted to ask.

And then she felt horrible and manipulative. That really wasn't fair of her. It was an emergency meeting, after all, so he must be up to his eyes.

She fed Tyler some puréed apple—his food repertoire

was expanding beautifully now—then gave him a bath, not minding that he kept banging his toy duck into the foamy water and splashing her. She put him to bed, sang to him and put his light show on, then changed into dry clothes and headed downstairs to the kitchen.

There was another text from Dylan on her phone. *On way now. Sorry.*

Oh, help. He'd be here before dinner was ready, at this rate.

She prepared the monkfish hastily and put it in the oven, then finished laying the table in the dining room.

Dylan walked in holding a bouquet of bright pink gerberas and deep blue irises, the kind of flowers she loved and bought herself as an occasional treat. 'For you,' he said, and handed it to her.

She stared at him, surprised. Why on earth would Dylan buy her flowers? It wasn't her birthday, and they weren't in the kind of relationship where he'd buy her flowers. 'Thank you. They're, um, lovely.'

'But?'

Obviously it was written all over her face. She gave him a rueful smile. 'I was just wondering why you'd bought me flowers.'

'Because I'm feeling guilty about being late,' he said.

Even if he said no to helping her, at least this late meeting had thawed the ice between them. And she was grateful for that.

'I bought them from the supermarket on the way home from the office. Sorry I'm late,' he said again.

'It's not a problem. You gave me as much notice as you could. Come and sit down in the dining room; dinner's almost ready. You've obviously had a tough day.'

'You could say that.' He didn't elaborate, and Emmy wasn't sure enough of herself to push him.

She poured him a glass of wine, then served dinner.

He frowned. 'This is a bit posh. And we normally eat in the kitchen. Is it some sort of special occasion? Your birthday?'

'No-o,' she hedged. 'I just wanted to make a bit of an effort, that was all.'

Except the second she took her first mouthful she realised that something had gone wrong. Really, *really* wrong. Instead of the nice, tender fish she'd expected, it was rubbery and tough, and the potato cakes she'd made were a bit too crisp at the edges.

'Oh, no—I'm sure I followed the recipe to the letter. I must've had the oven up too high or something.'

But Dylan didn't look annoyed, just rueful. 'Well, it *looked* nice.'

'And it tastes vile.' She grimaced. 'I'm so sorry.'

'Don't worry. Tell you what—get rid of this, and I'll order us pizza.' He took his mobile phone out of his pocket and tapped in a number.

She took their plates to the kitchen and scraped the food into the bin. Right then, she wanted to burst into tears. She'd ruined dinner. How could she ask him a favour now?

'Hey, it could easily have happened when I was cooking. Don't worry about it,' he said, coming into the kitchen to join her.

She wasn't worried about the *food*.

When she didn't reply, he rested a hand on her shoulder. 'Emmy, what's wrong?'

She took a deep breath. 'I was going to ask you a favour. I can't now.'

'Why not?'

'Because, instead of giving you a decent dinner, I served you something disgusting.'

He waved a dismissive hand. 'It's not a problem,

Emmy—though maybe in future it might be an idea to stick to stuff you actually know how to cook?'

'I guess so,' she said ruefully.

'So what did you want to ask me?'

She squirmed. 'There isn't an easy way to ask.'

'Straight out will do.'

'I got a call from one of the big glossy magazines. They want to do a feature on up-and-coming British jewellery designers and they want to interview me.'

'That's good, isn't it?' he asked.

'Ye-es.'

'But?'

She sighed. 'But they want me to make some jewellery and their deadline's massively tight. My guess is that someone dropped out at the last minute and I was a second choice, and I think there are another two designers they've asked as well, so there's no guarantee I'll be included anyway.'

'But they still asked you, and that's the main thing. How tight is the deadline?'

This was the deal-breaker, she knew. 'They've asked me to create something totally new for them. So I need to spend the next four days working solidly to get the pieces made on time for their shoot.'

'So you need me to take over Tyler's care for the next four days?'

She nodded. 'But you had an emergency project meeting tonight, so you're clearly up to your eyes and it's not doable.'

'I can delegate.'

'I'll just have to pass and ask if they'd consider me in the future. If I tell them about Ty, maybe then they'll be understanding and won't think I'm too lazy and just making up feeble excuses.'

He placed a finger over her mouth, making her skin tingle. 'Emmy, were you listening? I said I'd do it. I'll delegate.'

Her eyes went huge. 'Really?'

'Really,' he said softly.

Then he dropped his hand, before he did anything stupid—like moving it to cup her cheek and dip his head to kiss her. That kiss was still causing him to wake up at stupid o'clock in the morning and wonder what would happen if he did it again. He needed to keep a lid on his attraction towards Emmy. Now.

'Thank you,' she said. 'I—well, I feel bad about asking. Four days is a lot.'

'This is your big break, Emmy. And we're a team. Of course I'll do it.'

'Thank you.'

He couldn't resist teasing her. 'I will be exacting repayment, of course.'

Then he wished he hadn't said it when she blushed. Because now all sorts of things were running through his head, and none of them were sensible. All of them involved Emmy naked in his bed. Which would be a very, very bad idea for both of them. Hadn't he spent the last week or so trying to get his feelings under control and forcing himself to think of her as just his co-guardian?

'I mean, I want four days off in lieu,' he said.

She dragged in a shaky breath, and he had the feeling that her thoughts had been travelling along very similar lines to his own. 'That's a deal,' she said.

The doorbell rang, and the pizza delivery boy saved him from saying anything else stupid—such as suggesting they sealed the deal with a kiss. He made sure they had the full width of the kitchen table between them when they sat down to eat. Maybe, just maybe, his common sense would come back and do its usual job once he'd eaten. He needed carbs.

Sharing a house with a woman he knew he shouldn't be attracted to was turning out to be much harder than he'd expected. Though he knew that at least work was a safe topic. 'Tell me about the magazine,' he invited.

'It's one of the biggest women's monthly magazines, glossy and aspirational stuff.' She smiled. 'It's not exactly the kind of thing you'd be likely to read.'

No, but he knew the kind of thing that Nadine had flicked through and he had a pretty good idea of what they required.

'And they're featuring your work?'

'*If* they like it. There aren't any guarantees,' she warned. 'As I said, there are a couple of other designers in the running.'

'They'll like your work,' he said. 'What do they want you to make?'

'A pendant, rings, earrings, and a bangle—they want an ultra-modern set and an ultra-girly, almost old-fashioned set.'

'Like that filigree stuff you do.'

She nodded. 'Exactly that.'

A pendant, rings, earrings and a bangle. And his imagination *would* have to supply a vision of Emmy wearing said jewellery, and nothing but said jewellery.

'Are you going to show them your jet animals as well?' he asked, pushing the recalcitrant thoughts away.

She wrinkled her nose. 'No, they're just a bit of fun.'

'But they're different, Emmy. People might forget your name if they want to buy your jewellery, but they'll definitely remember your jet animals, so they'll look them up on the Internet and find you.'

She thought about it. 'Fair point.'

'Go for it,' he said. 'Maybe that little turtle you made for Ty last week. And the dolphin.'

'I could do a seahorse,' she said, seeming to warm to the idea.

'That would definitely do it,' he said. 'A jet seahorse.'

'I owe you,' she said, finishing her pizza. 'Would you mind...?'

'Go. You're off housework, childcare and everything else,' he said. 'Go beat that deadline.'

She went off to work, and he made a phone call to delegate his work for the next four days so he could take over from her. It was a lot to ask, but he also knew that if he'd been the one to ask the favour her reaction would've been the same: total support. And he could give her some help to chase her dream.

Over the next four days, Emmy worked crazy hours to get the pieces done—a solid jet heart with silver filigree radiating out into a larger heart-shaped pendant, matching earrings, and delicate filigree cuffs containing the shape of a heart in solid jet. The other set included a modern pendant of a jet cone with a slice of amber running through it, matching earrings, a jet ring that entwined with an amber one, and a bangle that replicated the same effect, a thin band of amber entwined with a thin band of jet. And to finish the collection she carved the jet seahorse she'd discussed with Dylan.

Outside her work, she didn't have time to do anything other than have a quick shower in the morning, then fall into bed exhausted at night. Dylan brought her coffee and fruit and sandwiches to keep her going during the day, but didn't stay long enough to disturb her. He did insist on her taking a short break in the evening, though, to eat a proper dinner. She gave him a grateful smile. 'Thank you, Dylan. You've been a real star.'

'You'd do the same for me. How's it going?'

'I'm getting there.'

When she'd finished, she showed him the two collections.

'This is beautiful. I know a lot of women who'd love something like this.' He smiled at her. 'You're definitely going to get this.'

'There are no guarantees,' she reminded him.

Emmy delivered the jewellery to the magazine offices by hand, including the jet seahorse. She knew she was being paranoid, but she couldn't trust them to anyone else. She'd put too much of her heart and soul into the project now for things to go wrong.

Then it was a matter of waiting.

Were they going to choose her?

And how long would they keep her waiting before they delivered the verdict?

Every second seemed to drag—even though she knew she was being ridiculous and she probably wouldn't hear for at least a week. But by the time she got back to the house in Islington, she felt flat.

Dylan took one look at her. 'Right. We're going out.'

'Where?' she asked.

'You need some fresh air, and Ty and I are going with you to keep you company—isn't that right, sweetheart?' he added to the baby. 'I've got his bag organised. All I need to do is get a couple of bottles from the fridge, and we're good to go.'

She gave in. 'Thank you, Dylan.'

'I know you like the sea,' he said as he finished packing the baby's bag. 'And I think it's what you need to blow the cobwebs out.'

'But it's nearly five hours from here to Whitby,' she blurted out.

He laughed. 'I know. I'm not taking you there. I thought we could go to Sussex.'

In the end he drove them to Brighton, where they crunched over the pebbles next to the sea. Part of Emmy was wistful for the fine, soft sand of the east coast she was used to, but she was seriously grateful that Dylan had thought of it. 'You're right. The sea's just what I need. Thank you so much.'

'My pleasure.' He smiled at her, and her heart did a flip. Which was totally ridiculous.

They ate fish and chips on the pier. He fed little bits of fish to Tyler, who absolutely loved it and opened his mouth for more.

'I think we've just found the next food for his list,' Dylan said with a grin.

The woman sitting on the bench next to them looked over. 'Oh, your baby's just adorable.'

Emmy froze.

But Dylan simply smiled. 'Thank you. We think so, too.'

For a moment Emmy wondered what it would be like if this were real—if Dylan were her partner and Tyler were their baby. Then she reminded herself that they were co-guardians. They'd agreed that kiss was a mistake. She'd be stupid to want more than she could have.

'You're quiet,' Dylan remarked when they were wandering through the narrow streets of boutique shops, with Tyler fast asleep in his pushchair.

'I'm just a bit tired,' she prevaricated.

'And worrying about whether they're going to like your designs?'

She frowned. 'How did you know?'

'I'm the same whenever I bid for a project. I always

know I've done my best, but I always worry whether the client will like what I've suggested.'

'And I guess you have the added pressure, because you have people relying on you for work.'

He shrugged. 'There is that.'

She grimaced. 'Sorry, that was patronising and a stupid thing to say.'

'It's OK. You've done the equivalent of a week and a half's normal office hours over four days. I'm not surprised your brain is a bit fried. Come on. Let's get an ice cream.'

'Good idea. And it's my shout.'

Emmy fell asleep in the car on the way back. Dylan glanced at her.

Now he understood exactly what Nadine had meant. The idea of having a partner and a child to complete his life. He hadn't understood it at the time. After his own experiences of growing up, he'd sworn never to have a child of his own. Even to the point where he'd split up from the woman he'd loved rather than have a child with her.

And yet here he was in exactly that position: a stand-in father to Tyler. Something he hadn't wanted to do, but guilt and duty had pushed him into it. He wasn't sure what surprised him more, the fact that he was actually capable of looking after the baby and giving him the love he needed, or the fact that he was actually *enjoying* it. Part of him felt guilty about that, too. He hadn't given Nadine that chance. Maybe if she'd forced his hand, stopped taking the Pill without telling him and just confronted him with the news that he was going to be a dad, he would've got used to the idea. She'd played fair with him by giving him the chance to say no; and he'd been stubborn enough and selfish enough to say exactly that.

On paper, Nadine had been the perfect choice: focused, career-orientated, organised. Just as he was. Except it hadn't worked, because she'd changed. She'd wanted something he'd always believed he hadn't wanted.

On paper, Emmy was just about the worst choice he could make. OK, she was more organised and together than he'd thought she was, but they were still so different. How could it possibly work between them?

Besides, this was meant to be a three-month trial in co-guardianship. Any relationship between them could potentially wreak huge havoc on Tyler's life. She'd said herself that her relationships always failed, and he'd made a mess of his marriage. He just couldn't let himself think of Emmy in any other role than that of co-guardian. No matter how attractive he found her. No matter how much he wanted to kiss those soft, sweet lips until her eyes went all wide and dark with passion.

Not happening, he told himself. Stick to the limits you agreed.

CHAPTER EIGHT

THE FOLLOWING WEEK, Emmy had a phone call that left her shrieking and dancing round the house. She called her mother, and then Dylan.

'Sorry to ring you at work,' she said, 'but I couldn't wait to tell you—the magazine just rang. They loved my designs and they're going to run the feature with me in it. Apparently what swayed them was the seahorse—which was your suggestion, so it's all thanks to you.'

'No worries,' he said, sounding pleased for her. 'But it was just a suggestion. You're the one who did all the hard work.'

'I'm going to stand you a decent meal to say thank you.' She laughed. 'Don't worry, I'm not cooking it myself, so you're in no danger of getting rubbery monkfish again. Mum says she can babysit Ty on Friday or Saturday, whichever suits you best.'

'Emmy, you don't need to take me out.'

'Yes, I do. You more than earned it, taking over all my duties and giving me the time to work, so don't argue. We'll sort out the time when you get home tonight, and I'll book somewhere.' She paused. 'One last thing. They want to take a few shots of me here, at my workbench. Um, this afternoon. Do you have a problem with that?'

'No, it's fine. Do you need me back early to look after Tyler?'

'Hopefully the photographer will be here while Tyler's taking a nap. Or, if he wakes, it won't matter if he's in the shots. If that's OK with you, that is.'

'It's fine,' he said again. 'I'll see you later.'

The journalist arrived while Tyler was still awake, so Emmy made her a coffee and played with the baby while she answered questions, hoping that she didn't come across as too flaky or too distracted. And Tyler decided to forego his nap, so when the photographer arrived—two hours later than they'd arranged—he ended up being in the shots.

They were halfway through the photo shoot when Dylan arrived.

'Sorry—am I in the way?' he asked, coming in to Emmy's workroom.

'No—we're running late,' Emmy said.

Tyler held out his hands to Dylan, who smiled and scooped him into his arms, then kissed him roundly. 'Hello, trouble. Aren't you supposed to be having a nap right now?' he asked.

The baby gurgled and clapped his hands.

'Come on. Let's give Emmy some peace and quiet.' He glanced over at Emmy, the journalist and the photographer. 'I'm about to put the kettle on. Coffee?'

'Thanks, that'd be great,' Emmy said gratefully. 'Oh, sorry, I haven't introduced you. Dylan, this is Mike and Flo from the magazine. Flo, Mike, this is Dylan Harper.'

'Nice to meet you,' Dylan said. 'Milk or sugar?'

'Just milk for me,' Flo said.

'Black, two sugars,' Mike said.

'Back in a tick,' Dylan said, winked at Emmy, and whisked Tyler out of the workroom.

'Wow, he's gorgeous *and* domesticated. The perfect man,' Flo said wistfully.

Just what Emmy was starting to think, though wild horses wouldn't make her admit it, especially if there was a danger of Dylan overhearing her. 'He has his moments,' she said gruffly.

'You're just so lucky. This house, that cute baby, and that gorgeous man. And you're talented as well. If you weren't so nice, I'd have to hate you,' Flo said.

'Hang on—you've got the wrong end of the stick. Ty's not ours. Well, he *is* ours,' Emmy said, 'but we're not his parents.'

'Adopted? That's lovely.'

'We're his guardians. We were his parents' best friends.' Emmy explained the situation with Ally and Pete as succinctly as she could. 'Dylan and I just share a house and Ty's care.'

Flo raised an eyebrow. 'Just housemates—with the way you two look at each other? Methinks the lady doth protest too much.'

Oh, help. Emmy didn't dare ask Flo to expand on that. Obviously she thought Dylan looked at her as if he were in love with her—which Emmy knew wasn't the case. But she really hoped that she didn't look at him as if she were mooning over him. Because she wasn't. Was she? 'We're just...' Her voice faded.

'Good friends?' Flo asked.

No. They weren't. Though they were on the way to becoming friends. There was a real easiness between them nowadays. 'Something like that,' Emmy said carefully.

'Gotcha.' Flo tapped her nose. 'So what does he do?'

'He's—well, I guess you'd call him a computer super-guru,' Emmy said.

Flo scribbled something on her notepad. 'Clever as well as easy on the eye. Nice.'

'Mmm.' Emmy wriggled uncomfortably, and was relieved when the photographer asked her to pose for some more shots and Flo changed the subject back to her work. Something safe. Whereas Dylan Harper was starting to become dangerous.

On Saturday evening, her planned thank-you meal with Dylan felt more like a date. Which was crazy. Though of course she'd had to dress up a bit for it; she couldn't just go out in her usual black trousers and a zany top.

And it felt even more like a date when the taxi arrived and her mother kissed them both goodbye at the door. 'Don't worry, Tyler's in safe hands—just go out and enjoy yourselves. And don't hurry back.'

Emmy felt almost shy with him, and she didn't manage to make any small talk in the taxi. Neither did he, she noticed. Was it because he was a geek with no social skills, or was it because he felt the same kind of awkwardness that she did? The same kind of awareness?

'Nice choice,' Dylan said approvingly when they reached the small Italian restaurant she'd booked. 'And I'm buying champagne. No arguments from you.'

Even though that was pretty much negating the point of the evening, it also broke the ice, and Emmy grinned. 'When have you known me argue with you, Dylan?' she teased.

He laughed back. 'Not for a few weeks, I admit.'

'I really appreciate your support over the article.'

'You would've done the same for me,' he pointed out.

'Well, yes. But it's still appreciated. You put yourself out.'

The waiter ushered them to their table, and the awkwardness returned. Emmy didn't have a clue what to say to Dylan. This was ridiculously like a first date, where you knew hardly anything about each other. She'd lived with him for weeks now and knew a fair bit about what made him tick—what brightened his day, and what he needed before he could be human first thing in the morning—but at the same time he was still virtually a stranger. He hadn't opened up to her about anything emotional. She knew nothing about his childhood or why his marriage broke up or what he really wanted out of life. He kept himself closed off. They were partners of a sort, stand-in parents to their godchild; and yet at the same time they weren't partners at all.

The champagne arrived and Dylan lifted his glass in a toast. 'To you, and every success in that magazine.'

'Thank you.' She lifted her own glass. 'To you, and thanks for—well, being there for me.'

'Any time.'

Given that Dylan didn't have a clue how to be nice to people for the sake of it, she knew he meant it, and it made her feel warm inside.

'It was good of your mum to babysit. She's really nice,' Dylan said.

Was she imagining things, or did he sound wistful? 'Isn't yours?' she asked, before she could stop herself.

'She travels a lot.'

Which told her precisely nothing. She could see that Dylan was busy putting up metaphorical barbed-wire fences with 'keep out' notices stuck to them, so she stuck with the safer topic. 'You're right, my mum's really nice. I'm lucky because she's always been really supportive.' She sighed. 'I just wish I could find someone for her who deserves her.'

Dylan raised an eyebrow. 'Your mum's single?'

She nodded. 'I nag her into dating sometimes. So does her best friend, but she always turns down a second date with whoever it is, or agrees they'd be better off as just friends. I guess she's never found anyone she really trusts.'

He sat and waited, and eventually Emmy found herself telling him the rest of it. 'My father pretty much broke her heart. While they were married, he had a lot of affairs. Now I'm older, I can see that it chipped away at her confidence every time she found out he was seeing someone.' Just as her own disastrous relationships had chipped away at her confidence, one by one. Every man who'd wanted to change something about her—and it had been a different thing, each time, until in the end the only thing she knew she was good at was her work.

She bit her lip. 'The worst thing is, Mum always wanted more children after me but couldn't have them. He refused to consider adoption or fostering. And then his current woman found out she was pregnant, and he left us for her. Mum felt she'd failed.'

Dylan knew exactly how it felt when your marriage failed and you were pretty sure it was all your fault. First-hand. And it wasn't a good feeling. 'It wasn't your mum's fault,' he said. 'I might be talking out of line, here, but sounds to me as if your dad was incredibly selfish.' Just like his mother. He knew how *that* felt, too, realising that you were way down someone's list of priorities. The amount of times he'd come home from school and let himself into a cold, empty house, and there was a note propped on the kitchen table telling him to go to his grandparents' house because they'd be looking after him for a few days. Days that stretched into weeks.

'My dad was incredibly selfish. He probably still is.'

'Probably?' Dylan was surprised. 'Don't you see him?'

'He didn't stay in touch with us, and for years I thought it was my fault that my parents split up. It was only later, when I'd left university and Mum told me what really went on when I was young, that I realised he was the one with the problem.'

And now Dylan understood why she'd accused him of breaking up his marriage because of an affair. She'd been caught in the fallout from her father's affairs, and it clearly still hurt.

She blew out a breath. 'I think he decided not to see me because whenever he did see me it reminded him of my mum, and that made him start to feel guilty about the way he treated her.'

'So is that why you're single? Because you don't trust men?' And that would certainly explain Spiky Emmy. It was clearly a defence mechanism, and it had definitely worked with him. He'd taken her at face value.

She frowned. 'Not quite. I just have a habit of picking the wrong ones. Men who want to change me—everything from the way I dress, to what I do for a living. Nothing about me is right.'

At one point Dylan would've wanted Emmy to change— but now he knew her better and he understood what made her tick. And he knew that she wasn't the woman he'd thought she was. 'You're fine as you are. There's nothing wrong with what you do for a living. Or how you dress.'

'I wasn't fishing for compliments.' She shrugged. 'I'm tired of dating men who can't see me for who I am or accept me for that. I'm tired of dating men who are all sweetness and light for a couple of weeks, then start making little "helpful" suggestions. All of which mean me changing to fit their expectations, rather than them looking at their expectations and maybe changing them.' She sighed. 'It's not that I think I'm perfect. Of course I'm not. I'm like everyone else, with good points and bad. I just wanted a partner who understands who I am and is OK with that.'

'Maybe,' he said, 'you should've got Ally to vet your dates before you went out with them.'

'I wish I had.' She sighed. 'The last one…' She grimaced and shook her head. 'No, I really don't want to talk about him. But he was definitely my biggest mistake. And he was my last mistake, too. So if you're worrying that I'm going to be flighty and disappear off with the first man who bats his eyelashes at me, leaving you to look after Tyler on your own, then don't. Because I'm not. I've given up looking for Mr Right. I know he isn't out there. My focus now is being there for Tyler while he grows up.'

'So you're not looking for a husband or a family, or what have you?'

'No. But I have Tyler. That's enough for me.'

Before they'd become co-guardians, the Emmy Jacobs Dylan knew was flighty as well as spiky. He'd disliked her because she'd reminded him so much of his mother. Selfish, always apologising for being late but never seeming sincere.

Now, he was seeing a different side of her. The way she looked after Tyler and put the baby's needs first: she was definitely responsible. She was kind; without being intrusive, she'd worked out what he liked to eat and the fact that he loathed lentils, and changed her meal plans to suit. She was thoughtful. And she was fiercely independent; from what she'd just told him about her childhood, he could understand exactly why she wouldn't want to rely on someone. She'd seen her mother's heart broken and had learned from that.

And he didn't want Spiky Emmy back. He liked the woman he'd got to know. More than liked her, if he was honest with himself. 'I'm not worried at all,' he said lightly.

'You didn't need to tell me that. I already know you're not flighty.'

'Oh.' She looked slightly deflated, as if she'd been gearing up to have a fight with him and now she didn't have to. 'So what about you? Are you looking for Ms Right?'

'No, I made enough of a mess of my marriage.' And then he surprised himself by adding, 'And it was my fault.'

'How? You didn't have an affair.'

'Neither did Nadine.'

'So what went wrong?' She put a hand to her mouth. 'Sorry. I know I shouldn't ask you personal stuff.'

Absolutely. He didn't want to talk about his feelings or his past. But he surprised himself even more by saying, 'Given our situation, you probably ought to know. And I know you're not going to gossip about me.'

'Of course I'm not.'

'Nadine and I—we wanted the same things, at first. A satisfying career, knowing we could reach the top of our respective trees. Neither of us wanted kids. Except then she changed her mind.'

'And you didn't?'

He shook his head. 'She gave me an ultimatum: baby or divorce. So I picked the latter.'

She blew out a breath. 'And now you're in exactly that situation with Tyler—a stand-in dad. Though obviously you and I—we're not…'

Her voice faded, and he wondered if she was thinking about that kiss. He most definitely was. He forced himself to focus. 'Yeah.' But his voice sounded slightly rusty to his ears. He hoped she wouldn't guess why.

'So does that mean…I mean, the three months are up in a couple of weeks. And you don't want to…?' She looked worried.

'I'm glad you brought that up,' he said. 'It's working for

me. I think we're a good team. I know we're never going to be as good as Pete and Ally, and I for one still have a lot to learn about babies, but Tyler seems happy with us.'

'Are *you* happy?' she asked.

'Yes. And I feel a bit guilty about it. I said I didn't want to be a parent. But, actually, I'm enjoying it,' he confessed. It was a relief to admit it out loud, at last. 'I like coming home to a baby. I like seeing him change. I like hearing him babble and I like seeing his face when he tries something new.'

'Me, too,' she said softly.

'So we keep going?' he asked.

'What about your ex?'

He grimaced. 'As I said, I feel guilty. Maybe it could've worked, if I hadn't been so stubborn. Or maybe it wouldn't. I don't know.'

'Why didn't you want a child?' she asked.

He blew out a breath. 'I just don't. Didn't.'

'You mean, back off because you don't want to talk about it?' she asked wryly.

He was slightly surprised that she'd read him so well. 'Yes. Tonight's meant to be about toasting your success, not dragging through my failures. So, yes, I'd rather change the subject. I'm not the kind of guy who talks about my feelings and wallows in things,' Dylan said. 'I just get things done. With the social skills of a rhino.'

She gave him a rueful smile. 'You're never going to let me forget that, are you?'

'No. Because, actually, it's true,' he said. 'Anyway. The main thing is that we both know where we stand—we're both single, and we're both planning to stay that way. And we can just get on with looking after Tyler.'

'Yeah.' She raised her glass again. 'To Tyler. I wish things could've been different—but I think we're managing to be the next best option for him. Even if we do have to rely on looking things up in a book or asking my mum, half the time.'

'Absolutely.' He clinked his glass against hers. 'To Tyler, and to being the best stand-in parents he could ever have.'

Somehow the awkwardness between them had vanished, and Emmy was surprised at how easy it was to talk to Dylan. And to discover that they had shared loves in music and places they wanted to visit.

She was beginning to see why Pete and Ally had made that decision, now. She and Dylan had their differences, which would be good for Tyler; but they also had much more overlap than either of them had ever imagined. She actually liked his company.

And she was shocked by how late it was when she finally glanced at her watch. 'We'd better call a taxi. And I'd better ring Mum and let her know we're on our way back.'

'You ring your mum, and I'll call the cab,' Dylan said.

In the taxi, their hands kept brushing against each other, and it felt as if little electric shocks were running through her veins. Which was crazy. Dylan was the last man she could afford to be attracted to. This shouldn't be happening.

But what if it did?

What if Dylan held her hand?

And then she stopped breathing for a second when his fingers curled round hers. Was he thinking the same as she was?

She met his gaze, and the remaining breath whooshed out of her lungs.

Yes. He was.

She wasn't sure which of them moved first, but then his hand was cupping her cheek, hers was curled into his hair, and his mouth was brushing against hers. Slow, soft, gentle kisses. Exploring. Enticing. Promising.

He drew her closer and the kiss deepened. Hot enough to make her toes curl and her skin feel too tight. This was what she wanted. What they both wanted.

And then she was horribly aware of a light going on and someone coughing.

The taxi driver.

Clearly they were home. And they'd been caught in a really embarrassing position.

She looked at Dylan, aghast. Oh, no. This was a bad move. Yes, she wanted him and he wanted her. But what would happen when it all went wrong? Tyler would be the one who paid the price.

So they were going to have to be sensible about this. Stop it before it started.

'Um. That shouldn't have happened,' she muttered, unable to look him in the eye.

'Absolutely,' he agreed, to her mingled relief and regret. 'Blame it on the champagne. And it won't happen again,' he added.

Which ought to make her feel relieved. Instead, it made her feel miserable.

'Go in. I'll pay the driver.'

'Thanks.' She fled before she said or did anything else stupid. And tonight, she thought, tonight she'd have a cold shower and hope that her common sense came back—and stayed there.

CHAPTER NINE

DYLAN PUT THE phone down and leaned back against his chair, his eyes closed.

This was potentially a huge deal.

And it came with an equally huge sticking point: the client was a family man who liked to work with people who had the same outlook on life.

Strictly speaking, Dylan wasn't a family man. He was an almost-divorcee who happened to have co-guardianship of his godson. His marriage breakdown would certainly count against him; and his arrangement with Emmy was hardly conventional.

Could he ask her to help him out?

After all, he'd helped her when she'd needed it. And she *had* offered…

He thought about buying her flowers, but that would be manipulative and tacky. No, he'd just ask her once Tyler was in bed. Talk it over with her. And maybe she'd have a creative way round the situation—because Emmy definitely had a different take on life from his.

It helped a bit that it was his turn to cook that night. And he totally appreciated now why she'd tried to cook the monkfish. Except he played it safe, with pasta. 'Emmy, can I ask you a favour?' he asked over dinner.

'Sure. What?'

'I've put in a tender for a project.'

She looked thoughtful. 'So you're going to be working longer hours and need me to pick up the slack for a bit? That's fine, because you did exactly that for me. Of course I'll do it.'

He grimaced. 'Not exactly. I'm learning to delegate, so I don't need you to pick up the slack. Anyway, I haven't got the deal yet.'

She frowned. 'So if you don't need me to take over from you, what's the favour, then?'

This was the biggie. 'The client. He's a family man. He likes to work with—well, people who have the same outlook.'

She raised an eyebrow. 'Isn't that discrimination?'

'It would be, if he was employing me,' Dylan agreed, 'but this is different. It's a project and my company's put in a bid for it, so the client can choose his contractor however he likes.'

'And you want him to think you're a family man?' She looked wary. 'Dylan, this is a seriously bad idea. You're not a family man.'

'I'm Tyler's co-guardian, so *technically* that makes me a family man.'

'But you and I...' Her voice faded and she looked slightly shocked. 'Oh, no. Please tell me you're not expecting me to lie for you and pretend that you and I are an item?'

'I'm not expecting you to lie. Just...' How could he put this nicely? 'Just fudge the issue a little.'

She shook her head. 'It'll backfire. When he realises you lied—and he *will* realise, if you get the contract and he works with you—then he'll have no faith in you. Professionally as well as personally. Which will be a disaster for your business.'

He folded his arms. 'What happened to looking out for each other?'

She narrowed her eyes at him. 'I *am* looking out for you, Dylan. This isn't the best way forward, and you know I'm right.'

There wasn't much he could say to that, so he remained silent.

'But,' she said, 'I'll help you. Invite him round to dinner. I'll cook.'

He looked at her. 'Thank you for the offer, but I think I'll pass on that one.'

She rolled her eyes. 'You're not going to let me forget that monkfish, are you?'

'It was pretty bad,' he said. 'Not that I could do any better myself. Which is why I think inviting him to dinner's a bad idea. The kitchen isn't my forte or yours.' He frowned. 'Though I suppose I could buy something from the supermarket that I just have to put in the oven and heat through.' His frown deepened. 'But could I ask you to do the table setting, please?'

She gave him a sidelong look. 'Because I'm a girl?'

'No. Because you have an artist's eye and you're good at that sort of thing,' he corrected.

He'd actually paid her a compliment. A genuine one. And Emmy was surprised by how warm it made her feel.

'Of course I'll do the table setting. But this meal needs to be home-cooked if you invite him round. We can't just give him a ready meal from the supermarket.' She thought for a moment. 'OK. If he's a family man, invite his wife and kids. We'll make it a family meal.'

His eyes narrowed. 'So what are you planning? Are you going to talk your mum into cooking for us?'

She shook her head. 'I don't need to. We'll keep it simple. Something like...hmm. A roast dinner.'

He grimaced. 'I remember the student house I shared with Pete. The four of us made our first Christmas dinner and the turkey wasn't properly cooked. We were all ill for three days afterwards.'

'This isn't a student house. And I'll ask my mum about timings so it won't go wrong. How old are his kids?'

'I have no idea.'

'Find out.' She looked thoughtful. 'Actually, if they're little, they won't have the patience for a starter, and if they're teens they probably won't want to come anyway. So we'll skip the starter. We can do a roast dinner for the main, and fresh fruit salad and ice cream for dessert. We're both working and we're looking after Tyler, so it's OK to take the odd short cut.'

'But you'll be there at the table, won't you? You're not just going to be in the kitchen?'

'Why, Dylan, anyone would think you wanted me there,' she teased.

He gave her a speaking look. 'All right. You can have your pound of flesh. I want you there. You have good social skills.'

'Thank you.' She grinned and punched his arm. 'And yours are a bit better than they were. Go and ring him. Find out if there's anything they can't eat—either because of allergies or because they hate it. And we definitely need to know if anyone's vegetarian.'

'Because then we'll have to rethink the menu?'

'Because then dinner will be pasta,' she said. 'We can both cook that. And we'll serve it with garlic bread and salad. Simple and homely.'

Dylan rang his potential client the next morning, and then rang Emmy. 'It'll be just Ted Burroughs and his wife.

You were right about the kids—they're teens, and he says they'll pass on the invite.' He smiled. 'Mind you, he has girls. If I'd said I live with a top jewellery designer...'

'No, they would've been bored with the conversation, so it's better that they don't come,' Emmy said. 'What about the food?'

'No allergies, and he appreciated you asking.' He paused. 'I appreciate you, too. I wouldn't have thought of that.'

'Which is because,' she said, 'you only have one X chromosome.'

'That's *so* sexist.'

She laughed. 'Bite me, Dylan.'

She was adorable in this playful mood.

Then Dylan caught his thoughts and was shocked at the fact he'd used the word 'adorable' about her. What was happening? Emmy Jacobs was his co-guardian, and that was all.

The kisses and the hand-holding in the taxi had been... well, mistakes.

Even if he did want to repeat them.

Even if a little, secret part of him thought that yes, he'd like to be partners with Emmy in more than just sharing Tyler's care.

'See you later,' he said. 'And thanks.'

The day of the dinner arrived, and Dylan made sure that he was home early to help. Emmy had already set the dining room table with candles, fresh flowers, a damask tablecloth and silverware, and the chicken was in the oven.

'Is there anything you need me to do?' he asked.

'Make a start on peeling the potatoes?' she suggested.

He did so, and noticed that there was a list held onto the fridge with a magnet. 'What's this?'

'The timing plan for dinner,' she said. 'And I'm using the oven timer to make sure I don't miss anything.'

She definitely looked strained, he thought. 'Stop worrying. I'm sure it will be fine.'

'That's not what you said when I first suggested cooking a roast dinner.'

He rolled his eyes. 'OK, O Wise One. You were right and you know better than I do.'

'I hope so.' Though she didn't sound convinced.

'So you got the timings from a book?' he asked.

'Better than that—Mum helped. She did offer to come and cook for us, but I thought that'd be cheating.'

Would it? he wondered.

She'd obviously caught the expression on his face just before he masked it, because she sighed. 'You think I should've taken her up on the offer, don't you?'

'No, I'm sure all will be just fine.' He finished peeling the potatoes. 'Do you want me to make the fruit salad?'

'It's already done so the flavours can mingle.' Almost on cue, there was the sound of gurgling and cooing from the baby listener. She smiled. 'It sounds like someone's just woken. Go and play with Tyler—you're getting under my feet and being annoying.' She shooed him out of the kitchen, though he was careful to make sure that she really didn't need any help before he agreed to go.

He spent some time playing with the baby. Again it surprised him just how much he was enjoying this domestic set-up. He'd never thought a family was for him; or maybe Nadine just hadn't been the right person for him to have a family with. He pushed away the thought that maybe Emmy was the right one. He knew she had issues about relationships, and he wasn't sure how it could work between them. They couldn't risk fracturing Tyler's world again.

* * *

Emmy ticked off everything she'd done on her list, checked the list a second time in case she'd missed anything, and then did a final read-through just to be absolutely certain.

Everything was ready, as far as it could be. Barring having to rescue everything from a last-minute catastrophe in the kitchen—and she hoped she'd done enough planning to avoid that—there was nothing else to do.

She changed into a simple black dress and some of her more delicate jewellery, and adopted the 'less is more' principle when it came to her make-up. She stared at herself critically in the mirror. How many of her ex-boyfriends hadn't been happy with the way she looked? The colour of her hair, the fact that it rarely stayed the same colour for more than a couple of months at a time, the way she dressed...

She took a deep breath. Dylan wasn't her boyfriend, and she looked just fine. Professional. Competent.

All the same, when she came back down into the kitchen, she grabbed an apron, just in case she spilled anything over herself while she was cooking.

Dylan was already there, feeding Tyler in his high chair. The baby beamed and banged his hands on his tray when he saw her.

'Hello, Gorgeous. Is Uncle Dylan in charge of dinner tonight?'

'Dih-dih.' Tyler gurgled with pleasure—and bits of carrot sprayed all over Dylan's shirt.

'Oops. Sorry,' she said.

He flapped a dismissive hand, then grinned.

'What?' she asked suspiciously.

'If anyone had ever told me I'd see you wearing an apron, looking all domestic...'

'Oh, ha ha.' She rolled her eyes. 'Ty, make sure you spit more carrot at him.'

Dylan just laughed. 'We're about done here. I'll sort out bath and bed. Is there anything else you need?'

'No—I'm fine. And you'd better change, Dylan—you've got mashed carrot on your shirt.'

'I guess so.'

It wasn't that long ago that Dylan had been so formal and stuffy that even his jeans were ironed and his T-shirts were pristine and white. He'd unbent an awful lot if he wasn't that fussed about mashed carrot on one of his work shirts, Emmy thought, especially as she knew carrot could stain.

She fussed around downstairs while Dylan sorted out Tyler's bath and bedtime, and changed his shirt. And then the doorbell went, and her stomach went into knots. This deal could mean as much for Dylan's business as the magazine thing meant for hers so she really couldn't afford to mess things up tonight. If the veg wasn't cooked enough or, worse, cooked to a mush...

Breathe, she told herself. Everything's going to be just fine. You've used the timer and ticked everything off the list. It's not going to let you down and you're not going to let Dylan down.

Dylan answered the door; she stayed in the kitchen for just a little longer, nerving herself, then came out to meet their guests.

'Emmy, this is Ted and Elaine Burroughs—Ted and Elaine, this is Emmy Jacobs,' Dylan introduced them.

'Delighted to meet you. Thank you for having us,' Ted said, and shook her hand warmly.

Emmy was horribly aware that she was still wearing her apron. So much for being sophisticated. 'Um, sorry,

I hope you'll excuse…' She indicated the apron with an embarrassed grimace.

'Of course,' Ted said.

'So how long have you been together?' Elaine asked.

Emmy and Dylan exchanged a glance.

Be honest, she willed him. Tell them the truth, or it'll come back to bite you.

'We're not actually a couple, as such,' Dylan said. 'We share a house. And we're also co-guardians of Tyler, our best friends' son—they were killed in a car crash three months ago. They'd asked us both to look after Tyler if anything happened to them. So here we are.'

'So you moved out of your own homes and in here together?' Elaine asked.

'It was the best thing for Tyler,' Emmy said. 'He needed to be somewhere familiar.'

'Plus my flat in Docklands wasn't really baby-friendly,' Dylan added.

'And mine in Camden was only big enough for me, not for the three of us,' Emmy explained.

'That must have been hard for you,' Ted said, his face full of sympathy.

'We've been thrown in a bit at the deep end,' Emmy said, 'but we're managing. I should tell you now that dinner's not totally a home-made thing. I'm afraid we cheated and bought the gravy and the ice cream, but I hope you'll forgive us for that.'

'My dear, it's very kind of you to invite us over—especially given your circumstances,' Elaine said.

'We support each other,' Emmy said. 'Sometimes Dylan has a late meeting and needs me to pick up the slack, and sometimes I have a rush on at work and need him to hold the fort for me.' She exchanged a glance with him. 'And he's better than I am at getting Ty to sleep. He sings better.'

'That always worked with our two,' Elaine said with a smile.

'Would you excuse me?' Emmy asked. 'I need to check on the veg. Dylan, can you—'

'—sort the drinks?' he finished. 'Sure. Would you like to come through to the dining room, Elaine and Ted?'

He sorted out the drinks while she did the last-minute things in the kitchen. She was putting the vegetables in serving dishes when she overheard Elaine complimenting the table setting.

'That's all down to Emmy,' Dylan said. 'She has an artist's eye. You should see her jewellery—it's amazing, so delicate and pretty.'

It warmed her to know he was being absolutely serious. Dylan never gushed.

She brought the serving dishes and warmed plates through, and Dylan carved the chicken.

To her relief, the food seemed to go down well. The vegetables were fine—not too hard or too soft—and she'd managed to get the potatoes crispy on the outside and fluffy inside, thanks to her mother's instructions.

'Dylan tells us you're a jeweller,' Elaine said. 'Our eldest daughter is about to turn sixteen, and I know she'd like some jewellery for her birthday. Could you make some for her?'

'Sure,' Emmy said. 'Most of the stuff on my website is either in stock or won't take long to make, or I could design something especially for her.'

'Why don't you show Elaine the pieces you made for the magazine?' Dylan suggested. 'Or is that embargoed?'

'Officially it's embargoed,' Emmy confirmed, 'but I guess it's OK for you to see the photographs I took. Excuse me a second?' She grabbed her phone from her bag, and showed Elaine the photographs.

'That really delicate stuff—that's so Claire. She'd love something like that,' Elaine said.

'Do you want it to be a surprise? If not, you could bring Claire over and I can talk to her about what she'd really like, and design it for her there and then.' Emmy smiled. 'Actually, why don't you do that and we can make it a really girly session? It'll make her feel special to have something designed just for her.' She put a hand on Dylan's arm. 'Sorry, this wasn't meant to be about my business tonight. I didn't mean to take over.'

He smiled. 'You weren't taking over. I just think what you make is really amazing. She does these jet carvings as well, little animals. She made me a fantastic bear.'

'Teddy?' Ted asked with a grin.

Dylan laughed back. 'Ah, no. It's a grizzly. She was making a point,' Dylan said.

'You're lucky I didn't make you a rhino,' she teased.

'A rhino?' Elaine looked mystified.

'Because she says I have the same level of social skills as a rhino,' Dylan explained. 'I guess it goes with being good at maths.'

'You're a total geek,' she said, but her tone was affectionate.

She cleared the table and brought out the fruit salad; she'd bought thin heart-shaped shortbread from the deli and vanilla ice cream to go with it.

'Pineapple, raspberries, kiwi and pomegranate,' Elaine said as she looked at the bowl. 'How lovely. I'd never thought of making a fruit salad like that. You really are good in the kitchen.'

'Not always,' Emmy confessed. 'I tried making monkfish in parma ham a few weeks back, and it was absolutely terrible. That's why we decided to cook a roast dinner tonight, because it's much simpler and less likely to go wrong. And I still had to call my mum for the timings and instructions on the roast potatoes.'

'You did her proud, love,' Ted said.

Emmy found herself relaxing now that the trickiest part of the meal was over. But then Tyler woke, and they could all hear him crying on the baby listener.

'I'll go,' Emmy said.

'No, it's my shift,' Dylan said.

'Not anymore,' she corrected him. 'I put a sticky note on the board so it's my shift. You stay with our guests.' She realised her slip almost immediately, but hoped she hadn't messed it up. It had felt so natural to call the Burroughses 'our' guests rather than 'your'.

'I'd love to see the baby,' Elaine said wistfully. 'But I guess you can't bring him down as it'll put him out of his routine.'

'You can come up to the nursery with me, if you like,' she offered impulsively, and Elaine beamed.

'I'd love to.'

And maybe this would give Dylan and Ted the chance to discuss business, Emmy thought.

Elaine clearly loved having the chance to cuddle a baby. 'How old is he?'

'Seven months, now.'

'You forget how cute they are at this age. He'll be crawling, next.'

'And we'll have baby gates all over the place,' Emmy said with a smile.

She settled the baby down in his cot again, and put his light show on.

'It's very sad about your friends,' Elaine said, 'and it must be difficult for you. How are you both coping?'

'It was pretty tough at first,' Emmy admitted. 'Dylan wasn't a very hands-on godfather when Tyler was really tiny. I guess he was waiting to do all the stuff like kicking a ball round in the park, going to the boating lake, and helping teach him to ride a bike—stuff I wouldn't do as a godmother, because I'd rather take him swimming or to baby music classes. But we've muddled through together for the last three months, and it helps that we take alternate night shifts.' She blew out a breath. 'It means we each manage to get one good night's sleep out of two. I have no idea how my best friend coped the way she did. She always looked fresh as a daisy, even if the baby had been up half a dozen times in the night.'

'You must miss her,' Elaine said.

'I do—and Dylan really misses Pete. They were the nearest we had to a brother and sister.'

'But Dylan helps you now.'

Emmy nodded. 'He's been brilliant. Actually, he's helped right from the start, even though he's never had anything to do with babies before and was obviously scared to death that he'd do something wrong and hurt the baby. He's never just left me to deal with everything; he's always done his fair share, even if it involves dirty nappies or having stuff dribbled all over him. He's stubborn and sometimes he comes across as a bit closed off or he says totally the wrong thing, but his heart's in the right place and he thinks things through properly.' She smiled. 'Don't tell him I said this, but when we do argue he's usually right.'

Elaine smiled back. 'He sounds like my Ted.'

Emmy checked the cot once more; satisfied that Tyler had settled again, she ushered Elaine back downstairs to the dining room. She made coffee and brought in the posh chocolate truffles she'd found in the deli, and helped Dylan make small talk until the Burroughses finally left.

Dylan helped her clear up. 'By the way, do you know

the baby listener was still on when you were upstairs with Elaine?'

Emmy looked at him, horrified. 'You're kidding!'

He shook his head.

'How much did you hear?' she demanded.

'Let me think.' He spread his hands. 'That would be...' He met her gaze. 'All of it.'

She closed her eyes briefly. Obviously she'd wrecked everything, because she just hadn't been able to keep her mouth shut. 'I'm so sorry, Dylan. Ted must've thought...' She bit her lip.

'He was laughing.' Dylan's eyes crinkled at the corners. 'Especially at the bit when you said I'm usually right. And I hope you realise I have every intention of using that one against you in the future.'

She knew that was an attempt to stop her worrying, and ignored it. 'I just hope I haven't screwed up the deal for you.'

'I think,' he said, 'you showed Ted what he wanted to know. That I'm not just this efficient machine.'

'Well, you're that as well.'

Dylan raised an eyebrow. 'Thank you. If that was meant to be a compliment.'

'A backhanded one,' she confirmed.

He smiled at her. 'That's what I like about you. You never sugar-coat stuff.'

'There's no point. I've had it with charm.'

'Ouch.' He looked serious. 'Want to talk about it?'

'We already have. I told you I had rubbish taste in men. That's just another example. I fall for the charm every time—hook, line and sinker.'

He reached over and stroked her cheek, and every nerve-end in her skin zinged. 'Something I should tell you. You're usually right, too, when we argue. You make me think things through in a different way. And that's a good thing.'

'Think outside the regular tetrahedron?' she asked

'There's absolutely nothing regular tetrahedron about you, Emmy.'

'Thank you. If that was meant to be a compliment,' she threw back at him.

His eyes crinkled at the corners again. And how ridiculous that it made her heart skip a beat.

'It was. And thank you for your help. You might just have made the difference.' He looked at her mouth. 'Emmy. You were brilliant, tonight.' His voice deepened, grew huskier. And then he leaned forward and pressed the lightest, sweetest kiss against her lips.

It was anatomically impossible, but he made her feel as if her heart had just turned over. How could she help herself resting her palm against his cheek, feeling the faint prickle of stubble against her fingertips? Especially when his hands slid down her sides, resting lightly against her hips as he drew her closer.

Then she panicked. She couldn't feel like this about Dylan. She just couldn't. She took a step back. 'We...'

'Yeah. I know. Sorry.' He raked a hand through his hair. 'That didn't happen.'

'No. It was just adrenaline, because we were both panicking about dinner.'

'Absolutely,' he said as she took another step back. 'I'll finish up in here. You go and...' He blew out a breath. 'Whatever. I'll see you later.'

She took the hint and made herself scarce. Before she did something really stupid, like kissing him again.

CHAPTER TEN

DYLAN WAS TWITCHY for the next couple of days, though Emmy understood why. She'd been in the same situation herself, not so long ago.

On Saturday morning at breakfast, she said, 'Right, you need to get out of the house.'

'What?' Dylan looked at her as if she were speaking Martian.

'Waiting. It's the pits. And if you stay in and try and concentrate on work, you'll end up brooding. So you're coming out with Ty and me to get some fresh air. Isn't he, Ty?'

The baby gurgled and banged his spoon against the tray of his high chair. 'Dih-dih!'

'It sounds as if you have something in mind,' Dylan said.

Emmy nodded. 'I've been making a list of places to go with him. We can always go to the park with the slide and the swings on sunny days, but it's no good on rainy or cold days. And this is one I've been looking forward to.'

She was mysterious about where they were going, and Dylan didn't have a clue until they were standing outside what looked like an Edwardian greenhouse with a large banner that proclaimed it to be the House of Butterflies.

When they were inside, he discovered that the green-house was full of lush vegetation and had a slightly humid, warm atmosphere. He could hear the sound of water falling, so he realised there must be a fountain somewhere. There were butterflies of all sizes and colours, some huge and vivid. He'd never seen so many in one place before.

Ty seemed to love it, watching the butterflies opening and closing their wings as they perched on a flower or fluttered overhead. He reached out to them, waggling his fingers as if copying the movement of their wings.

'Look—those people over there are standing very still, and the butterflies are landing on them,' Emmy exclaimed, looking enchanted.

She tried it herself, and her face was suffused with wonder when a butterfly landed on her. Dylan wished for a second that he had a camera to capture that expression.

They wandered through the different sections of the enormous greenhouse, looking at the butterflies and the flowers; Dylan was surprised by how much it made him relax.

'Thank you for bringing me here. I was getting a bit scratchy. Sorry, I haven't been very nice to live with.'

She patted his arm, and the feel of her skin against his made him tingle. 'That's OK. I was the same when I was waiting. And you did the same for me, when you took me to the sea,' she said. 'I just thought this might be something different.'

'I would never have thought to go to a butterfly house.'

'To be fair, it hasn't been open for that long, so you probably wouldn't have known about it.' She smiled at him. 'Do you mind if I take a few photos?'

'Sure, go ahead. I'll take Ty.'

He took over the pushchair, and she took various photographs with her phone. Including, to his surprise, the roof of the greenhouse. He'd expected her to concentrate on the butterflies. Then again, Emmy seemed to see things in a different way from most people.

In the next section, there was a terrarium full of chrysalises, and they could actually see some of the pupae emerging from their cocoons.

'That's amazing. I never saw anything like that when I was a kid,' Dylan said.

'Did you have a garden?'

He nodded. 'My grandparents had a huge garden, and my gran loved butterflies and bees—she had shrubs to attract them. My grandfather preferred the more practical stuff, growing fruit and vegetables. And I used to have to help weed the garden whenever I was there.'

'Sounds as if you weren't keen.'

'I was a child,' he said. 'But I've never had a garden since.'

And they'd neglected Pete and Ally's garden, just mowing the lawn.

In the section after, there was a waterfall and a pond with huge red and white goldfish. Emmy unbuckled Tyler from his pushchair and held him up so he had a good view of the pond. 'See the red fish, Ty?'

'Fiiih,' said the little boy.

He saw the shock on Emmy's face and the way she suddenly held Tyler that little bit tighter, as if she'd been near to dropping him. 'Did you hear that, Dylan? He said "fish"!'

'I heard.' And it was crazy to feel so proud of him. Then again, Tyler was the nearest he'd ever get to having a son. Something he'd always thought he didn't want, but now he knew he did.

Tyler clapped his hands with delight, and Emmy beamed at him. 'Clever boy.'

* * *

This, Emmy thought, was the perfect day. Tyler learning a new word. Sharing this amazing spectacle with him and with Dylan. And the butterfly house definitely seemed to have taken Dylan's mind off the wait to hear from Ted Burroughs.

In the next section, Dylan found a giant stripy caterpillar and pointed it out to the baby. 'Hey, Tyler, what pillar doesn't need holding up? A caterpillar!'

He chuckled, and the baby laughed back. And Emmy was enchanted. The joke was terrible, but Stuffy Dylan would never have done something like that. He was definitely changing and she really liked the man he was becoming.

'We'll have to take him to the zoo. I've noticed he really likes that tiger story you bought him,' she said.

'Maybe we could go next weekend?' he suggested. 'Though it's your weekend off.'

'No, that'd be good. I'd like that.'

'And maybe we can look at planting things in the garden,' he said, 'flowers that butterflies really like. Then, next summer, when Tyler plays in the garden he might get to see a few butterflies.'

And maybe it would also bring back nice memories of his grandmother, Emmy thought. Dylan had mentioned her before; and she had the strongest feeling that he'd been closer to his grandmother than he was to his mother. He certainly missed her, from what he'd let slip.

'That's a great idea,' she said. 'Though I had a flat so I'm afraid I'm not much of a gardener. I tended to have cut flowers rather than houseplants. Ally bought me a couple and…well, let's just say I don't have green fingers.'

'We'll learn,' he said. 'Looking after a garden can't be

any harder than bringing up a baby, and we're managing fine with Tyler.'

Emmy felt warm inside that not only were they working together as a team, he was also acknowledging that. And this was beginning to feel like being part of a real family. It was taking time, but they were finally bonding.

She was fascinated by the terrarium with the dragonflies in the next section. 'Just look at the colours,' she said, pointing them out to Tyler. 'Blue and green dragonflies.'

'Fiiih,' the baby said again.

She laughed and rubbed the tip of her nose against his. 'Fly, sweetie, not fish. But I guess they both sort of have scales.'

When they stopped in the café, she mashed a banana for Tyler and leaned down to feed him in his pushchair while Dylan went to get the coffee. When Tyler had finished, she scooped him onto her lap and cuddled him with one arm while she made a couple of quick sketches in the notebook she always carried in her handbag.

Dylan put the coffees on the table, out of Tyler's reach. 'What are you doing?' he asked.

'Just noting down a couple of ideas for jewellery.'

He looked intrigued. 'So this sort of thing is where you get your inspiration?'

'Sort of,' she hedged.

'Sorry, is this a creative thing? You don't like to talk about work in progress?'

'No, it's fine.' She felt relaxed enough with him to know that he wasn't like her exes—he was asking because he was interested, not because he wanted her to stop or thought he had better ideas that she ought to go along with. She pushed her notebook across the table to him. 'Have a look through if you want to. Sometimes I take pictures, sometimes I sketch.'

He flicked through the pages. 'That spiderweb reminds me a bit of that necklace you made.'

'With the heart in the middle rather than the spider?' She smiled. 'You're right, that was the inspiration. It was a frosty morning and the cobwebs were really visible. They looked incredibly pretty, delicate yet strong at the same time.'

He reached the page where she'd sketched a couple of pictures of Tyler asleep. 'I had no idea you could draw. I mean, I knew you designed stuff, but that's not the same as a portrait. These are really good.'

'Thank you. I was working while he was napping and I just thought he looked so cute and peaceful. I couldn't resist it.'

He handed the book back to her. 'Very cute. So you carry a notebook all the time?'

'Yes. Because you never know when you're going to see something that sets off an idea,' she explained. 'Though I guess it's not quite like that with your job.'

He smiled. 'No, it's talking to the client that does that.' He indicated the slice of chocolate cake he'd bought. 'Would you like some of this?'

'Thanks, but I'm fine.' Mr Stuffy had changed absolutely, Emmy thought. A couple of months ago, he would barely have spoken to her. Now he was offering to share cake with her, for all the world as if they were partners.

Though she knew better than to kid herself. Yes, Dylan was attractive. Especially when you saw past the superficial eye-candy stuff to the real smile, the one that lit up his eyes. He could tempt her to break every single one of her rules and fall in love with him.

But then what? She couldn't take the risk. If she had an affair with Dylan, she knew it would be amazing at first.

But then it would go the way of all her other relationships and end in tears. Hers.

Dylan flicked through the leaflet he'd picked up at the counter. 'Did you know that a butterfly tastes through its feet?'

She raised an eyebrow. 'You expect me to believe that?'

'Seriously, a butterfly can't bite or chew food. It just sucks everything up with a proboscis, so it has to taste things through sensors in its feet.'

'Did you hear that, Ty?' She traced circles on his palm, making the baby giggle.

'Round and round the garden,' Dylan said.

He knew this? Then again, she'd noticed what he'd been reading. He'd left child development books in the living room. Being Dylan, he took things seriously and did it the geek way. 'Like a teddy bear,' she said.

'One step.' He put a finger on Tyler's wrist.

'Two step.' She put a finger on Tyler's elbow.

'And a tickle under there.' He tickled Tyler under the armpit, and the baby's rich chuckle rang out.

'Come to me so Em can drink her coffee?' Dylan asked, holding his arms out.

Tyler echoed him, holding his arms out to be picked up. 'Dih-dih!'

Dylan scooped him up. 'How did he do with the banana?'

'He ate about three-quarters of it.'

'Good boy. Is the milk in his bag?'

'Sure is.' And how Dylan had come on as a father, she thought. In the early days, he'd been wary, unsure of himself. Now, he was confident, and Tyler responded to that. The baby clearly adored him.

She could easily adore Dylan, too—the man he'd become.

But she needed to keep her burgeoning feelings under control. This was as good as it was going to get, so she was going to enjoy it for what it was and not let herself wish for more. Even though, secretly, she did wish for more.

They really did look cute together, Tyler cuddled on Dylan's lap, holding his own bottle and yet with Dylan's hand held just under it as a safety net. She couldn't resist taking a picture on her phone. 'That's lovely. I'll send it to Ally's and Pete's parents.'

'I was talking to them the other night,' Dylan said. 'They told me you write to them every week with pictures and updates.'

She shrugged. 'Well, they don't really use email. It's nearly the same, just that I print it out rather than send it electronically. It's not a big deal.'

'It's nice of you to bother, though.'

'Just because they've lost their children, it doesn't mean they have to lose their grandson as well,' she said. Then an idea hit her. 'Would you like to send a copy of this photo to your mum? I could send it to your phone, or even directly to her if that's easier for you.'

'No, it's OK.' But it was as if she'd thrown up a brick wall between them, because he went quiet on her.

What had she said?

They'd talked about sending a picture to Tyler's grandparents and she'd suggested sending it to his own mother, too. And it wasn't the first time he'd gone quiet on her after the subject of his parents had cropped up.

Clearly there was some kind of rift there, and she'd just trampled on a really sore spot.

'I'm sorry, Dylan. I didn't mean to…' Help. Given that the intensely private man seemed to be back, how could she phrase this without making it worse? 'I'm sorry,' she said again.

He sighed. 'It's not your fault. Sorry. I'm stressing about the contract. I shouldn't take it out on you.'

She let it go, but still she wondered. She'd noticed that Dylan's mother had never visited or even called the house. He'd said before that his mother was travelling, so maybe she was somewhere with poor phone connections, or maybe she just called him during office hours, when he wasn't in the house. But it was as if almost everything to do with Dylan's family was in a box marked 'extra private, do not touch'.

They still hadn't quite got that easiness and family feeling back by the time they'd finished in the café and went to the gift shop.

Until she spied the butterfly mobile. 'That's lovely. We can put it over his cot. It'd look great with the stars from his nightlight floating over it, and he'll see it first thing in the morning when he wakes.'

'Mmm.' Dylan didn't sound that enthusiastic, but she knew he secretly liked the nightlight.

They continued to browse, and Dylan picked up a board book. 'We need to get this.'

She glanced at it; it was a story about a caterpillar, and there was a finger puppet. So New Dylan was back. Stuffy Dylan might have read a grudging bedtime story, but New Dylan would read it with voices and props so a child would really enjoy it. She grinned. 'You like doing bedtime stories, don't you?'

'Yes. If anyone had told me I'd like doing all the voices, I would've said they were crazy. But I do.' He looked a bit wistful. 'I wish Pete was here to share it. He would've loved this.'

'So would Ally,' she said softly. 'And you know what? I think they're looking down on us right now, hugging each other and saying they made exactly the right choice.'

To her surprise, he reached over to touch her cheek. 'Know what? I agree.'

Emmy felt warm all over. Right now they were definitely in accordance. And nothing felt better than this.

CHAPTER ELEVEN

TWO NIGHTS LATER, Tyler wasn't settling in his cot as he usually did after a bath and a story; he was just grizzling and looking unhappy. It didn't look like teething, because although his cheeks were red he wasn't dribbling. Emmy laid her fingertips against his forehead and bit her lip. He felt a bit too hot for her liking.

Where was the thermometer?

She looked through the top drawer of Tyler's dressing table. Ally had shown it to her when she'd bought it. All she had to do now was put a thin plastic cone over the tip of the digital thermometer, place it in the baby's ear, and press a button.

Except she couldn't get the thermometer to switch on.

Oh, no. And she had a nasty feeling that they didn't have any spare batteries that would fit.

Although it was her night on duty, she wanted a second opinion—especially as the thermometer was out of action.

'Shh, sweetie, we'll do something to make you feel better,' she said, scooping the baby up and holding him close. She carried him down to the living room, where Dylan was working on his laptop.

'Sorry to interrupt you,' she said, 'but I need a second opinion.'

'What's up?' he asked.

'The thermometer battery's run out and we don't have a spare. Does Tyler feel hot to you, or am I just being paranoid?'

He felt the baby's forehead. 'No, he feels hot to me, too. What do we do now? Where's the book?' He grabbed *The Baby Bible* and looked something up in the index. He frowned as he swiftly read the relevant page. 'Do we have any baby paracetamol?'

'It's in the kitchen with the medicine cabinet.'

'Good. We need to give him that to help bring his temperature down, and while that's working we have to strip him down to his vest and sponge him down with tepid water.' He held out his arms for the baby. 'I'll give him a cuddle and sing to him while you go and get the stuff. I'll meet you in the bathroom.'

The baby was still crying softly when Emmy came upstairs with the baby paracetamol and the syringe. Dylan had taken the babygro off and was rocking Tyler and singing to him.

Dylan glanced at the syringe and his eyes widened. 'What, we have to give him an injection?'

'No. The instructions say it's easier to give medicine to babies with an oral syringe than a spoon,' she explained.

'Right.'

Between them, they managed to administer the medicine, then sponged the baby with tepid water.

'Sorry, I interrupted you from your work.' She blew out a breath. 'It's my shift, and I should be able to cope. It's just… This is what keeps me awake at night. I worry about him. I worry that every cough and sneeze will turn into meningitis. That he'll die and it'll be all my fault for not looking after him properly.'

'Emmy, he doesn't have meningitis. He doesn't have a rash.'

'There isn't one at first. We could blink and he'll be covered in purple stuff that won't go away when you press a glass against it.' She'd read all the books. She knew the signs. And she had nightmares about it. Terror that made her breathing go shallow.

'We're both keeping an eye on him, so we won't miss anything between us.' He rested his fingertips against her cheek, his touch calming her. 'Deep breaths, Emmy. He's not going to die and you're doing a great job of looking after him. And don't apologise for interrupting me.' He cradled the baby tenderly. 'He's not well, and he needs to come first. I would've done the same if it was my shift.'

'I'll get him a drink of cooled boiled water. It might help him feel better.'

'Good idea. It must be some sort of bug. There are quite a few people at work with rotten colds.' He looked stricken. 'Oh, no. I probably brought the germs home with me.'

She shook her head. 'It's not your fault, Dylan. He could have caught a virus absolutely anywhere.'

Three hours later, the baby was fast asleep, but Emmy was still worried about him. 'I think I'll sleep in his room tonight.'

'You're not going to get a lot of rest on the floor,' Dylan pointed out.

'I know.' She sighed. 'Or maybe I'll bring him in with me. Except I'm a bit scared of rolling over in the night and squishing him.'

He looked at her. 'If it was my shift tonight, you still wouldn't be able to sleep because you'd be worrying about him, right?'

'I guess so.'

'Don't take this the wrong way,' he warned, 'but maybe we could both look after him, tonight. I do trust you—of *course* I do—but this is the first time he's been ill since we've been looking after him, and it worries me.'

'Me, too,' she admitted.

'We could take two-hour shifts, so one of us stays awake and keeps an eye on him while the other of us has a nap,' he suggested

She nodded. 'But it isn't fair to keep moving him between our rooms—and, as you said, the nursery floor isn't that comfortable.' The sensible course was obvious. But actually saying it... She took a deep breath. 'OK. Your bed or mine?'

Dylan gave her a rueful smile. 'I never thought I'd hear those words from you, Em.'

'Believe you me, I never thought I'd say them to you,' she said dryly. 'And this is only because we both need to look after him. I'm not coming on to you.' Though even as she said it, she felt her face flood with colour. She was horribly aware that, in another life, she *would* be coming on to Dylan—because she liked the man he'd become. And she definitely found him attractive.

Which was why she found her most frumpy pair of pyjamas before she showered, just to make the point that there was nothing sexual about this. She felt amazingly shy as she changed into her nightwear—which was ridiculous, considering that she was covered from head to toe and she knew that Dylan had seen more of her body when she was wearing a dress. Even so, she kept the bedside light on its lowest setting.

There was a knock on the door.

And how stupid that her heart missed a beat.

'Come in,' she called, hoping that her voice didn't sound as husky and nervous to him as it did to her.

He walked in wearing just a pair of pyjama bottoms, carrying the sleeping baby.

'I, um, don't tend to wear a pyjama top because I get too hot at night. Is that a problem for you?'

'No, it's fine.' She really hoped he hadn't heard that little shiver in her voice. *Too hot at night.* Oh-h-h. He looked amazingly hot right now. She could really see that he worked out at the gym regularly because his muscles were beautifully sculpted; he had good abs and strong arms, and he wouldn't have looked out of place in a perfume ad. Especially dressed the way he was, right now.

And that was totally inappropriate. He was here in her bedroom because Tyler was sick and they were sharing his care, that was all.

'Which side of the bed do you prefer to sleep on?' he asked.

'The right side—nearest the door,' she said.

'Fine by me.' He pulled the covers back and gently laid Tyler in the middle of the bed. He touched the baby's forehead and grimaced. 'He still feels hot.'

'We'd better not put a cover over him, then.'

They both climbed into bed, on either side of the baby.

'Poor little mite,' Emmy said softly. 'I wish I could have that high temperature for him.'

'Me, too,' Dylan said. 'It's weird how protective I feel about him. I never thought I'd ever feel this way about a baby.'

It was as if Tyler were their natural child, Emmy thought. She wasn't his birth mother, but she was in the position of his mother, now, and she loved him deeply. Dylan clearly felt the same way, as if he were Tyler's real father.

'We're privileged,' she said softly.

'Yes, we are.' He paused. 'Shall I take the first shift while you try to get some sleep for a couple of hours? I'll wake you when it's your turn.'

'OK. Thanks, Dylan. I appreciate the backup.'

'You'd have done the same if it'd been my turn to look after him,' he said. 'Try to get some sleep.'

She turned over so her back was to him, but she was so aware of him. He was in her bed, barely an arm's reach away. And if Tyler hadn't been there…

No, no and *no*. She was not going to allow herself to think about the possibilities.

Eventually Emmy managed to get to sleep. Then she became aware of someone stroking her arm and shaking her shoulder very gently. 'Emmy? Wake up.'

'Uhh.' It took a second for her to think why Dylan would be shaking her awake; then she remembered and sat up with a jolt. 'Is Tyler OK?'

'He's still a bit warm, but I put a single sheet over him because his legs and arms seemed a bit cold.'

'Good idea. You get some sleep now. I'll stay awake.'

Still feeling groggy, she placed her fingertips on Tyler's forehead. Dylan's assessment was spot on.

She was glad that Dylan turned his back to her to go to sleep, because she really didn't want him to catch her looking lustfully at him. Even his back was beautiful. She itched to sketch him, though it was years since she'd taken her Art A level and sketched a life model. Apart from those brief sketches she'd made of Tyler, she'd stuck mainly to abstracts and the designs for her jewellery. But Dylan was beautiful. He'd be a joy to sketch. She fixed the picture in her mind, intending to indulge herself later, then watched Tyler sleeping. The baby looked angelic with that mop of dark curls; and she was glad to see, even in the low light in the room, that his cheeks didn't look quite so red.

In his sleep, Dylan shifted to face her. In repose, he looked younger. It took Emmy a while to realise what the difference was, and then she worked it out: he didn't have that slight air of wariness she was used to.

Someone had hurt him pretty deeply, Emmy was sure. Nadine was the obvious candidate, but Emmy had a feeling that it went deeper than that. Why had he been so resistant to the idea of having a child of his own? Had he had a rotten childhood?

Not that he'd tell her, she knew. Even if she asked him straight out. He was way too private for that, and it was surprising that he'd already let this much slip to her.

Finally her two-hour watch was over. She checked Tyler's temperature again. Good. It was definitely going down. She reached over to lay a hand on Dylan's arm. His skin felt so good against her fingertips. Soft and smooth. Tempting her to explore further.

Get a grip, Emmy Jacobs, she lambasted herself silently. This isn't about you.

She patted his arm lightly, but it didn't wake him at all. She shook his shoulder, and there was still no response. Dylan was clearly in a really deep sleep. And he had taken the first shift; he must've been exhausted. She decided to leave him sleeping for another hour, then tried to wake him again. This time, she climbed out of bed and went round to his side, so she could shake him harder without waking the baby.

In response, Dylan reached out to her and mumbled something she didn't quite catch. It sounded like 'Mmm, Dee'.

'Dylan,' she said in an urgent whisper.

'Mmm,' he muttered. This time, he actually pulled her into his arms and snuggled closer.

Oh, help.

If it weren't for the baby lying next to him, she could be oh, so tempted. All she had to do was to move her head slightly and her mouth would touch against his. She could kiss him awake. See where it led them.

But he'd said 'Dee', and she had a nasty feeling that he was dreaming about his ex. Mmm, Dee. Nadine. They sounded the same, mumbled in sleep. And how stupid she was to think that Dylan would get over his wife that quickly. He was obviously still in love with his ex. Yes, there was a definite attraction between the two of them, but physical attraction wasn't enough. Her relationships never lasted. If she had a fling with Dylan, it would make everything way too complicated. She really couldn't do this.

She managed to resist the temptation—only just—and wriggled out of his arms.

'Dylan,' she said, more loudly this time.

He woke with a start and looked at her in utter confusion. Then his expression cleared as he obviously remembered where he was and why. 'How's Tyler?'

'Still a little bit warm, but nowhere near as hot as he was. He's asleep.'

'Good. Is it three o'clock?'

'Four.'

He looked shocked. 'You were supposed to wake me at three.'

'Dylan, you sleep like a log. I couldn't wake you.'

He grimaced. 'I'm sorry. OK. I'll take the next three hours and I'll wake you at seven, not six, OK?'

'OK.' She was still feeling slightly lightheaded; but that had to be from lack of sleep. It had absolutely nothing to do with the way Dylan had pulled her into his arms and held her close. Did it?

Emmy looked absolutely shattered, Dylan thought—and no wonder, since her shift had lasted longer than his. He felt guilty about it, and lapsed into silence to let her sleep.

He touched Tyler's forehead, just to check; she was right, the baby felt cooler.

He shifted onto his side to watch the baby. Emmy had turned away from him to sleep, but he could still feel her warmth in his arms. When she'd woken him, for a moment he'd been confused and thought he was back in his old house, the one he'd shared with Nadine before he'd moved into the Docklands flat. It had seemed natural to draw her closer, hold her.

Hopefully she'd forget about that by the morning. He didn't want her to think he was coming on to her, because it could make things so awkward between them. And he didn't want it to go back to the bad old days, when they hadn't got on.

Funny, sharing a house with Emmy hadn't been like sharing with Nadine, even in the early days when he and Nadine had been happy. With Emmy, he didn't feel any pressure. He didn't have anything to live up to, because they'd started from the lowest possible point and thought the worst of each other.

And these past few months had been a revelation. He'd been so sure that he didn't want a family. That he didn't want to risk things going wrong and for his child to grow up as unhappy as he'd been. Even when Nadine had given him an ultimatum, his feelings hadn't changed and he knew he'd made the right decision.

Yet, ever since he'd become a stand-in father, things had been different. Over the months, he'd grown to love his godson. He loved seeing all the little changes every day, hearing the little boy's vocabulary grow from a simple da-da, ba-ba, through to 'Dih-dih' for Dylan and 'Ehhhm,' for Emmy, and sounds that resembled real words—like the time in the butterfly house when Emmy had been convinced that he'd said 'fish'. He enjoyed seeing Tyler's anticipation as they read through a story and were about to reach his favourite bits. He enjoyed the simple clapping games Emmy had taught him to play with the little boy.

And Emmy herself...

There was the rub.

She was Tyler's stand-in mother. Dylan's co-guardian and housemate.

They were well on the way to becoming friends. He enjoyed her company, and he thought she enjoyed his, too. And, although they'd agreed to have alternate weekends off from childcare, in recent weeks they'd ended up spending a fair bit of those weekends together.

It felt like being a family. What he'd always said he didn't want. And what he'd discovered that, actually, yes, he did want. Very much indeed.

She shifted in bed, turning to face him, and he held his breath.

Spiky Emmy, the cynical and brittle woman he'd loathed so much in the past, wasn't here. This was sweet, gentle, soft Emmy. Vulnerable Emmy, who'd had her confidence chipped away by exes who couldn't see her for who she was, only what they wanted her to be. Emmy, who didn't really believe in herself.

Dylan could see her for who she was. And he liked her. More than liked her.

But could he ask her to take a chance with him—to make their unexpected family a real one?

It would be a risk. A huge risk. It had gone wrong with Nadine; he couldn't make any promises that he'd get it right, second time round, with Emmy. And he knew she shared similar fears, given that she'd been let down in the past.

Somehow he'd have to overcome those fears. Teach her

that he wasn't like the men she'd dated before: that he saw her for who she was and he liked her just the way she was. And then maybe, just maybe, they'd stand a chance.

CHAPTER TWELVE

A WEEK LATER, Emmy opened the thick brown envelope that had just been delivered, to discover an early copy of the glossy magazine that had interviewed her.

'Ty, look—it's Aunty Emmy's feature,' she said, waving the magazine at him.

Tyler was much more interested in picking up the bricks they'd been playing with, and dropping them.

She built him another tower to enjoy knocking down, counting the bricks for him as she did so, then flicked through the magazine to the article. There was a nice picture of her with Tyler, and they'd really showcased her jewellery beautifully. But her delight turned to dismay as she skimmed through the text.

She'd explained the situation to the journalist. She'd made it totally clear that she and Dylan were Tyler's co-guardians and they weren't an item. So why did the article make reference to Dylan being her partner?

Oh, no. He wasn't going to be happy about that. At all.

She paced the house all morning. What was the best way to deal with this?

In the end, she decided to tell him straight. Sooner rather than later.

She waited until Tyler took his late morning nap, then called Dylan at work.

He answered immediately. 'Is Tyler all right?'

'Yes, he's fine.'

Her shakiness must've shown in her voice, because he asked, 'What's wrong?'

'There's something you need to know. It's pretty bad.' She took a deep breath. 'The magazine's coming out next week. They sent me an early copy today.'

'And they didn't use your jewellery in the end?' He sounded sympathetic. 'More fool them.'

'It's not that. They did use my pieces.' She swallowed hard. 'But they've used a picture of me with Tyler—and they've said in the piece that you're my partner. They actually named you as computer superguru Dylan Harper. And it—well, basically it implied that Tyler's our child. I told the journalist why we were sharing a house and sharing Tyler's care. I can't believe they got it wrong like this! I'm so sorry. If this causes you any problems...' Her voice faded. If it caused him problems, she had no idea what she could do to fix it. Would it make his divorce more difficult?

'They got the wrong end of the stick. So what? It doesn't matter. Stop worrying,' he said, surprising her. She'd been so sure he'd be annoyed about it. 'The main thing is that they showcased your jewellery.'

'They did. And the jet animals.'

'Good. Now breathe, Emmy.'

'Thank you,' she said in a small voice. 'I thought you'd be livid.'

'It could be a lot worse. Most people know the press exaggerate, so don't worry about it. Just wait for people to start contacting you with commissions—and then you'll be so busy you won't have time to worry about it anymore.'

It was another week until the magazine was in the shops. Although Dylan had told her not to worry about it, Emmy still couldn't help fretting. If anyone who knew him read the piece, they'd get completely the wrong idea.

The day before the magazine came out Dylan distracted her when he called her from work.

'Don't tell me—an emergency project meeting and you're going to be late?' she asked.

'No—and I'm bringing champagne home. I got some good news this afternoon.'

'You got the Burroughs contract?'

'I certainly did.'

'Fantastic.' Emmy was genuinely pleased for him. 'Well done.'

'It was partly thanks to you,' Dylan pointed out.

'No, it's because he recognises your skill. Actually, I have some news for you. Elaine Burroughs rang. She's bringing her daughter over to see me next week.'

'For a commission? That's great. Well done. Got to go but I'll see you later. Oh—and please don't cook monkfish.'

She just laughed. 'For that, I'm ordering a takeaway. See you later.' She replaced the phone and cuddled Tyler. 'You know what? This is all starting to work out. It's not quite how Dylan and I wanted things—we'd both do anything to have your mum and dad back with us. But, as second-best goes, this is pretty good.'

Over champagne, that evening, Dylan said, 'I want to take you out to dinner to say thanks—being here with us really made a difference to Ted's decision to give us the project. Do you think your mum would babysit Ty for us?'

'Probably. I'll ask her,' Emmy said.

'Do you mind if I ask her?' Dylan asked.

She smiled. 'You know her number.' Dylan might not be that close to his own mother, she thought, but he definitely got on well with hers.

The following evening was Dylan's turn to cook. Over pasta, he told her, 'I spoke to your mum this morning. It's all arranged; we're going tomorrow.'

'Going where?' she asked.

'Out to lunch,' he said. 'Except we need to leave really early tomorrow morning, and you'll need your passport.'

She frowned. 'Why do I need my passport?'

'Don't be difficult,' he said. 'I was going to take you out to dinner, but I thought lunch might be more fun.'

'Lunch is fine, but what does that have to do with my passport?'

'Surprise.'

She sighed. 'You do know I hate surprises, don't you?'

'I think you'll like this one.' Annoyingly, he refused to be drawn on any further details.

'Are you at least going to tell me the dress code?' she asked in exasperation.

He thought about it for a moment. 'Smart casual—probably a little bit more on the smart side. You definitely need shoes you can walk in.'

'So we're walking somewhere?'

'End of information bulletin. No more answers,' he said, and gave her the most infuriating grin. Worse still, he refused to be drawn for the rest of the evening.

'I swear I'm never playing poker with you,' she said. 'You're inscrutable.'

He just laughed. 'I've been called worse.'

The next morning, Dylan knocked on Emmy's bedroom door at what felt like just before the crack of dawn. 'We're leaving in half an hour.'

Which gave her just enough time to shower, wash her hair, dress, and check in on Tyler. Her mother was already in the kitchen when Emmy came downstairs, and the kettle was on. 'Hi, Mum. Thanks for babysitting. Tyler's still asleep, given it's the crack of dawn.' She greeted her mother with a hug and kiss. 'Coffee and toast?'

'We don't have time,' Dylan said.

She gave him a sceptical look. 'You know I'm horrible if I haven't eaten. And why do we have to leave so early if we're going out to lunch, which won't be for hours?'

He answered her question with one of his own. 'You've definitely got your passport in your bag?'

She gave him a withering look. 'I'm not *that* flaky, Dylan.'

'Sorry. Old habits die hard.' He ruffled her hair. 'Let's go. We have a train to catch.'

So wherever they were going, it was by Tube. She still had no idea why he wanted her to bring her passport; though, knowing Dylan, that could be a red herring. She kissed her mum goodbye; to her surprise, so did he. Together, they headed for the Tube station, a ten-minute walk away.

Emmy noticed that although Dylan was wearing one of his work suits, teamed with a white shirt and highly polished shoes, at least for once he wasn't wearing a tie. She'd opted for a simple black shift dress teamed with black tights and flat shoes; a silver and turquoise choker; and a turquoise pashmina.

'You look lovely,' he said.

She inclined her head. 'Thank you, kind sir. Actually, you don't look so bad yourself.'

He smiled back at her. 'Why, thank you.'

Ten minutes later, they arrived at King's Cross. The second he directed her through the exit to St Pancras, she realised where they were going. 'We're going to *Paris* for lunch, Dylan? That's incredibly decadent!'

'Not really. It's as quick to take the train from London to

Paris as it is to drive from London to Brighton,' he pointed out. 'Anyway, I love Paris. It's a beautiful city.'

To her delight, he'd booked them in business class so they could have breakfast on the train.

'So this is why you wouldn't let me have even a piece of toast at home,' she said, surveying the feast in front of her. Champagne with fresh orange juice, smoked salmon and scrambled egg, fresh strawberries, and good coffee. 'This has to be the most perfect breakfast ever. I feel totally spoiled.'

He smiled. 'Good.'

'I've never been in business class before.' Because she could only really afford standard class. And only then if she booked the seat early enough to get the supercheap rate.

He shrugged. 'The seats are more comfortable.'

'Thank you, Dylan. This is a real treat.'

Dylan watched her selecting what to have next; he loved the fact that she was enjoying her food rather than picking at it, the way Nadine always had.

She caught him watching her. 'Sorry. Am I being greedy?'

He laughed. 'No, I was just thinking how nice it is that you enjoy your food instead of nibbling on a lettuce leaf.'

'This is a lot better than you or I can cook,' she said with a smile. 'And if we're going to Paris, I take it we're walking, so I'm going to burn all this off anyway.'

The journey to the Gare du Nord was quick and uneventful; a short trip on the Métro took them to the Champs Elysées.

'It's too long since I've been to Paris. I'd almost forgotten how lovely it is—all that space in the streets, all the windows and the balconies.' She gestured across to a terrace on the other side of the street. 'I love that wrought ironwork.'

He smiled at her; he recognised that light in her eyes. The same as it had been at the butterfly house, and he'd seen drafts of designs that reminded him of the metalwork in the old Edwardian conservatory. 'Are you going to get your notebook out and start sketching?'

She smiled back. 'Not in the middle of the street. But would you mind if I took some photographs to remind me later?'

''Course not. Enjoy.'

They wandered down the street and stopped in a small café. Macaroons were arranged in a cone shape on the counter, showcasing all the different colours available, from deep pink through to browns, yellows and pistachio green.

'I guess we have to try them, as we're in Paris,' he said, and ordered macaroons with their coffee.

'This is just *lovely*. The perfect day.' Her eyes were all huge and shiny with pleasure—and that in turn made Dylan feel happy, too.

This was definitely as good as it got.

And taking her to Paris was the best idea he'd ever had. Romantic and sweet—and this might be the place where he could ask her to change their relationship. Be more than just his co-guardian. If he could find the right words.

'What would you like to do before lunch?' he asked.

'Are you planning to go somewhere in particular for lunch?'

'Yes. We need to be in the fourth arrondissement at one o'clock, but before then we can go wherever you like. I assume you'd like to go to an art gallery?'

'That's a tough one,' she said. 'Even at this time of day, I think there will be too much of a queue at the Louvre.'

She looked at him. 'You said the fourth arrondissement, so that means the old quarter. Could we go to Notre Dame and see the grotesques?'

'Sure,' he said. 'I've never been. It'd be interesting to see them.' He'd visited most of the art galleries and museums, as well as the Sacré-Coeur and Montmartre, but he'd never actually been to Notre Dame.

'It's a bit of a trek up the tower,' she warned.

'I don't mind. I know you said you wanted to walk, but how do you feel about going by river?'

She nodded. 'That works for me. I love boat trips.'

He made a mental note; it might be nice to take Tyler to Kew on the river, in the spring.

When they'd finished their coffee, they took the Batobus along the Seine to the Île de la Cité, with Emmy exclaiming over several famous buildings on the way. They walked up the steps from the bridge, then across the square with the famous vista of Notre Dame and its square double tower and rose window. The stone of the cathedral looked brilliant white against the blue sky.

'I love the shape of the rose window, the way it fans out—almost like the petals of a gerbera crossed with a spiderweb,' she said.

'Are you thinking a pendant?' he asked.

She nodded. 'Do you mind if I take some pictures?'

He laughed. 'You really don't have to ask me every time, Emmy. Just do it. Today's for you to enjoy.'

'Thank you.' She took several photos on her phone, and then they queued at the side of the cathedral to walk up the tower to the galleries.

'I always think of poor Quasimodo, here,' Emmy said. 'So deeply in love with Esmeralda, yet afraid she'll despise him like everyone else does.'

'So you cried over the film?'

'No, over the book,' she said, surprising him.

'You read Victor Hugo?' He hadn't expected that.

She looked at him. 'It was one of my set texts for A level.'

'English?'

'French,' she corrected.

He blinked. 'You let everyone think you're this ditzy designer, but you're really bright, aren't you?'

'Don't sound so surprised. It kind of spoils the compliment.' She rolled her eyes. 'I'm really going to have to make you that jet rhino, aren't I?'

'Hey.' He gave her a brief hug. 'I didn't mean it like that. But you do keep your light under a bushel.'

'Maybe.'

They walked up the hundreds of spiral steps; the stone was worn at the edges where thousands of people had walked up those steps before them. At the first stage, they had amazing views of the square and the Seine, with the Eiffel Tower looming in the background. They carried on up to the next stage and saw the famous chimera grotesques in the Grande Galerie. Dylan was fascinated by the pelican. 'And that elephant would look great carved in jet,' he said.

'For Ty's Noah's Ark? Good idea,' she said.

'So why are the gargoyles here?' he asked.

'Strictly speaking, gargoyles carry rainwater away from the building. These ones don't act as conduits; they're just carvings, so they're called grotesques. These are Victorian ones, done at the same time as the restoration. And there's a fabulous legend—see the one sitting over there, looking over the Seine?'

'Yes.'

'Apparently it watches out for people who are drowning, then swoops down and rescues them.'

He raised an eyebrow. 'Is that something else you learned for your A level?'

'No. Actually, I can't even remember where I heard it, but I think it's a lovely story.'

Emmy liked the brighter side of life, he noticed. Trust her to know about that sort of legend.

They walked across to the other tower to see the bell, then back down all the steps.

'Did you want to go inside the cathedral?' he asked.

'Yes, please. I love the stained glass,' she said.

As he'd half expected, she took several photographs of the rose window with its beautiful blue and red glass.

'Is this a Victorian renovation, too?' he asked.

'Most of this one's original thirteenth-century glass. If I were you, I'd tell me to shut up, now,' she said with a grin, 'because stained glass was one of the modules in my degree, and Ally says I get really boring about it, always dragging her off to tiny churches to see rare specimens.' Her smile faded. 'Said,' she corrected herself.

He took her hand and squeezed it. 'You really miss her, don't you?'

'Yes. But I'm glad we have Tyler. We'll see her and Pete in him as he grows up.'

And then he forgot to release her hand. She didn't make a protest; it was only as they strolled through the streets of the old quarter that he realised he was still holding her hand. And that he was actually *happy*. Happier than he could remember being for a long, long time.

Maybe he didn't need to struggle with words, after all. Maybe all he had to do was *be*.

She insisted on stopping at one of the stalls and buying a baby-sized beret for Tyler. She gave him a sidelong look. 'I'm tempted to get you one as well.'

'You expect me to wear a beret?' he scoffed.

'Mmm, and you could have a Dali moustache to go with it.'

He shuddered. 'What next, a stripy jumper and a red scarf?'

She laughed. 'OK, so a beret is a bit too avant-garde for you—but men can look good in a beret, you know.'

'I think I'll pass,' he said. 'Though I admit Tyler will look cute.'

As they crossed the bridge she asked, 'Where are we going?'

'Time for lunch,' he said.

They stopped outside a restaurant in the old quarter right next to the Seine with view of Notre Dame. She looked at him, wide-eyed. 'I know of this place. Zola, Dumas and de Maupassant all used to come here—it's hideously expensive, Dylan. It's Michelin starred.'

And it had a great reputation, which was why he'd booked it. He simply shrugged. 'They might have monk-fish.'

She let the teasing comment pass. 'I've never eaten in a restaurant with a Michelin star.'

'Good. That means you'll enjoy this,' he said.

Enjoy?

This was way, way out of her experience. Dylan, despite the fact that he wasn't keen on cooking, clearly liked good food and was used to eating at seriously swish restaurants like this one.

Enjoy.

OK. She'd give it a go. Even if she did feel a bit intimidated.

The maître d' showed them to a table in a private salon. She'd never been to such an amazing place before; the décor was all gilded wood and hand-painted wallpaper.

There was a white damask cloth on the table along with lit white candles and silverware, and gilded Louis XIV chairs. The windows were covered with dark voile curtains, making the room seem even more intimate. And the maître d' told them that the waiter would be along whenever they rang the bell.

Emmy's eyes met Dylan's as they were seated. For a moment, she allowed herself to think what it would be like if this were a proper romantic date. A total sweep-you-off-your-feet date.

He'd held her hand as they'd wandered through the city together; so was this Dylan's way of taking her on a date without having to ask her? He didn't like emotional stuff, so she knew he'd shy away from the words; but this definitely felt like more than a thank you. More like the fact that he wanted to be with her. Some time for just the two of them. Together.

Unless she was projecting her own wants on him and seeing what she wanted to see...

When she looked at her menu, she noticed that there were no prices. In her experience, this meant the food was seriously expensive. And it made her antsy.

She coughed. 'Dylan, there aren't any prices on my menu.'

He spread his hands. 'And?'

She bit her lip. 'I'm used to paying my way.'

'Not on this occasion. I'm taking you out to lunch to say thank you.'

So not a date, then. She tried not to feel disappointed.

'Just as you took me out to dinner,' he reminded her.

'But when I took you out, it wasn't somewhere as swish as this.'

He sighed. 'Emmy, if you're worrying about the bill, then please don't. I can afford this. My business is doing just fine—and, thanks to this new contract, it's going to be doing even better. I couldn't have got this contract without your help, so please let me say thank you.'

'Can I at least buy the wine?' she asked.

'No. This one is all on me. And, I don't know about you, but I've got to the stage where I fall asleep if I drink at lunchtime, so I was going to suggest champagne by the glass.' His eyes crinkled at the corners. 'But I might let you buy me a crêpe later.'

A crêpe. Which would only cost a couple of Euros, whereas she was pretty sure the bill here was going to be nearer half a month's mortgage payment for her. 'I feel really guilty about this.'

'Don't. I'm doing it because I want to treat you. So enjoy it. What would you like for lunch?'

Protesting any more would be churlish. Emmy scanned the menu. 'It's all so fantastic, I don't know what to choose. I'm torn between lobster and asparagus.'

'We could,' he said, 'order both—and share them.'

Now it was starting to feel like a date again. And that made her all quivery inside. 'Sounds good,' she said.

She actually enjoyed sharing forkfuls of starter with him. Especially as it gave her an excuse to look at his mouth as much as she liked. And she noticed he was looking at her mouth, too. As if he wanted to kiss away a stray crumb and make her forget the rest of the meal.

Oh, help. She really had to keep a lid on this.

After that, she had crayfish with satay and lime, and he chose lamb.

'Look at this. It's beautifully cooked and beautifully presented,' she said. 'I can see exactly why they have a Michelin star. This is *sublime*.'

He chuckled, and she narrowed her eyes at him. 'What's so funny?'

'That you're such a foodie—and, um, in the kitchen…'

She rolled her eyes. 'Yeah, yeah. I'm never going to live that monkfish down. You'll still tease me about it when we're ninety.'

Oh, help. Had she really said that? Implied that they were going to be together forever and ever?

'Yes. I will,' he said softly, and it suddenly made it hard for her to breathe.

She fell back on teasing. Just to defuse the intensity before she said something really, really clueless. 'I could point out that this is a bit of a pots and kettles conversation, given that you're clearly a foodie and you're about the same as I am in the kitchen.'

He laughed. 'I admit my monkfish would've been just as terrible. But you're right. This is sublime. Try it.' He offered her a forkful of lamb.

'Mmm. And try this.' She offered him some crayfish.

'So are you going to tell me that lunch in Paris was the best idea ever?' he prompted.

'That,' she said, 'depends on the dessert.'

They scanned the menu when they'd finished. 'How can you not order madeleines in France?' she asked with a smile.

'When there's chocolate soufflé on the menu,' he retorted, and she laughed.

Again they shared tastes of each other's pudding, and she enjoyed making him lean over to reach the spoon—especially when he retaliated and did likewise.

'That was fantastic,' she said when the meal was over. 'A real treat. I admit, yes, it's the best idea ever. Thank you so much.'

'My pleasure. I enjoyed it, too.'

And his smile reached his eyes; he wasn't just being polite.

They spent the rest of the afternoon browsing in little boutiques. Again, he held her hand; and again, neither of them commented on it.

Emmy bought a box of shiny macaroons for her mother. 'And I think we should go to a toy shop, so we can bring something more than just a beret back for Ty.'

Dylan smiled. 'He probably hasn't even noticed we're gone. Unless that's just a flimsy excuse for toy shopping, Ms Jacobs.'

'It's a really flimsy excuse,' she said with a grin. 'I love toy shops.'

'I'd already noticed that,' he said, 'given how much Tyler's toy box seems to have grown recently.' He checked on his phone to find the nearest toy shop, and when they looked along the shelves Emmy was thrilled to discover a soft plush teddy bear with a beret and stripy shirt. 'This is perfect,' she said, and gave Dylan an arch look. 'Beret and stripy shirt. Hmm.'

He laughed. 'Don't you dare call it Dylan.'

'Spoilsport,' she teased.

'You know, we'll have to bring Ty to Paris when he's a little older. He'll love seeing the Eiffel Tower sparkle at night,' Dylan said.

Making plans for the future, she thought. Neither of them had said it. This was too new, too fragile. But she was beginning to think that there was a future...

When they'd finished shopping, Dylan allowed Emmy to buy him a coffee before they headed back to the Gare du Nord to catch the train to London.

Back in London, Emmy shivered when they came out of the Tube station and pulled her pashmina closer round her. 'I wish I'd brought a proper coat with me, now. It's colder than I expected.'

'Have my jacket,' he offered, starting to shrug it off.

'No, because then you'll be cold. And it's only a few minutes until we get home.'

'I'll call a taxi.'

'By the time it gets here, we could've walked home,' she pointed out.

'OK. Then let's do it this way.' He put his arm round her shoulders, drawing her close to him.

Oh, help. Her skin actually tingled where he touched her. And the whole thing sent her brain into such a flutter that she couldn't utter a word until he opened the front door and ushered her inside.

Her mum greeted them warmly. 'Did you have a good time?'

'The best,' Emmy said. 'Oh, and these are for you.' She handed her mother the bag from the patisserie. 'How's Tyler?'

'Asleep, and he's been absolutely fine all day.' She hugged them both. 'I'll call you tomorrow.'

'Thanks for babysitting for us.' Dylan hugged her back. 'I only had one glass of champagne at lunchtime, so I'm OK to drive. I'll run you home.'

'That's sweet of you.'

Emmy checked on Tyler while Dylan drove her mother home.

Today had been magical. The way Dylan had fed her morsels from his plate at lunchtime, and walked through Paris hand in hand with her; the way he'd automatically offered her his jacket and then, when she'd refused, put his arm round her to keep her warm... Was she adding two and two and making five, or was it the same for him? Had they become something more than co-guardians? Was this a real relationship—one for keeps?

Dylan was back by the time she came downstairs.

'Everything OK?' he asked.

'Tyler's fine. Thank you for today. It really was special.' She stood up, intending to kiss his cheek. But somehow she ended up brushing her mouth against his instead.

She pulled back and looked up at him.

His eyes were intense, darkened from their normal cornflower-blue to an almost stormy navy. She shivered, and couldn't help looking at his mouth again.

He leaned forward and touched his mouth to hers in the lightest, sweetest kiss. Automatically, she parted her lips and tipped her head back in offering. He drew her closer and she could feel the lean, hard strength of his body. So much for Dylan being a geek; he felt more like the athlete she'd once dated, all muscular. And she couldn't help remembering the way he'd looked in her bed, half-naked and asleep.

Her hands were tangled in his hair and his arms were wrapped tightly round her as he deepened the kiss. Her head was spinning, and it felt as if the room were lit by a hundred stars.

He shuddered as he broke the kiss. 'Emmy.'

'I know.' She reached up to trace his lower lip with the tip of her forefinger.

'Are we going to regret this in the morning?' he asked, his voice huskier this time.

'I don't know. Maybe not.' She shivered as he drew the tip of her forefinger into his mouth and sucked; she closed her eyes and tipped her head back, inviting another kiss.

He released her hand. 'Emmy. My common sense is deserting me. If you don't tell me to stop…' he warned.

Then she knew what was going to happen.

And every nerve in her body longed for it.

She opened her eyes and looked at him. 'Yes.'

Still holding her gaze, he scooped her up and carried her up the stairs.

CHAPTER THIRTEEN

EMMY LAY IN the dark, curled against Dylan.

Are we going to regret this in the morning? His words from earlier echoed in her head.

Would they?

Part of her regretted it already. Because she was scared that now everything could go *really* wrong. When had she ever managed to make a relationship last? When had she ever picked the right man? What if Dylan changed his mind about her?

'I can almost hear you thinking,' he said softly, stroking her hair.

'Panicking,' she admitted. 'Dylan—I'm not good at this stuff. I've messed up every relationship I've ever had.'

'You're good at picking Mr Wrong,' he said. 'And you think I might be another.' He shifted so he could brush his mouth against hers. 'Maybe I'm not.'

She swallowed hard. 'I swore I'd never risk anything like this again, not after the last time.'

'What happened? He was another one who wanted you to change?'

'No,' she said miserably. 'Far worse. I should've told you before. He was married.' She grimaced. 'Finding out that I was the other woman...I hated myself for that.'

'You didn't know?'

'No. Especially after what happened to my mum, no way would I ever have tried to break up a family like that. I found out when I called his mobile phone and his wife answered.' Her breath hitched. 'I wasn't the first. Far from it. But I felt so horrible that I'd done that to someone. My mum was devastated when my father had affairs; and I felt like the lowest of the low for making someone else feel like that.'

'It's not your fault if he lied to you,' Dylan pointed out. He sighed. 'Though I don't have room to talk, do I? Technically, I'm married.'

'You've been separated for months, and you're just waiting for that last bit of paper to come through. That's totally different. You've been honest with me. He wasn't. Though I should've worked it out for myself,' Emmy said. 'Afterwards, when I thought about it, it was really obvious. We always went to my place rather than his, and he never stayed overnight. If we did go out, we only ever went to obscure places, and half the time we'd have to call it off—he said it was because of work, but it was obviously because he was doing family things. I should've seen it.'

'It wasn't your fault,' Dylan said again. 'You wouldn't have had anything to do with him if you'd known he was married. He was the cheat, not you.' He sighed. 'And his wife…maybe she loved him very much, but it's still a shame that she'd let herself be treated like that. It sounds to me as if she deserved better. And so do you.'

'I don't know, Dylan. Sometimes my judgement is atrocious.'

'Mine, too,' he said. 'But it's late, we've had a long day, and now maybe isn't the best time to talk. Go to sleep, Em.' He drew her closer.

Well, at least he hadn't walked away, she thought.

Yet.

* * *

The next morning, Emmy was dimly aware of crying. *Loud* crying, which was turning into screams.

She sat up, suddenly wide awake. Tyler. She hadn't put the baby listener on last night. Because she'd...

Oh, no.

She looked at the other side of her bed.

Where Dylan was also sitting up. Completely naked. And looking shocked, embarrassed and awkward.

That made two of them. They'd complicated things hugely, last night. How were they ever going to fix this?

She glanced at the clock: half past nine. A good two and a half hours later than they were usually up. No wonder Tyler was crying. She'd missed her Pilates class. And Dylan would be lucky to get to the office on time for a meeting she knew he had this morning.

'Oh, my God. We're really late,' she said. 'And Tyler's screaming.'

Dylan looked at her. 'Emmy, we need to talk about this, but—'

'You have a meeting, and I need to feed Tyler.'

'I feel bad about leaving without...' He grimaced.

'We'll talk about it later,' she said. 'Can you close your eyes for a moment?' It was ridiculous, she knew, considering they'd both explored each other's bodies in considerable detail the night before; but she felt shy and exposed.

He mumbled something, clearly feeling as embarrassed as she did, and closed his eyes; she fled to the door, grabbed her bathrobe, and put it on as she raced to the baby's room.

And hopefully by the time she and Dylan talked, she would've rediscovered her common sense and worked out how they could deal with this with the minimum fallout for Tyler.

She scooped Tyler out of his cot and held him close. 'OK, babe, Aunty Emmy and Uncle Dylan messed up. But we'll fix things.' And they would fix things, because they didn't have any other option. 'Come on, let's get you some breakfast.'

The crying subsided, and Tyler was back to being all smiles and gurgled after she'd fed him his usual baby porridge and some puréed apple, and given him some milk.

Dylan was clearly as glad as she was of the respite, because she didn't see him at all before he left the house.

She put Tyler back in his cot with some toys to keep him amused, while she had a shower and dressed. Then she scooped him back out of his cot, changed him, and took him downstairs to play.

'I might've just made the biggest mistake of my life, Ty,' she said. 'Or it might've been the best idea ever. Right now, I just don't know.' And it terrified her. She'd already made too many mistakes. 'I don't know how Dylan really feels about me. But we both love you.' She was sure about that. 'And, whatever happens between us, we'll make sure that your world stays safe and secure and happy.'

She still didn't have any solutions by the time that Tyler had his morning nap.

And then a mobile phone shrilled. It wasn't her ringtone, so the phone must be Dylan's. He'd obviously left it behind and was probably ringing to find out where he'd left it.

She found the phone and picked it up, intending to answer and tell him yes, he'd left it here, and yes, she could drop it in to the office if he needed it. It wasn't his name on the screen; but she recognised it immediately. *Nadine.*

What should she do?

This might be important. She ought to answer it. On the other hand, if she answered the phone and Nadine demanded to know who she was, or got the wrong idea, it could make everything much more complicated.

She grabbed the landline and rang Dylan. 'You left your mobile behind.'

He groaned. 'Sorry. Well, don't think you have to bring it out to me or anything. I'll manage without it for today.'

'You might not be able to. Um, Nadine just rang.'

'Why?' He sounded shocked. 'What did she say?'

'I don't know. When I saw her name, I was too much of a coward to answer. Sorry.'

'It's fine. Probably just as well.' He sighed. 'Did she leave a message?'

She glanced at the screen of his phone. 'It looks like it.'

'What does it say?'

'How would I know? I don't listen in to your messages, Dylan.'

'It's probably something to do with paperwork for the divorce,' he said, and sighed. 'I'll sort it out. And I'll see you later. Em...'

'Yes?'

'Never mind. We'll talk when I get home.'

Emmy spent the morning playing with Tyler. But when the baby had a nap, she looked a few things up on the Internet. And then she really wished that she'd let it go. Now she'd seen a picture of Nadine, she could see that Dylan's ex was perfect for him. Poised, sleekly groomed, very together—everything that Emmy wasn't.

And the divorce was taking a very long time to come through. Assuming that they'd split up before Tyler was born...why hadn't it been settled yet? Did Nadine want him back? Had she heard from a colleague that Dylan was guardian to the baby she'd wanted, and did she think that Dylan might be prepared to give their marriage another chance?

She blew out a breath. OK. Dylan wasn't a liar and a cheat. He wouldn't have slept with her if he'd still been in love with his ex. She knew that.

But...

Her relationships always went wrong. What was to say that this would be any different? And there had been that night where he'd pulled her close and murmured Nadine's name...

The doubts flooded through her, and she just couldn't shift them. What if Dylan had changed his mind about her? What if, when he came home tonight, he wanted them to go back to their old relationship—at arm's length and only sharing the baby's care? What if they got together and, once the first flush of desire had worn off, he started realising how many flaws she had, just as her exes always had? What if he started wanting her to change, and she couldn't be who he wanted her to be?

Tyler woke; feeding him distracted her for a little bit, but still the thoughts whizzed round her head. And the doubts grew and grew and grew until she felt suffocated by them.

'I need to think about this,' she told the baby. 'I need to work out what I want. Find out what Dylan wants. And I think we need to be apart while we work it out.'

She knew exactly where she could go. Where she'd be welcomed, where the baby would be fussed over, where she'd be able to walk for miles next to the sea. Where she could talk to someone clear-sighted who'd listen and let her work it out.

She rang her great-aunt to check that it was convenient for her to visit, then packed swiftly. 'We're going to the sea,' she told the baby, who cooed at her and clapped his hands. 'Where I used to go when I was tiny. You'll like it.'

Then she picked up the phone again. It was only fair to tell Dylan what she planned. Except he was unavailable, in a meeting with a client. This wasn't the kind of thing she wanted to leave in a message, and she could hardly text him because his mobile phone was still here.

But she could leave him a voicemail.

She dialled his mobile number swiftly and waited for the phone to click through to his voicemail. 'Dylan, I need some space to think about things,' she said. 'To get my head straight. I'm staying at Great-Aunt Syb's. I'll text you when I get there so you know we've arrived safely.' Given what had happened to Ally and Pete, she would've wanted him to text her if he'd been the one travelling. It was only fair.

Honestly, Dylan thought, if you were going to leave a message on someone's voicemail, you could at least make sure you were around to accept the return call.

On the third attempt, he finally got through to Nadine. 'You wanted to talk to me,' he said.

'Yes. I saw that article in the magazine.'

'Uh-huh.'

'And Jenny at the office said you were looking after Pete's son since the accident.'

Where was she going with this? He had a nasty feeling about it. 'My godson. Yes.'

She dragged in a breath. 'So you're a dad.'

Uh-oh. This was exactly what he'd thought she wanted to talk to him about. 'A stand-in one.'

'So we could—'

'No,' he cut in gently before she could finish her suggestion. 'Nadine, you're seeing someone else.'

'On the rebound from you. I still love you, Dylan. We can stop the divorce going through. All you have to do is say yes. We can make a family together.'

'It's not quite the same thing, Nadine. You wanted a baby of your own,' he reminded her.

'And we still can. We can have a brother or sister for Tyler.'

'No. Nadine, it's over,' he said, as gently as he could. 'I'm sorry.'

'So you're really—' she took a deep breath '—with that jeweller?'

'I am,' he confirmed. And it shocked him how good that made him feel. Tonight, he'd leave the office and go home to Emmy and Tyler. His partner and his child. His unexpected family.

Her voice wobbled. 'What does she have that I don't?'

'That isn't a fair conversation,' he said. 'You're very different. Opposites, even. But she complements me. And it works.' He paused. 'Be happy, Nadine. And try to be happy for me. We've both got a chance to make a new life now, to get what we wanted.'

'I wanted it with you.'

'I'm sorry,' he said, guilt flooding through him. 'But there's no going back for us. I know that now. We wouldn't make each other happy.'

'We could try.' Hope flared in her voice.

'I'm sorry,' he said again. 'Goodbye, Nadine. And good luck.' He cut the connection.

And now he could go home. See Emmy. Tell her that everything was going to be just fine.

Except, when he opened the front door, he realised that the house was empty.

Maybe she'd taken Tyler to the park or something. He tried calling her mobile phone from the house landline, but there was no answer. Maybe she was somewhere really noisy and hadn't heard the phone, or maybe she was in the middle of a nappy change. 'It's me. I'm home,' he said when the line clicked through to voicemail. 'See you later.'

He went in search of his mobile phone. Emmy had left it in the middle of the kitchen table. He flicked into the first screen, intending to check his text messages, and noticed that he had two voicemail messages. The first was Nadine's from earlier, asking him to call. He sighed and deleted it.

The second was probably work. He'd sneak some in until Emmy got home, and then—well. Then he could kiss her stupid, for starters.

He smiled at the thought, and listened to the message.

And then his smile faded.

I need some space.

Uh-oh. That wasn't good. Did that mean she'd changed her mind about what had happened between them? That she didn't want to be with him?

Or had he been right about her all along and she was like his mother, unable to stick to any decisions and dropping everything at a moment's notice to go off and 'find herself'?

Feeling sick, he listened to the rest of the message.

So she was going up north. To the sea. That figured. And she'd left the message two hours ago, so right now she was probably in the car. Of course she wouldn't answer while she was driving. She'd never put Tyler at risk like that.

OK. He'd talk to her when she got there. And in the meantime he'd get on with some work.

Though it was almost impossible to concentrate. The house just didn't feel right without her and Tyler. Going for a run didn't take his mind off things, either, and nor did his shower afterwards. And he was even crosser with himself when he saw the text from Emmy when he got out of the shower. *Here safely. E.*

Just his luck that she'd texted when he wouldn't hear it. He called her back immediately, but a recorded voice informed him that the phone was unavailable. Switched off? Or was she in an area with a poor signal?

'Leave a message, or send a text,' the recorded voice told him.

Right.

'Emmy, call me. Please. We need to talk.' They really had to sort this out. Did she want him, or didn't she?

Except she didn't call him.

And Dylan was shocked to find out how much he missed them both. How much he wanted them home safely with him.

Maybe she wanted space because she wasn't sure of him. Maybe he hadn't made her realise exactly how he felt about her. Maybe she needed something from him that he wasn't good at—emotional stuff. The right words.

Maybe his mother went to find herself because she had nobody to find her. But Emmy had someone to find *her*. She had him. And he needed to tell her that.

It was too late to drive to Whitby now. It'd be stupid o'clock in the morning before he got there. But he could go and find her tomorrow. Tell her how he felt. And hope that she'd agree to come back with him.

First, though, where did Syb live? He had a feeling that if he did manage to get through to Emmy's phone to ask for the address, she'd come up with an excuse. And this was too important to put off. He needed to see her *now*.

Knowing Emmy, all her contacts would be on her phone rather than written down somewhere. But he knew she was savvy enough to keep a backup. If she had a password on her computer at all, he reasoned, it would be an easy one to crack. He switched on the machine, waited for the programs to load, and typed in Tyler's birthdate when the computer prompted him for a password.

Bingo.

It was a matter of seconds to find Syb's address in Emmy's contacts file. He made a note of the address for his GPS system and shut down the computer.

Tomorrow—he just hoped that tomorrow would see his life getting back on track. Back where he belonged.

CHAPTER FOURTEEN

AT FIVE O'CLOCK the next morning, Dylan gave up trying to get back to sleep. He had a shower, chugged down some coffee, and headed for Whitby.

He'd connected his phone to the car and switched it into hands-free mode, so he was able to call his second in command on his way up north to brief him on the most urgent stuff he had scheduled for the day. And, with that worry off his mind, it let him concentrate on Emmy.

As he drove over the Yorkshire moors the heather looked resplendently purple, and there was a huge rainbow in the sky. When he was small, his grandmother used to tell him there was a pot of gold at the end of a rainbow. Well, he didn't want gold. He wanted something much more precious: he wanted Emmy and Tyler.

At last he could see the sea and the spooky gothic ruin of Whitby Abbey that loomed over the town. Almost there. He didn't want to turn up empty-handed, so he stopped at a petrol station to refuel and buy flowers for both Emmy and her great-aunt. He managed to find a parking space near the house; when he rang the doorbell and waited, his heart was beating so hard that he was sure any passers-by could hear it. Finally, the door was opened by an elderly lady. 'Yes?'

'Would you be Emmy's great-aunt Syb?' he asked.

She looked wary. 'Who wants to know?'

'My name's Dylan Harper,' he said.

'Ah. So *you're* Dylan.'

Emmy had obviously talked to her great-aunt about him. And probably not in glowing terms, either. He took a deep breath. 'Please, may I see her?'

'I'm afraid she's not here.'

His heart stopped for a moment. OK, so she'd probably guess that he'd lose patience with the situation and come to see her, but surely she hadn't disappeared already? 'Where is she?' he asked.

'Walking by the sea. I told her to leave Tyler with me—she needed some fresh air and time to think. It's hard to think when you're looking after a baby.'

'Is he OK?'

'He's absolutely fine and he's having a nap, so don't worry. Just go and find her. She'll be on the east foreshore.' He must've looked as mystified as he felt, because Syb added, 'Head for the Abbey, then instead of going up the steps just keep going forward until you get to the beach, then hug the cliffs and keep heading to the right. You'll see her.'

'Thank you.' He thrust the flowers at her. 'These are for you—well, one bunch is. The other's for Emmy.'

'Thank you, Dylan,' Syb said gently.

A cheap bunch of flowers. How pathetic was he? And the only other thing he had to give Emmy was his heart. Which was incredibly scary. What if she rejected him? What if she was here because she was trying to work out how to tell him that it was a huge mistake and she didn't want to be with him in that way? 'I, um…'

'Go and find her,' Syb said. 'Talk to her. Sort it out between you. I'm here for Tyler, so don't rush. Take your time.'

As Dylan walked through the town he felt sick. What if she wouldn't talk to him, wouldn't listen to what he had to say? What if she didn't want him?

There were a few families on the beach, and his stomach clenched as he saw them. That was exactly what he wanted—to be able to do simple things like building a sandcastle on the beach with Tyler, and playing with him and Emmy at the edge of the sea. Family things. A *forever* family.

Please let her listen to him.

There were a few people beachcombing on the foreshore; some had hammers and chisels, and Dylan assumed they were collecting fossils. Then he rounded a corner and saw her. She bent down to pick up something from the sand; probably some jet, he thought. Syb had sent Emmy out to do something to soothe her soul, and he already knew how much she loved the sea.

He quickened his pace and nearly slipped on the treacherous surface; he blew out a breath and picked his way more steadily over towards her.

She looked up as he reached her side. 'What are you doing here?'

'I've come to see you. Talk to you.' He took a deep breath. 'Emmy, I'm good at business words and computer code and geek. I'm rubbish at the emotional stuff. I know I'm going to make a mess of this, but...' His voice faded.

She nodded. 'What did Nadine want? Was it about the paperwork?'

'No. She'd seen the article.'

'You said she wanted a baby. You have a baby, now.' Her voice wobbled. 'Is that what she wants?'

He knew with blinding clarity what she was really asking. Was that what he wanted, too? 'I'm not going to lie to you, Emmy,' he said softly. 'She did suggest it. But I said no. Because that's not what I want.'

She bit her lip. 'You don't want a child.'

He squirmed. There was no way out of this. He was going to have to bare his heart to her, even though he hated making himself that vulnerable. 'Not with her. We're not right for each other.' He dragged in a breath. 'I guess that's something else you need to know. I didn't want a child,' he said slowly, 'because of the way I grew up.'

She waited. And eventually the words flooded in to fill the silence.

'I never knew who my dad was. My mum used to go off to "find herself" every time she broke up with whoever she was dating, and she always dumped me on the nearest relative. Usually my grandparents.' He looked away. 'My grandmother loved me and had time for me but my grandfather always made me feel I was a nuisance and a burden.'

She reached out and linked her fingers through his; it gave him the strength to go on, and he looked back at her.

'I hated it. I hated feeling that I was always in the way. Then, as I grew older, I was scared that maybe I wouldn't be able to bond with a child because my parental role models were—well, not what I would've chosen myself. I was scared that I wouldn't be any good as a parent, and I never wanted a child to feel the way I did when I grew up, so I decided that I was never going to have children.' He blew out a breath. 'I suppose I married Nadine because I thought she was safe. Because I thought she wanted the same thing that I did, that her job was enough for her. But then she changed her mind about what she wanted and I just couldn't change with her. I couldn't give her what she wanted, because I was too selfish. Because I was a coward. Because I was scared I'd fail at it, and I walked away rather than trying to make it work.'

KATE HARDY

'And yet you stepped up to the mark when Ty needed you,' Emmy said softly.

'I didn't have a clue what I was doing. I still don't,' he confessed wryly.

'Me, neither—but we're muddling through, and Ty definitely feels loved and settled.' She paused. 'Is that why you didn't like me? Because you thought I was flaky and selfish and just thought of myself, like your mum? Because my relationships never lasted and Ally always had to pick up the pieces?'

He bit his lip. 'I was wrong about that. But—yes, I admit, I did.'

She sighed. 'I don't blame you. I probably would've thought the same, in your shoes.' She paused. 'Is that why you think I went away? To find myself?'

'You said you needed space. Time to think.' He paused. 'I think my mum went away to find herself, because there wasn't anyone to find her.' He looked her straight in the eye. 'But I came to find you, Emmy.'

She dragged in a breath. 'I'd never dump Ty on anyone. The only reason he's with Syb is because he's asleep—and I have my mobile phone with me. She promised to call me the second he woke up, if I wasn't already back by then.'

'I know,' he said softly. 'She told me to take our time. To talk. She's wise, your great-aunt.'

She nodded.

'So why did you leave?'

'Because I was scared,' she admitted. 'I had doubts.'

'Doubts about me, or doubts about being with me?'

'I was scared that things would change. Scared that you'd compare me to Nadine and find me wanting.' She looked anguished. 'I always pick the wrong guy. It starts off well, I think it's going to work—and then I find out that there are things he doesn't like about me. Things he expects me to change. And you used to loathe me.'

Hope flooded through him. She didn't have doubts about being with him; what she doubted was herself. Which meant she needed total honesty from him. 'Yes, I used to loathe you. But that was before I knew you properly. I don't loathe you now. And I don't want to change you, Emmy. I don't want to change a single thing.' He drew her hand to his mouth and kissed it. 'I'm sorry. I should've cancelled my meeting yesterday morning and talked to you, instead.'

'You couldn't. You were late, and it was important.'

'I never thought I'd ever say this to anyone, but I don't care if it was important. You're more important to me than work,' he said.

She stared at him, as if not quite daring to believe that he meant it.

'I should've stayed with you. Better still, instead of telling you to go to sleep, the night before, I should've talked to you about what happened between us. Listened to you. Soothed your worries, and asked you to soothe mine. But I'm rubbish at the emotional stuff, so I bailed out on you. I thought it'd give me time to work out what to say.'

'Did it?'

'No,' he admitted. 'I still don't know what to say. Or how to say it without it coming out all wrong. But…' He took a deep breath. 'My world doesn't feel right without you in it.' His heart was racing. Had he got this wrong? This could all implode, become so messy. But he owed it to their future to take that risk. 'I love you, Emmy.'

Hope blossomed in her expression. 'You love me?'

'I don't know when it happened. Or how. Or why. I just know I do. And Paris clinched it for me. I finally got why they call it the City of Light. Because you were there with me, and I was so happy.' He took a deep breath. 'It isn't the same thing I felt with Nadine. You're not safe, like I thought she was. I'm not entirely sure what makes you tick. I think we're always going to have fights—you're going to think I'm stuffy and I'm going to think you're flaky. But that's OK. We can agree to disagree. What I do know is that I love you. I want to be with you. And I want you, me and Tyler to be a proper family. Maybe we could have a little brother or sister for him. If you...' He broke off. 'Sorry. That's too much pressure. I never expected to feel like this. I've made a mess of one marriage. I can't guarantee I'll get it right with you. But I'll try. Believe me, I'll try.'

She reached up and stroked his face. 'Dylan. I'm rubbish at relationships, too. It scares me that everything's going to go wrong.'

'But maybe it won't. Not if you want me the way I want you.'

'I do.'

'Are you sure?' She'd already walked away from him.

'I've worked you out, now. You're a goalpost shifter,' Emmy said. 'You never think you're good enough—and that's not your fault, it's because your mum's as selfish as my dad and she made you feel you weren't good enough. Except you are good enough. You *are*. You've got the biggest heart. And I...' She swallowed hard. 'I love you too, Dylan. So the answer's yes. Yes, I want to make you, me and Dylan a forever family. Yes, if we're blessed and when Ty's a little bit older, it might be nice to have another baby.' She smiled. 'We might even have more of a clue what we're doing as parents, the second time round.'

The trickle of hope became a flood. He dropped to one knee, not caring that the foreshore was rocky and slippery and wet. 'Emmy Jacobs, I know I ought to wait for that piece of paper to come through before I ask you, but

I can't. I want the rest of my life to start right now. Will you marry me?'

She leaned down to kiss him. 'Yes. We'll still make mistakes, Dylan. Neither of us is perfect. But we'll be in it together. We'll talk it through and we'll make it work.'

He got to his feet and kissed her lingeringly. 'You're right. And we don't have to be perfect. We just have to be ourselves. Together. I love you, Emmy.'

'I love you, too.' Her phone rang, and she smiled at him. 'I think that might be Syb. Our cue to go home.'

Home, Dylan thought. He was home at last. Because home was wherever Emmy was. 'To our baby. Because he is ours, Emmy. Just as you're mine.'

'And you're mine.'

He nodded. 'For now and forever'.

* * * * *

A BUSINESS
ENGAGEMENT

MERLINE LOVELACE

To Susan and Monroe and Debbie and Scott
and most especially, le beau Monsieur Al.
Thanks for those magical days in Paris.
Next time, I promise not to break
a foot—or anything else!

A career Air Force officer, **Merline Lovelace** served at bases all over the world. When she hung up her uniform for the last time, she decided to try her hand at storytelling. Since then more than twelve million copies of her books had been published in over thirty countries. Check her website at www.merlinelovelace.com or friend Merline on Facebook for news and information about her latest releases.

Prologue

Ah, the joys of having two such beautiful, loving granddaughters. And the worries! Eugenia, my joyful Eugenia, is like a playful kitten. She gets into such mischief but always seems to land on her feet. It's Sarah I worry about. So quiet, so elegant and so determined to shoulder the burdens of our small family. She's only two years older than her sister but has been Eugenia's champion and protector since the day those darling girls came to live with me.

Now Sarah worries about *me*. I admit to a touch of arthritis and have one annoying bout of angina, but she insists on fussing over me like a mother hen. I've told her repeatedly I won't have her putting her life on hold because of me, but she won't listen. It's time, I think, to take more direct action. I'm not quite certain at this point just what action, but something will come to me. It must.

From the diary of Charlotte,
Grand Duchess of Karlenburgh

One

Sarah heard the low buzz but didn't pay any attention to it. She was on deadline and only had until noon to finish the layout for *Beguile*'s feature on the best new ski resorts for the young and ultrastylish. She wanted to finish the mock-up in time for the senior staff's weekly working lunch. If she didn't have it ready, Alexis Danvers, the magazine's executive editor, would skewer her with one of the basilisk-like stares that had made her a legend in the world of glossy women's magazines.

Not that her boss's stony stares particularly bothered Sarah. They might put the rest of the staff in a flophouse sweat, but she and her sister had been raised by a grandmother who could reduce pompous officials or supercilious headwaiters to a quivering bundle of nerves with the lift of a single brow. Charlotte St. Sebastian had once moved in the same circles as Princess Grace and Jackie O. Those days were long gone, Sarah acknowledged, as she switched the headline font from Futura to Trajan, but Grandmama still adhered to the unshakable belief that good breeding and quiet elegance could see a woman through anything life might throw at her.

Sarah agreed completely. Which was one of the reasons she'd refined her own understated style during her three years as layout editor for a magazine aimed at thirtysomethings determined to be chic to the death. Her vintage Chanel suits and Dior gowns might come from Grandmama's closet, but she teamed the gowns with funky costume jewelry and the suit jackets with slacks or jeans and boots. The result was a stylishly retro look that even Alexis approved of.

The primary reason Sarah stuck to her own style, of course, was that she couldn't afford the designer shoes and bags and clothing featured in *Beguile*. Not with Grandmama's medical bills. Some of her hand-me-downs were starting to show their wear, though, and…

The buzz cut into her thoughts. Gaining volume, it rolled in her direction. Sarah was used to frequent choruses of oohs and aahs. Alexis often had models parade through the art and production departments to field test their hair or makeup or outfits on *Beguile*'s predominantly female staff.

Whatever was causing this chorus had to be special. Excitement crackled in the air like summer lightning. Wondering what new Jimmy Choo beaded boots or Atelier Versace gown was creating such a stir, Sarah swung her chair around. To her utter astonishment, she found herself looking up into the face of Sexy Single Number Three.

"Ms. St. Sebastian?"

The voice was cold, but the electric-blue eyes, black hair and rugged features telegraphed hot, hot, hot. Alexis had missed the mark with last month's issue, Sarah thought wildly. This man should have *topped* the magazine's annual Ten Sexiest Single Men in the World list instead of taking third place.

The artist in her could appreciate six-feet-plus of hard, muscled masculinity cloaked in the civilized veneer of a hand-tailored suit and Italian-silk tie. The professional in her responded to the coldness in his voice with equally cool civility.

"Yes?"

"I want to talk to you." Those devastating blue eyes cut to the side. "Alone."

Sarah followed his searing gaze. An entire gallery of female faces peered over, around and between the production department's chin-high partitions. A few of those faces were merely curious. Most appeared a half breath away from drooling.

She turned back to Number Three. Too bad his manners didn't live up to his looks. The aggressiveness in both his tone and his stance were irritating and uncalled for, to say the least.

"What do you want to talk to me about, Mr. Hunter?"

He didn't appear surprised that she knew his name. She did, after all, work at the magazine that had made hunky Devon Hunter the object of desire by a good portion of the female population at home and abroad.

"Your sister, Ms. St. Sebastian."

Oh, no! A sinking sensation hit Sarah in the pit of her stomach. What had Gina gotten into now?

Her glance slid to the silver-framed photo on the credenza beside her workstation. There was Sarah, dark-haired, green-eyed, serious as always, protective as always. And Gina. Blonde, bubbly, affectionate, completely irresponsible.

Two years younger than Sarah, Gina tended to change careers with the same dizzying frequency she tumbled in and out of love. She'd texted just a few days ago, gushing about the studly tycoon she'd hooked up with. Omitting, Gina style, to mention such minor details as his name or how they'd met.

Sarah had no trouble filling in the blanks now. Devon Hunter was founder and CEO of a Fortune 500 aerospace corporation headquartered in Los Angeles. Gina was in

L.A. chasing yet another career opportunity, this time as a party planner for the rich and famous.

"I think it best if we make this discussion private, Ms. St. Sebastian."

Resigned to the inevitable, Sarah nodded. Her sister's flings tended to be short and intense. Most ended amicably, but on several occasions Sarah had been forced to soothe some distinctly ruffled male feathers. This, apparently, was one of those occasions.

"Come with me, Mr. Hunter."

She led the way to a glass-walled conference room with angled windows that gave a view of Times Square. Framed prominently in one of the windows was the towering Condé Nast Building, the center of the universe for fashion publications. The building was home to *Vogue, Vanity Fair, Glamour* and *Allure*. Alexis often brought advertisers to the conference room to impress them with *Beguile*'s proximity to those icons in the world of women's glossies.

The caterers hadn't begun setting up for the working lunch yet but the conference room was always kept ready for visitors. The fridge discreetly hidden behind oak panels held a half-dozen varieties of bottled water, sparkling and plain, as well as juices and energy drinks. The gleaming silver coffee urns were replenished several times a day.

Sarah gestured to the urns on their marble counter. "Would you care for some coffee? Or some sparkling water, perhaps?"

"No. Thanks."

The curt reply decided her against inviting the man to sit. Crossing her arms, she leaned a hip against the conference table and assumed a look of polite inquiry.

"You wanted to talk about Gina?"

He took his time responding. Sarah refused to bristle as his killer blue eyes made an assessing trip from her face to her Chanel suit jacket with its black-and-white checks and signature logo to her black boots and back up again.

"You don't look much like your sister."

"No, I don't."

She was comfortable with her slender build and what her grandmother insisted were classic features, but she knew she didn't come close to Gina's stunning looks.

"My sister's the only beauty in the family."

Politeness dictated that he at least make a show of disputing the calm assertion. Instead, he delivered a completely unexpected bombshell.

"Is she also the only thief?"

Her arms dropped. Her jaw dropped with them. "I beg your pardon?"

"You can do more than beg my pardon, Ms. St. Sebastian. You can contact your sister and tell her to return the artifact she stole from my house."

The charge took Sarah's breath away. It came back on a hot rush. "How dare you make such a ridiculous, slanderous accusation?"

"It's neither ridiculous nor slanderous. It's fact."

"You're crazy!"

She was in full tigress mode now. Years of rushing to her younger sibling's defense spurred both fury and passion.

"Gina may be flighty and a little careless at times, but she would never take anything that didn't belong to her!"

Not intentionally, that is. There was that nasty little Pomeranian she'd brought home when she was eight or nine. She'd found it leashed to a sign outside a restaurant in one-hundred-degree heat and "rescued" it. And it was true Gina and her teenaged friends used to borrow clothes from each other constantly, then could never remember what belonged to whom. And, yes, she'd been known to overdraw her checking account when she was strapped for cash, which happened a little too frequently for Sarah's peace of mind.

But she would never commit theft, as this…this boor was suggesting. Sarah was about to call security to have the man escorted from the building when he reached into his suit pocket and palmed an iPhone.

"Maybe this clip from my home surveillance system will change your mind."

He tapped the screen, then angled it for Sarah to view. She saw a still image of what looked like a library or study, with the focus of the camera on an arrangement of glass shelves. The objects on the shelves were spaced and spotlighted for maximum dramatic effect. They appeared to be an eclectic mix. Sarah noted an African buffalo mask, a small cloisonné disk on a black lacquer stand and what looked like a statue of a pre-Columbian fertility goddess.

Hunter tapped the screen again and the still segued into a video. While Sarah watched, a tumble of platinum-blond curls came into view. Her heart began to thump painfully even before the owner of those curls moved toward the shelving. It picked up more speed when the owner showed her profile. That was her sister. Sarah couldn't even pretend to deny it.

Gina glanced over her shoulder, all casual nonchalance, all smiling innocence. When she moved out of view again, the cloisonné medallion no longer sat on its stand. Hunter froze the frame again, and Sarah stared at the empty stand as though it was a bad dream.

"It's Byzantine," he said drily. "Early twelfth century, in case you're interested. One very similar to it sold recently at Sotheby's in London for just over a hundred thousand."

She swallowed. Hard. "Dollars?"

"Pounds."

"Oh, God."

She'd rescued Gina from more scrapes than she could count. But this… She almost yanked out one of the chairs and collapsed in a boneless heap. The iron will she'd inherited from Grandmama kept her spine straight and her chin up.

"There's obviously a logical explanation for this, Mr. Hunter."

"I very much hope so, Ms. St. Sebastian."

She wanted to smack him. Calm, refined, always polite Sarah had to curl her hands into fists to keep from slapping that sneer off his too-handsome face.

He must have guessed her savagely suppressed urge. His jaw squared and his blue eyes took on a challenging glint, as if daring her to give it her best shot. When she didn't, he picked up where they'd left off.

"I'm very interested in hearing that explanation before I refer the matter to the police."

The police! Sarah felt a chill wash through her. Whatever predicament Gina had landed herself in suddenly assumed a very ominous tone. She struggled to keep the shock and worry out of her voice.

"Let me get in touch with my sister, Mr. Hunter. It may... it may take a while. She's not always prompt about returning calls or answering emails right away."

"Yeah, I found that out. I've been trying to reach her for several days."

He shot back a cuff and glanced at his watch.

"I've got meetings scheduled that will keep me tied up for the rest of this afternoon and well into the night. I'll make dinner reservations for tomorrow evening. Seven o'clock. Avery's, Upper West Side." He turned that hard blue gaze on her. "I assume you know the address. It's only a few blocks from the Dakota."

Still stunned by what she'd seen in the surveillance clip, Sarah almost missed his last comment. When it penetrated, her eyes widened in shock. "You know where I live?"

"Yes, Lady Sarah, I do." He tipped two fingers to his brow in a mock salute and strode for the door. "I'll see you tomorrow."

* * *

Lady Sarah.

Coming on top of everything else, the use of her empty title shouldn't have bothered her. Her boss trotted it out frequently at cocktail parties and business meetings. Sarah had stopped being embarrassed by Alexis's shameless peddling of a royal title that had long since ceased to have any relevance.

Unfortunately, Alexis wanted to do more than peddle the heritage associated with the St. Sebastian name. Sarah had threatened to quit—twice!—if her boss went ahead with the feature she wanted to on *Beguile*'s own Lady Sarah Elizabeth Marie-Adele St. Sebastian, granddaughter to Charlotte, the Destitute Duchess.

God! Sarah shuddered every time she remembered the slant Alexis had wanted to give the story. That destitute tag, as accurate as it was, would have shattered Grandmama's pride.

Having her younger granddaughter arrested for grand larceny wouldn't do a whole lot for it, either.

Jolted back to the issue at hand, Sarah rushed out of the conference room. She had to get hold of Gina. Find out if she'd really lifted that medallion. She was making a dash for her workstation when she saw her boss striding toward her.

"What's this I just heard?"

Alexis's deep, guttural smoker's rasp was always a shock to people meeting her for the first time. *Beguile*'s executive editor was paper-clip thin and always gorgeously dressed. But she would rather take her chances with cancer than quit smoking and risk ballooning up to a size four.

"Is it true?" she growled. "Devon Hunter was here?"

"Yes, he…"

"Why didn't you buzz me?"

"I didn't have time."

"What did he want? He's not going to sue us, is he?

Dammit, I told you to crop that locker-room shot above the waist."

"No, Alexis. You told me to make sure it showed his butt crack. And I told *you* I didn't think we should pay some smarmy gym employee to sneak pictures of the man without his knowledge or consent."

The executive editor waved that minor difference of editorial opinion aside. "So what did he want?"

"He's, uh, a friend of Gina's."

Or was, Sarah thought grimly, until the small matter of a twelfth-century medallion had come between them. She had to get to a phone. Had to call Gina.

"Another one of your sister's trophies?" Alexis asked sarcastically.

"I didn't have time to get all the details. Just that he's in town for some business meetings and wants to get together for dinner tomorrow."

The executive editor cocked her head. An all-too-familiar gleam entered her eyes, one that made Sarah swallow a groan. Pit bulls had nothing on Alexis when she locked her jaws on a story.

"We could do a follow-up," she said. "How making *Beguile*'s Top Ten list has impacted our sexy single's life. Hunter's pretty much a workaholic, isn't he?"

Frantic to get to the phone, Sarah gave a distracted nod. "That's how we portrayed him."

"I'm guessing he can't take a step now without tripping over a half-dozen panting females. Gina certainly smoked him out fast enough. I want details, Sarah. Details!"

She did her best to hide her agitation behind her usual calm facade. "Let me talk to my sister first. See what's going on."

"Do that. And get me details!"

Alexis strode off and Sarah barely reached the chair at her worktable before her knees gave out. She snatched up her iPhone and hit the speed-dial number for her sister. Of course, the call went to voice mail.

"Gina! I need to talk to you! Call me."

She also tapped out a text message and zinged off an email. None of which would do any good if her sister had forgotten to turn on her phone. Again. Knowing the odds of that were better than fifty-fifty, she tried Gina's current place of employment. She was put through to her sister's distinctly irate boss, who informed her that Gina hadn't shown up for work. Again.

"She called in yesterday morning. We'd catered a business dinner at the home of one our most important clients the night before. She said she was tired and was taking the day off. I haven't heard from her since."

Sarah had to ask. "Was that client Devon Hunter, by any chance?"

"Yes, it was. Look, Ms. St. Sebastian, your sister has a flair for presentation but she's completely unreliable. If you speak to her before I do, tell her not to bother coming in at all."

Despite the other, far more pressing problem that needed to be dealt with, Sarah hated that Gina had lost yet another job. She'd really seemed to enjoy this one.

"I'll tell her," she promised the irate supervisor. "And if she contacts you first, please tell her to call me."

She got through the working lunch somehow. Alexis, of course, demanded a laundry list of changes to the ski-resort layout. Drop shadows on the headline font. Less white space between the photos. Ascenders, not descenders, for the first letter of each lead paragraph.

Sarah made the fixes and shot the new layout from her computer to Alexis's for review. She then tried to frame another article describing the latest body-toning techniques. In between, she made repeated calls to Gina. They went unanswered, as did her emails and text messages.

Her concentration in shreds, she quit earlier than usual and hurried out into the April evening. A half block away, Times Square glowed in a rainbow of white, blue and brilliant-red lights. Tourists were out in full force, crowding the sidewalks and snapping pictures. Ordinarily Sarah took the subway to and from work, but a driving sense of urgency made her decide to splurge on a cab. Unbelievably, one cruised up just when she hit the curb. She slid in as soon as the previous passenger climbed out.

"The Dakota, please."

The turbaned driver nodded and gave her an assessing glance in the rearview mirror. Whatever their nationality, New York cabbies were every bit as savvy as any of *Beguile*'s fashion-conscious editors. This one might not get the label on Sarah's suit jacket exactly right but he knew quality when he saw it. He also knew a drop-off at one of New York City's most famous landmarks spelled big tips.

Usually. Sarah tried not to think how little of this month's check would be left after paying the utilities and maintenance fees for the seven-room apartment she shared with her grandmother. She also tried not to cringe when the cabbie scowled at the tip she gave him. Muttering something in his native language, he shoved his cab in gear.

Sarah hurried toward the entrance to the domed and turreted apartment building constructed in the 1880s and nodded to the doorman who stepped out of his niche to greet her.

"Good evening, Jerome."

"Good evening, Lady Sarah."

She'd long ago given up trying to get him to drop the empty title. Jerome felt it added to the luster of "his" building.

Not that the Dakota needed additional burnishing. Now a National Historic Landmark, its ornate exterior had been featured in dozens of films. Fictional characters in a host of novels claimed the Dakota as home. Real-life celebrities like Judy Garland, Lauren Bacall and Leonard Bernstein had lived there. And, sadly, John Lennon. He'd been shot just a short distance away. His widow, Yoko Ono, still owned several apartments in the building.

"The Duchess returned from her afternoon constitutional about an hour ago," Jerome volunteered. The merest hint of a shadow crossed his lean face. "She was leaning rather heavily on her cane."

Sharp, swift fear pushed aside Sarah's worry about her sister. "She didn't overdo it, did she?"

"She said not. But then, she wouldn't say otherwise, would she?"

"No," Sarah agreed in a hollow voice, "she wouldn't.

Charlotte St. Sebastian had witnessed the brutal execution of her husband and endured near-starvation before she'd escaped her war-ravaged country with her baby in her arms and a king's ransom in jewels hidden inside her daughter's teddy bear. She'd fled first to Vienna, then New York, where she'd slipped easily into the city's intellectual and social elite. The discreet, carefully timed sale of her jewels had allowed her to purchase an apartment at the Dakota and maintain a gracious lifestyle.

Tragedy struck again when she lost both her daughter and son-in-law in a boating accident. Sarah was just four and Gina still in diapers at the time. Not long after that, an unscrupulous Wall Street type sank the savings the duchess had managed to accrue into a Ponzi scheme that blew up in his and his clients' faces.

Those horrific events might have crushed a lesser woman. With two small girls to raise, Charlotte St. Sebastian wasted little time on self-pity. Once again she was forced to sell her heritage. The remaining jewels were discreetly disposed of over the years to provide her granddaughters with the education and lifestyle she insisted was their birthright. Private schools. Music tutors. Coming-out balls at the Waldorf. Smith College and a year at the Sorbonne for Sarah, Barnard for Gina.

Neither sister had a clue how desperate the financial situation had become, however, until Grandmama's heart attack. It was a mild one, quickly dismissed by the iron-spined duchess as a trifling bout of angina. The hospital charges weren't trifling, though. Nor was the stack of bills Sarah had found stuffed in Grandmama's desk when she sat down to pay what she'd thought were merely recurring monthly expenses. She'd nearly had a heart attack herself when she'd totaled up the amount.

Sarah had depleted her own savings account to pay that daunting stack of bills. Most of them, anyway. She still had to settle the charges for Grandmama's last echocardiogram. In the meantime, her single most important goal in life was to avoid stressing out the woman she loved with all her heart.

She let herself into their fifth-floor apartment, as shaken by Jerome's disclosure as by her earlier meeting with Devon Hunter. The comfortably padded Ecuadoran who served as maid, companion to Charlotte and friend to both Sarah and her sister for more than a decade was just preparing to leave.

"*Hola,* Sarah."

"*Hola,* Maria. How was your day?"

"Good. We walked, *la duquesa* and me, and shopped a little." She shouldered her hefty tote bag. "I go to catch my bus now. I'll see you tomorrow."

"Good night."

When the door closed behind her, a rich soprano voice only slightly dimmed by age called out, "Sarah? Is that you?"

"Yes, Grandmama."

She deposited her purse on the gilt-edged rococo sideboard gracing the entryway and made her way down a hall tiled in pale pink Carrara marble. The duchess hadn't been reduced to selling the furniture and artwork she'd acquired when she'd first arrived in New York, although Sarah now knew how desperately close she'd come to it.

"You're home early."

Charlotte sat in her favorite chair, the single aperitif she allowed herself despite the doctor's warning close at hand. The sight of her faded blue eyes and aristocratic nose brought a rush of emotion so strong Sarah had to swallow before she could a reply past the lump in her throat.

"Yes, I am."

She should have known Charlotte would pick up on the slightest nuance in her granddaughter's voice.

"You sound upset," she said with a small frown. "Did something happen at work?"

"Nothing more than the usual." Sarah forced a wry smile and went to pour herself a glass of white wine. "Alexis was on a tear about the ski-resort mock-up. I had to rework everything but the page count."

The duchess sniffed. "I don't know why you work for that woman."

"Mostly because she was the only one who would hire me."

"She didn't hire you. She hired your title."

Sarah winced, knowing it was true, and her grandmother instantly shifted gears.

"Lucky for Alexis the title came with an unerring eye for form, shape and spatial dimension," she huffed.

"Lucky for *me*," Sarah countered with a laugh. "Not everyone can parlay a degree in Renaissance-era art into a job at one of the country's leading fashion magazines."

"Or work her way from junior assistant to senior editor in just three years," Charlotte retorted. Her face softened into an expression that played on Sarah's heartstrings like a finely tuned Stradivarius. "Have I told you how proud I am of you?"

"Only about a thousand times, Grandmama."

They spent another half hour together before Charlotte decided she would rest a little before dinner. Sarah knew better than to offer to help her out of her chair, but she wanted to. God, she wanted to! When her grandmother's cane had thumped slowly down the hall to her bedroom, Sarah fixed a spinach salad and added a bit more liquid to the chicken Maria had begun baking in the oven. Then she washed her hands, detoured into the cavernous sitting room that served as a study and booted up her laptop.

She remembered the basics from the article *Beguile* had run on Devon Hunter. She wanted to dig deeper, uncover every minute detail she could about the man before she crossed swords with him again tomorrow evening.

Two

Seated at a linen-draped table by the window, Dev watched Sarah St. Sebastian approach the restaurant's entrance. Tall and slender, she moved with restrained grace. No swinging hips, no ground-eating strides, just a smooth symmetry of motion and dignity.

She wore her hair down tonight. He liked the way the mink-dark waves framed her face and brushed the shoulders of her suit jacket. The boxy jacket was a sort of pale purple. His sisters would probably call that color lilac or heliotrope or something equally girlie. The skirt was black and just swished her boot tops as she walked.

Despite growing up with four sisters, Dev's fashion sense could be summed up in a single word. A woman either looked good, or she didn't. This one looked good. *Very* good.

He wasn't the only one who thought so. When she entered the restaurant and the greeter escorted her to the table by the window, every head in the room turned. Males without female companions were openly admiring. Those with women at their tables were more discreet but no less appreciative. Many of the women, too, slanted those seemingly casual, careless glances that instantly catalogued every detail of hair, dress, jewelry and shoes.

How the hell did they do that? Dev could walk into the belly of a plane and tell in a single glance if the struts were buckling or the rivets starting to rust. As he'd discovered since that damned magazine article came out, however, his powers of observation paled beside those of the female of the species.

He'd treated the Ten Sexiest Singles list as a joke at first. He could hardly do otherwise, with his sisters, brothers-in-law and assorted nieces and nephews ragging him about it nonstop. And okay, being named one of the world's top ten hunks did kind of puff up his ego.

That was before women began stopping him on the street to let him know they were available. Before waitresses started hustling over to take his order and make the same pronouncement. Before the cocktail parties he was forced to attend as the price of doing business became a total embarrassment.

Dev had been able to shrug off most of it. He couldn't shrug off the wife of the French CEO he was trying to close a multibillion dollar deal with. The last time Dev was in Paris, Elise Girault had draped herself all over him. He knew then he had to put a stop to what had become more than just a nuisance.

He'd thought he'd found the perfect tool in Lady Eugenia Amalia Therése St. Sebastian. The blonde was gorgeous, vivacious and so photogenic that the vultures otherwise known as paparazzi wouldn't even glance at Dev if she was anywhere in the vicinity.

Thirty minutes in Gina St. Sebastian's company had deep-sixed that idea. Despite her pedigree, the woman was as bubbleheaded as she was sumptuous. Then she'd lifted the Byzantine medallion and the game plan had changed completely. For the better, Dev decided as he rose to greet the slender brunette being escorted to his table.

Chin high, shoulders back, Sarah St. Sebastian carried herself like the royalty she was. Or would have been, if her grandmother's small Eastern European country hadn't dispensed with royal titles about the same time Soviet tanks had rumbled across its border. The tanks had rumbled out again four decades later. By that time the borders of Eastern Europe had been redrawn several times and the duchy that had been home to the St. Sebastians for several centuries had completely disappeared.

Bad break for Charlotte St. Sebastian and her granddaughters. Lucky break for Dev. Lady Sarah didn't know it yet, but she was going to extract him from the mess she and her magazine had created.

"Good evening, Mr. Hunter."

The voice was cool, the green eyes cold.

"Good evening, Ms. St. Sebastian."

Dev stood patiently while the greeter seated her. A server materialized instantly.

"A cocktail or glass of wine before dinner, madam?"

"No, thank you. And no dinner." She waved aside the gilt-edged menu he offered and locked those forest-glade eyes on Dev. "I'll just be here a few minutes, then I'll leave Mr. Hunter to enjoy his meal."

The server departed, and Dev reclaimed his seat. "Are you sure you don't want dinner?"

"I'm sure." She placed loosely clasped hands on the table and launched an immediate offensive. "We're not here to exchange pleasantries, Mr. Hunter."

Dev sat back against his chair, his long legs outstretched beneath the starched tablecloth and his gaze steady on her face. Framed by those dark, glossy waves, her features fascinated him. The slight widow's peak, the high cheekbones, the aquiline nose—all refined and remote and in seeming contrast to those full, sensual lips. She might have modeled for some famous fifteenth- or sixteen-century sculptor. Dev was damned if he knew which.

"No, we're not," he agreed, still intrigued by that face. "Have you talked to your sister?"

The clasped hands tightened. Only a fraction, but that small jerk was a dead giveaway.

"I haven't been able to reach her."

"Neither have I. So what do you propose we do now?"

"I propose you wait." She drew in a breath and forced a small smile. "Give me more time to track Gina down before you report your medallion missing or...or..."

"Or stolen?"

The smile evaporated. "Gina didn't steal that piece, Mr. Hunter. I admit it appears she took it for some reason, but I'm sure...I *know* she'll return it. Eventually."

Dev played with the tumbler containing his scotch, circling it almost a full turn before baiting the trap.

"The longer I wait to file a police report, Ms. St. Sebastian, the more my insurance company is going to question why. A delay reporting the loss could void the coverage."

"Give me another twenty-four hours, Mr. Hunter. Please."

She hated to beg. He heard it in her voice, saw it in the way her hands were knotted together now, the knuckles white.

"All right, Ms. St. Sebastian. Twenty-four hours. If your sister hasn't returned the medallion by then, however, I..."

"She will. I'm sure she will."

"And if she doesn't?"

She drew in another breath: longer, shakier. "I'll pay you the appraised value."

"How?"

Her chin came up. Her jaws went tight. "It will take some time," she admitted. "We'll have to work out a payment schedule."

Dev didn't like himself much at the moment. If he didn't have a multibillion-dollar deal hanging fire, he'd call this farce off right now. Setting aside the crystal tumbler, he leaned forward.

"Let's cut to the chase here, Ms. St. Sebastian. I had my people run an in-depth background check on your feather-headed sister. On you, too. I know you've bailed Gina out of one mess after another. I know you're currently providing your grandmother's sole support. I also know you barely make enough to cover her medical co-pays, let alone re-imburse me for a near-priceless artifact."

Every vestige of color had drained from her face, but pride sparked in those mesmerizing eyes. Before she could tell him where to go and how to get there, Dev sprang the trap.

"I have an alternate proposal, Ms. St. Sebastian."

Her brows snapped together. "What kind of a proposal?"

"I need a fiancée."

For the second time in as many days Dev saw her composure crumble. Her jaw dropping, she treated him to a disbelieving stare.

"Excuse me?"

"I need a fiancée," he repeated. "I was considering Gina for the position. I axed that idea after thirty minutes in her company. Becoming engaged to your sister," he drawled, "is not for the faint of heart."

He might have stunned her with his proposition. That didn't prevent her from leaping to the defense. Dev suspected it came as natural to her as breathing.

"My sister, Mr. Hunter, is warm and generous and open-hearted and…"

"Gone to ground." He drove the point home with the same swift lethality he brought to the negotiating table. "You, on the other hand, are available. And you owe me."

"*I* owe you?"

"You and that magazine you work for." Despite his best efforts to keep his irritation contained, it leaked into his voice. "Do you have any idea how many women have accosted me since that damned article came out? I can't even grab a meatball sub at my favorite deli without some female writing her number on a napkin and trying to stuff it into my pants pocket."

Her shock faded. Derision replaced it. She sat back in her chair with her lips pooched in false sympathy.

"Ooh. You poor, poor sex object."

"You may think it's funny," he growled. "I don't. Not with a multibillion-dollar deal hanging in the balance."

That wiped the smirk off her face. "Putting you on our Ten Sexiest Singles list has impacted your business? How?"

Enlightenment dawned in almost the next breath. The smirk returned. "Oh! Wait! I've got it. You have so many women throwing themselves at you that you can't concentrate."

"You're partially correct. But it's not a matter of not being able to concentrate. It's more that I don't want to jeopardize the deal by telling the wife of the man I'm negotiating with to keep her hands to herself."

"So instead of confronting the woman, you want to hide behind a fiancée."

The disdain was cool and well-bred, but it was there. Dev was feeling the sting when he caught a flutter of movement from the corner of one eye. A second later the flutter evolved into a tall, sleek redhead being shown to an empty table a little way from theirs. She caught Dev's glance, arched a penciled brow and came to a full stop beside their table.

"I know you." She tilted her head and put a finger to her chin. "Remind me. Where have we met?"

"We haven't," Dev replied, courteous outside, bracing inside.

"Are you sure? I never forget a face. Or," she added as her lips curved in a slow, feline smile, "a truly excellent butt."

The grimace that crossed Hunter's face gave Sarah a jolt

of fierce satisfaction. Let him squirm, she thought glee-
fully. Let him writhe like a specimen under a microscope.
He deserved the embarrassment.

Except...

He didn't. Not really. *Beguile* had put him under the microscope. *Beguile* had also run a locker-room photo with
the face angled away from the camera just enough to keep
them from getting sued. And as much as Sarah hated to
admit it, the man had shown a remarkable degree of restraint by not reporting his missing artifact to the police
immediately.

Still, she didn't want to come to his rescue. She *really*
didn't. It was an innate and very grudging sense of fair
play that compelled her to mimic her grandmother in one
of Charlotte's more imperial moods.

"I beg your pardon," she said with icy hauteur. "I believe my fiancé has already stated he doesn't know you.
Now, if you don't mind, we would like to continue our
conversation."

The woman's cheeks flushed almost the same color as
her hair. "Yes, of course. Sorry for interrupting."

She hurried to her table, leaving Hunter staring after her
while Sarah took an unhurried sip from her water goblet.

"That's it." He turned back to her, amusement slashing
across his face. "That's exactly what I want from you."

Whoa! Sarah gripped the goblet's stem and tried to blunt
the impact of the grin aimed in her direction. Devon Hunter
all cold and intimidating she could handle. Devon Hunter
with crinkly squint lines at the corners of those killer blue
eyes and his mouth tipped into a rakish smile was something else again.

The smile made him look so different. That, and the
more casual attire he wore tonight. He was in a suit again,
but he'd dispensed with a tie and his pale blue shirt was
open at the neck. This late in the evening, a five-o'clock
shadow darkened his cheeks and chin, giving him the so-

phisticated bad-boy look so many of *Beguile*'s male models tried for but could never quite pull off.

The research Sarah had done on the man put him in a different light, too. She'd had to dig hard for details. Hunter was notorious about protecting his privacy, which was why *Beguile* had been forced to go with a fluff piece instead of the in-depth interview Alexis had wanted. And no doubt why he resented the article so much, Sarah acknowledged with a twinge of guilt.

The few additional details she'd managed to dig up had contributed to an intriguing picture. She'd already known that Devon Hunter had enlisted in the Air Force right out of high school and trained as a loadmaster on big cargo jets. She hadn't known he'd completed a bachelor's *and* a master's during his eight years in uniform, despite spending most of those years flying into combat zones or disaster areas.

On one of those combat missions his aircraft had come under intense enemy fire. Hunter had jerry-rigged some kind of emergency fix to its damaged cargo ramp that had allowed them to take on hundreds of frantic Somalian refugees attempting to escape certain death. He'd left the Air Force a short time later and patented the modification he'd devised. From what Sarah could gather, it was now used on military and civilian aircraft worldwide.

That enterprise had earned Hunter his first million. The rest, as they say, was history. She hadn't found a precise estimate of the man's net worth, but it was obviously enough to allow him to collect hundred-thousand-pound museum pieces. Which brought her back to the problem at hand.

"Look, Mr. Hunter, this whole…"

"Dev," he interrupted, the grin still in place. "Now that we're engaged, we should dispense with the formalities. I know you have a half-dozen names. Do you go by Sarah or Elizabeth or Marie-Adele?"

"Sarah," she conceded, "but we are *not* engaged."

He tipped his chin toward the woman several tables away, her nose now buried in a menu. "Red there thinks we are."

"I simply didn't care for her attitude."

"Me, either." The amusement left his eyes. "That's why I offered you a choice. Let me spell out the basic terms so there's no misunderstanding. You agree to an engagement. Six months max. Less, if I close the deal currently on the table. In return, I destroy the surveillance tape and don't report the loss."

"But the medallion! You said it was worth a hundred thousand pounds or more."

"I'm willing to accept your assurances that Gina will return it. Eventually. In the meantime..." He lifted his tumbler in a mock salute. "To us, Sarah."

Feeling much like the proverbial mouse backed into a corner, she snatched at her last lifeline. "You promised me another twenty-four hours. The deal doesn't go into effect until then. Agreed?"

He hesitated, then lifted his shoulders in a shrug. "Agreed."

Surely Gina would return her calls before then and this whole, ridiculous situation would be resolved. Sarah clung to that hope as she pushed away from the table.

"Until tomorrow, Mr. Hunter."

"Dev," he corrected, rising, as well.

"No need for you to walk me out. Please stay and enjoy your dinner."

"Actually, I got hungry earlier and grabbed a Korean taco from a street stand. Funny," he commented as he tossed some bills on the table, "I've been in and out of Korea a dozen times. Don't remember ever having tacos there."

He took her elbow in a courteous gesture Grandmama would approve of. Very correct, very polite, not really possessive but edging too close to it for Sarah's comfort. Walking beside him only reinforced the impression she'd gained yesterday of his height and strength.

They passed the redhead's table on the way to the door. She glanced up, caught Sarah's dismissive stare and stuck her nose back in the menu.

"I'll hail you a cab," Hunter said as they exited the restaurant.

"It's only a few blocks."

"It's also getting dark. I know this is your town, but I'll feel better sending you home in a cab."

Sarah didn't argue further, mostly because dusk had started to descend and the air had taken on a distinct chill. Across the street, the lanterns in Central Park shed their golden glow. She turned in a half circle, her artist's eye delighting in the dots of gold punctuating the deep purple of the park.

Unfortunately, the turn brought the redhead into view again. The picture there wasn't as delightful. She was squinting at them through the restaurant's window, a phone jammed to her ear. Whoever she was talking to was obviously getting an earful.

Sarah guessed instantly she was spreading the word about Sexy Single Number Three and his fiancée. The realization gave her a sudden, queasy feeling. New York City lived and breathed celebrities. They were the stuff of life on *Good Morning America,* were courted by Tyra Banks and the women of *The View,* appeared regularly on *Late Show with David Letterman*. The tabloids, the glossies, even the so-called "literary" publications paid major bucks for inside scoops.

And Sarah had just handed them one. Thoroughly disgusted with herself for yielding to impulse, she smothered a curse that would have earned a sharp reprimand from Grandmama. Hunter followed her line of sight and spotted the woman staring at them through the restaurant window, the phone still jammed to her ear. He shared Sarah's pessimistic view of the matter but didn't bother to swallow his curse. It singed the night air.

"This is going turn up in another rag like *Beguile,* isn't it?"

Sarah stiffened. True, she'd privately cringed at some of the articles Alexis had insisted on putting in print. But that didn't mean she would stand by and let an outsider disparage her magazine.

"*Beguile* is hardly a rag. We're one of the leading fashion publications for women in the twenty to thirty-five age range, here and abroad."

"If you say so."

"I do," she ground out.

The misguided sympathy she'd felt for the man earlier had gone as dry and stale as yesterday's bagel. It went even staler when he turned to face her. Devon Hunter of the crinkly squint lines and heart-stuttering grin was gone. His intimidating alter ego was back.

"I guess if we're going to show up in some pulp press, we might as well give the story a little juice."

She saw the intent in his face and put up a warning palm. "Let's not do anything rash here, Mr. Hunter."

"Dev," he corrected, his eyes drilling into hers. "Say it, Sarah. Dev."

"All right! Dev. Are you satisfied?"

"Not quite."

His arm went around her waist. One swift tug brought them hip to hip. His hold was an iron band, but he gave her a second, maybe two, to protest.

Afterward Sarah could list in precise order the reasons she should have done exactly that. She didn't like the man. He was flat-out blackmailing her with Gina's rash act. He was too arrogant, and too damned sexy, for his own good.

But right then, right there, she looked up into those

dangerous blue eyes and gave in to the combustible mix of guilt, nagging worry and Devon Hunter's potent masculinity.

Three

Sarah had been kissed before. A decent number of times, as a matter of fact. She hadn't racked up as many admirers as Gina, certainly, but she'd dated steadily all through high school and college. She'd also teetered dangerously close to falling in love at least twice. Once with the sexy Italian she'd met at the famed Uffizi Gallery and spent a dizzying week exploring Florence with. Most recently with a charismatic young lawyer who had his eye set on a career in politics. That relationship had died a rather painful death when she discovered he was more in love with her background and empty title than he was with her.

Even with the Italian, however, she'd never indulged in embarrassingly public displays of affection. In addition to Grandmama's black-and-white views of correct behavior, Sarah's inbred reserve shied away from the kind of exuberant joie de vivre that characterized her sister. Yet here she was, locked in the arms of a near stranger on the sidewalk of one of New York's busiest avenues. Her oh-so-proper self shouted that she was providing a sideshow for everyone in and outside the restaurant. Her other self, the one she let off its leash only on rare occasions, leaped to life.

If *Beguile* ever ran a list of the World's Ten Best Kissers, she thought wildly, she would personally nominate Devon Hunter for the top slot. His mouth fit over hers as though it was made to. His lips demanded a response.

Sarah gave it. Angling her head, she planted both palms on his chest. The hard muscles under his shirt and suit coat provided a feast of tactile sensations. The fine bristles scraping her chin added more. She could taste the faint, smoky hint of scotch on his lips, feel the heat that rose in his skin.

There was nothing hidden in Hunter's kiss. No attempt to impress or connect or score a victory in the battle of the sexes. His mouth moved easily over hers. Confidently. Hungrily.

Her breath came hard and fast when he raised his head. So did his. Sarah took immense satisfaction in that—and the fact that he looked as surprised and disconcerted as she felt at the moment. When his expression switched to a frown, though, she half expected a cutting remark. What she got was a curt apology.

"I'm sorry." He dropped his hold on her waist and stepped back a pace. "That was uncalled for."

Sarah wasn't about to point out that she hadn't exactly resisted. While she struggled to right her rioting senses, she caught a glimpse of a very interested audience backlit inside the restaurant. Among them was the redhead, still watching avidly, only this time she had her phone aimed in their direction.

"Uncalled for or not," Sarah said with a small groan, "be prepared for the possibility that kiss might make its way into print. I suspect your friend's phone is camera equipped."

He shot a glance over his shoulder and blew out a disgusted breath. "I'm sure it is."

"What a mess," she murmured half under her breath. "My boss will *not* be happy."

Hunter picked up on the ramifications of the comment instantly. "Is this going to cause a problem for you at work? You and me, our engagement, getting scooped by some other rag, uh, magazine?"

"First, we're not engaged. Yet. Second, you don't need to worry about my work."

Mostly because he wouldn't be on scene when the storm hit. If *Beguile*'s executive editor learned from another source that Sarah had locked lips with Number Three on busy Central Park West, she'd make a force-five hurricane seem like a spring shower.

Then there was the duchess.

"I'm more concerned about my grandmother," Sarah admitted reluctantly. "If she should see or hear something before I get this mess straightened out…"

She gnawed on her lower lip, trying to find a way out of what was looking more and more like the kind of dark, tangly thing you find at the bottom of a pond. To her surprise, Hunter offered a solution to at least one of her problems.

"Tell you what," he said slowly. "Why don't I take you home tonight? You can introduce me to your grandmother. That way, whatever happens next won't come as such a bolt from the blue."

It was a measure of how desperate Sarah was feeling that she actually considered the idea.

"I don't think so," she said after a moment. "I don't want to complicate the situation any more at this point."

"All right. I'm staying at the Waldorf. Call me when you've had time to consider my proposal. If I don't hear from you within twenty-four hours, I'll assume your tacit agreement."

With that parting shot, he stepped to the curb and flagged down a cab for her. Sarah slid inside, collapsed against the seat and spent the short ride to the Dakota alternately feeling the aftereffects of that kiss, worrying about her sister and cursing the mess Gina had landed her in.

When she let herself in to the apartment, Maria was emptying the dishwasher just prior to leaving.

"*Hola*, Sarah."

"*Hola*, Maria. How did it go today?"

"Well. We walk in the park this afternoon."

She tucked the last plate in the cupboard and let the dishwasher close with a quiet whoosh. The marble counter got a final swipe.

"We didn't expect you home until late," the housekeeper commented as she reached for the coat she'd draped over a kitchen chair. "*La duquesa* ate an early dinner and retired to her room. She dozed when I checked a few minutes ago."

"Okay, Maria. Thanks."

"You're welcome, *chica*." The Ecuadoran shrugged into her coat and hefted her suitcase-size purse. Halfway to the hall, she turned back. "I almost forgot. Gina called."

"*When!*"

"About a half hour ago. She said you texted her a couple times."

"A couple? Try ten or twenty."

"Ah, well." A fond smile creased the maid's plump cheeks. "That's Gina."

"Yes, it is," Sarah agreed grimly. "Did she mention where she was?"

"At the airport in Los Angeles. She said she just wanted to make sure everything was all right before she got on the plane."

"What plane? Where was she going?"

Maria's face screwed up in concentration. "Switzerland, I think she said. Or maybe…Swaziland?"

Knowing Gina, it could be either. Although, Sarah thought on a sudden choke of panic, Europe probably boasted better markets for twelfth-century Byzantine artifacts.

She said a hurried good-night to Maria and rummaged

frantically in her purse for her phone. She had to catch her sister before her plane took off.

When she got the phone out, the little green text icon indicated she had a text message. And she'd missed hearing the alert. Probably because she was too busy letting Devon Hunter kiss her all the way into next week.

The message was brief and typical Gina.

Met the cuddliest ski instructor.
Off to Switzerland. Later.

Hoping against hope it wasn't too late, Sarah hit speed dial. The call went immediately to voice mail. She tried texting and stood beside the massive marble counter, scowling at the screen, willing the little icon to pop back a response.

No luck. Gina had obviously powered down her phone. If she ran true to form, she would forget to power the damned thing back up for hours—maybe days—after she landed in Switzerland.

Sarah could almost hear a loud, obnoxious clock ticking inside her head as she went to check on her grandmother. Hunter had given her an additional twenty-four hours. Twenty-three now, and counting.

She knocked lightly on the door, then opened it as quietly as she could. The duchess sat propped against a bank of pillows. Her eyes were closed and an open book lay in her lap.

The anxiety gnawing at Sarah's insides receded for a moment, edged aside by the love that filled her like liquid warmth. She didn't see her grandmother's thin, creased cheeks or the liver spots sprinkled across the back of her hands. She saw the woman who'd opened her heart and her arms to two scared little girls. Charlotte St. Sebastian had nourished and educated them. She'd also shielded them from as much of the world's ugliness as she could. Now it was Sarah's turn to do the same.

She tried to ease the book out of the duchess's lax fingers without waking her. She didn't succeed. Charlotte's papery eyelids fluttered up. She blinked a couple of times to focus and smiled.

"How was your dinner?"

Sarah couldn't lie, but she could dodge a bit. "The restaurant was definitely up to your standards. We'll have to go there for your birthday."

"Never mind my birthday." She patted the side of the bed. "Sit down and tell me about this friend of Eugenia's. Do you think there's anything serious between them?"

Hunter was serious, all right. Just not in any way Charlotte would approve of.

"They're not more than casual acquaintances. In fact, Gina sent me a text earlier this evening. She's off to Switzerland with the cuddliest ski instructor. Her words, not mine."

"That girl," Charlotte huffed. "She'll be the death of me yet."

Not if Sarah could help it. The clock was pounding away inside her head, though. In desperation, she took Hunter's advice and decided to lay some tentative groundwork for whatever might come tomorrow.

"I actually know him better than Gina does, Grandmama."

"The ski instructor?"

"The man I met at the restaurant this evening. Devon Hunter." Despite everything, she had to smile. "You know him, too. He came in at Number Three on our Ten Sexiest Singles list."

"Oh, for heaven's sake, Sarah. You know I only peruse *Beguile* to gain an appreciation for your work. I don't pay any attention to the content."

"I guess it must have been Maria who dog-eared that particular section," she teased.

Charlotte tipped her aristocratic nose. The gesture was

instinctive and inbred and usually preceded a withering set-down. To Sarah's relief, the nose lowered a moment later and a smile tugged at her grandmother's lips.

"Is he as hot in real life as he is in print?"

"Hotter." She drew a deep mental breath. "Which is why I kissed him outside the restaurant."

"You kissed him? In public?" Charlotte *tch-tched,* but it was a halfhearted effort. Her face had come alive with interest. "That's so déclassé, dearest."

"Yes, I know. Even worse, there was a totally obnoxious woman inside the restaurant. She recognized Devon and made a rather rude comment. I suspect she may have snapped a picture or two. The kiss may well show up in some tabloid."

"I should hope not!"

Her lips thinning, the duchess contemplated that distasteful prospect for a moment before making a shrewd observation.

"Alexis will throw a world-class tantrum if something like this appears in any magazine but hers. You'd best fore-warn her."

"I intend to." She glanced at the pillbox and crystal water decanter on the marble-topped nightstand. "Did you take your medicine?"

"Yes, I did."

"Are you sure? Sometimes you doze off and forget."

"I took it, Sarah. Don't fuss at me."

"It's my job to fuss." She leaned forward and kissed a soft, lily-of-the-valley-scented cheek. "Good night, Grand-mama."

"Good night."

She got as far as the bedroom door. Close, so close, to making an escape. She had one hand on the latch when the duchess issued an imperial edict.

"Bring this Mr. Hunter by for drinks tomorrow evening, Sarah. I would like to meet him."

"I'm not certain what his plans are."

"Whatever they are," Charlotte said loftily, "I'm sure he can work in a brief visit."

Sarah went to sleep trying to decide which would be worse: entering into a fake engagement, informing Alexis that a tabloid might beat *Beguile* to a juicy story involving one of its own editors or continuing to feed her grandmother half-truths.

The first thing she did when she woke up the next morning was grab her cell phone. No text from Gina. No email. No voice message.

"You're a dead woman," she snarled at her absent sibling. "Dead!"

Throwing back the covers, she stomped to the bathroom. Like the rest of the rooms in the apartment, it was high ceilinged and trimmed with elaborate crown molding. Most of the fixtures had been updated over the years, but the tub was big and claw-footed and original. Sarah indulged in long, decadent soaks whenever she could. This morning she was too keyed up and in too much of a hurry for anything more than a quick shower.

Showered and blow-dried, she chose one of her grandmama's former favorites—a slate-gray Pierre Balmain minidress in a classic A-line. According to Charlotte, some women used to pair these thigh-skimming dresses with white plastic go-go boots. *She* never did, of course. Far too gauche. She'd gone with tasteful white stockings and Ferragamo pumps. Sarah opted for black tights, a pair of Giuseppi Zanottis she'd snatched up at a secondhand shoe store and multiple strands of fat faux pearls.

Thankfully, the duchess preferred a late, leisurely breakfast with Maria, so Sarah downed her usual bagel and black coffee and left for work with only a quick goodbye.

She got another reprieve at work. Alexis had called in to say she was hopping an early shuttle to Chicago for a short-notice meeting with the head of their publishing group. And to Sarah's infinite relief, a computer search of stories in print for the day didn't pop with either her name or a lurid blowup of her wrapped in Devon Hunter's arms.

That left the rest of the day to try to rationalize her unexpected reaction to his kiss and make a half-dozen futile attempts to reach Gina. All the while the clock marched steadily, inexorably toward her deadline.

Dev shot a glance at the bank of clocks lining one wall of the conference room. Four-fifteen. A little less than four hours to the go/no-go point.

He tuned out the tanned-and-toned executive at the head of the gleaming mahogany conference table. The man had been droning on for almost forty minutes now. His equally slick associates had nodded and ahemed and interjected several editorial asides about the fat military contract they were confident their company would win.

Dev knew better. They'd understated their start-up costs so blatantly the Pentagon procurement folks would laugh these guys out of the competition. Dev might have chalked this trip to NYC as a total waste of time if not for his meeting with Sarah St. Sebastian.

Based on the profile he'd had compiled on her, he'd expected someone cool, confident, levelheaded and fiercely loyal to both the woman who'd raised her and the sibling who gave her such grief. What he hadn't expected was her inbred elegance. Or the kick to his gut when she'd walked into the restaurant last night. Or the hours he'd spent afterward remembering her taste and her scent and the press of her body against his.

His visceral reaction to the woman could be a potential glitch in his plan. He needed a decoy. A temporary fiancée to blunt the effect of that ridiculous article. Someone to act as a buffer between him and the total strangers hitting on him everywhere he went—and the French CEO's wife who'd whispered such suggestive obscenities in his ear.

Sarah St. Sebastian was the perfect solution to those embarrassments. She'd proved as much last night when she'd cut Red off at the knees. Problem was the feel of her, the taste of her, had damned near done the same to Dev. The delectable Sarah could well prove more of a distraction than the rest of the bunch rolled up together.

So what the hell should he do now? Call her and tell her the deal he'd offered was no longer on the table? Write off the loss of the medallion? Track Gina down and recover the piece himself?

The artifact itself wasn't the issue, of course. Dev had lost more in the stock market in a single day than that bit of gold and enamel was worth. The only reason he'd pursued it this far was that he didn't like getting ripped off any more than the next guy. That, and the damned Ten Sexiest Singles article. He'd figured he could leverage the theft of the medallion into a temporary fiancée.

Which brought him full circle. What should he do about Sarah? His conscience had pinged at him last night. It was lobbing 50mm mortar shells now.

Dev had gained a rep in the multibillion-dollar world of aerospace manufacturing for being as tough as boot leather, but honest. He'd never lied to a competitor or grossly underestimated a bid like these jokers were doing now. Nor had he ever resorted to blackmail. Dev shifted uncomfortably, feeling as prickly about the one-sided deal he'd offered Sarah as by the patently false estimates Mr. Smooth kept flashing up on the screen.

To hell with it. He could take care of at least one of those itches right now.

"Excuse me, Jim."

Tanned-and-toned broke off in midspiel. He and his associates turned eager faces to Dev.

"We'll have to cut this short," he said without a trace of

apology. "I've got something hanging fire that I thought could wait. I need to take care of it now."

Jim and company concealed their disappointment behind shark-toothed smiles. Professional courtesy dictated that Devon offer a palliative.

"Why don't you email me the rest of your presentation? I'll study it on the flight home."

Tanned-and-toned picked up an in-house line and murmured an order to his AV folks. When he replaced the receiver, his smile sat just a few degrees off center.

"It's done, Dev."

"Thanks, Jimmy. I'll get back to you when I've had a chance to review your numbers in a little more depth."

Ole Jim's smile slipped another couple of degrees but he managed to hang on to its remnants as he came around the table to pump Devon's hand.

"I'll look forward to hearing from you. Soon, I hope."

"By the end of the week," Devon promised, although he knew Mr. Smooth wouldn't like what he had to say.

He decided to wait until he was in the limo and headed back to his hotel to contact Sarah. As the elevator whisked him down fifty stories, he tried to formulate exactly what he'd say to her.

His cell phone buzzed about twenty stories into the descent. Dev answered with his customary curt response, blissfully unaware a certain green-eyed brunette was just seconds away from knocking his world off its axis.

"Hunter."

"Mr. Hunter… Dev… It's Sarah St. Sebastian."

"Hello, Sarah. Have you heard from Gina?"

"Yes. Well, sort of."

Hell! So much for his nagging guilt over coercing this woman into a fake engagement. All Devon felt now was a searing disappointment that it might not take place. The feeling was so sharp and surprisingly painful he almost missed her next comment.

"Gina's on her way to Switzerland. Or she was when she texted me last night."

"What's in…?"

He broke off, knowing the answer before he asked the question. Bankers in Switzerland would commit hara-kiri before violating the confidentiality of deals brokered under their auspices. What better place to sell—and deposit the proceeds of—a near-priceless piece of antiquity?

"So where does that leave us?"

It came out stiffer than he'd intended. She responded in the same vein.

"I'm still trying to reach Gina. If I can't…"

The elevator reached the lobby. Dev stepped out, the phone to his ear and his adrenaline pumping the way it did when his engineers were close to some innovative new concept or major modification to the business of hauling cargo.

"If you can't?" he echoed.

"I don't see I have any choice but to agree to your preposterous offer."

She spelled it out. Slowly. Tightly. As if he'd forgotten the conditions he'd laid down last night.

"Six months as your fiancée. Less if you complete the negotiations you're working on. In return, you don't press charges against my sister. Correct?"

"Correct." Crushing his earlier doubts, he pounced. "So we have a deal?"

"On one condition."

A dozen different contingency clauses flashed through his mind. "And that is?" he said cautiously.

"You have to come for cocktails this evening. Seven o'clock. My grandmother wants to meet you."

Four

Dev frowned at his image in the elevator's ornate mirror and adjusted his tie. He was damned if he knew why he was so nervous about meeting Charlotte St. Sebastian.

He'd flown into combat zones more times than he could count, for God's sake. He'd also participated in relief missions to countries devastated by fires, tsunamis, earthquakes, horrific droughts and bloody civil wars. More than once his aircraft had come under enemy fire. And he still carried the scar from the hit he'd taken while racing through a barrage of bullets to get a sobbing, desperate mother and her wounded child aboard before murderous rebels overran the airport.

Those experiences had certainly shaped Dev's sense of self. Building an aerospace design-and-manufacturing empire from the ground up only solidified that self-confidence. He now rubbed elbows with top-level executives and power brokers around the world. Charlotte St. Sebastian wouldn't be the first royal he'd met, or even the highest ranking.

Yet the facts Dev had gathered about the St. Sebastian family painted one hell of an intimidating picture of its matriarch. The woman had once stood next in line to rule a duchy with a history that spanned some seven hundred years. She'd been forced to witness her husband's execution by firing squad. Most of her remaining family had disappeared forever in the notorious gulags. Charlotte herself had gone into hiding with her infant daughter and endured untold hardships before escaping to the West.

That would be heartbreak enough for anyone. Yet the duchess had also been slammed with the tragic death of her daughter and son-in-law, then had raised her two young granddaughters alone. Few, if any, of her friends and acquaintances were aware that she maintained only the facade of what appeared to be a luxurious lifestyle. Dev knew because he'd made it his business to learn everything he could about the St. Sebastians after beautiful, bubbly Lady Eugenia had lifted the Byzantine medallion.

He could have tracked Gina down. Hell, anyone with a modicum of computer smarts could track a GPS-equipped cell phone these days. Dev had considered doing just that until he'd realized her elder sister was better suited for his purposes. Plus, there was the bonus factor of where Sarah St. Sebastian worked. It had seemed only fair that he get a little revenge for the annoyance caused by that article.

Except, he thought as he exited the elevator, revenge had a way of coming back to bite you in the ass. What had seemed like a solid plan when he'd first devised it was now generating some serious doubts. Could he keep his hands off the elegant elder sister and stick to the strict terms of their agreement? Did he want to?

The doubts dogged him right up until he pressed the button for the doorbell. He heard a set of melodic chimes, and his soon-to-be fiancée opened the door to him.

"Hello, Mr.... Dev."

She was wearing chunky pearls, a thigh-skimming little dress and black tights tonight. The pearls and gray dress gave her a personal brand of sophistication, but the tights showcased her legs in a way that made Dev's throat go bone-dry. He managed to untangle his tongue long enough to return her greeting.

"Hello, Sarah."

"Please, come in."

She stood aside to give him access to a foyer longer than the belly of a C-17 and almost as cavernous. Marble tiles, ornate wall sconces, a gilt-edged side table and a crystal bowl filled with something orange blossomy. Dev absorbed the details along with the warning in Sarah's green eyes.

"I've told my grandmother that you and Gina are no more than casual acquaintances," she confided in a low voice.

"That's true enough."

"Yes, well…" She drew in a breath and squared shoulders molded by gray silk. "Let's get this over with."

She led the way down the hall. Dev followed and decided the rear view was as great as the front. The dress hem swayed just enough to tease and tantalize. The tights clung faithfully to the curve of her calves.

He was still appreciating the view when she showed him into a high-ceilinged room furnished with a mix of antiques and a few pieces of modern technology. The floor here was parquet; the wood was beautifully inlaid, but cried for the cushioning of a soft, handwoven carpet to blunt some of its echo. Windows curtained in pale blue velvet took up most of two walls and gave what Dev guessed was one hell of a view of Central Park. Flames danced in the massive fireplace fronted in black marble that dominated a third wall.

A sofa was angled to catch the glow from the fire. Two high-backed armchairs faced the sofa across a monster coffee table inset with more marble. The woman on one of those chairs sat ramrod straight, with both palms resting on the handle of an ebony cane. Her gray hair was swept up into a curly crown and anchored by ivory combs. Lace wrapped her throat like a muffler and was anchored by a cameo brooch. Her hawk's eyes skewered Dev as he crossed the room.

Sarah summoned a bright smile and performed the introductions. "Grandmama, this is Devon Hunter."

"How do you do, Mr. Hunter?"

The duchess held out a veined hand. Dev suspected that courtiers had once dropped to a knee and kissed it reverently. He settled for taking it gently in his.

"It's a pleasure to meet you, ma'am. Gina told me she'd inherited her stunning looks from her grandmother. She obviously had that right."

"Indeed?" Her chin lifted. Her nose angled up a few degrees. "You know Eugenia well, then?"

"She coordinated a party for me. We spoke on a number of occasions."

"Do sit down, Mr. Hunter." She waved him to the chair across from hers. "Sarah, dearest, please pour Mr. Hunter a drink."

"Certainly. What would you like, Dev?"

"Whatever you and your grandmother are having is fine."

"I'm having white wine." Her smile tipped into one of genuine affection as she moved to a side table containing an opened bottle of wine nested in a crystal ice bucket and an array of decanters. "Grandmama, however, is ignoring her doctor's orders and sipping an abominable brew concocted by our ancestors back in the sixteenth century."

"Žuta Osa is hardly abominable, Sarah," the duchess countered. She lifted a tiny liqueur glass and swirled its amber-colored contents before treating her guest to a bland look. "It simply requires a strong constitution."

Dev recognized a challenge when one smacked him in the face. "I'll give it a try."

"Are you sure?" Sarah shot him a warning glance from behind the drinks table. "The name translates roughly to yellow wasp. That might give you an idea of what it tastes like."

"Really, Sarah! You must allow Mr. Hunter to form his own opinion of what was once our national drink."

Dev was already regretting his choice but concealed it behind a polite request. "Please call me Dev, ma'am."

He didn't presume to address the duchess by name or by rank. Mostly because he wasn't sure which came first. European titles were a mystery wrapped up in an enigma to most Americans. Defunct Eastern European titles were even harder to decipher. Dev had read somewhere that the form of address depended on whether the rank was inherited or bestowed, but that didn't help him a whole lot in this instance.

The duchess solved his dilemma when she responded to his request with a gracious nod. "Very well. And you may call me Charlotte."

Sarah paused with the stopper to one of the decanters in hand. Her look of surprise told Dev he'd just been granted a major concession. She recovered a moment later and filled one of the thimble-size liqueur glasses. Passing it to Dev, she refilled her wineglass and took a seat beside her grandmother.

As he lifted the glass in salute to his hostess, he told himself a half ounce of yellow wasp couldn't do much damage. One sip showed just how wrong he was. The fiery, plum-based liquid exploded in his mouth and damned near burned a hole in his esophagus.

"Holy sh…!"

He caught himself in time. Eyes watering, he held the glass at arm's length and gave the liqueur the respect it deserved. When he could breathe again, he met the duchess's amused eyes.

"This puts the stuff we used to brew in our helmets in Iraq to shame."

"You were in Iraq?" With an impatient shake of her

head, Charlotte answered her own question. "Yes, of course you were. Afghanistan, too, if I remember correctly from the article in *Beguile*."

Okay, now he was embarrassed. The idea of this gray-haired matriarch reading all that nonsense—and perusing the picture of his butt crack!—went down even rougher than the liqueur.

To cover his embarrassment, Dev took another sip. The second was a little easier than the first but still left scorch marks all the way to his gullet.

"So tell me," Charlotte was saying politely, "how long will you be in New York?"

"That depends," he got out.

"Indeed?"

The duchess did the nose-up thing again. She was good at it, Dev thought as he waited for the fire in his stomach to subside.

"On what, if I may be so bold to ask?"

"On whether you and your granddaughter will have dinner with me this evening. Or tomorrow evening."

His glance shifted to Sarah. The memory of how she'd fit against him, how her mouth had opened under his, hit with almost the same sucker punch as the *Žuta Osa*.

"Or any evening," he added, holding her gaze.

Sarah gripped her wineglass. She didn't have any trouble reading the message in his eyes. It was a personal challenge. A not-so-private caress. Her grandmother would have to be blind to miss either.

Okay. All right. She'd hoped this meeting would blunt the surprise of a sudden engagement. Dev had done his part. The ball was now in her court.

"I can't speak for Grandmama, but I'm free tomorrow evening. Or any evening," she added with what felt like a silly, simpering smile.

She thought she'd overplayed her hand. Was sure of it when the duchess speared her with a sharp glance.

The question in her grandmother's eyes ballooned Sarah's guilt and worry to epic proportions. She couldn't do this. She couldn't deceive the woman who'd sold every precious family heirloom she owned to provide for her granddaughters. A confession trembled on her lips. The duchess forestalled it by turning back Devon Hunter.

"I'm afraid I have another engagement tomorrow evening."

Both women knew that to be a blatant lie. Too caught up in her own web of deceit to challenge her grandmother, Sarah tried not to squirm as the duchess slipped into the role of royal matchmaker.

"But I insist you take my granddaughter to dinner tomorrow. Or any evening," she added drily. "Right now, however, I'd like to know a little more about you."

Sarah braced herself. The duchess didn't attack with the same snarling belligerence as Alexis, but she was every bit as skilled and tenacious when it came to extracting information. Dev didn't stand a chance.

She had to admit he took the interrogation with good grace. Still, her nerves were stretched taunt when she went to bed some hours later. At least she'd mitigated the fallout from one potentially disastrous situation. If—*when*—she and Devon broke the news of their engagement, it wouldn't come as a complete shock to Grandmama.

She woke up the next morning knowing she had to defuse another potentially explosive situation. A quick scan of her phone showed no return call or text from Gina. An equally quick scan of electronic, TV and print media showed the story hadn't broken yet about Sarah and Number Three. It would, though. She sensed it with every instinct she'd developed after three years in the dog-eat-dog publishing business.

Alexis. She had to tell Alexis some version of her involvement with Devon Hunter. She tried out different slants as she hung from a handrail on the subway. Several more in the elevator that zoomed her up to *Beguile*'s offices. Every possible construction but one crumbled when Alexis summoned her into her corner office. Pacing like a caged tiger, the executive editor unleashed her claws.

"Jesus, Sarah!" Anger lowered Alexis's smoker's rasp to a frog-like croak. "You want to tell me why I have to hear secondhand that one of my editors swapped saliva with Sexy Single Number Three? On the street. In full view of every cabbie with a camera phone and an itch to sell a sensational story."

"Come on, Alexis. How many New York cabbies read *Beguile* enough to recognize Number Three?"

"At least one, apparently."

She flung the sheet of paper she was holding onto the slab of Lucite that was her desk. Sarah's heart tripped as she skimmed the contents. It was a printed email, and below the printed message was a grainy color photo of a couple locked in each other's arms. Sarah barely had time for a mental apology to Red for thinking she'd be the one to peddle the story before Alexis pounced.

"This joker wants five thousand for the picture."

"You're kidding!"

"See this face?" The executive editor stabbed a finger at her nose. "Does it look like I'm kidding?"

"This...this isn't what you think, Alexis."

"So maybe you'll tell me what the hell it is, Lady Sarah."

It might have been the biting sarcasm. Or the deliberate reference to her title. Or the worry about Gina or the guilt over lying to her grandmother or the pressure Devon Hunter had laid on her. Whatever caused Sarah's sudden meltdown, the sudden burst of tears shocked her as much as it did Alexis.

"Oh, Christ!" Her boss flapped her hands like a PMS-ing

hen. "I'm sorry. I didn't mean to come at you so hard. Well, maybe I did. But you don't have to cry about it."

"Yes," Sarah sobbed, "I do!"

The truth was she couldn't have stopped if she wanted to. All the stress, all the strain, seemed to boil out of her. Not just the problems that had piled up in the past few days. The months of worrying about Grandmama's health. The years of standing between Gina and the rest of the world. Everything just seemed to come to a head. Dropping into a chair, she crossed her arms on the half acre of unblemished Lucite and buried her face.

"Hey! It's okay." Alexis hovered over her, patting her shoulder, sounding more desperate and bullfroggish by the moment. "I'll sit on this email. Do what I can to kill the story before it leaks."

Sarah raised her head. She'd struck a deal. She'd stand by it. "You don't have to kill it. Hunter... He and I..."

"You and Hunter...?"

She dropped her head back onto her arms and gave a muffled groan. "We're engaged."

"What! When? Where? How?"

Reverting to her natural self, Alexis was relentless. Within moments she'd wormed out every succulent detail. Hunter's shocking accusation. The video with its incontrovertible proof. The outrageous proposal. The call from Gina stating that she was on her way to Switzerland.

"Your sister is a selfish little bitch," Alexis pronounced in disgust. "When are you going to stop protecting her?"

"Never!" Blinking away her tears, Sarah fired back with both barrels. "Gina's all I have. Gina and Grandmama. I'll do whatever's necessary to protect them."

"That's all well and good, but your sister..."

"*Is* my sister."

"Okay, okay." Alexis held up both palms. "She's your sister. And Devon Hunter's your fiancé for the next six months. Unless..."

Her face took on a calculating expression. One Sarah knew all too well. She almost didn't want to ask, but the faint hope that her boss might see a way out of the mess prompted a tentative query.

"Unless what?"

"What if you keep a journal for the next few weeks? Better yet, a photo journal?"

Deep in thought, Alexis tapped a bloodred nail against her lips. Sarah could almost see the layout taking shape in her boss's fertile mind.

"You and Hunter. The whirlwind romance. The surprise proposal. The romantic dinners for two. The long walks in Central Park. Our readers would eat it up."

"Forget it, Alexis. I'm not churning out more juicy gossip for our readers."

"Why not?"

The counter came as swift and as deadly as an adder. In full pursuit of a feature now, Alexis dropped into the chair next to Sarah and pressed her point.

"You and I both know celebrity gossip sells. And this batch comes with great bonus elements. Hunter's not only rich, but handsome as hell. You're a smart, savvy career woman with a connection to royalty."

"A connection to a royal house that doesn't exist anymore!"

"So? We resurrect it. Embellish it. Maybe send a photographer over to shoot some local color from your grandmother's homeland. Didn't you say you still had some cousins there?"

"Three or four times removed, maybe, but Grandmama hasn't heard from anyone there in decades."

"No problem. We'll make it work."

She saw the doubt on Sarah's face and pressed her point with ruthless determination.

"If what you give me is as full of glam and romance as I think it could be, it'll send our circulation through the roof. And that, my sweet, will provide you with enough of a bonus to reimburse Hunter for his lost artifact. *And* pay off the last of your grandmother's medical bills. *And* put a little extra in your bank account for a rainy day or two."

The dazzling prospect hung before Sarah's eyes for a brief, shining moment. She could extricate Gina from her latest mess. Become debt-free for the first time in longer than she could remember. Splurge on some totally unnecessary luxury for the duchess. Buy a new suit instead of retrofitting old classics.

She came within a breath of promising Alexis all the photos and R-rated copy she could print. Then her irritating sense of fair play raised its head.

"I can't do it," she said after a bitter internal struggle. "Hunter promised he wouldn't file charges against Gina if I play the role of adoring fiancée. I'll try to get him to agree to a photo shoot focusing on our—" she stopped, took a breath, continued "—on our engagement. I'm pretty sure he'll agree to that."

Primarily because it would serve his purpose. Once the word hit the street that he was taken, all those women shoving their phone numbers at him would just have to live with their disappointment. So would Alexis.

"That's as far as I'll go," Sarah said firmly.

Her boss frowned and was priming her guns for another salvo when her intercom buzzed. Scowling, she stabbed at the instrument on her desk.

"Didn't I tell you to hold all calls?"

"Yes, but…"

"What part of 'hold' don't you understand?"

"It's…"

"It's what, dammit?"

"Number Three," came the whispered reply. "He's here."

Five

If Dev hadn't just run past a gauntlet of snickering females, he might have been amused by the almost identical expressions of surprise on the faces of his fiancée and her boss. But he had, so he wasn't.

Alexis Danvers didn't help matters by looking him up and down with the same scrutiny an auctioneer might give a prize bull. As thin as baling wire, she sized him up with narrowed, calculating eyes before thrusting out a hand tipped with scarlet talons.

"Mr. Hunter. Good to meet you. Sarah says you and she are engaged."

"Wish I could say the same, Ms. Danvers. And yes, we are."

He shifted his gaze to Sarah, frowning when he noted her reddened eyes and tearstained cheeks. He didn't have to search far for the reason behind them. The grainy color photo on Danvers's desk said it all.

Hell! Sarah had hinted the crap would hit the fan if some magazine other than hers scooped the story. Looked as if it had just hit. He turned back to the senior editor and vectored the woman's anger in his direction.

"I'm guessing you might be a little piqued that Sarah didn't clue you in to our relationship before it became public knowledge."

Danvers dipped her chin in a curt nod. "You guessed right."

"I'm also guessing you understand why I wasn't real anxious for another avalanche of obnoxious publicity."

"If you're referring to the Ten Sexiest Singles article..."

"I am."

"Since you declined to let us interview you for that article, Mr. Hunter, everything we printed was in the public domain. Your military service. That cargo thingamajig you patented. Your corporation's profits last quarter. Your marital status. All we did was collate the facts, glam them up a little, toss in a few pictures and offer you to an admiring audience."

"Any more admiration from that audience and I'll have to hire a bodyguard."

"Or a fiancée?"

She slipped that in with the precision of a surgeon. Dev had to admire her skill even as he acknowledged the hit.

"Or a fiancée," he agreed. "Luckily I found the perfect one right here at *Beguile*."

Which reminded him of why he'd made a second trek to the magazine's offices.

"Something's come up," he told Sarah. "I was going to explain it to you privately, but..."

"You heard from Gina?"

Her breathless relief had Dev swearing silently. Little Miss Gina deserved a swift kick in the behind for putting her sister through all this worry. And he might just be the one to deliver it.

"No, I haven't."

The relief evaporated. Sarah's shoulders slumped. Only for a moment, though. The St. Sebastian steel reasserted itself almost immediately. Good thing, as she'd need every ounce of it for the sucker punch Dev was about to deliver.

"But I did hear from the CEO I've been negotiating with for the past few months. He's ready to hammer out the final details and asked me to fly over to Paris."

She sensed what was coming. He saw it in the widening of her green eyes, the instinctive shake of her head. Dev ignored both and pressed ahead.

"I told him I would. I also told him I might bring my fiancée. I explained we just got engaged, and that I'm thinking of taking some extra time so we can celebrate the occasion in his beautiful city."

"Excuse me!" Danvers butted in, her expression frigid. "Sarah has an important job here at *Beguile,* with deadlines to meet. She can't just flit off to Paris on your whim."

"I appreciate that. It would only be for a few days. Maybe a week."

Dev turned back to Sarah, holding her gaze, holding her to their bargain at the same time.

"We've been working this deal for months. I need to wrap it up. Monsieur Girault said his wife would be delighted to entertain you while we're tied up in negotiations."

He slipped in that veiled reminder of one of his touchiest problems deliberately. He'd been up front with her. He wanted her to provide cover from Elise Girault. In exchange, he'd let her light-fingered sister off the hook.

Sarah got the message. Her chin inched up. Her shoulders squared. The knowledge she would stick to her side of the bargain gave him a fiercer sense of satisfaction than he had time to analyze right now.

"When are you thinking of going?" she asked.

"My executive assistant has booked us seats on a seven-ten flight out of JFK."

"Tonight?"

"Tonight. You have a current passport, don't you?"

"Yes, but I can't just jet off and leave Grandmama!"

"Not a problem. I also had my assistant check with the top home health-care agencies in the city. A licensed, bonded RN can report for duty this afternoon and stay with your grandmother until you get back."

"Dear God, no!" A shudder shook her. "Grandmama would absolutely hate that invasion of her privacy. I'll ask our housekeeper, Maria, to stay with her."

"You sure?"

"I'm sure."

"Since I'm springing this trip on you with such short notice, please tell your housekeeper I'll recompense her for her time."

"That's not necessary," she said stiffly.

"Of course it is."

She started to protest, but Dev suggested a daily payment for Maria's services that made Sarah blink and her boss hastily intervene.

"The man's right, kiddo. This is his gig. Let him cover the associated costs."

She left unsaid the fact that Dev could well afford the generous compensation. It was right there, though, like the proverbial elephant in the room, and convinced Sarah to reluctantly agree.

"We're good to go, then."

"I…I suppose." She chewed on her lower lip for a moment. "I need to finish the Sizzling Summer Sea-escapes layout, Alexis."

"And the ad for that new lip gloss," her boss put in urgently. "I want it in the June edition."

"I'll take my laptop. I can do both layouts on the plane." She pushed out of her chair and faced Dev. "You understand that my accompanying you on this little jaunt is contingent on Maria's availability."

"I understand. Assuming she's available, can you be ready by three o'clock?"

"Isn't that a little early for a seven-ten flight?"

"It is, but we need to make a stop on the way out to JFK. Or would you rather go to Cartier now?"

"Cartier? Why do we…? Oh." She gave a low groan. "An engagement ring, right?"

"Right."

She shook her head in dismay. "This just keeps getting better and better."

Her boss took an entirely different view. With a hoarse whoop, she reached for the phone on her desk.

"Perfect! We'll send a camera crew to Cartier with you." She paused with the phone halfway to her ear and raked her subordinate with a critical glance. "Swing by makeup on your way out, Sarah. Have them ramp up your color. Wouldn't hurt to hit wardrobe, too. That's one of your grandmother's Dior suits, right? It's great, but it needs something. A belt, maybe. Or…"

Sarah cut in, alarm coloring her voice. "Hold on a minute, Alexis."

"What's to hold? This is exactly what we were talking about before Hunter arrived."

Sarah shot Dev a swift, guilty glance. It didn't take a genius for him to fill in the blanks. Obviously, her boss had been pressing to exploit the supposed whirlwind romance between one of her own and Number Three.

As much as it grated, Dev had to admit a splashy announcement of his engagement to Sarah St. Sebastian fell in with his own plans. If nothing else, it would get the word out that he was off the market and, hopefully, keep Madame Girault's claws sheathed.

"I'll consent to a few pictures, if that's what Sarah wants."

"A few pictures," she agreed with obvious reluctance, leveling a pointed look at her boss. "Just this *one* time."

"Come on, Sarah. How much more romantic can you get than April in Paris? The city of light and love. You and Hunter here strolling hand in hand along the Quai de Conti…"

"No, Alexis."

"Just think about it."

"No, Alexis."

There was something in the brief exchange Dev couldn't quite get a handle on. The communication between the two women was too emphatic, too terse. He didn't have time to decipher it now, however.

"Your people get this one shoot," he told Danvers, putting an end to the discussion. "They can do it at Cartier." He checked his watch. "Why don't you call your housekeeper now, Sarah? Make sure she's available. If she is, we'll put a ring on your finger and get you home to pack."

Sarah battled a headache as the limo cut through the Fifth Avenue traffic. Devon sat beside her on the cloud-soft leather, relaxed and seemingly unperturbed about throwing her life into total chaos. Seething, she threw a resentful glance at his profile.

Was it only two days ago he'd stormed into her life? Three? She felt as though she'd been broadsided by a semi. Okay, so maybe she couldn't lay all the blame for the situation she now found herself in on Dev. Gina had certainly contributed her share. Still…

When the limo pulled up at the front entrance to Cartier's iconic flagship store, the dull throb in her temples took on a sharper edge. With its red awnings and four stories of ultra high-end merchandise, the store was a New York City landmark.

Sarah hadn't discovered until after her grandmother's heart attack that Charlotte had sold a good portion of her jewels to Cartier over the years. According to a recent invoice, the last piece she'd parted with was still on display in their Estate Jewelry room.

Dev had called ahead, so they were greeted at the door

by the manager himself. "Good afternoon, Mr. Hunter. I'm Charles Tipton."

Gray-haired and impeccably attired, he shook Dev's hand before bowing over Sarah's with Old World courtesy.

"It's a pleasure to meet you, Ms. St. Sebastian. I've had the honor of doing business with your grandmother several times in the past."

She smiled her gratitude for his discretion. "Doing business with" stung so much less than "helping her dispose of her heritage."

"May I congratulate you on your engagement?"

She managed not to wince, but couldn't help thinking this lie was fast taking on a life of its own.

"Thank you."

"I'm thrilled, of course, that you came to Cartier to shop for your ring. I've gathered a selection of our finest settings and stones. I'm sure we'll find something exactly to your…"

He broke off as a cab screeched over to the curb and the crew from *Beguile* jumped out. Zach Zimmerman— nicknamed ZZ, of course—hefted his camera bags while his assistant wrestled with lights and reflectors.

"Hey, Sarah!" Dark eyed and completely irreverent about everything except his work, ZZ stomped toward them in his high-top sneakers. "You really engaged to Number Three or has Alexis been hitting the sauce again?"

She hid another wince. "I'm really engaged. ZZ, this is my fiancé, Devon…"

"Hunter. Yeah, I recognize the, uh, face."

He smirked but thankfully refrained from referring to any other part of Dev's anatomy.

"If you'll all please come with me."

Mr. Tipton escorted them through the first-floor show-room with its crystal chandeliers and alcoves framed with white marble arches. Faint strains of classical music floated on the air. The seductive scent of gardenia wafted from strategically positioned bowls of potpourri.

A short elevator ride took them to a private consultation room. Chairs padded in gold velvet were grouped on either side of a gateleg, gilt-trimmed escritoire. Several cases sparkling with diamond engagement sets sat on the desk's burled wood surface.

The manager gestured them to the chairs facing the desk but before taking his own he detoured to a sideboard holding a silver bucket and several Baccarat flutes.

"May I offer you some champagne? To toast your engagement, perhaps?"

Sarah glanced at Dev, saw he'd left the choice up to her, and surrendered to the inevitable.

"Thank you. That would be delightful."

The cork had already been popped. Tipton filled flutes and passed them to Sarah and Dev. She took the delicate crystal, feeling like the biggest fraud on earth. Feeling as well the stupidest urge to indulge in another bout of loud, sloppy tears.

Like many of *Beguile*'s readers, Sarah occasionally got caught up in the whole idea of romance. You could hardly sweat over layouts depicting the perfect engagement or wedding or honeymoon without constructing a few private fantasies. But this was about as far from those fantasies as she could get. A phony engagement. A pretend fiancé. A ring she would return as soon as she fulfilled the terms of her contract.

Then she looked up from the pale gold liquid bubbling in her flute and met Dev's steady gaze. His eyes had gone deep blue, almost cobalt, and something in their depths made her breath snag. When he lifted his flute and tipped it to hers, the fantasies begin to take on vague form and shape.

"To my..." he began.

"Wait!" ZZ pawed through his camera bag. "I need to catch this."

The moment splintered. Like a skater on too-thin ice,

Sarah felt the cracks spidering out beneath her feet. Panic replaced the odd sensation of a moment ago. She had to fight the urge to slam down the flute and get off the ice before she sank below the surface.

She conquered the impulse, but couldn't summon more than a strained smile once ZZ framed the shot.

"Okay," the photographer said from behind a foot-long lens, "go for it!"

Dev's gesture with his flute was the same. So was the caress in his voice. But whatever Sarah had glimpsed in his blue eyes a moment ago was gone.

"To us," he said as crystal clinked delicately against crystal.

"To us," she echoed.

She took one sip, just one, and nixed ZZ's request to repeat the toast so he could shoot it from another angle. She couldn't ignore him or his assistant, however, while she tried on a selection of rings. Between them, they made the process of choosing a diamond feel like torture.

According to Tipton, Dev had requested a sampling of rings as refined and elegant as his fiancée. Unfortunately, none of the glittering solitaires he lifted from the cases appealed to Sarah. With an understanding nod, he sent for cases filled with more elaborate settings.

Once again Sarah could almost hear a clock ticking inside her head. She needed to make a decision, zip home, break the startling news of her engagement to Grandmama, get packed and catch that seven-ten flight. Yet none of the rings showcased on black velvet triggered more than a tepid response.

Like it mattered. Just get this over with, she told herself grimly.

She picked up a square cut surrounded by glittering baguettes. Abruptly, she returned it to the black velvet pad.

"I think I would prefer something unique." She looked Tipton square in the eye. "Something from your estate sales, perhaps. An emerald, for my birth month. Mounted in gold."

Her birthday was in November, and the stone for that month was topaz. She hoped Hunter hadn't assimilated that bit of trivia. The jeweler had, of course, but he once again proved himself the soul of discretion.

"I believe we might have just the ring for you."

He lifted a house phone and issued a brief instruction. Moments later, an assistant appeared and deposited an intricately wrought ring on the display pad.

Thin ropes of gold were interwoven to form a wide band. An opaque Russian emerald nested in the center of the band. The milky green stone was the size and shape of a small gumball. When Sarah turned the ring over, she spotted a rose carved into the stone's flat bottom.

Someone with no knowledge of antique jewelry might scrunch their noses at the overly fussy setting and occluded gemstone. All Sarah knew was that she had to wear Grandmama's last and most precious jewel, if only for a week or so. Her heart aching, she turned to Dev.

"This is the one."

He tried to look pleased with her choice but didn't quite get there. The price the manager quoted only increased his doubts. Even fifteen-karat Russian emeralds didn't come anywhere close to the market value of a flawless three- or four-karat diamond.

"Are you sure this is the ring you want?"

"Yes."

Shrugging, he extracted an American Express card from his wallet. When Tipton disappeared to process the card, he picked up the ring and started to slip it on Sarah's finger.

ZZ stopped him cold. "Hold it!"

Dev's blue eyes went glacial. "Let us know when you're ready."

"Yeah, yeah, just hang on a sec."

ZZ thrust out a light meter, scowled at the reading and

barked orders to his assistant. After a good five minutes spent adjusting reflectors and falloff lights, they were finally ready.

"Go," the photographer ordered.

Dev slipped the ring on Sarah's finger. It slid over her knuckle easily, and the band came to rest at the base of her finger as though it had been sized especially for her.

"Good. Good." ZZ clicked a dozen fast shots. "Look up at him, Sarah. Give him some eye sex."

Heat rushed into her cheeks but she lifted her gaze. Dev wore a cynical expression for a second or two before exchanging it for one more lover-like.

Lights heated the room. Reflectors flashed. The camera shutter snapped and spit.

"Good. Good. Now let's have the big smooch. Make it hot, you two."

Tight lines appeared at the corners of Dev's mouth. For a moment he looked as though he intended to tell ZZ to take his zoom lens and shove it. Then he rose to his feet with lazy grace and held out a hand to Sarah.

"We'll have to try this without an audience sometime," he murmured as she joined him. "For now, though…"

She was better prepared this time. She didn't stiffen when he slid an arm around her waist. Didn't object when he curled his other hand under her chin and tipped her face to his. Yet the feel of his mouth, the taste and the scent of him, sent tiny shock waves rippling through her entire body.

A lyric from an old song darted into her mind. Something about getting lost in his kiss. That was exactly how she felt as his mouth moved over hers.

"Good. Good."

More rapid-fire clicks, more flashes. Finally ZZ was done. He squinted at the digital screen and ran through the entire sequence of images before he gave a thumbs-up.

"Got some great shots here. I'll edit 'em and email you

the best, Sarah. Just be sure to credit me if you use 'em on your bridal website."

Right. Like that was going to happen. Still trying to recover from her second session in Devon Hunter's arms, Sarah merely nodded.

While ZZ and his assistant packed up, Dev checked his watch. "Do you want to grab lunch before I take you home to pack?"

Sarah thought for a moment. Her number-one priority right now was finding some way to break the news to the duchess that her eldest granddaughter had become engaged to a man she'd met only a few days ago. She needed a plausible explanation. One that wouldn't trigger Charlotte's instant suspicion. Or worse, so much worse, make her heart stutter.

Sarah's glance dropped to the emerald. The stone's cloudy beauty gave her the bravado to respond to Dev's question with a completely false sense of confidence.

"Let's have lunch with Grandmama and Maria. We'll make it a small celebration in honor of the occasion, then I'll pack."

Six

Dev had employed a cautious, scope-out-the-territory approach for his first encounter with the duchess. For the second, he decided on a preemptive strike. As soon as he and Sarah were in the limo and headed uptown, he initiated his plan of attack.

"Do you need to call your grandmother and let her know we're coming?"

"Yes, I should." She slipped her phone out of her purse. "And I'll ask Maria to put together a quick lunch."

"No need. I'll take care of that. Does the duchess like caviar?"

"Yes," Sarah replied, a question in her eyes as he palmed his own phone, "but only Caspian Sea osetra. She thinks beluga is too salty and sevruga too fishy."

"What about Maria? Does she have a favorite delicacy?"

She had to think for a moment. "Well, on All Saints Day she always makes *fiambre*."

"What's that?"

"A chilled salad with fifty or so ingredients. Why?" she asked as he hit a speed-dial key. "What are you…?"

He held up a hand, signaling her to wait, and issued a

quick order. "I need a champagne brunch for four, delivered to Ms. St. Sebastian's home address in a half hour. Start with osetra caviar and whatever you can find that's close to... Hang on." He looked to Sarah. "What was that again?"

"Fiambre."

"Fiambre. It's a salad...Hell, I don't know...Right. Right. Half an hour."

Sarah was staring at him when he cut the connection. "Who was that?"

"My executive assistant."

"She's here, in New York?"

"It's a he. Patrick Donovan. We used to fly together. He's back in L.A."

"And he's going to have champagne and caviar delivered to our apartment in half an hour?"

"That's why he gets paid the big bucks." He nodded to the phone she clutched in her hand. "You better call the duchess. With all this traffic, lunch will probably get there before we do."

Despite his advance preparations, Dev had to shake off a serious case of nerves when he and Sarah stepped out of the elevator at the Dakota. His introduction to Charlotte St. Sebastian last night had given him a keen appreciation of both her intellect and her fierce devotion to her grand-daughters. He had no idea how she'd react to this sudden engagement, but he suspected she'd make him sweat.

Sarah obviously suspected the same thing. She paused at the door to their apartment, key in hand, and gave him a look that was half challenge, half anxious appeal.

"She...she has a heart condition. We need to be careful how we orchestrate this."

"I'll follow your lead."

Pulling in a deep breath, she squared her shoulders. The key rattled in the lock, and the door opened on a parade of white-jacketed waiters just about to exit the apartment. Their arms full of empty cartons, they stepped aside.

"Your grandmother told us to set up in the dining room," the waiter in charge informed Sarah. "And may I say, ma'am, she has exquisite taste in crystal. Bohemian, isn't it?"

"Yes, it is."

"I thought so. No other lead crystal has that thin, liquid sheen."

Nodding, Sarah hurried down the hall. Dev lingered to add a hefty tip to the service fee he knew Patrick would have already taken care of. Gushing their thanks, the team departed and Dev made his way to the duchess's high-ceilinged dining room.

He paused on the threshold to survey the scene. The mahogany table could easily seat twelve, probably twenty or more with leaves in, but had been set with four places at the far end. Bone-white china gleamed. An impressive array of ruby-red goblets sparkled at each place setting. A sideboard held a row of domed silver serving dishes, and an opened bottle of champagne sat in a silver ice bucket.

Damn! Patrick would insist Dev add another zero to his already astronomical salary for pulling this one off.

"I presume this is your doing, Devon."

His glance zinged to the duchess. She stood ramrod straight at the head of the table, her hands folded one atop the other on the ivory handle of her cane. The housekeeper, Maria, hovered just behind her.

"Yes, ma'am."

"I also presume you're going to tell me the reason for this impromptu celebration."

Having agreed to let Sarah take the lead, Dev merely moved to her side and eased an arm around her waist. She stiffened, caught herself almost instantly and relaxed.

"We have two reasons to celebrate, Grandmama. Dev's asked me to go to Paris with him."

"So I understand. Maria informed me you asked her to stay with me while you're gone."

Her arctic tone left no doubt as to her feelings about the matter.

"It's just for a short while, and more for me than for you. This way I won't feel so bad about rushing off and leaving you on such short notice."

The duchess didn't unbend. If anything, her arthritic fingers clutched the head of her cane more tightly.

"And the second reason for this celebration?"

Sarah braced herself. Dev could feel her body go taut against his while she struggled to frame their agreement in terms her grandmother would accept. It was time for him to step in and draw the duchess's fire.

"My sisters will tell you I'm seriously deficient in the romance department, ma'am. They'll also tell you I tend to bulldoze over any and all obstacles when I set my sights on something. Sarah put up a good fight, but I convinced her we should get engaged before we take off for Paris."

"Madre de Dios!" The exclamation burst from Maria, who gaped at Sarah. "You are *engaged?* To this man?"

When she nodded, the duchess's chin shot up. Her glance skewered Dev where he stood. In contrast to her stark silence, Maria gave quick, joyous thanks to the Virgin Mary while making the sign of the cross three times in rapid succession.

"How I prayed for this, *chica!*"

Tears sparkling in her brown eyes, she rushed over to crush Sarah against her generous bosom. Dev didn't get a hug, but he was hauled down by his lapels and treated to a hearty kiss on both cheeks.

The duchess remained standing where she was. Dev was damned if he could read her expression. When Sarah approached, Charlotte's narrow-eyed stare shifted to her granddaughter.

"We stopped by Cartier on our way here, Grandmama. Dev wanted to buy me an engagement ring."

She raised her left hand, and the effect on the duchess was instant and electric.

"Dear God! Is that…? Is that the Russian Rose?"

"Yes," Sarah said gently.

Charlotte reached out a veined hand and stroked the emerald's rounded surface with a shaking fingertip. Dev felt uncomfortably like a voyeur as he watched a succession of naked emotions cross the older woman's face. For a long moment, she was in another time, another place, reliving memories that obviously brought both great joy and infinite sadness.

With an effort that was almost painful to observe, she returned to the present and smiled at Sarah.

"Your grandfather gave me the Rose for my eighteenth birthday. I always intended you to have it."

Her glance shifted once again to Dev. Something passed between them, but before he could figure out just what the hell it was, the duchess became all brisk efficiency.

"Well, Sarah, since you're traipsing off to Paris on such short notice, I think we should sample this sumptuous feast your…your fiancé has so generously arranged. Then you'll have to pack. Devon, will you pour the champagne?"

"Yes, ma'am."

Dev's misguided belief that he'd escaped unscathed lasted only until they'd finished brunch and Sarah went to pack. He got up to help Maria clear the table. She waved him back to his seat.

"I will do this. You sit and keep *la duquesa* company."

The moment Maria bustled through the door to the kitchen, *la duquesa* let loose with both barrels. Her pale eyes dangerous, she unhooked her cane from her chair arm and stabbed it at Dev like a sword.

"Let's be sure we understand each other, Mr. Hunter. I

may have been forced to sell the Russian Rose, but if you've purchased it with the mistaken idea you can also purchase my granddaughter, you'd best think again. One can't buy class or good genes. One either has both—" she jabbed his chest with the cane for emphasis "—or one doesn't."

Geesh! Good thing he was facing this woman over three feet of ebony and not down the barrel of an M16. Dev didn't doubt she'd pull the trigger if he answered wrong.

"First," he replied, "I had no idea that emerald once belonged to you. Second, I'm perfectly satisfied with my genes. Third…"

He stopped to think about that one. His feelings for Sarah St. Sebastian had become too confused, too fast. The way she moved…. The smile in her green eyes when she let down her guard for a few moments…. Her fierce loyalty to her grandmother and ditz of a sister…. Everything about her seemed to trigger both heat and hunger.

"Third," he finally admitted, "there's no way I'll ever match Sarah's style or elegance. All I can do is appreciate it, which I most certainly do."

The duchess kept her thoughts hidden behind her narrowed eyes for several moments. Then she dropped the tip of the cane and thumped the floor.

"Very well. I'll wait to see how matters develop."

She eased back against her chair and Dev started to breathe again.

"I'm sure you're aware," she said into the tentative truce, "that Paris is one of Sarah's favorite cities?"

"We haven't gotten around to sharing all our favorites yet," he replied with perfect truthfulness. "I do know she attended the Sorbonne for a year as an undergraduate."

That much was in the background dossier, as was the fact she'd majored in art history. Dev planned to use whatever spare time they might have in Paris to hit a few museums with her. He looked forward to exploring the Louvre or the Cluny with someone who shared his burgeoning interest in art. He was certainly no expert, but his appreciation of art in its various forms had grown with each incremental increase in his personal income...as evidenced by the Byzantine medallion.

The belated reminder of why he was here, being poked in the chest by this imperious, indomitable woman, hit with a belated punch. He'd let the side details of his "engagement" momentarily obscure the fact that he'd arm-twisted Sarah into it. He was using her, ruthlessly and with cold deliberation, as a tool to help close an important deal. Once that deal was closed...

To borrow the duchess's own words, Dev decided, they'd just have to wait and see how matters develop. He wouldn't employ the same ruthlessness and calculation to seduce the eminently seductive Lady Sarah as he had to get a ring on her finger. But neither would he pass up the chance to finesse her into bed if the opportunity offered.

The possibility sent a spear of heat into his belly. With a sheer effort of will, he gave the indomitable Charlotte St. Sebastian no sign of the knee-jerk reaction. But he had to admit he was now looking forward to this trip with considerably more anticipation than when Jean-Jacques Girault first requested it.

Seven

Three hours out over the Atlantic Sarah had yet to get past her surprise.

"I still can't believe Grandmama took it so well," she said, her fingers poised over the keyboard of her laptop. "Not just the engagement. This trip to Paris. The hefty bonus you're paying Maria. Everything!"

Dev looked up from the text message he'd just received. Their first-class seat pods were separated by a serving console holding his scotch, her wine and a tray of appetizers, but they were seated close enough for him to see the lingering disbelief in her jade-green eyes.

"Why shouldn't she take it well?" he countered. "She grilled me last night about my parents, my grandparents, my siblings, my education, my health, my club memberships and my bank account. She squeezed everything else she wanted to know out of me today at lunch. It was a close call, but evidently I passed muster."

"I think it was the ring," Sarah murmured, her gaze on the milky stone that crowned her finger. "Her whole attitude changed when she spotted it."

Dev knew damn well it was the ring, and noted with

interest the guilt and embarrassment tinging his fiancée's cheeks.

"I supposed I should have told you at Cartier that the Russian Rose once belonged to Grandmama."

"Not a problem. I'm just glad it was available."

She was quiet for a moment, still pondering the luncheon.

"Do you know what I find so strange? Grandmama didn't once ask how we could have fallen in love so quickly."

"Maybe because she comes from a different era. Plus, she went through some really rough times. Could be your security weighs as heavily in her mind as your happiness."

"That can't be it. She's always told Gina and me that her marriage was a love match. She had to defy her parents to make it happen."

"Yes, but look what came next," Dev said gently. "From what I've read, the Soviet takeover of her country was brutal. She witnessed your grandfather's execution. She barely escaped the same fate and had to make a new life for herself and her baby in a different country."

Sarah fingered the emerald, her profile etched with sadness. "Then she lost my parents and got stuck with Gina and me."

"Why do I think she didn't regard it as getting stuck? I suspect you and your sister went a long way to filling the hole in her heart."

"Gina more than me."

"I doubt that," Dev drawled.

As he'd anticipated, she jumped instantly to her sister's defense.

"I know you think Gina's a total airhead…"

"I do."

"…but she's so full of joy and life that no one—I repeat, *no one*—can be in her company for more than three minutes without cracking a smile."

Her eyes fired lethal darts, daring him to disagree. He didn't have to. He'd achieved his objective and erased the sad memories. Rather than risk alienating her, he changed the subject.

"I just got a text from Monsieur Girault. He says he's delighted you were able to get away and accompany me."

"Really?" Sarah hiked a politely skeptical brow. "What does his wife say?"

To Dev's chagrin, heat crawled up his neck. He'd flown in and out of a dozen different combat zones, for God's sake! Could stare down union presidents and corporate sharks with equal skill. Yet Elise Girault had thrown him completely off stride when he'd bent to give her the obligatory kiss on both cheeks. Her whispered suggestion was so startling—and so erotic—he'd damned near gotten whiplash when he'd jerked his head back. Then she'd let loose with a booming, raucous laugh that invited him to share in their private joke.

"He didn't say," Dev said in answer to Sarah's question, "but he did ask what you would like to do while we're locked up in a conference room. He indicated his wife is a world-class shopper. Apparently she's well-known at most of the high-end boutiques."

He realized his mistake the moment the words were out. He'd run Sarah St. Sebastian's financials. He knew how strapped she was.

"That reminds me," he said with deliberate nonchalance. "I don't intend for you to incur any out-of-pocket expenses as part of our deal. There'll be a credit card waiting for you at the hotel."

"Please tell me you're kidding."

Her reaction shouldn't have surprised him. Regal elegance was only one of the traits Lady Sarah had inherited from her grandmother. Stiff-necked pride had to rank right up near the top of the list.

"Be reasonable, Sarah. You're providing me a personal service."

Which was becoming more personal by the hour. Dev was getting used to her stimulating company. The heat she ignited in him still took him by surprise, though. He hadn't figured that into his plan.

"Of course I'll cover your expenses."

Her expression turned glacial. "The hotel, yes. Any meals we take with Madame and Monsieur Girault, yes. A shopping spree on the rue du Faubourg Saint-Honoré, no."

"Fine. It's your call."

He tried to recover with an admiring survey of her petal-pink dress. The fabric was thick and satiny, the cut sleek. A coat in the same style hung in their cabin's private closet.

"The rue du Whatever has nothing on Fifth Avenue. That classy New York look will have Elise Girault demanding an immediate trip to the States."

She stared at him blankly for a moment, then burst into laughter. "You're not real up on haute couture, are you?"

"Any of my sisters would tell you I don't know haute from hamburger."

"I wouldn't go that far," she said, still chuckling. "Unless I miss my guess, your shoes are Moroccan leather, the suit's hand-tailored and the tie comes from a little shop just off the Grand Canal in Venice."

"Damn, you're good! Although Patrick tells me he orders the ties from Milan, not Venice. So where did that dress come from?"

"It's vintage Balenciaga. Grandmama bought it in Madrid decades ago."

The smile remained, but Dev thought it dimmed a few degrees.

"She disposed of most of her designer originals when… when they went out of style, but she kept enough to provide a treasure trove for me. Thank goodness! Retro is the new 'new,' you know. I'm the envy of everyone at *Beguile*."

Dev could read behind the lines. The duchess must have sold off her wardrobe as well as her jewelry over the years. It was miracle she'd managed to hang on to the apartment at the Dakota. The thought of what the duchess and Sarah had gone through kicked Dev's admiration for them both up another notch. Also, his determination to treat Sarah to something new and obscenely expensive. He knew better than to step on her pride again, though, and said merely, "Retro looks good on you."

"Thank you."

After what passed for the airline's gourmet meal, Dev used his in-flight wireless connection to crunch numbers for his meetings with Girault and company while Sarah went back to work on her laptop. She'd promised Alexis she would finish the layout for the Summer Sea-escapes but the perspectives just wouldn't gel. After juggling Martha's Vineyard with Catalina Island and South Padre Island with South Georgia Island, she decided she would have to swing by *Beguile*'s Paris offices to see how the layout looked on a twenty-five-inch monitor before shooting it off to Alexis for review.

Dev was still crunching numbers when she folded down the lid of her computer. With a polite good-night, she tugged up the airline's fleecy blue blanket and curled into her pod.

A gentle nudge brought her awake some hours later. She blinked gritty eyes and decided reality was more of a fantasy than her dreams. Dev had that bad-boy look again. Tie loosened. Shirt collar open. Dark circles below his blue eyes.

"We'll be landing in less than an hour," he told her.

As if to emphasize the point, a flight attendant appeared with a pot of fresh-brewed coffee. Sarah gulped down a half cup before she took the amenity kit provided to all business- and first-class passengers to the lavatory. She emerged with her face washed, teeth brushed, hair combed and her soul ready for the magic that was springtime in Paris.

Or the magic that might have been.

Spring hadn't yet made it to northern France. The temperature hovered around fifty, and a cold rain was coming down in sheets when Sarah and Dev emerged from the terminal and ducked into a waiting limo. The trees lining the roads from the airport showed only a hint of new green and the fields were brown and sere.

Once inside the city, Paris's customary snarl of traffic engulfed them. Neither the traffic nor the nasty weather could dim the glory of the 7th arrondissement, however. The townhomes and ministries, once the residences of France's wealthiest nobility, displayed their mansard roofs and wrought-iron balconies with haughty disregard for the pelting rain. Sarah caught glimpses of the Eiffel Tower's iron symmetry before the limo rolled to a stop on a quiet side street in the heart of Saint-Germain. Surprise brought her around in her seat to face Dev.

"We're staying at the Hôtel Verneuil?"

"We are."

"Gina and I and Grandmama stayed here years ago, on our last trip abroad together."

"So the duchess informed me." His mouth curved. "She also informed me that I'm to take you to Café Michaud to properly celebrate our engagement," he said with a smile.

Sarah fell a little bit in love with him at that moment. Not because he'd booked them into this small gem of a palace instead of a suite at the much larger and far more expensive Crillon or George V. Because he'd made such an effort with her grandmother.

Surprised and shaken by the warmth that curled around her heart, she tried to recover as they exited the limo. "From what I remember, the Verneuil only has twenty-five or twenty-six rooms. The hotel's usually full. I'm surprised you could get us in with such short notice."

"I didn't. Patrick did. After which he informed me that I'd just doubled his Christmas bonus."

"I have to meet this man."

"That can be arranged."

He said it with a casualness that almost hid the implication behind his promise. Sarah caught it, however. The careless words implied a future beyond Paris.

She wasn't ready to think about that. Instead she looked around the lobby while Dev went to the reception desk. The exposed beams, rich tapestries and heavy furniture covered in red velvet hadn't changed since her last visit ten or twelve years ago. Apparently the management hadn't, either. The receptionist must have buzzed her boss. He emerged from the back office, his shoulders stooped beneath his formal morning coat and a wide smile on his face.

"*Bonjour,* Lady Sarah!"

A quick glance at his name tag provided his name. "*Bonjour,* Monsieur LeBon."

"What a delight to have you stay with us again," he exclaimed in French, the Parisian accent so different from that of the provinces. "How is the duchess?"

"She's very well, thank you."

"I'm told this trip is in honor of a special occasion," the manager beamed. "May I offer you my most sincere congratulations?"

"Thank you," she said again, trying not to cringe at the continuation of their deception.

LeBon switched to English to offer his felicitations to Dev. "If I may be so bold to say it, Monsieur Hunter, you are a very lucky man to have captured the heart of one such as Lady Sarah."

"Extremely lucky," Dev agreed.

"Allow me to show you to your floor."

He pushed the button to summon the elevator, then stood aside for them to enter the brass-bedecked cage. While it lifted them to the upper floors, he apologized profusely for not being able to give them adjoining rooms as had been requested.

"We moved several of our guests as your so very capable assistant suggested, Monsieur Hunter, and have put you and Lady Sarah in chambers only a short distance apart. I hope they will be satisfactory."

Sarah's was more than satisfactory. A mix of antique, marble and modern, it offered a four-poster bed and a lovely sitting area with a working fireplace and a tiny balcony. But it was the view from the balcony that delighted her artist's soul.

The rain had softened to a drizzle. It glistened on the slate-gray rooftops of Paris. Endless rows of chimneys rose from the roofs like sentries standing guard over their city. And in the distance were the twin Gothic towers and flying buttresses of Notre Dame.

"I don't have anything scheduled until three this afternoon," Dev said while Monsieur LeBon waited to escort him to his own room. "Would you like to rest awhile, then go out for lunch?"

The city beckoned, and Sarah ached to answer its call. "I'm not tired. I think I'd like to take a walk."

"In the rain?"

"That's when Paris is at its best. The streets, the cafés, seem to steal the light. Everything shimmers."

"Okay," Dev said, laughing, "you've convinced me. I'll change and rap on your door in, say, fifteen minutes?"

"Oh, but…"

She stopped just short of blurting out that she hadn't intended that as an invitation. She could hardly say she didn't want her fiancé's company with Monsieur LeBon beaming his approval of a romantic stroll.

"…I'll need a bit more time than that," she finished. "Let's say thirty minutes."

"A half hour it is."

As she changed into lightweight wool slacks and a hip-length, cherry-red sweater coat that belted at the waist, Sarah tried to analyze her reluctance to share these first hours in Paris with Dev. She suspected it stemmed from the emotion that had welled up when they'd first pulled up at the Hôtel Verneuil. She knew then that she could fall for him, and fall hard. What worried her was that it wouldn't take very much to push her over the precipice.

True, he'd blackmailed her into this uncomfortable charade. Also true, he'd put a ring on her finger and hustled her onto a plane before she could formulate a coherent protest. In the midst of those autocratic acts, though, he'd shown incredible forbearance and generosity.

Then there were the touches, the kisses, the ridiculous whoosh every time he smiled at her. Devon Hunter had made *Beguile*'s list based on raw sex appeal. Sarah now realized he possessed something far more potent…and more dangerous to her peace of mind.

She had to remember this was a short-term assignment. Dev had stipulated it would last only until he wrapped up negotiations on his big deal. It looked now as though that might happen within the next few days. Then this would all be over.

The thought didn't depress her. Sarah wouldn't let it. But worked hard to keep the thought at bay.

She was ready when Dev knocked. Wrapping on a biscuit-colored rain cape, she tossed one of its flaps over a shoulder on her way to the door. With her hair tucked up under a flat-brimmed Dutch-boy cap, she was rainproof and windproof.

"Nice hat," Dev said when she stepped into the hall.

"Thanks."

"Nice everything, actually."

She could have said the same. This was the first time she'd seen him in anything other than a suit. The man was made for jeans. Or vice versa. Their snug fit emphasized his flat belly and lean flanks. And, she added with a gulp when he turned to press the button for the elevator, his tight, trim butt.

He'd added a cashmere scarf in gray-and-blue plaid to his leather bomber jacket, but hadn't bothered with a hat. Sarah worried that it would be too cold for him, but when they exited the hotel, they found the rain was down to a fine mist and the temperature had climbed a few degrees.

Dev took her arm as they crossed the street, then tucked it in his as they started down the boulevard. Sarah felt awkward with that arrangement at first. Elbow to elbow, shoulder to shoulder, strolling along the rain-washed boulevard, they looked like the couple they weren't.

Gradually, Sarah got used to the feel of him beside her, to the way he matched his stride to hers. And bit by bit, the magic of Paris eased her nagging sense that this was all just a charade.

Even this late in the morning the *boulangeries* still emitted their seductive, tantalizing scent of fresh-baked bread. Baguettes sprouted from tall baskets and the racks were crammed with braided loaves. The pastry shops, too, had set out their day's wares. The exquisitely crafted sweets, tarts, chocolate éclairs, gâteaux, caramel mousse, napoleons, macaroons—all were true works of art, and completely impossible to resist.

"God, these look good," Dev murmured, his gaze on the colorful display. "Are you up for a coffee and an éclair?"

"Always. But my favorite patisserie in all Paris is just a couple of blocks away. Can you hold out a little longer?"

"I'll try," he said, assuming an expression of heroic resolution.

Laughing, Sarah pressed his arm closer to her side and guided him the few blocks. The tiny patisserie was nested between a bookstore and a bank. Three dime-size wrought-iron tables sat under the striped awning out front; three more were wedged inside. Luckily two women were getting up from one of the tables when Dev and Sarah entered.

Sarah ordered an espresso and *tart au citron* for herself, and a café au lait for Dev, then left him debating his choice of pastries while she claimed the table. She loosed the flaps of her cape and let it drift over the back of her chair while she observed the drama taking place at the pastry case.

With no other customers waiting, the young woman behind the counter inspected Dev with wide eyes while he checked out the colorful offerings. When he made his selection, she slid the pastry onto a plate and offered it with a question.

"You are American?"

He flashed her a friendly smile. "I am."

Sarah guessed what was coming even before the woman's face lit up with eager recognition.

"Aah, I knew it. You are Number Three, yes?"

Dev's smile tipped into a groan, but he held his cool as she called excitedly to her coworkers.

"C'est lui! C'est lui! Monsieur Hunter. Numéro trois."

Sarah bit her lip as a small bevy of females in white aprons converged at the counter. Dev took the fuss with good grace and even autographed a couple of paper napkins before retreating to the table with his chocolate éclair.

Sarah felt the urge to apologize but merely nodded when he asked grimly if *Beguile* had a wide circulation in France.

"It's our third-largest market."

"Great."

He stabbed his éclair and had to dig deep for a smile when the server delivered their coffees.

"In fact," Sarah said after the girl giggled and departed,

"*Beguile* has an office here in the city. I was going to swing by there when you go for your meeting."

"I'll arrange a car for you."

The reply was polite, but perfunctory. The enchantment of their stroll through Paris's rain-washed streets had dissipated with the mist.

"No need. I'll take the subway."

"Your call," Dev replied. "I'll contact you later and let you know what time we're meeting the Giraults for dinner tonight."

Eight

The French offices of *Beguile* were located only a few blocks from the Arc de Triomphe, on rue Balzac. Sarah always wondered what that famed French novelist and keen observer of human absurdities would think of a glossy publication that pandered to so many of those absurdities.

The receptionist charged with keeping the masses at bay glanced up from her desk with a polite expression that morphed into a welcoming smile when she spotted Sarah.

"*Bonjour,* Sarah! So good to see you again!"

"*Bonjour,* Madeline. Good to see you, too. How are the twins?"

"Horrors," the receptionist replied with a half laugh, half groan. "Absolute horrors. Here are their latest pictures."

After duly admiring the impish-looking three-year-olds, Sarah rounded the receptionist's desk and walked a corridor lined with framed, poster-size copies of *Beguile* covers. Paul Vincent, the senior editor, was pacing his glass cage of an office and using both hands to emphasize whatever point he was trying to make to the person on the speakerphone. Sarah tipped him a wave and would have proceeded to the production unit, but Paul gestured her inside and abruptly terminated his call.

"Sarah!"

Grasping her hands, he kissed her on both cheeks. She bent just a bit so he could hit the mark. At five-four, Paul tended to be as sensitive about his height as he was about the kidney-shaped birthmark discoloring a good portion of his jaw. Yet despite what he called his little imperfections, his unerring eye for color and style had propelled him from the designers' cutting rooms to his present exalted position.

"Alexis emailed to say you would be in Paris," he informed Sarah. "She's instructed me to put François and his crew at your complete disposal."

"For what?"

"To take photos of you and your fiancé. She wants all candids, no posed shots and plenty of romantic backdrop in both shallow and distant depth of field. François says he'll use wide aperture at the Eiffel Tower, perhaps F2.8 to…"

"No, Paul."

"No F2.8? Well, you'll have to speak with François about that."

"No, Paul. No wide aperture, no candids, no Eiffel Tower, no François!"

"But Alexis…."

"Wants to capitalize on my engagement to Number Three. Yes, I know. My fiancé agreed to a photo shoot in New York, but that's as far as either he or I will go. We told Alexis that before we left."

"Then you had better tell her again."

"I will," she said grimly. "In the meantime, I need to use Production's monitors to take a last look at the layout I've been working on. When I zap it to Alexis, I'll remind her of our agreement."

She turned to leave, but Paul stopped her. "What can you tell me of the Chicago meeting?"

The odd inflection in his voice gave Sarah pause. Wondering what was behind it, she searched her mind. So much had happened in the past few days that she'd forgotten about the shuttle Alexis had jumped for an unscheduled meeting with the head of their publishing group. All she'd thought about her boss's unscheduled absence at the time was that it had provided a short reprieve. Paul's question now brought the Chicago meeting forcibly to mind.

"I can't tell you anything," she said honestly. "I didn't have a chance to talk to Alexis about it before I left. Why, what have you heard?"

He folded his arms, bent an elbow and tapped two fingers against the birthmark on his chin. It was a nervous gesture, one he rarely allowed. That he would give in to it now generated a distinct unease in Sarah.

"I've heard rumors," he admitted. "Only rumors, you understand."

"What rumors?"

The fingers picked up speed, machine-gunning his chin.

"Some say... Not me, I assure you! But some say that Alexis is too old. Too out of touch with our target readership. Some say the romance has gone out of her, and out of our magazine. Before, we used to beguile, to tantalize. Now we titillate."

Much to her chagrin, Sarah couldn't argue the point. The butt shot of Dev that Alexis had insisted on was case in point. In the most secret corners of her heart, she agreed with the ambiguous, unnamed "some" Paul referenced.

Despite her frequent differences of opinion with her boss, however, she owed Alexis her loyalty and support. She'd hired Sarah right out of college, sans experience, sans credentials. Grandmama might insist Sarah's title had influenced that decision. Maybe so, but the title hadn't done more than get a neophyte's foot in the door. She'd sweated blood to work her way up to layout editor. And now, apparently, it was payback time.

Alexis confirmed that some time later in her response to Sarah's email.

Sea-escapes layout looks good. We'll go with it. Please re-think the Paris photo shoot. Chicago feels we need more romance in our mag. You and Hunter personify that, at least as far as our readers are concerned.

The email nagged at Sarah all afternoon. She used the remainder of her private time to wander through her favorite museum, but not even the Musée d'Orsay could resolve her moral dilemma. Questions came at her, dive-bombing like suicidal mosquitoes as she strolled through the converted railroad station that now housed some of the world's most celebrated works of art.

All but oblivious to the Matisses and Rodins, she weighed her options. Should she support her boss or accede to Dev's demand for privacy? What about the mess with Gina? Would Alexis exploit that, too, if pushed to the wall? Would she play up the elder sister's engagement as a desperate attempt to save the younger from a charge of larceny?

She would. Sarah knew damned well she would. The certainty curdled like sour milk in the pit of her stomach. Whom did she most owe her loyalty to? Gina? Dev? Alexis? Herself?

The last thought was so heretical it gnawed at Sarah's insides while she prepped for her first meeting with the Giraults early that evening. Dev had told her this would be an informal dinner at the couple's Paris town house.

"Ha!" she muttered as she added a touch of mascara. "I'll bet it's informal."

Going with instinct, she opted for a hip-length tuxedo jacket that had been one of Grandmama's favorite pieces. Sarah had extracted the jacket from the to-be-sold pile on at least three separate occasions. Vintage was vintage, but

Louis Féraud was art. He'd opened his first house of fashion in Cannes 1950, became one of Brigitte Bardot's favorite designers and grew into a legend in his own lifetime.

This jacket was quintessential Féraud. The contour-hugging design featured wide satin lapels and a double-breasted, two-button front fastening. Sarah paired it with a black, lace-edged chemise and wide-pegged black satin pants. A honey-colored silk handkerchief peeked from the breast pocket. A thin gold bangle circled her wrist. With her hair swept up in a smooth twist, she looked restrained and refined.

For some reason, though, restrained just didn't hack it tonight. Not while she was playing tug-of-war between fiercely conflicting loyalties. She wanted to do right by Dev. And Alexis. And Gina. And herself. Elise Girault could take a flying leap.

Frowning, she unclipped her hair and let the dark mass swirl to her shoulders. Then she slipped out of the jacket and tugged off the chemise. When she pulled the jacket on again, the two-button front dipped dangerously low. Grandmama would have a cow if she saw how much shadowy cleavage her Sarah now displayed. Dev, she suspected, would approve.

He did. Instantly and enthusiastically. Bending an arm against the doorjamb, he gave a long, low whistle.

"You look fantastic."

"Thanks." Honesty compelled her to add, "So do you."

If the afternoon negotiating session with Monsieur Girault had produced any stress, it didn't show in his face. He was clean shaven, clear eyed and smelled so darned good Sarah almost leaned in for a deeper whiff. His black hair still gleamed with damp. From a shower, she wondered as she fought the urged to feather her fingers through it, or the foggy drizzle that had kept up all day?

His suit certainly wasn't vintage, but had obviously been

tailored with the same loving skill as Grandmama's jacket. With it he wore a crisp blue shirt topped by a blue-and-silver-striped tie.

"What was it Oscar Wilde said about ties?" Sarah murmured, eyeing the expensive neckwear.

"Beats me."

"Something about a well-tied tie being the first serious step in a man's life. Of course, that was back when it took them hours to achieve the perfect crease in their cravat."

"Glad those days are gone. Speaking of gone… The car's waiting." He bowed and swept a hand toward the door. "Shall we go, *ma chérie?*"

Her look of surprise brought a smug grin.

"I had some time after my meeting so I pulled up a few phrases on Google Translate. How's the accent?"

"Well…"

"That bad, huh?"

"I've heard worse."

But not much worse. Hiding a smile, she picked up her clutch and led the way to the door.

"How did the meeting go, by the way?"

"We're making progress. Enough that my chief of production and a team of our corporate attorneys are in the air as we speak. We still need to hammer out a few details, but we're close."

"You *must* be making progress if you're bringing in a whole team."

Sarah refused to acknowledge the twinge that gave her. She hadn't really expected to share much of Paris with Dev. He was here on business. And she was here to make sure that business didn't get derailed by the wife of his prospective partner. She reminded herself of that fact as the limo glided through the lamp-lit streets.

Jean-Jacques Girault and his wife greeted them at the door to their magnificent town house. Once inside the palatial foyer, the two couples engaged in the obligatory cheek-kissing. Madame Girault behaved herself as she congratulated her guests on their engagement, but Dev stuck close to his fiancée just in case.

The exchange gave Sarah time to assess her hostess. The blonde had to be in her mid-fifties, but she had the lithe build and graceful carriage of a ballerina...which she used to be, she informed Sarah with a nod toward the portrait holding place of honor in the palatial foyer. The larger-than-life-size oil depicted a much younger Elise Girault costumed as Odile, the evil black swan in Tchaikovsky's *Swan Lake.*

"I loved dancing that part." With a smile as wicked as the one she wore in the portrait, Madame Girault hooked an arm in Sarah's and led her through a set of open double doors into a high-ceilinged salon. "Being bad is so much more fun than being good, yes?"

"Unless, as happens to Odile in some versions of *Swan Lake,* being bad gets you an arrow through the heart."

The older woman's laugh burst out, as loud and booming as a cannon. "Aha! You are warning me, I think, to keep my hands off your so-handsome Devon."

"If the ballet slipper fits..."

Her laugh foghorned again, noisy and raucous and totally infectious. Sarah found herself grinning as Madame Girault spoke over her shoulder.

"I like her, Devon."

She pronounced it Dee-vón, with the accent on the last syllable.

"I was prepared not to, you understand, as I want you for myself. Perhaps we can arrange a ménage à trois, yes?"

With her back to Dev, Sarah missed his reaction to the suggestion. She would have bet it wasn't as benign as Monsieur Girault's.

"Elise, my pet. You'll shock our guests with these little jokes of yours."

The look his wife gave Sarah brimmed with mischief and the unmistakable message that she was *not* joking.

Much to Sarah's surprise, she enjoyed the evening. Elise Girault didn't try to be anything but herself. She was at times sophisticated, at other times outrageous, but she didn't cross the line Sarah had drawn in the sand. Or in this case, in the near-priceless nineteenth-century Aubusson carpet woven in green-and-gold florals.

The Giraults and their guests took cocktails in the salon and dinner in an exquisitely paneled dining room with windows overlooking the Seine. The lively conversation ranged from their hostess's years at the Ballet de l'Opéra de Paris to Sarah's work at *Beguile* to, inevitably, the megabusiness of aircraft manufacturing. The glimpse into a world she'd had no previous exposure to fascinated Sarah, but Elise tolerated it only until the last course was cleared.

"Enough, Jean-Jacques!"

Pushing away from the table, she rose. Her husband and guests followed suit.

"We will take coffee and dessert in the petite salon. And you," she said, claiming Dev's arm, "will tell me what convinced this delightful woman to marry you. It was the story in *Beguile,* yes?" Her wicked smile returning, she threw Sarah an arch look. "The truth, now. Is his derriere as delicious as it looked in your magazine?"

Her husband shook his head. "Be good, Elise."

"I am, *mon cher.* Sooo good."

"I'm good, Dee-vón." Grinning, Sarah batted her lashes as the Hôtel Verneuil's elevator whisked them upward. "Sooo good."

Amused, Dev folded his arms and leaned his shoulders against the cage. She wasn't tipsy—she'd restricted her alcoholic intake to one aperitif, a single glass of wine and a few sips of brandy—but she was looser than he'd yet seen her.

He liked her this way. Her green eyes sparkling. Her hair windblown and brushing her shoulders. Her tuxedo jacket providing intermittent and thoroughly tantalizing glimpses of creamy breasts.

Liked, hell. He wanted to devour her whole.

"You were certainly good tonight," he agreed. "Especially when Elise tried to pump you for details about our sex life. I still don't know how you managed to give the impression of torrid heat when all you did was arch a brow."

"Ah, yes. The regal lift. It's one of Grandmama's best weapons, along with the chin tilt and the small sniff."

She demonstrated all three and had him grinning while he walked her to her door.

"Elise may be harder to fend off when she and I have lunch tomorrow," Sarah warned as she extracted the key card from her purse. "I may need to improvise."

His pulse jumping, Dev took the key and slid it into the electronic lock. The lock snicked, the door opened and he made his move.

"No reason you should have to improvise."

She turned, her expression at once wary and disbelieving. "Are you suggesting we go to bed together to satisfy Elise Girault's prurient curiosity?"

"No, ma'am." He bent and brushed his lips across hers. "I'm suggesting we go to bed together to satisfy ours."

Her jaw sagged. "You're kidding, right?"

"No, ma'am," he said again, half laughing, wholly serious.

She snapped her mouth shut, but the fact that she didn't stalk inside and slam the door in his face set Dev's pulse jumping again.

"Maybe," she said slowly, her eyes locked with his, "we could go a little way down that road. Just far enough to provide Elise with a few juicy details."

That was all the invitation he needed. Scooping her into his arms, he strode into the room and kicked the door shut. The maid had left the lamps on and turned down the duvet on the bed. Much as Dev ached to vector in that direction, he aimed for the sofa instead. He settled on its plush cushions with Sarah in his lap.

Exerting fierce control, he slid a palm under the silky splash of her hair. Her nape was warm, her lips parted, her gaze steady. The thought flashed into Dev's mind that he was already pretty far down the road.

Rock hard and hurting, he bent his head again. No mere brush of lips this time. No tentative exploration. No show for the cameras. This was hunger, raw and hot. He tried to throttle it back, but Sarah sabotaged that effort by matching him kiss for kiss, touch for touch. His fingers speared through her hair. Hers traced the line of his jaw, slipped inside his collar, found the knot of his tie.

"To hell with Oscar Wilde," she muttered after a moment. "The tie has to go."

The tie went. So did the suit coat. When she popped the top two buttons of his dress shirt, he reached for the ones on her jacket. The first one slid through its opening and Dev saw she wasn't wearing a bra. With a fervent prayer of thanks, he fingered the second button.

"I've been fantasizing about doing this from the moment you opened the door to me this evening," he admitted, his voice rough.

"I fantasized about it, too. Must be why I discarded the chemise I usually wear with this outfit."

Her honesty shot straight to his heart. She didn't play games. Didn't tease or go all pouty and coy. She was as hungry as Dev and not ashamed to show it.

Aching with need, he slid the second button through its opening. The satin lapels gaped open, baring her breasts. They were small and proud and tipped with dark rose nipples that Dev couldn't even begin to resist. Hefting her a little higher, he trailed a line of kisses down one slope and caught a nipple between his lips.

Her neck arched. Her head tipped back. With a small groan, Sarah reveled in the sensations that streaked from her breast to her belly. They were so deep, so intense, she purred with pleasure.

It took her a few moments to realize she wasn't actually emitting that low, humming sound. It was coming from the clutch purse she'd dropped on the sofa table.

"That's my cell phone," she panted through waves of pleasure. "I put it on vibrate at the Giraults."

"Ignore it."

Dev turned his attention to her other breast and Sarah was tempted, so tempted, to follow his gruff instruction.

"I can't," she groaned. "It could be Grandmama. Or Maria," she added with a little clutch of panic.

She scrambled upright and grabbed her bag. A glance at the face associated in her address book with the incoming number made her sag with relief.

Only for a moment, however. What could Alexis want, calling this late? Remembering her conversation with Paul Vincent at *Beguile*'s Paris office this afternoon, Sarah once again felt the tug of conflicting loyalties.

"Sarah? Are you there?" Alexis's hoarse rasp rattled through voice mail. "Pick up if you are."

Sarah sent Dev an apologetic glance and hit Answer. "I'm here, Alexis."

"Sorry, kiddo, I didn't think about the time difference. Were you in bed?"

"Almost," Dev muttered.

Sarah made a shushing motion with her free hand but it was too late. Alexis picked up the scent like a bloodhound.

"Is that Hunter? He's with you?"

"Yes. We just got in from a late dinner."

Not a lie, exactly. Not the whole truth, either. There were some things her boss simply didn't need to know.

"Good," Alexis was saying. "He can look over the JPEGs I just emailed you from the photo shoot at Cartier. I marked the one we're going to use with the blurb about your engagement."

"We'll take a look at them and get back to you."

"Tonight, kiddo. I want the story in this month's issue."

"Okay." Sighing, Sarah closed the flaps of her jacket and fastened the top button one-handed. "Shoot me the blurb, too."

"Don't worry about it. It's only a few lines."

The too-bland assurance set off an internal alarm.

"Send it, Alexis."

"All right, all right. But I want it back tonight, too."

She cut the connection, and Sarah sank back onto the cushions. Dev sat in his corner, one arm stretched across the sofa back. His shirttails hung open and his belt had somehow come unbuckled. He looked more than willing to pick up where they'd left off, but Sarah's common sense had kicked in. Or rather her sense of self-preservation.

"Saved by the bell," she said with an attempt at lightness. "At least now I won't have to improvise when Elise starts digging for details."

The phone pinged in her hand, signaling the arrival of a text message.

"That's the blurb Alexis wants to run with the pictures from Cartier. I'll pull it up with the photos so you can review them."

"No need." Dev pushed off the sofa, stuffed in his shirt and buckled his belt. "I trust you on this one."

"I'll make sure there are no naked body parts showing," she promised solemnly.

"You do that, and I'll make sure we're not interrupted next time."

"Next time?"

He dropped a quick kiss on her nose and grabbed his discarded suit coat.

"Oui, ma chérie," he said in his truly execrable French. "Next time."

Nine

Dev had a breakfast meeting with his people, who'd flown in the night before. That gave Sarah the morning to herself. A shame, really, because the day promised glorious sunshine and much warmer temperatures. Perfect for strolling the Left Bank with that special someone.

Which is what most of Paris seemed to be doing, she saw after coffee and a croissant at her favorite patisserie. The sight of so many couples, young, old and in between, rekindled some of the raw emotions Dev had generated last night.

In the bright light of day, Sarah couldn't believe she'd invited him to make love to her. Okay, she'd practically demanded it. Even now, as she meandered over the Pont de l'Archevêché, she felt her breasts tingle at the memory of his hands and mouth on them.

She stopped midway across the bridge. Pont de l'Archevêché translated to the Archbishop's Bridge in English, most likely because it formed a main means of transit for the clerics of Notre Dame. The cathedral's square towers rose on the right. Bookseller stalls and cafés crowded the broad avenue on the left. The Seine flowed dark and silky below. What intrigued her, though, were the padlocks of all shapes and sizes hooked through the bridge's waist-high, iron-mesh scrollwork. Some locks had tags attached, some were decorated with bright ribbons, some included small charms.

She'd noticed other bridges sporting locks, although none as heavily adorned as this one. They'd puzzled her but she hadn't really wondered about their significance. It became apparent a few moments after she spotted a pair of tourists purchasing a padlock from an enterprising lock seller at the far end of the bridge. The couple searched for an empty spot on the fancy grillwork to attach their purchase. Then they threw the key into the Seine and shared a long, passionate kiss.

When they walked off arm in arm, Sarah approached the lock seller. He was perched on an upturned wooden crate beside a pegboard displaying his wares. His hair sprouted like milky-white dandelion tufts from under his rusty-black beret. A cigarette hung from his lower lip.

"I've been away for a while," she said in her fluent Parisian. "When did this business with the locks begin?"

"Three years? Five? Who can remember?" His shoulders lifted in the quintessential Gallic shrug. "At first the locks appeared only at night, and they would be cut off each day. Now they are everywhere."

"So it seems."

Mistaking her for a native, he winked and shared his personal opinion of his enterprise. "The tourists, they eat this silly stuff up. As if they can lock in the feelings they have right now, today, and throw away the key. We French know better, yes?"

His cigarette bobbed. His gestures grew extravagant as he expounded his philosophy.

"To love is to take risks. To be free, not caged. To walk away if what you feel brings hurt to you or to your lover. Who would stay, or want to stay, where there is pain?"

The question was obviously rhetorical, so Sarah merely spread her hands and answered with a shrug.

She was still thinking about the encounter when she met Madame Girault for lunch later that day. She related the lock seller's philosophy to Elise, who belted out a raucous laugh that turned heads throughout the restaurant.

"My darling Sarah, I must beg to disagree!"

With her blond hair drawn into a tight bun that emphasized her high cheekbones and angular chin, Elise looked more like the Black Swan of her portrait. Her sly smile only heightened the resemblance.

"Locks and, yes, a little pain can add a delicious touch to an affair," she said, her eyes dancing. "And speaking of which…"

Her mouth took a sardonic tilt as a dark-haired man some twenty-five or thirty years her junior rose from his table and approached theirs.

"Ah, Elise, only one woman in all Paris has a laugh like yours. How are you, my love?"

"Very well. And you, Henri? Are you still dancing attendance on that rich widow I saw you with at the theater?"

"Sadly, she returned to Argentina before I extracted full payment for services rendered." His dark eyes drifted to Sarah. "But enough of such mundane matters. You must introduce me to your so-lovely companion."

"No, I must not. She's in Paris with her fiancé and has no need of your special skills." Elise flapped a hand and shooed him off. "Be a good boy and go away."

"If you insist…"

He gave a mocking half bow and returned to his table, only to sign the check and leave a few moments later. A fleeting look of regret crossed Elise's face as he wove his way toward the exit. Sighing, she fingered her glass.

"He was so inventive in bed, that one. So *very* inventive. But always in need of money. When I tired of emptying my purse for him, he threatened to sell pictures of me in certain, shall we say, exotic positions."

Sarah winced, but couldn't say anything. Any mention of the paparazzi and sensational photographs struck too close to home.

"Jean-Jacques sent men to convince him that would not be wise," Elise confided. "The poor boy was in a cast for weeks afterward."

The offhand comment doused the enjoyment Sarah had taken in Elise's company up to that point. Madame Girault's concept of love suddenly seemed more tawdry than amusing. Deliberately, Sarah changed the subject.

"I wonder how the negotiations are going? Dev said he thought they were close to a deal."

Clearly disinterested, Elise shrugged and snapped her fingers to summon their waiter.

Halfway across Paris, Dev had to force himself to focus on the columns of figures in the newly restructured agreement. It didn't help that his seat at the conference table offered a panoramic view of the pedestrians-only esplanade and iconic Grande Arche that dominated Paris's financial district. Workers by the hundreds were seated on the steps below the Grande Arche, their faces lifted to the sun while they enjoyed their lunch break.

One couple appeared to be enjoying more than the sun. Dev watched them share a touch, a laugh, a kiss. Abruptly, he pushed away from the table.

"Sorry," he said to the dozen or so startled faces that turned in his direction. "I need to make a call."

Jean-Jacques Girault scooted his chair away from the table, as well. "Let's all take a break. We'll reconvene in thirty minutes, yes? There'll be a catered lunch waiting when we return."

Dev barely waited for Girault to finish his little speech. The urge to talk to Sarah, to hear her voice, drove him through the maze of outer offices and into the elevator. A short while later he'd joined the throng on the steps below the Grande Arche.

It took him a moment to acknowledge the unfamiliar sensation that knifed through him as he dialed Sarah's number. It wasn't just the lust that had damned near choked him last night. It was that amorphous, indefinable feeling immortalized in so many sappy songs. Grimacing, he admitted the inescapable truth. He was in love, or close enough to it to make no difference.

Sarah answered on the second ring. "Hello, Dev. This must be mental telepathy. I was just talking about you."

"You were, huh?"

"How are the negotiations going?"

"They're going."

The sound of her voice did something stupid to his insides. To his head, too. With barely a second thought, he abandoned Girault and company to the team of sharks he'd flown in last night.

"We've been crunching numbers all morning. I'm thinking of letting my people handle the afternoon session. What do you have planned?"

"Nothing special."

"How about I meet you back at the hotel and we'll do nothing special together?"

He didn't intend to say what came next. Didn't have any control over the words. They just happened.

"Or maybe," he said, his voice going husky, "we can work on our next time."

A long silence followed his suggestion. When it stretched for several seconds, Dev kicked himself for his lack of finesse. Then she came back with a low, breathless response that damned near stopped his heart.

"I'll catch a cab and meet you at the hotel."

* * *

Sarah snapped her phone shut and sent Madame Girault a glance that was only a shade apologetic. "That was Dev. I'm sorry, but I have to go."

Elise looked startled for a moment. But only a moment. Then her face folded into envious lines.

"Go," she ordered with a wave of one hand. "Paris is the city of love, after all. And I think yours, *ma petite,* is one that deserves a lock on the Archbishop's Bridge."

Sarah wanted to believe that was what sent her rushing out of the restaurant. Despite the lock seller's philosophical musings, despite hearing the details of Elise's sordid little affair, she wanted desperately to believe that what she felt for Dev could stand the test of time.

That hope took a temporary hit when she caught up with the dark-haired, dark-eyed Henri on the pavement outside of the restaurant. He'd just hailed a cab, but generously offered it to her instead.

Or not so generously. His offer to escort her to her hotel and fill her afternoon hours with unparalleled delight left an unpleasant taste in Sarah's mouth. Unconsciously, she channeled Grandmama.

"I think not, monsieur."

The haughty reply sent him back a pace. The blank surprise on his face allowed Sarah more than enough time to slide into the cab and tell the driver her destination. Then she slammed the door and forgot Henri, forgot Elise, forgot everything but the instant hunger Dev's call had sparked in her.

She wrestled with that hunger all the way back to the hotel. Her cool, rational, practical-by-necessity self kept asserting that her arrangement with Dev Hunter was just that, an arrangement. A negotiated contract that would soon conclude. If she made love with him, as she desperately wanted to do, she'd simply be satisfying a short-term physical need while possibly setting herself up for long-term regrets.

The other side of her, the side she usually kept so sternly repressed, echoed Gina at her giddiest. Why not grab a little pleasure? Taste delight here, now, and let tomorrow take care of itself?

As was happening all too frequently with Dev, giddy and greedy vanquished cool and rational. By the time Sarah burst out of the elevator and headed down the hall toward her room, heat coursed through her, hot and urgent. The sight of Dev leaning against the wall beside the door to her room sent her body temperature soaring up another ten degrees.

"What took you so long?" he demanded.

Snatching the key card from her hand, he shoved it into the lock. Two seconds after the door opened, he had her against the entryway wall.

"I hope you had a good lunch. We won't be coming up for food or drink anytime soon."

The bruising kiss spiked every one of Sarah's senses. She tasted him, drank in his scent, felt his hips slam hers against the wall.

He kicked the door shut. Or did she? She didn't know, didn't care. Dev's hands were all over her at that point. Unbuttoning her blouse. Hiking up her skirt. Shoving down her bikini briefs.

Panting, greedy, wanting him so much she ached with it, she struggled out of her blouse. Kicked her shoes off and the panties free of her ankles. Hooked one leg around his thighs.

"Sarah." It was a groan and a plea. "Let's take this to the bedroom."

Mere moments later she was naked and stretched out on the king-size bed. Her avid gaze devoured Dev as he stood beside the bed and shed his clothing.

She'd seen portions of him last night. Enough to confirm that he ranked much higher than number three on her personal top ten list. Those glimpses didn't even begin to compare with the way he looked now with his black hair catching the afternoon light and his blue eyes fired with need. Every muscle in his long, lean body looked taut and eager. He was hard for her, and hungry, and so ready that Sarah almost yelped when he turned away.

"What are you doing?"

"Making sure you don't regret this."

Her dismay became a wave of relief when she saw him extract a condom from the wallet in his discarded pants. She wasn't on the pill. She'd stopped months ago. Or was it years? Sarah couldn't remember. She suspected her decision to quit birth control had a lot to do with the realization that taking care of Grandmama and keeping a roof over their heads were more important to her than casual sex.

Showed what she knew. There was nothing casual about this sex, however. The need for it, the gnawing hunger for it, consumed her.

No! Her mind screamed the denial even as she opened her arms to Dev. This wasn't just sex. This wasn't just raw need. This was so elemental. So...so French. Making love in the afternoon. With a man who filled her, physically, emotionally, every way that mattered.

His hips braced against hers. His knees pried hers apart. Eagerly, Sarah opened her legs and her arms and her heart to him. When he eased into her, she hooked her calves around his and rose up to meet his first, slow thrusts. Then the pace picked up. In. Out. In again.

Soon, *too* soon, dammit, her vaginal muscles began to quiver and her belly contracted. She tried to suppress the spasms. Tried to force her muscles to ease their greedy grip. She wanted to build to a steady peak, spin the pleasure as long as she could.

Her body refused to listen to her mind. The tight, spiraling sensation built to a wild crescendo. Panting, Sarah arched her neck. A moment later, she was flying, sailing, soaring. Dev surged into her, went taut and rode to the crest with her. Then he gave a strangled grunt and collapsed on top of her.

* * *

Sarah was still shuddering with the aftershocks when he whispered a French phrase into her ear. Her eyes flew open. Her jaw dropped.

"What did you say?"

He levered up on one elbow. A flush rode high in his cheeks and his blue eyes were still fever bright, but he managed a semicoherent reply.

"I was trying to tell you I adore you."

Sarah started giggling and couldn't stop. No easy feat with 180 plus pounds of naked male pinning her to the sheets.

A rueful grin sketched across Dev's face. "Okay, what did I really say?"

"It sounded...it sounded..." Helpless with laughter, she gasped for breath. "It sounded like you want to hang an ornament on me."

"Yeah, well, that, too." His grin widening, he leaned down and dropped a kiss on her left breast. "Here. And here..."

He grazed her right breast, eased down to her belly.

"And here, and..."

"Dev!"

Pleasure rippled in waves across the flat plane of her stomach. She wouldn't have believed she could become so aroused so fast. Particularly after that shattering orgasm. Dev, on the other hand, was lazy and loose and still flaccid.

"Don't you need to, uh, take a little time to recharge?"

"I do." His voice was muffled, his breath hot against her skin. "Doesn't mean you have to. Unless you want to?"

He raised his head and must have seen the answer in her face. Waggling his brows, he lowered his head again. Sarah gasped again when his tongue found her now supersensitized center.

The climax hit this time without warning. She'd just reached up to grip the headboard and bent a knee to avoid a cramp when everything seemed to shrink to a single, white-hot nova. The next second, the star exploded. Pleasure pulsed through her body. Groaning, she let it flow before it slowly, exquisitely ebbed.

When she opened her eyes again, Dev looked smug and pretty damn pleased with himself. With good reason, she thought, drifting on the last eddies. She sincerely hoped he still needed some time to recharge. She certainly did!

To her relief, he stretched out beside her and seemed content to just laze. She nestled her head on his arm and let her thoughts drift back to his mangled French. He said he'd been trying to tell her that he adored her. What did that mean, exactly?

She was trying to find a way to reintroduce the subject when the phone buzzed. His this time, not hers. With a muffled grunt, Dev reached across her and checked his phone's display.

"Sorry," he said with a grimace. "I told them not to call unless they were about to slam up against our own version of a fiscal cliff. I'd better take this."

"Go ahead. I'll hit the bathroom."

She scooped up the handiest article of clothing, which happened to be Dev's shirt, and padded into the bathroom. The tiles felt cool and smooth against her bare feet. The apparition that appeared in the gilt-edged mirrors made her gasp.

"Good grief!"

Her hair could have provided a home for an entire flock of sparrows. Whatever makeup she'd started out with this morning had long since disappeared. She was also sporting one whisker burn on her chin and another on her neck. Shuddering at the thought of what Elise Girault would say if she saw the telltale marks, Sarah ran the taps and splashed cold water on her face and throat.

That done, she eyed the bidet. So practical for Europeans, so awkward for most Americans. Practical won hands down in this instance. Clean and refreshed, Sarah reentered the bedroom just as Dev was zipping up his pants.

"Uh-oh. Looks like your negotiators ran into that cliff."

"Ran into it, hell. According to my chief of production, they soared right over the damned thing and are now in a free fall."

"That doesn't sound good."

Detouring to her closet, she exchanged Dev's shirt for the thigh-length, peony-decorated silk robe Gina had given her for her birthday last year.

"It's all part of the game," he said as she handed him back his shirt. "Girault's just a little better at it than I gave him credit for."

The comment tripped a reminder of Elise's disclosures at lunch. Sarah debated for a moment over whether she should share them with Dev, then decided he needed to know the kind of man he would be doing business with.

"Elise said something today about her husband that surprised me."

Dev looked up from buttoning his shirt. "What was that?"

"Supposedly, Jean-Jacques sent some goons to rough up one of her former lovers. The guy had threatened to sell pictures of her to the tabloids."

"Interesting. I would have thought Girault man enough to do the job himself. I certainly would have." He scooped up his tie and jacket and gave her a quick kiss. "I'll call as soon as I have a fix on when we'll break for dinner."

Sarah nodded, but his careless remark about going after Elise's lover for trying to sell pictures of her had struck home. The comment underscored his contempt for certain members of her profession. How much would it take, she wondered uneasily, for him to lump her in with the sleaziest among them?

Ten

Still troubled by Dev's parting comment, Sarah knotted the sash to her robe and stepped out onto her little balcony. She'd lost herself in the view before, but this time the seemingly endless vista of chimneys and gray slate roofs didn't hold as much interest as her bird's-eye view of the street four stories below.

The limo Dev had called for idled a few yards from the hotel's entrance. When he strode out of the hotel, the sight of him once again outfitted in his business attire gave Sarah's heart a crazy bump. She couldn't help contrasting that with the image of his sleek, naked body still vivid in her mind.

The uniformed driver jumped out to open the rear passenger door. Dev smiled and said a few words to him, inaudible from Sarah's height, and ducked to enter the car. At the last moment he paused and glanced up. When he spotted her, the friendly smile he'd given the driver warmed into something so private and so sensual that she responded without thinking.

Touching her fingers lightly to her lips, she blew him a kiss—and was immediately embarrassed by the gesture. It was so schmaltzy, and so out of character for her. More like something Gina might do. Yet she remained on the balcony like some lovelorn Juliet long after Dev had driven off.

Even worse, she couldn't summon the least desire to get dressed and meander through the streets. Peering into shop windows or people watching at a café didn't hold as much allure as it had before. She would rather wait until Dev finished with his meeting and they could meander together.

She'd take a long, bubbly bath instead, she decided. But first she had catch up on her email. And call Grandmama. And try Gina again. Maybe this time her sister would answer the damned phone.

Gina didn't, but Sarah caught the duchess before she went out for her morning constitutional. She tried to temper her habitual concern with a teasing note.

"You won't overdo it, will you?"

"My darling Sarah," Charlotte huffed. "If I could walk almost forty miles through a war-torn country with an infant in my arms, I can certainly stroll a few city blocks."

Wisely, Sarah refrained from pointing out that the duchess had made the first walk more than fifty years ago.

"Have you heard from Gina?" she asked instead.

"No, have you?"

"Not since she texted me that she was flitting off to Switzerland."

She'd tried to keep her the response casual, but the duchess knew her too well.

"Listen to me, Sarah Elizabeth Marie-Adele. Your sister may act rashly on occasion, but she's a St. Sebastian. Whatever you think she may be up to, she won't bring shame on her family or her name."

The urge to tell her grandmother about the missing medallion was so strong that Sarah had to bite her lip to keep from blurting it out. That would only lead to a discussion of how she'd become involved with Dev, and she wasn't ready to explain that, either. Thankfully, her grandmother was content to let the subject drop.

"Now tell me about Paris," she commanded. "Has Devon taken you to Café Michaud yet?"

"Not yet, but he said you'd given him strict orders to do so. Oh, and he had his people work minor miracles to get us into the Hôtel Verneuil on such short notice."

"He did? How very interesting."

She sounded so thoughtful—and so much like a cat that had just lapped up a bowl of cream—that Sarah became instantly suspicious.

"What other instructions did you give him?"

"None."

"Come on. Fess up. What other surprises do I have in store?"

A soft sigh came through the phone. "You're in Paris, with a handsome, virile man. One whom I suspect is more than capable of delivering surprises of his own."

Sarah gave a fervent prayer of thanks that the duchess hadn't yet mastered the FaceTime app on her phone. If she had, she would have seen her elder granddaughter's cheeks flame at the thought of how much she'd *already* enjoyed her handsome, virile fiancé.

"I'll talk to you tomorrow, Grandmama. Give Maria my love."

She hung up, marveling again at how readily everyone seemed to have accepted Dev Hunter's sudden appearance in their lives. Grandmama. Maria. Alexis. Sarah herself. Would they accept his abrupt departure as readily?

Would they have to?

Sarah was no fool. Nor was she blind. She could tell Dev felt at least some of the same jumbled emotions she did. Mixed in with the greedy hunger there was the shared laughter, the seduction of this trip, the growing delight in each other's company. Maybe, just maybe, there could be love, too.

She refused to even speculate about anything beyond that. Their evolving relationship was too new, too fragile, to project vary far ahead. Still, she couldn't help humming the melody from Edith Piaf's classic, "La Vie En Rose," as she started for the bathroom and a long, hot soak.

The house phone caught her halfway there. She detoured to the desk and answered. The caller identified himself as Monsieur LeBon, the hotel's manager, and apologized profusely for disturbing her.

"You're not disturbing me, monsieur."

"Good, good." He hesitated, then seemed to be choosing his words carefully. "I saw Monsieur Hunter leave a few moments ago and thought perhaps I might catch you alone."

"Why? Is there a problem?"

"I'm not sure. Do you by chance know a gentleman by the name of Henri Lefèvre?"

"I don't recognize the name."

"Aha! I thought as much." LeBon gave a small sniff. "There was something in his manner..."

"What has this Monsieur Lefèvre to do with me?"

"He approached our receptionist earlier this afternoon and claimed you and he were introduced by a mutual acquaintance. He couldn't remember your name, however. Only that you were a tall, slender American who spoke excellent French. And that you mentioned you were staying at the Hôtel Verneuil."

The light dawned. It had to be Elise's former lover. He must have heard her give the cabdriver instructions to the hotel.

"The receptionist didn't tell him my name, did she?"

"You may rest assured she did not! Our staff is too well trained to disclose information on any of our guests. She referred the man to me, and I sent him on his way."

"Thank you, Monsieur LeBon. Please let me know immediately if anyone else inquires about me."

"Of course, Lady Sarah."

The call from the hotel manager dimmed a good bit of Sarah's enjoyment in her long, bubbly soak. She didn't particularly like the fact that Elise's smarmy ex-lover had tracked her to the hotel.

Dev called just moments after she emerged from the tub. Sounding totally disgusted, he told her he intended to lock everyone in the conference room until they reached a final agreement.

"The way it looks now that might be midnight or later. Sorry, Sarah. I won't be able to keep our dinner date."

"Don't worry about that."

"Yeah, well, I'd much rather be with you than these clowns. I'm about ready to tell Girault and company to shove it."

Sarah didn't comment. She couldn't, given the staggering sums involved in his negotiations. But she thought privately he was taking a risk doing business with someone who hired thugs to pound on his wife's lover.

Briefly, she considered telling Dev that same lover had shown up at the hotel this afternoon but decided against it. He had enough on his mind at the moment and Monsieur LeBon appeared to have taken care of the matter.

She spent what remained of the afternoon and most of the evening on her laptop, with only a short break for soup and a salad ordered from room service. She had plenty of work to keep her busy and was satisfied with the two layouts she'd mocked up when she finally quit. She'd go in to the offices on rue Balzac tomorrow to view the layouts on the twenty-five-inch monitor.

Unless Dev finished negotiations tonight as he swore he would do. Then maybe they'd spend the day together. And the night. And...

Her belly tightening at the possibilities, she curled up in bed with the ebook she'd downloaded. She got through only a few pages before she dozed off.

* * *

The phone jerked her from sleep. She fumbled among the covers, finally found it and came more fully awake when she recognized Dev's number.

"Did you let them all out of the conference room?" she asked with a smile.

"I did. They're printing the modified contracts as we speak. They'll be ready to sign tomorrow morning."

"Congratulations!"

She was happy for him, she really was, even if it meant the termination of their arrangement.

"I'm on my way back to the hotel. Is it too late for a celebration?"

"I don't know. What time is it?"

"Almost one."

"No problem. Just give me a few minutes to get dressed. Do you have someplace special in mind? If not, I know several great cafés that stay open until 2:00 a.m."

"Actually, I was hoping for a private celebration. No dressing required."

She could hear the smile in his voice, and something more. Something that brought Gina forcefully to mind. Her sister always claimed she felt as though she was tumbling through time and space whenever she fell in love. Sarah hadn't scoffed but she *had* chalked the hyperbole up to another Gina-ism.

How wrong she was. And how right Gina was. That was exactly how Sarah felt now. As though Dev had kicked her feet out from under her and she was on some wild, uncontrollable slide.

"A private celebration sounds good to me," she got out breathlessly.

She didn't change out of the teddy and bikini briefs she'd worn to bed, but she did throw on the peony robe and make a dash to the bathroom before she answered Dev's knock.

As charged up as he'd sounded on the phone, she half expected him to kick the door shut and pin her against the wall again. Okay, she kind of hoped he would.

He didn't, but Sarah certainly couldn't complain about his altered approach. The energy was there, and the exultation from having closed his big deal. Yet the hands that cupped her face were incredibly gentle, and the kiss he brushed across her mouth was so tender she almost melted from the inside out.

"Jean-Jacques told me to thank you," he murmured against her lips.

"For what?"

"He thinks I finally agreed to his company's design for the pneumatic turbine assembly because I was so damned anxious to get back to you."

"Oh, no!"

She pulled back in dismay. She had no idea what a pneumatic turbine assembly was, but it sounded important.

"You didn't concede anything critical, did you?"

"Nah. I always intended to accept their design. I just used it as my ace in the hole to close the deal. *And* to get back to you."

He bent and brushed her mouth again. When he raised his head, the look in his eyes started Sarah on another wild spin through time and space.

"I don't want to risk any more mangled verbs," he said with a slow smile, "so I'll stick to English this time. I love you, Sarah St. Sebastian."

"Since...? Since when?"

He appeared to give the matter some consideration. "Hard to say. I have to admit it started with a severe case of lust."

She would have to admit the same thing. Later. Right now she could only try to keep breathing as he raised her hand and angled it so the emerald caught the light.

"By the time I put this on your finger, though, I was

already strategizing ways to keep it there. I know I black-mailed you into this fake engagement, Sarah, but if I ask very politely and promise to be nice to your ditz of a sister, would you consider making it real?"

Although it went against a lifetime of ingrained habit, she didn't fire up in Gina's defense. Instead she drew her brows together.

"I need a minute to think about it."

Surprise and amusement and just a touch of uncertainty colored Dev's reply. "Take all the time you need."

She pursed her lips and gave the matter three or four seconds of fierce concentration.

"Okay."

"Okay you'll consider it, or okay you'll make it real?"

Laughing, Sarah hooked her arms around his neck. "I'm going with option B."

Dev hadn't made a habit of going on the prowl like so many crew dogs he'd flown with, but he'd racked up more than a few quality hours with women in half a dozen countries. Not until *this* woman, however, did he really appreciate the difference between having sex and making love. It wasn't her smooth, sleek curves or soft flesh or breathless little pants. It was the sum of all parts, the whole of her, the elegance that was Sarah.

And the fact that she was his.

He'd intended to make this loving slow and sweet, a sort of unspoken acknowledgment of the months and years of nights like this they had ahead. She blew those plans out of the water mere moments after Dev positioned her under him. Her body welcomed him, her heat fired his. The primitive need to possess her completely soon had him pinning her wrists to the sheets, his thrusts hard and deep. Her head went back. Her belly quivered. A moan rose from deep in her throat, and Dev took everything she had to give.

* * *

She was still half-asleep when he leaned over her early the next morning. "I've got to shower and change and get with Girault to sign the contracts. How about we meet for lunch at your grandmother's favorite café?"

"Mmm."

"Tell me the name of it again."

"Café Michaud," she muttered sleepily, "rue de Monttessuy."

"Got it. Café Michaud. Rue de Monttessuy. Twelve noon?"

"Mmm."

He took his time in the shower, answered several dozen emails, reviewed a bid solicitation on a new government contract and still made the ten o'clock signing session at Girault's office with time to spare.

The French industrialist was in a jovial mood, convinced he'd won a grudging, last-minute concession. Dev didn't disabuse him. After initialing sixteen pages and signing three, the two chief executives posed for pictures while their respective staffs breathed sighs of relief that the months of intense negotiations were finally done.

"How long do you remain in Paris?" Girault asked after pictures and another round of handshakes.

"I had planned to fly home as soon as we closed this deal, but I think now I'll take some downtime and stay over a few more days."

"A very wise decision," Girault said with a wink. "Paris is a different city entirely when explored with one you love. Especially when that one is as delightful as your Sarah."

"I won't argue with that. And speaking of my Sarah, we're meeting for lunch. I'll say goodbye now, Jean-Jacques."

"But no! Not goodbye. You must have dinner with Elise and me again before you leave. Now that we are partners, yes?"

"I'll see what Sarah has planned and get back to you."

* * *

The rue de Monttessuy was in the heart of Paris's 7th arrondissement. Tall, stately buildings topped with slate roofs crowded the sidewalks and offered a glimpse of the Eiffel Tower spearing into the sky at the far end of the street. Café Michaud sat midway down a long block, a beacon of color with its bright red awnings and window boxes filled with geraniums.

Since he was almost a half hour early, Dev had his driver drop him off at the intersection. He needed to stretch his legs, and he preferred to walk the half block rather than wait for Sarah at one of the café's outside tables. Maybe he could find something for her in one of the shops lining the narrow, cobbled street. Unlike the high-end boutiques and jeweler's showrooms on some of the more fashionable boulevards, these were smaller but no less intriguing.

He strolled past a tiny grocery with fresh produce displayed in wooden crates on either side of the front door, a chocolatier, a wine shop and several antique shops. One in particular caught his attention. Its display of military and aviation memorabilia drew him into the dim, musty interior.

His eyes went instantly to an original lithograph depicting Charles Lindbergh's 1927 landing at a Paris airfield after his historic solo transatlantic flight. The photographer had captured the shadowy images of the hundreds of Model As and Ts lined up at the airfield, their headlamps illuminating the grassy strip as the *Spirit of St. Louis* swooped out of the darkness.

"I'll take that," he told the shopkeeper.

The man's brows soared with surprise and just a touch of disdain for this naive American who made no attempt to bargain. Dev didn't care. He would have paid twice the price. He'd never thought of himself as particularly sentimental, but the key elements in the print—aviation and Paris—were what had brought him and Sarah together.

As if to compensate for his customer's foolishness, the shopkeeper threw in at no cost the thick cardboard tube the print had been rolled in when he himself had discovered it at a flea market.

Tube in hand, Dev exited the shop and started for the café. His pulse kicked when he spotted Sarah approaching from the opposite direction. She was on the other side of the street, some distance from the café, but he recognized her graceful walk and the silky brown hair topped by a jaunty red beret.

He picked up his pace, intending to cross at the next corner, when a figure half-hidden amid a grocer's produce display brought him to a dead stop. The man had stringy brown hair that straggled over the shoulders and a camera propped on the top crate. Its monster zoom lens was aimed directly at Sarah. While Dev stood there, his jaw torquing, the greaseball clicked off a half-dozen shots.

"What the hell are you doing?"

The photographer whipped around. He said something in French, but it was the careless shrug that fanned Dev's anger into fury.

"Bloodsucking parasites," he ground out.

The hand gripping the cardboard tube went white at the knuckles. His other hand bunched into a fist. Screw the lawsuits. He'd flatten the guy. The photographer read his intent and jumped back, knocking over several crates of produce in the process.

"*Non, non!*" He stumbled back, his face white with alarm under the greasy hair. "You don't...you don't understand, Monsieur Hunter. I am François. With *Beguile*. I shoot the photos for the story."

For the second time in as many moments, Dev froze. "The story?"

"*Oui.* We get the instructions from New York."

He thrust out the camera and angled the digital display.

His thumb beat a rapid tattoo as he clicked through picture after picture.

"But look! Here are you and Sarah having coffee. And here you walk along the Seine. And here she blows you a kiss from the balcony of her hotel room."

Pride overrode the photographer's alarm. A few clicks of the zoom button enlarged the shot on the screen.

"Do you see how perfectly she is framed? And the expression on her face after you drive away. Like one lost in a dream, yes? She stays like that long enough for me to shoot from three different angles."

The anger still hot in Dev's gut chilled. Ice formed in his veins.

"She posed for you?" he asked softly, dangerously.

The photographer glanced up, nervous again. He stuttered something about New York, but Dev wasn't listening. His gaze was locked on Sarah as she approached the café.

She'd posed for this guy. After making all those noises about allowing only that one photo shoot at Cartier, she'd caved to her boss's demands. He might have forgiven that. He had a harder time with the fact that she'd set this all up without telling him.

Dev left the photographer amid the produce. Jaw tight, he stalked toward the café. Sarah was still a block away on the other side of the street. He was about to cross when a white delivery van slowed to a rolling stop and blocked her from view. A few seconds later, Dev heard the thud of its rear doors slam. When the van cut a sharp left and turned down a narrow side street, the sidewalk Sarah had been walking along was empty.

Eleven

Dev broke into a run even before he fully processed what had just happened. All he knew for sure was that Sarah had been strolling toward him one moment and was gone the next. His brain scrambled for a rational explanation of her sudden disappearance. She could have ducked into a shop. Could have stopped to check something in a store window. His gut went with the delivery van.

Dev hit the corner in a full-out sprint and charged down the side street. He dodged a woman pushing a baby carriage, earned a curse from two men he almost bowled over. He could see the van up ahead, see its taillights flashing red as it braked for a stop sign.

He was within twenty yards when the red lights blinked off. Less than ten yards away when the van began another turn. The front window was halfway down. Through it Dev could see the driver, his gaze intent on the pedestrians streaming across the intersection and his thin black cigarillo sending spirals of smoke through the half-open window.

Dev calculated the odds on the fly. Go for the double rear doors or aim for the driver? He risked losing the van if the rear doors were locked and the vehicle picked up speed after completing the turn. He also risked causing an accident if he jumped into traffic in the middle of a busy intersection and planted himself in front of the van.

He couldn't take that chance on losing it. With a desperate burst of speed, he cut the corner and ran into the street right ahead of an oncoming taxi. Brakes squealing, horn blaring, the cab fishtailed. Dev slapped a hand on its hood, pushed off and landed in a few yards ahead of the now-rolling van. He put up both hands and shouted a fierce command.

"Stop!"

He got a glimpse, just a glimpse, of the driver's face through the windshield. Surprise, fear, desperation all flashed across it in the half second before he hit the gas.

Well, hell! The son of a bitch was gunning straight for him.

Dev jumped out of the way at the last second and leaped for the van's door as the vehicle tried to zoom past. The door was unlocked, thank God, although he'd been prepared to hook an arm inside the open window and pop the lock if necessary. Wrenching the panel open, he got a bulldog grip on the driver's leather jacket.

"Pull over, dammit."

The man jerked the wheel, cursing and shouting and trying frantically to dislodge him. The van swerved. More horns blasted.

"Dev!"

The shout came from the back of the van. From Sarah. He didn't wait to hear more. His fist locked on the driver's leather jacket, he put all his muscle into a swift yank. The bastard's face slammed into the steering wheel. Bone crunched. Blood fountained. The driver slumped.

Reaching past him, Dev tore the keys from the ignition. The engine died, but the van continued to roll toward a car that swerved wildly but couldn't avoid a collision. Metal crunched metal as both vehicles came to an abrupt stop, and Dev fumbled for the release for the driver's seat belt. He dragged the unconscious man out and let him drop to the pavement. Scrambling into the front seat, he had one leg over the console to climb into the rear compartment when the back doors flew open and someone jumped out.

It wasn't Sarah. She was on her knees in the back. A livid red welt marred one cheek. A roll of silver electrical tape dangled from a wide strip wrapped around one wrist. Climbing over the console, Dev stooped beside her.

"Are you okay?"

"Yes."

Her eyes were wide and frightened, but the distant wail of a siren eased some of their panic. Dev tore his glance from her to the open rear doors and the man running like hell back down the side street.

"Stay here and wait for the police. I'm going after that bastard."

"Wait!" She grabbed his arm. "You don't need to chase him! I know who he is."

He swung back. "You *know* him?"

When she nodded, suspicion knifed into him like a serrated blade. His fists bunched, and a distant corner of his mind registered the fact that he'd lost the lithograph sometime during the chase. The rest of him staggered under a sudden realization.

"This is part of it, isn't it? This big abduction scene?"

"Scene?"

She sounded so surprised he almost believed her. Worse, dammit, he wanted to believe her!

"It's okay," he ground out. "You can drop the act. I bumped into the photographer from *Beguile* back there on rue de Monttessuy. We had quite a conversation."

Her color drained, making the red welt across her cheek look almost obscene by contrast. "You...you talked to a photographer from my magazine?"

"Yeah, Lady Sarah, I did. François told me about the shoot. Showed me some of the pictures he's already taken. I'll have to ask him to send me the one of you on the balcony. You make a helluva Juliet."

The sirens were louder now. Their harsh, up-and-down bleat almost drowned out her whisper.

"And you think we...me, this photographer, my magazine...you think we staged an abduction?"

"I'm a little slow. It took me a while to understand the angle. I'm betting your barracuda of a boss dreamed it up. Big, brave Number Three rescues his beautiful fiancée from would-be kidnappers."

She looked away, and her silence cut even deeper than Dev's suspicion. He'd hoped she would go all huffy, deny at least some of her part in this farce. Apparently, she couldn't.

Well, Sarah and her magazine could damned well live with the consequences of their idiotic scheme. At the least, they were looking at thousands of dollars in vehicle damage. At the worst, reconstructive surgery for the driver whose face Dev had rearranged.

Thoroughly disgusted, he took Sarah's arm to help her out of the van. She shook off his hold without a word, climbed down and walked toward the squad car now screeching to a halt. Two officers exited. One went to kneel beside the moaning van driver. The other soon centered on Sarah as the other major participant in the incident. She communicated with him in swift, idiomatic French. He took notes the entire time, shooting the occasional glance at Dev that said his turn would come.

It did, but not until an ambulance had screamed up and two EMTs went to work on the driver. At the insistence of the officer who'd interviewed Sarah, a third medical tech examined her. The tech was shining a penlight into her pupils when the police officer turned his attention to Dev. Switching to English, he took down Dev's name, address while in Paris and cell-phone number before asking for his account of the incident.

He'd had time to think about it. Rather than lay out his suspicion that the whole thing was a publicity stunt, he stuck to the bare facts. He'd spotted Sarah walking toward him. Saw the van pull up. Saw she was gone. Gave chase.

The police officer made more notes, then flipped back a few pages. "So, Monsieur Hunter, are you also acquainted with Henri Lefèvre?"

"Who?"

"The man your fiancée says snatched her off the street and threw her into the back of this van."

"No, I'm not acquainted with him."

"But you know Monsieur Girault and his wife?"

Dev's eyes narrowed as he remembered Sarah telling him about the goons Girault had employed to do his dirty work. Was Lefèvre one of those goons? Was Jean-Jacques somehow mixed up in all this?

"Yes," he replied, frowning, "I know Monsieur Girault and his wife. How are they involved in this incident?"

"Mademoiselle St. Sebastian says Lefèvre is Madame Girault's former lover. He came to their table while they were at lunch yesterday. She claims Madame Girault identified him as a gigolo, one who tried to extort a large sum of money from her. We'll verify that with madame herself, of course."

Dev's stomach took a slow dive. Christ! Had he misread the situation? The kidnapping portion of it, anyway?

"Your fiancée also says that the manager of your hotel told her Lefèvre made inquiries as to her identity." The officer glanced up from his notes. "Are you aware of these inquiries, Monsieur Hunter?"

"No."

The police officer's expression remained carefully neutral, but he had to be thinking the same thing Dev was.

What kind of a man didn't know a second- or third-class gigolo was sniffing after his woman?

"Do you have any additional information you can provide at this time, Monsieur Hunter?"

"No."

"Very well. Mademoiselle St. Sebastian insists she sustained no serious injury. If the EMTs agree, I will release her to return to your hotel. I must ask you both not to leave Paris, however, until you have spoken with detectives from our *Brigade criminelle*. They will be in touch with you."

Dev and Sarah took a taxi back to the hotel. She stared out the window in stony silence while he searched for a way to reconcile his confrontation with the photographer and his apparently faulty assumption about the attempted kidnapping. He finally decided on a simple apology.

"I'm sorry, Sarah. I jumped too fast to the wrong conclusion."

She turned her head. Her distant expression matched her coolly polite tone. "No need to apologize. I can understand how you reached that conclusion."

Dev reached for her hand, trying to bridge the gap. She slid it away and continued in the same, distant tone.

"Just for the record, I didn't know the magazine had put a photographer on us."

"I believe you."

It was too little, too late. He realized that when she shrugged his comment aside.

"I am aware, however, that Alexis wanted to exploit the story, so I take full responsibility for this invasion of your privacy."

"*Our* privacy, Sarah."

"Your privacy," she countered quietly. "There is no us. It was all just a facade, wasn't it?"

"That's not what you said last night," Dev reminded her, starting to get a little pissed.

How the hell did he end up as the bad guy here? Okay, he'd blackmailed Sarah into posing as his fiancée. And, yes, he'd done his damnedest to finesse her into bed. Now that he had her there, though, he wanted more. Much more!

So did she. She'd admitted that last night. Dev wasn't about to let her just toss what they had together out the window.

"What happened to option B?" he pressed. "Making it real?"

She looked at him for a long moment before turning her face to the window again. "I have a headache starting. I'd rather not talk anymore, if you don't mind."

He minded. Big time. But the angry bruise rising on her cheek shut him up until they were back at the hotel.

"We didn't have lunch," he said in an effort to reestablish a common ground. "Do you want to try the restaurant here or order something from room service?"

"I'm not hungry." Still so cool, still so distant. "I'm going to lie down."

"You need ice to keep the swelling down on your cheek. I'll bring some to your room after I talk to Monsieur LeBon."

"There's ice in the minifridge in my room."

She left him standing in the lobby. Frustrated and angry and not sure precisely where he should target his ire, he stalked to the reception desk and asked to speak to the manager.

Sarah's first act when she reached her room was to call *Beguile*'s Paris offices. Although she didn't doubt Dev's account, she couldn't help hoping the photographer he'd spoken to was a freelancer or worked for some other publication. In her heart of hearts, she didn't want to believe *her* magazine had, in fact, assigned François to shoot pictures of her and Dev. Paul Vincent, the senior editor, provided the corroboration reluctantly.

"Alexis insisted, Sarah."

"I see."

She disconnected and stared blankly at the wall for several moments. How naive of her to trust Alexis to hold to her word. How stupid to feel so hurt that Dev would jump to the conclusion he had. Her throat tight, she tapped out a text message. It was brief and to the point.

I quit, effective immediately.

Then she filled the ice bucket, wrapped some cubes in a hand towel and shed her clothes. Crawling into bed, she put the ice on her aching cheek and pulled the covers over her head.

The jangle of the house phone dragged her from a stew of weariness and misery some hours later.

"I'm sorry to disturb you, Lady Sarah."

Grimacing, she edged away from the wet spot on the pillow left by the soggy hand towel. "What is it, Monsieur LeBon?"

"You have a call from *Brigade criminelle*. Shall we put it through?"

"Yes."

The caller identified herself as Marie-Renee Delacroix, an inspector in the division charged with investigating homicides, kidnappings, bomb attacks and incidents involving personalities. Sarah wanted to ask what category this investigation fell into but refrained. Instead she agreed to an appointment at police headquarters the next morning at nine.

"I've already spoken to Monsieur Hunter," the inspector said. "He'll accompany you."

"Fine."

"Just so you know, Mademoiselle St. Sebastian, this

meeting is a mere formality, simply to review and sign the official copy of your statement."

"That's all you need from me?"

"It is. We already had the van driver in custody, and we arrested Henri Lefèvre an hour ago. They've both confessed to attempting to kidnap you and hold you for ransom. Not that they could deny it," the inspector added drily. "Their fingerprints were all over the van, and no fewer than five witnesses saw Lefèvre jump out of it after the crash. We've also uncovered evidence that he's more than fifty thousand Euros in debt, much of which we believe he owes to a drug dealer not known for his patience."

A shudder rippled down Sarah's spine. She couldn't believe how close she'd come to being dragged into such a dark, ugly morass.

"Am I free to return to the United States after I sign my statement?"

"I'll have to check with the prosecutor's office, but I see no reason for them to impede your return given that Lefèvre and his accomplice have confessed. I'll confirm that when you come in tomorrow, yes?"

"Thank you."

She hung up and was contemplating going back to bed when there was a knock on her door.

"It's Dev, Sarah."

She wanted to take the coward's way out and tell him she didn't feel up to company, but she couldn't keep putting him off.

"Just a minute," she called through the door.

She detoured into the bedroom and threw on the clothes she'd dropped to the floor earlier. She couldn't do much about the bruise on her cheek, but she did rake a hand through her hair. Still, she felt messy and off center when she opened the door.

Dev had abandoned his suit coat but still wore the pleated pants and pale yellow dress shirt he'd had on earlier. The shirt was open at the neck, the cuffs rolled up. Sarah had to drag her reluctant gaze up to meet the deep blue of his eyes. They were locked on her cheek.

"Did you ice that?"

"Yes, I did. Come in."

He followed her into the sitting room. Neither of them sat. She gravitated to the window. He shoved his hands into his pants pockets and stood beside the sofa.

"Have you heard from Inspector Delacroix?"

"She just called. I understand we have an appointment with her at nine tomorrow morning."

"Did she tell you they've already obtained confessions?"

Sarah nodded and forced a small smile. "She also told me I could fly home after I signed the official statement. I was just about to call and make a reservation when you knocked."

"Without talking to me first?"

"I think we've said everything we needed to."

"I don't agree."

She scrubbed a hand down the side of her face. Her cheek ached. Her heart hurt worse. "Please, Dev. I don't want to beat this into the ground."

Poor verb choice, she realized when he ignored her and crossed the room to cup her chin. The ice hadn't helped much, Sarah knew. The bruise had progressed from red to a nasty purple and green.

"Did Lefèvre do this to you?"

The underlying savagery in the question had her pulling hastily away from his touch.

"No, he didn't. I hit something when he pushed me into the van."

The savagery didn't abate. If anything, it flared hotter and fiercer. "Good thing the bastard's in police custody."

Sarah struggled to get the discussion back on track. "Lefèvre doesn't matter, Dev."

"The hell he doesn't."

"Listen to me. What matters is that I didn't know Alexis had sicced a photographer on us. But even if she hadn't, some other magazine or tabloid would have picked up the story sooner or later. I'm afraid that kind of public scrutiny is something you and whoever you *do* finally get engaged to will have to live with."

"I'm engaged to you, Sarah."

"Not any longer."

Shoving her misery aside, she slid the emerald off her finger and held it out. He refused to take it.

"It's yours," he said curtly. "Part of your heritage. Whatever happens from here on out between us, you keep the Russian Rose."

The tight-jawed response only added to her aching unhappiness. "Our arrangement lasted only until you and Girault signed your precious contracts. That's done now. So are we."

She hadn't intended to sound so bitter. Dev had held to his end of their bargain. Every part of it. She was the one who'd almost defaulted. If not personally, then by proxy through Alexis.

But would Dev continue to hold to his end? The sudden worry that he might take his anger out on Gina pushed her into a rash demand for an assurance.

"I've fulfilled the conditions of our agreement, right? You won't go after my sister?"

She'd forgotten how daunting he could look when his eyes went hard and ice blue.

"No, Lady Sarah, I won't. And I think we'd better table this discussion until we've had more time to think things through."

"I've thought them through," she said desperately. "I'm going home tomorrow, Dev."

He leaned in, all the more intimidating because he didn't touch her, didn't raise his voice, didn't so much as blink.

"Think again, sweetheart."

Twelve

Left alone in her misery, Sarah opened her hand and stared at the emerald-and-gold ring. No matter what Dev said, she couldn't keep it.

Nor could she just leave it lying around. She toyed briefly with the thought of taking it downstairs and asking Monsieur LeBon to secure it in the hotel safe, but didn't feel up to explaining either her bruised cheek or the call from *Brigade criminelle*.

With an aching sense of regret for what might have been, she slipped the ring back on her finger. It would have to stay there until she returned it to Dev.

She was trying to make herself go into the bedroom and pack when a loud rumble from the vicinity of her middle reminded her she hadn't eaten since her breakfast croissant and coffee. She considered room service but decided she needed to get out of her room and clear her head. She also needed, as Dev had grimly instructed, to think more.

After a fierce internal debate, she picked up the house phone. A lifetime of etiquette hammered in by the duchess demanded she advise Dev of her intention to grab a bite at a local café. Fiancé or not, furious or not, he deserved the courtesy of a call.

Relief rolled through her in waves when he didn't answer. She left a quick message, then took the elevator to the lobby. Slipping out one of the hotel's side exits, she hiked up the collar of her sweater coat. It wasn't dusk yet, but the temperature was skidding rapidly from cool to cold.

As expected this time of day, the sidewalks and streets were crowded. Parisians returning from work made last-minute stops at grocers and patisseries. Taxis wove their erratic path through cars and bicycles. Sarah barely noticed the throng. Her last meeting with Dev still filled her mind. Their tense confrontation had shaken her almost as much as being snatched off the street and tossed into a delivery van like a sack of potatoes.

He had every right to be angry about the photographer, she conceded. She was furious, too. What had hurt most, though, was Dev's assumption that *Beguile* had staged the kidnapping. And that Sarah was part of the deception. How could he love her, yet believe she would participate in a scam like that?

The short answer? He couldn't.

As much as she wanted to, Sarah couldn't escape that brutal truth. She'd let Paris seduce her into thinking she and Dev shared something special. Come so close to believing that what they felt for each other would merit a padlock on the Archbishop's Bridge. Aching all over again for what might have been, she ducked into the first café she encountered.

A waiter with three rings piercing his left earlobe and a white napkin folded over his right forearm met her at the door. His gaze flickered to the ugly bruise on her cheek and away again.

"Good evening, madame."

"Good evening. A table for one, please."

Once settled at a table in a back corner, she ordered

without glancing at the menu. A glass of red table wine and a croque-monsieur—the classic French version of a grilled ham and cheese topped with béchamel sauce—was all she wanted. All she could handle right now. That became apparent after the first few sips of wine.

Her sandwich arrived in a remarkably short time given this was Paris, where even the humblest café aimed for gastronomic excellence. Accompanied by a small salad and thin, crisp fries, it should have satisfied her hunger. Unfortunately, she never got to enjoy it. She took a few forkfuls of salad and nibbled a fry, but just when she was about to bite into her sandwich she heard her name.

"Lady Sarah, granddaughter to Charlotte St. Sebastian, grand duchess of the tiny duchy once known as Karlenburgh."

Startled, she glanced up at the flat screen TV above the café's bar. While Sarah sat frozen with the sandwich halfway to her mouth, one of a team of two newscasters gestured to an image that came up on the display beside her. It was a photo of her and Gina and Grandmama, one of the rare publicity shots the duchess had allowed. It'd been taken at a charity event a number of years ago, before the duchess had sold her famous pearls. The perfectly matched strands circled her neck multiple times before draping almost to her waist.

"The victim of an apparent kidnapping attempt," the announcer intoned, "Lady Sarah escaped injury this afternoon during a dramatic rescue by her fiancé, American industrialist Devon Hunter."

Dread churned in the pit of Sarah's stomach as the still image gave way to what looked like an amateur video captured on someone's phone camera. It showed traffic swerving wildly as Dev charged across two lanes and planted himself in front of oncoming traffic.

Good God! The white van! It wasn't going to stop!

Her heart shot into her throat. Unable to breathe, she saw

Dev dodge aside at the last moment, then leap for the van door. When he smashed the driver's face into the wheel, Sarah gasped. Blobs of béchamel sauce oozed from the sandwich hanging from her fork and plopped unnoticed onto her plate. She'd been in the back of the van. She hadn't known how Dev had stopped it, only that he had.

Stunned by his reckless courage, she watched as the street scene gave way to another video. This one was shot on the steps of the Palais de Justice. Henri Lefèvre was being led down the steps to a waiting police transport. Uniformed officers gripped his arms. Steel cuffs shackled his wrists. A crowd of reporters waited at the bottom of the steps, shouting questions that Lefèvre refused to answer.

When the news shifted to another story, Sarah lowered her now-mangled sandwich. Her mind whirled as she tried to sort through her chaotic thoughts. One arrowed through all the others. She knew she had to call her grandmother. Now. Before the story got picked up by the news at home, if it hadn't already. Furious with herself for not thinking of that possibility sooner, she hit speed dial.

To her infinite relief, the duchess had heard nothing about the incident. Sarah tried to downplay it by making the kidnappers sound like bungling amateurs. Charlotte was neither amused nor fooled.

"Were you the target," she asked sharply, "or Devon?"

"Devon, of course. Or rather his billions."

"Are you sure? There may still be some fanatics left in the old country. Not many after all this time, I would guess. But your grandfather… Those murderous death squads…" Her voice fluttered. "They hated everything our family stood for."

"These men wanted money," Sarah said gently, "and Dev made them extremely sorry they went after it the way they did. One of them is going to need a whole new face."

"Good!"

The duchess had regained her bite, and her granddaughter breathed a sigh of relief. Too soon, it turned out.

"Bring Devon home with you, Sarah. I want to thank him personally. And tell him I see no need for a long engagement," Charlotte added briskly. "Too many brides today spend months, even years, planning their weddings. I thank God neither of my granddaughters are prone to such dithering."

"Grandmama…"

"Gina tends to leap before she looks. You, my darling, are more cautious. More deliberate. But when you choose, you choose wisely. In this instance, I believe you made an excellent choice."

Sarah couldn't confess that she hadn't precisely chosen Dev. Nor was she up to explaining that their relationship was based on a lie. All she could do was try to rein in the duchess.

"I'm not to the point of even thinking about wedding plans, Grandmama. I just got engaged."

And unengaged, although Dev appeared to have a different take on the matter.

"You don't have to concern yourself with the details, dearest. I'll call the Plaza and have Andrew take care of everything."

"Good grief!" Momentarily distracted, Sarah gasped. "Is Andrew still at the Plaza?"

Her exclamation earned an icy retort. "The younger generation may choose to consign seniors to the dustbin," the duchess returned frigidly. "Some of us are not quite ready to be swept out with the garbage."

Uh-oh. Before Sarah could apologize for the unintended slight, Charlotte abandoned her lofty perch and got down to business.

"How about the first weekend in May? That's such a lovely month for a wedding."

"Grandmama! It's mid-April now!"

"Didn't you hear me a moment ago? Long engagements are a bore."

"But...but..." Scrambling, Sarah grabbed at the most likely out. "I'm sure the Plaza is booked every weekend in May for the next three years."

Her grandmother heaved a long-suffering sigh. "Sarah, dearest, did I never tell you about the reception I hosted for the Sultan of Oman?"

"I don't think so."

"It was in July...no, August of 1962. Quite magnificent, if I do say so myself. President Kennedy and his wife attended, of course, as did the Rockefellers. Andrew was a very new, very junior waiter at the time. But the letter I sent to his supervisor commending his handling of an embarrassingly inebriated presidential aide helped catapult him to his present exalted position."

How could Sarah possibly respond to that? Swept along on a relentless tidal wave, she gripped the phone as the duchess issued final instructions. "Talk to Devon, dearest. Make sure the first weekend in May is satisfactory for him. And tell him I'll take care of everything."

Feeling almost as dazed as she had when Elise Girault's smarmy ex-lover manhandled her into that white van, Sarah said goodbye. Her meal forgotten, she sat with her phone in hand for long moments. The call to her grandmother had left her more confused, more torn.

Dev had risked his life for her. And that was after he'd confronted the photographer from *Beguile*. As angry as he'd been about her magazine stalking him, he'd still raced to her rescue. Then, of course, he'd accused her of being party to the ruse. As much as she wanted to, Sarah couldn't quite get past the disgust she'd seen in his face at that moment.

Yet he'd also shown her moments of incredible tenderness in their short time together. Moments of thoughtfulness and laughter and incredible passion. She couldn't get past those, either.

Or the fact that she'd responded to him so eagerly. So damned joyously. However they'd met, whatever odd circumstances had thrown them together, Dev Hunter stirred—and satisfied—a deep, almost primal feminine hunger she'd never experienced before.

The problem, Sarah mused as she paid her check and walked out into the deepening dusk, was that everything had happened so quickly. Dev's surprise appearance at her office. His bold-faced offer of a deal. Their fake engagement. This trip to Paris. She'd been caught up in the whirlwind since the day Dev had showed up at her office and tilted her world off its axis. The speed of it, the intensity of it, had magnified emotions and minimized any chance to catch her breath.

What they needed, she decided as she keyed the door to her room, was time and some distance from each other. A cooling-off period, after which they could start over. Assuming Dev wanted to start over, of course. Bracing herself for what she suspected would be an uncomfortable discussion, she picked up the house phone and called his room.

He answered on the second ring. "Hunter."

"It's Sarah."

"I got your message. Did you have a good dinner?"

She couldn't miss the steel under the too-polite query. He wasn't happy that she'd gone to eat without him.

"I did, thank you. Can you come down to my room? Or I'll come to yours, if that's more convenient."

"More convenient for what?"

All right. She understood he was still angry. As Grandmama would say, however, that was no excuse for boorishness.

"We need to finish the conversation we started earlier," she said coolly.

He answered with a brief silence, followed by a terse agreement. "I'll come to your room."

Dev thought he'd done a damned good job of conquering his fury over that business with the photographer. Yes, he'd let it get the better of him when he'd accused Sarah's magazine of staging her own abduction. And yes, he'd come on a little strong earlier this evening when she'd questioned whether he'd hold to his end of their agreement.

He'd had plenty of time to regret both lapses. She'd seen to that by slipping out of the hotel without him. The brief message she'd left while he was in the shower had pissed him off all over again.

Now she'd issued a summons in that aristocratic lady-of-the-manor tone. She'd better not try to shove the emerald at him again. Or deliver any more crap about their "arrangement" being over. They were long past the arrangement stage, and she knew it. She was just too stubborn to admit it.

She'd just have to accept that he wasn't perfect. He'd screwed up this afternoon by throwing that accusation at her. He'd apologize again. Crawl if he had to. Whatever it took, he intended to make it clear she wasn't rid of him. Not by a long shot.

That was the plan, anyway, right up until she opened the door. The mottled purple on her cheek tore the heart and the heat right out of him. Curling a knuckle, he brushed it gently across the skin below the bruise.

"Does this hurt as bad as it looks?"

"Not even close."

She didn't shy away from his touch. Dev took that as a hopeful sign. That, and the fact that some of the stiffness went out of her spine as she led him into the sitting area.

Nor did it escape his attention that she'd cut off the view that had so enchanted her before. The heavy, room-darkening drapes were drawn tight, blocking anyone from seeing out…or in.

"Would you like a drink?" she asked politely, gesturing to the well-stocked minibar.

"No, thanks, I'm good."

As he spoke, an image on the TV snagged his glance. The sound was muted but he didn't need it to recognize the amateur video playing across the screen. He'd already seen it several times.

Sarah noticed what had caught his attention and picked up the remote. "Have you seen the news coverage?"

"Yeah."

Clicking off the TV, she sank into an easy chair and raised a stockinged foot. Her arms locked around her bent knee and her green eyes regarded him steadily.

"I took your advice and thought more about our…our situation."

"That's one way to describe it," he acknowledged. "You come to any different conclusions about how we should handle it?"

"As a matter of fact, I did."

Dev waited, wanting to hear her thoughts.

"I feel as though I jumped on a speeding train. Everything happened so fast. You, me, Paris. Now Grandmama is insisting on…" She broke off, a flush rising, and took a moment to recover. "I was afraid the news services might pick up the kidnapping story, so I called her and tried to shrug off the incident as the work of bumbling amateurs."

"Did she buy that?"

"No."

"Smart woman, your grandmother."

"You might not agree when I tell you she segued immediately from that to insisting on a May wedding."

Well, what do you know? Dev was pretty sure he'd passed inspection with the duchess. Good to have it confirmed, especially since he apparently had a number of hurdles to overcome before he regained her granddaughter's trust.

"I repeat, your grandmother's a smart woman."

"She is, but then she doesn't know the facts behind our manufactured engagement."

"Do you think she needs to?"

"What I think," Sarah said slowly, "is that we need to put the brakes on this runaway train."

Putting the brakes on was a long step from her earlier insistence they call things off. Maybe he didn't face as many hurdles as he'd thought.

His tension easing by imperceptible degrees, Dev cocked his head. "How do you propose we do that?"

"We step back. Take some time to assess this attraction we both seem to…"

"Attraction?" He shook his head. "Sorry, sweetheart, I can't let you get away with that one. You and I both know we've left attraction in the dust."

"You're right."

She rested her chin on her knee, obviously searching for the right word. Impatience bit at him, but he reined it in. If he hadn't learned anything else today, he'd discovered Sarah could only be pushed so far.

"I won't lie," she said slowly. "What I feel for you is so different from anything I've ever experienced before. I think it's love. No, I'm pretty sure it's love."

That was all he needed to hear. He started toward her, but she stopped him with a quick palms-up gesture.

"What I'm *not* sure of, Dev, is whether love's enough to overcome the fact that we barely know each other."

"I know all I need to know about you."

"Oh. Right." She made a wry face. "I forgot about the background investigation."

He wouldn't apologize. He'd been up front with her about that. But he did attempt to put it in perspective.

"The investigation provided the externals, Sarah. The

time we've spent together, as brief as it's been, provided the essentials."

"Really?" She lifted a brow. "What's my favorite color? Am I a dog or a cat person? What kind of music do I like?"

"You consider those essentials?" he asked, genuinely curious.

"They're some of the bits and pieces that constitute the whole. Don't you think we should see how those pieces fit together before getting in any deeper?"

"I don't, but you obviously do."

If this was a business decision, he would ruthlessly override what he privately considered trivial objections. He'd made up his mind. He knew what he wanted.

Sarah did, too, apparently. With a flash of extremely belated insight, Dev realized she wanted to be courted. More to the point, she *deserved* to be courted.

Lady Sarah St. Sebastian might work at a magazine that promoted flashy and modern and ultrachic, but she held to old-fashioned values that he'd come to appreciate as much as her innate elegance and surprising sensuality. Her fierce loyalty to her sister, for instance. Her bone-deep love for the duchess. Her refusal to accept anything from him except her grandmother's emerald ring, and then only on a temporary basis.

He could do old-fashioned. He could do slow and courtly. Maybe. Admittedly, he didn't have a whole lot of experience in either. Moving out and taking charge came as natural to him as breathing. But if throttling back on his more aggressive instincts was what she wanted, that was what she'd get.

"Okay, we'll do it your way."

He started toward her again. Surprised and more than a little wary of his relatively easy capitulation, Sarah let her raised foot slip to the floor and pushed out of her chair.

He stopped less than a yard away. Close enough to kiss,

which she had to admit she wouldn't have minded all that much at this point. He settled for a touch instead. He kept it light, just a brush of his fingertips along the underside of her chin.

"We'll kick off phase two," he promised in a tone that edged toward deep and husky. "No negotiated contracts this time, no self-imposed deadlines. Just you and me, learning each other's little idiosyncrasies. If that's what you really want…?"

She nodded, although the soft dance of his fingers under her chin and the proximity of his mouth made it tough to stay focused.

"It's what I really want."

"All right, I'll call Patrick."

"Who? Oh, right. Your executive assistant. Excuse me for asking, but what does he have to do with this?"

"He's going to clear my calendar. Indefinitely. He'll blow every one of his fuses, but he'll get it done."

His fingers made another pass. Sarah's thoughts zinged wildly between the little pinpricks of pleasure he was generating and that "indefinitely."

"What about your schedule?" he asked. "How much time can you devote to phase two?"

"My calendar's wide-open, too. I quit my job."

"You didn't have to do that. I'm already past the business with the photographer."

"You may be," she retorted. "I'm not."

He absorbed that for a moment. "All right. Here's what we'll do, then. We give our statements to the *Brigade criminelle* at nine tomorrow morning and initiate phase two immediately after. Agreed?"

"Agreed."

"Good. I'll have a car waiting at eight-thirty to take us downtown. See you down in the lobby then."

He leaned in and brushed his lips over hers.

"Good night, Sarah."

She'd never really understood that old saying about
being hoisted with your own petard. It had something to do
with getting caught up in a medieval catapult, she thought.
Or maybe hanging by one foot in a tangle of ropes from
the mast of a fourteenth-century frigate.

Either situation would pretty much describe her feelings
when Dev crossed the room and let himself out.

Thirteen

Sarah spent hours tossing and turning and kicking herself for her self-imposed celibacy. As a result, she didn't fall asleep until almost one and woke late the next morning.

The first thing she did was roll over in bed and grab her cell phone from the nightstand to check for messages. Still nothing from Gina, dammit, but Alexis had left two voice mails apologizing for what she termed an unfortunate misunderstanding and emphatically refusing to accept her senior layout editor's resignation.

"Misunderstanding, my ass."

Her mouth set, Sarah deleted the voice mails and threw back the covers. She'd have to hustle to be ready for the car Dev had said would be waiting at eight-thirty. A quick shower eliminated most of the cobwebs from her restless night. An equally quick cup of strong brew from the little coffeemaker in her room helped with the remainder.

Before she dressed, she stuck her nose through the balcony doors to assess the weather. No fog or drizzle, but still chilly enough to make her opt for her gray wool slacks and cherry-red sweater coat. She topped them with a scarf doubled around her throat European-style and a black beret tilted to a decidedly French angle.

She rushed down to the lobby with two minutes to spare and saw Dev had also prepared for the chill. But in jeans, a black turtleneck and a tan cashmere coat this morning instead of his usual business suit. He greeted her with a smile and a quick kiss.

"*Bonjour, ma chérie.* Sleep well?"

She managed not to wince at his accent. "Fairly well."

"Did you have time for breakfast?"

"No."

"I was running a little late, too, so I had the driver pick up some chocolate croissants and coffees. Shall we go?"

He offered his arm in a gesture she was beginning to realize was as instinctive as it was courteous. When she tucked her hand in the crook of his elbow, she could feel his warmth through the soft wool. Feel, too, the ripple of hard muscle as he leaned past her to push open the hotel door.

Traffic was its usual snarling beast, but the coffee and chocolate croissants mitigated the frustration. They were right on time when they pulled up at the block-long building overlooking the Seine that housed the headquarters of the *Brigade criminelle*. A lengthy sequence of security checkpoints, body scans and ID verification made them late for their appointment, however.

Detective Inspector Marie-Renée Delacroix waved aside their apologies as unnecessary and signed them in. Short and barrel-shaped, she wore a white blouse, black slacks and rubber-soled granny shoes. The semiautomatic nested in her shoulder holster belied her otherwise unprepossessing exterior.

"Thank you for coming in," she said in fluent English. "I'll try to make this as swift and painless as possible. Please, come with me."

She led them up a flight of stairs and down a long corridor interspersed with heavy oak doors. When Delacroix pushed through the door to her bureau, Sarah looked about with interest. The inspector's habitat didn't resemble the bull pens depicted on American TV police dramas. American bull pens probably didn't, either, she acknowledged wryly.

There were no dented metal file cabinets or half-empty cartons of doughnuts. No foam cups littering back-to-back desks or squawking phones. The area was spacious and well lit and smoke free. Soundproofing dividers offered at least the illusion of privacy, while monitors mounted high on the front wall flashed what looked like real-time updates on hot spots around Paris.

"Would you like coffee?" Delacroix asked as she waved them to seats in front of her desk.

Sarah looked to Dev before answering for them both. "No, thank you."

The inspector dropped into the chair behind the desk. Shoulders hunched, brows straight-lined, she dragged a wireless keyboard into reach and attacked it with two stubby forefingers. The assault was merciless, but for reasons known only to French computer gods, the typed versions of the statements Sarah and Dev had given to the responding officers wouldn't spit out of the printer.

"Merde!"

Muttering under her breath, she jabbed at the keyboard yet again. She looked as though she'd like to whip out her weapon and deliver a lethal shot when she finally admitted defeat and slammed away from her desk.

"Please wait. I need to find someone who can kick a report out of this piece of sh— Er, crap."

She returned a few moments later with a colleague in a blue-striped shirt and red suspenders. Without a word, he pressed a single key. When the printer began coughing up papers, he rolled his eyes and departed.

"I hate these things," Delacroix muttered as she dropped into her chair again.

Sarah and Dev exchanged a quick look but refrained from comment. Just as well, since the inspector became all brisk efficiency once the printer had disgorged the documents she wanted. She pushed two ink pens and the printed statements in their direction.

"Review these, please, and make any changes you feel necessary."

The reports were lengthy and correct. Delacroix was relieved that neither Sarah nor Dev had any changes, but consciously did her duty.

"Are you sure, mademoiselle? With that nasty bruise, we could add assault to the kidnapping charge."

Sarah fingered her cheek. Much as she'd like to double the case against Lefèvre, he hadn't directly caused the injury.

"I'm sure."

"Very well. Sign here, please, and here."

She did as instructed and laid down her pen. "You said you were going to talk to the prosecuting attorney about whether we need to remain in Paris for the arraignment," she reminded Delacroix.

"Ah, yes. He feels your statements, the evidence we've collected and the confessions from Lefèvre and his associate are more than sufficient for the case against them. As long as we know how to contact you and Monsieur Hunter if necessary, you may depart Paris whenever you wish."

Oddly, the knowledge that she could fly home at any time produced a contradictory desire in Sarah to remain in Paris for the initiation of phase two. That, and the way Dev once again tucked her arm in his as they descended the broad staircase leading to the main exit. There was still so much of the city—*her* city—she wanted to share with him.

The moment they stepped out into the weak sunshine, a blinding barrage of flashes sent Sarah stumbling back. Dismayed, she eyed the wolf pack crowding the front steps, their news vans parked at the curb behind them. While sound handlers thrust their boom mikes over the reporters' heads, the questions flew at Sarah like bullets. She heard her name and Dev's and Lefèvre's and Elise Girault's all seemingly in the same sentences.

She ducked her chin into her scarf and started to scramble back into police headquarters to search out a side exit. Dev stood his ground, though, and with her arm tucked tight against his side, Sarah had no choice but to do the same.

"Might as well give them what they want now," he told her. "Maybe it'll satisfy their appetites and send them chasing after their next victim."

Since most of the questions zinged at them were in French, Sarah found herself doing the translating and leaving the responding to Dev. He'd obviously fielded these kinds of rapid-fire questions before. He deftly avoided any that might impact the case against the kidnappers and confirmed only that he and Sarah were satisfied with the way the police were handling the matter.

The questions soon veered from the official to the personal. To Sarah's surprise, Dev shelved his instinctive dislike of the media and didn't cut them off at the knees. His responses were concise and to the point.

Yes, he and Lady Sarah had only recently become engaged. Yes, they'd known each other only a short time. No, they hadn't yet set a date for the wedding.

"Although," he added with a sideways glance at Sarah, "her grandmother has voiced some thoughts in that regard."

"Speaking of the duchess," a sharp-featured reporter commented as she thrust her mike almost in Sarah's face, "Charlotte St. Sebastian was once the toast of Paris and New York. From all reports, she's now penniless. Have you insisted Monsieur Hunter include provisions for her maintenance in your prenup agreement?"

Distaste curled Sarah's lip but she refused to give the

vulture any flesh to feed on. "As my fiancé has just stated," she said with a dismissive smile, "we've only recently become engaged. And what better place to celebrate that engagement than Paris, the City of Lights and Love? So now you must excuse us, as that's what we intend to do."

She tugged on Dev's arm and he took the hint. When they cleared the mob and started for the limo waiting a half block away, he gave her a curious look.

"What was that all about?"

She hadn't translated the last question and would prefer not to now. Their engagement had been tumultuous enough. Despite her grandmother's insistence on booking the Plaza, Sarah hadn't really thought as far ahead as marriage. Certainly not as far as a prenup.

They stopped beside the limo. The driver had the door open and waiting but Dev waved him back inside the car.

"Give us a minute here, Andre."

"*Oui*, monsieur."

While the driver slid into the front seat, Dev angled Sarah to face him. Her shoulders rested against the rear door frame. Reluctantly, she tipped up her gaze to meet his.

"You might as well tell me," he said. "I'd rather not be blindsided by hearing whatever it was play on the five-o'clock news."

"The reporter wanted details on our prenup." She hunched her shoulders, feeling awkward and embarrassed. "I told her to get stuffed."

His grin broke out, quick and slashing. "In your usual elegant manner, of course."

"Of course."

Still grinning, he studied her face. It must have reflected her acute discomfort because he stooped to speak to the driver.

"We've decided to walk, Andre. We won't need you anymore today."

When the limo eased away from the curb, he hooked

Sarah's arm through his again and steered her into the stream of pedestrians.

"I know how prickly you are about the subject of finances, so we won't go there until we've settled more important matters, like whether you're a dog or cat person. Which are you, by the way?"

"Dog," she replied, relaxing for the first time that morning. "The bigger the better, although the only one we've ever owned was the Pomeranian that Gina brought home one day. She was eight or nine at the time and all indignant because someone had left it leashed outside a coffee shop in one-hundred-degree heat."

Too late she realized she might have opened the door for Dev to suggest Gina had developed kleptomaniac tendencies early. She glanced up, met his carefully neutral look and hurried on with her tale.

"We went back and tried to find the owner, but no one would claim it. We soon found out why. Talk about biting the hand that feeds you! The nasty little beast snapped and snarled and wouldn't let anyone pet him except Grandmama."

"No surprise there. The duchess has a way about her. She certainly cowed me."

"Right," Sarah scoffed. "I saw how you positively quaked in her presence."

"I'm still quaking. Finish the story. What happened to the beast?"

"Grandmama finally palmed him off on an acquaintance of hers. What about you?" she asked, glancing up at him again. "Do you prefer dogs or cats?"

"Bluetick coonhounds," he answered without hesitation. "Best hunters in the world. We had a slew of barn cats, though. My sisters were always trying to palm their litters off on friends, too."

Intrigued, Sarah pumped him for more details about

his family. "I know you grew up on a ranch. In Nebraska, wasn't it?"

"New Mexico, but it was more like a hardscrabble farm than a ranch."

"Do your parents still work the farm?"

"They do. They like the old place and have no desire to leave it, although they did let me make a few improvements."

More than a few, Sarah guessed.

"What about your sisters?"

He had four, she remembered, none of whom had agreed to be interviewed for the *Beguile* article. The feeling that their business was nobody else's ran deep in the Hunter clan.

"All married, all comfortable, all happy. You hungry?"

The abrupt change of subject threw Sarah off until she saw what had captured his attention. They'd reached the Pont de l'Alma, which gave a bird's-eye view of the glass-roofed barges docked on the north side of the Seine. One boat was obviously set for a lunch cruise. Its linen-draped tables were set with gleaming silver and crystal.

"Have you ever taken one of these Seine river cruises?" Dev asked.

"No."

"Why not?"

"They're, uh, a little touristy."

"This is Paris. Everyone's a tourist, even the Parisians."

"Good God, don't let a native hear you say that!"

"What do you say? Want to mingle with the masses for a few hours?"

She threw a glance at a tour bus disgorging its load of passengers and swallowed her doubts.

"I'm game if you are."

He steered her to the steps that led down to the quay. Sarah fully expected them to be turned away at the ticket office. While a good number of boats cruised the Seine,

picking up or letting off passengers at various stops, tour
agencies tended to book these lunch and dinner cruises for
large groups months in advance.

Whatever Dev said—or paid—at the ticket booth not
only got them on the boat, it garnered a prime table for two
beside the window. Their server introduced herself and
filled their aperitif glasses with kir. A smile in his eyes,
Dev raised his glass.

"To us."

"To us," Sarah echoed softly.

The cocktail went down with velvet smoothness. She
savored the intertwined flavors while Dev gave his glass
a respectful glance.

"What's in this?"

"*Crème de cassis*—black-currant liqueur—topped with
white wine. It's named for Félix Kir, the mayor of Dijon,
who popularized the drink after World War II."

"Well, it doesn't have the same wallop as your grandmother's *Žuta Osa* but it's good."

"'Scuse me."

The interruption came from the fortyish brunette at the
next table. She beamed Sarah a friendly smile.

"Y'all are Americans, aren't you?"

"Yes, we are."

"So are we. We're the Parkers. Evelyn and Duane Parker,
from Mobile."

Sarah hesitated. She hated to be rude, but Evelyn's
leopard-print Versace jacket and jewel-toed boots indicated
she kept up with the latest styles. If she read *Beguile,* she
would probably recognize Number Three from the Sexiest
Singles article. Or from the recent news coverage.

Dev solved her dilemma by gesturing to the cell phone
Evelyn clutched in one hand. "I'm Dev and this is my fiancée, Sarah. Would you like me to take a picture of you
and your husband?"

"Please. And I'll do one of y'all."

The accordion player began strolling the aisle while cell phones were still being exchanged and photos posed for. When he broke into a beautiful baritone, all conversation on the boat ceased and Sarah breathed easy again.

Moments later, they pulled away from the dock and glided under the first of a dozen or more bridges yet to come. Meal service began then. Sarah wasn't surprised at the quality of the food. This was Paris, after all. She and Dev sampled each of the starters: foie gras on a toasted baguette; Provençal smoked salmon and shallots; duck magret salad with cubes of crusty goat cheese; tiny vegetable egg rolls fried to a pale golden brown. Sarah chose honey-and-sesame-seed pork tenderloin for her main dish. Dev went with the veal blanquette. With each course, their server poured a different wine. Crisp, chilled whites. Medium reds. Brandy with the rum baba they each selected for dessert.

Meanwhile, Paris's most famous monuments were framed in the windows. The Louvre. La Conciergerie. Notre Dame. The Eiffel Tower.

The boat made a U-turn while Sarah and Dev lingered over coffee, sharing more of their pasts. She listened wide-eyed to the stories Dev told of his Air Force days. She suspected he edited them to minimize the danger and maximize the role played by others on his crew. Still, the war-torn countries he'd flown into and the horrific disasters he'd helped provide lifesaving relief for made her world seem frivolous by comparison.

"Grandmama took us abroad every year," she related when he insisted it was her turn. "She was determined to expose Gina and me to cultures other than our own."

"Did she ever take you to Karlenburgh?"

"No, never. That would have been too painful for her. I'd like to go someday, though. We still have cousins there, three or four times removed."

She traced a fingertip around the rim of her coffee cup.

Although it tore at her pride, she forced herself to admit the truth.

"Gina and I never knew what sacrifices Grandmama had to make to pay for those trips. Or for my year at the Sorbonne."

"I'm guessing your sister still doesn't know."

She jerked her head up, prepared to defend Gina yet again. But there was nothing judgmental in Dev's expression. Only quiet understanding.

"She has a vague idea," Sarah told him. "I never went into all the gory details, but she's not stupid."

Dev had to bite down on the inside of his lower lip. Eugenia Amalia Thérése St. Sebastian hadn't impressed him with either her intelligence or her common sense. Then again, he hadn't been particularly interested in her intellectual prowess the few times they'd connected.

In his defense, few horny, heterosexual males could see beyond Gina's stunning beauty. At least not until they'd spent more than an hour or two in the bubbleheaded blonde's company. Deciding discretion was the better part of valor, he chose not to share that particular observation.

He couldn't help comparing the sisters, though. No man in his right mind would deny that he'd come out the winner in the St. Sebastian lottery. Charm, elegance, smarts, sensuality and...

He'd better stop right there! When the hell had he reached the point where the mere thought of Sarah's smooth, sleek body stretched out under his got him rock hard? Where the memory of how she'd opened her legs for him damned near steamed up the windows beside their table?

Suddenly Dev couldn't wait for the boat to pass under the last bridge. By the time they'd docked and he'd hustled Sarah up the gangplank, his turtleneck was strangling him. The look of confused concern she flashed at him as they climbed the steps to street level didn't help matters.

"Are you all right?"

He debated for all of two seconds before deciding on the truth. "Not anywhere close to all right."

"Oh, no! Was it the foie gras?" Dismayed, she rushed to the curb to flag down a cab. "You have to be careful with goose liver."

"Sarah…"

"I should have asked if it had been wrapped in grape leaves and slow cooked. That's the safest method."

"Sarah…"

A cab screeched to the curb. Forehead creased with worry, she yanked on the door handle. Dev had to wait until they were in the taxi and heading for the hotel to explain his sudden incapacitation.

"It wasn't the foie gras."

Concern darkened her eyes to deep, verdant green. "The veal, then? Was it bad?"

"No, sweetheart. It's you."

"I beg your pardon?"

Startled, she lurched back against her seat. Dev cursed his clumsiness and hauled her into his arms.

"As delicious as lunch was, all I could think about was how you taste." His mouth roamed hers. His voice dropped to a rough whisper. "How you fit against me. How you arch your back and make that little noise in your throat when you're about to climax."

She leaned back in his arms. She wanted him as much as he wanted her. He could see it in the desire that shaded her eyes to deep, dark emerald. In the way her breath had picked up speed. Fierce satisfaction knifed into him. She was rethinking the cooling-off period, Dev thought exultantly. She had to recognize how unnecessary this phase two was.

His hopes took a nosedive—and his respect for Sarah's

willpower kicked up a grudging notch—when she drew in a shuddering breath and gave him a rueful smile.

"Well, I'm glad it wasn't the goose liver."

Fourteen

As the cab rattled along the quay, Sarah wondered how she could be such a blithering idiot. One word from her, just one little word, and she could spend the rest of the afternoon and evening curled up with Dev in bed. Or on the sofa. Or on cushions tossed onto the floor in front of the fire, or in the shower, soaping his back and belly, or...

She leaned forward, her gaze suddenly snagged by the green bookstalls lining the riverside of the boulevard. And just beyond the stalls, almost directly across from the renowned bookstore known as Shakespeare and Company, was a familiar bridge.

"Stop! We'll get out here!"

The command surprised both Dev and the cabdriver, but he obediently pulled over to the curb and Dev paid him off.

"Your favorite bookstore?" he asked with a glance at the rambling, green-fronted facade of the shop that specialized in English-language books. Opened in 1951, the present store had assumed the mantle of the original Shakespeare and Company, a combination bookshop, lending library and haven for writers established in 1917 by American expatriate Sylvia Beach and frequented by the likes of Ernest Hemingway, Ezra Pound and F. Scott Fitzgerald. During her year at the Sorbonne, Sarah had loved exploring the shelves crammed floor to ceiling in the shop's small, crowded rooms. She'd never slept in one of the thirteen beds available to indigent students or visitors who just wanted to sleep in the rarified literary atmosphere, but she'd hunched for hours at the tables provided for scholars, researchers and book lovers of all ages.

It wasn't Shakespeare and Company that had snagged her eye, though. It was the bridge just across the street from it.

"That's the Archbishop's Bridge," she told Dev with a smile that tinged close to embarrassment.

She'd always considered herself the practical sister, too levelheaded to indulge in the kind of extravagant flights of fancy that grabbed Gina. Yet she'd just spent several delightful hours on a touristy, hopelessly romantic river cruise. Why not cap that experience with an equally touristy romantic gesture?

"Do you see these locks?" she asked as she and Dev crossed the street and approached the iron bridge.

"Hard to miss 'em," he drawled, eyeing the almost solid wall of brass obscuring the bridge's waist-high grillwork. "What's the story here?"

"I'm told it's a recent fad that's popping up on all the bridges of Paris. People ascribe wishes or dreams to locks and fasten them to the bridge, then throw the key in the river."

Dev stooped to examine some of the colorful ribbons, charms and printed messages dangling from various locks. "Here's a good one. This couple from Dallas wish their kids great joy, but don't plan to produce any additional offspring. Evidently seven are enough."

"Good grief! Seven would be enough for me, too."

"Really?"

He straightened and leaned a hip against the rail. The breeze ruffled his black hair and tugged at the collar of his camel-hair sport coat.

"I guess that's one of those little idiosyncrasies we should find out about each other, almost as important as whether we prefer dogs or cats. How many kids *do* you want, Sarah?"

"I don't know." She trailed a finger over the oblong hasp of a bicycle lock. "Two, at least, although I wouldn't mind three or even four."

As impulsive and thoughtless as Gina could be at times, Sarah couldn't imagine growing up without the joy of her bubbly laugh and warm, generous personality.

"How about you?" she asked Dev. "How many offspring would you like to produce?"

"Well, my sisters contend that the number of kids their husbands want is inversely proportional to how many stinky diapers they had to change. I figure I can manage a couple of rounds of diapers. Three or maybe even four if I get the hang of it."

He nodded to the entrepreneur perched on his over-turned crate at the far end of the bridge. The man's peg-board full of locks gleamed dully in the afternoon sun.

"What do you think? Should we add a wish that we survive stinky diapers to the rest of these hopes and dreams?"

Still a little embarrassed by her descent into sappy sentimentality, Sarah nodded. She waited on the bridge while Dev purchased a hefty lock. Together they scouted for an open spot. She found one two-thirds of the way across the bridge, but Dev hesitated before attaching his purchase.

"We need to make it more personal." Frowning, he eyed the bright ribbons and charms dangling from so many of the other locks. "We need a token or something to scribble on."

He patted the pockets of his sport coat and came up

with the ticket stubs from their lunch cruise. "How about one of these?"

"That works. The cruise gave me a view of Paris I'd never seen before. I'm glad I got to share it with you, Dev."

Busy scribbling on the back of a ticket, he merely nodded. Sarah was a little surprised by his offhanded acceptance of her tribute until she read what he'd written.

To our two or three or four or more kids,
we promise you one cruise each on the Seine.

"And I thought *I* was being mushy and sentimental," she said, laughing.

"Mushy and sentimental is what phase two is all about." Unperturbed, he punched the hasp through the ticket stub. "Here, you attach it."

When the lock clicked into place, Sarah knew she'd always remember this moment. Rising up on tiptoe, she slid her arms around Dev's neck.

She'd remember the kiss, too. Particularly when Dev valiantly stuck to their renegotiated agreement later that evening.

After their monster lunch, they opted for supper at a pizzeria close to the Hôtel Verneuil. One glass of red wine and two mushroom-and-garlic slices later, they walked back to the hotel through a gray, soupy fog. Monsieur LeBon had gone off duty, but the receptionist on the desk relayed his shock over the news of the attack on Lady Sarah and his profound regret that she had suffered such an indignity while in Paris.

Sarah smiled her thanks and made a mental note to speak to the manager personally tomorrow. Once on her floor, she slid the key card into her room lock and slanted Dev a questioning look.

"Do you want to come in for a drink?"

"A man can only endure so much torture." His expression rueful, he traced a knuckle lightly over the bruise she'd already forgotten. "Unless you're ready to initiate phase three, we'd better call it a night."

She was ready. More than ready. But the companionship she and Dev had shared after leaving Inspector Delacroix's office had delivered as much punch as the hours they'd spent tangled up in the sheets. A different kind of punch, admittedly. Emotional rather than physical, but every bit as potent.

Although she knew she'd regret it the moment she closed the door, Sarah nodded. "Let's give phase two a little more time."

She was right. She did regret it. But she decided the additional hours she spent curled up on the sofa watching very boring TV were appropriate punishment for being so stupid. She loved Dev. He obviously loved her. Why couldn't she just trust her instincts and…

The buzz of her cell phone cut into her disgusted thoughts. She reached for the instrument, half hoping it was Alexis trying to reach her again. Sarah was in the mood to really, really unload on her ex-boss. When her sister's picture flashed up on the screen, she almost dropped the phone in her excitement and relief.

"Gina! Where are you?"

"Lucerne. I…I waited until morning in New York to call you but…"

"I'm not in New York. I'm in Paris, as you would know if you'd bothered to answer any of my calls."

"Thank God!"

The moaned exclamation startled her, but not as much as the sobs her sister suddenly broke into. Sarah lurched upright on the sofa, the angry tirade she'd intended to deliver instantly forgotten.

"What's wrong? Gina! What's happened?"

A dozen different disasters flooded into her mind. Gina had taken a tumble on the ski slopes. Broken a leg or an arm. Or her neck. She could be paralyzed. Breathing by machine.

"Are you hurt?" she demanded, fear icing her heart. "Gina, are you in the hospital?"

"Nooo."

The low wail left her limp with relief. In almost the next heartbeat, panic once again fluttered like a trapped bird inside her chest. She could count on the fingers of one hand the times she'd heard her always-upbeat, always-sunny sister cry.

"Sweetie, talk to me. Tell me what's wrong."

"I can't. Not…not over the phone. Please come, Sarah. *Please!* I need you."

It didn't even occur to her to say no. "I'll catch the next flight to Lucerne. Tell me where you're staying."

"The Rebstock."

"The hotel Grandmama took us to the summer you turned fourteen?"

That set off another bout of noisy, hiccuping sobs. "Don't…don't tell Grandmama about this."

About *what?* Somehow, Sarah choked back the shout and offered a soothing promise.

"I won't. Just keep your phone on, Gina. I'll call you as soon as I know when I can get there."

She cut the connection, switched to the phone's internet browser and pulled up a schedule of flights from Paris to Lucerne. Her pulse jumped when she found a late-night shuttle to Zurich that departed Charles de Gaulle Airport at 11:50 p.m. From there she'd have to rent a car and drive the sixty-five kilometers to Lake Lucerne.

She could make the flight. She had to make it. Her heart racing, she reserved a seat and scrambled off the sofa. She started for the bedroom to throw some things together but made a quick detour to the sitting room desk and snatched up the house phone.

"Come on, Dev. Answer!"

Her quivering nerves stretched tighter as it rang six times, then cut to the hotel operator.

"May I help you, Lady Sarah?"

"I'm trying to reach Monsieur Hunter, but he doesn't answer."

"May I take a message for you?"

"Yes, please. Tell him to call me as soon as possible."

Hell! Where was he?

Slamming the phone down, she dashed into the bedroom. She didn't have time to pack. Just shove her laptop in her shoulder tote, grab her sweater coat, make sure her purse held her passport and credit cards and run.

While the elevator made its descent, she tried to reach Dev by cell phone. She'd just burst into the lobby when he answered on a husky, teasing note.

"Please tell me you've decided to put me out of my misery."

"Where are you?" The phone jammed to her ear, she rushed through the lobby. "I called your room but there wasn't any answer.

"I couldn't sleep. I went out for a walk." He caught the tension in her voice. The teasing note dropped out of his. "Why? What's up?"

"Gina just called."

"It's about time."

She pushed through the front door. The fog had cleared, thank God, and several taxis still cruised the streets. She waved a frantic arm to flag one down, the phone clutched in her other fist.

"She's in some kind of trouble, Dev."

"So what else is new?"

If she hadn't been so worried, the sarcastic comment might not have fired her up as hot and fast as it did.

"Spare me the editorial," she snapped back angrily. "My sister needs me. I'm on my way to Switzerland."

"Whoa! Hold on a minute…"

The taxi rolled up to the curb. She jumped in and issued a terse order. "De Gaulle Airport. Hurry, please."

"Dammit, Sarah, I can't be more than ten or fifteen minutes from the hotel. Wait until I get back and we'll sort this out together."

"She's *my* sister. I'll sort it out." She was too rushed and too torqued by his sarcasm to measure her words. "I'll call you as soon as I know what's what."

"Yeah," he bit out, as pissed off now as she was. "You do that."

In no mood to soothe his ruffled feathers, she cut the connection and leaned into the Plexiglas divider.

"I need to catch an eleven-fifty flight," she told the cab-driver. "There's an extra hundred francs in it for you if I make it."

The Swiss Air flight was only half-full. Most of the passengers looked like businessmen who wanted to be on scene when Zurich's hundreds of banks opened for business in the morning. There were a few tourists scattered among them, and several students with crammed backpacks getting a jump start on spring break in the Alps.

Sarah stared out the window through most of the ninety-minute flight. The inky darkness beyond the strobe lights on the wing provided no answers to the worried questions tumbling through her mind.

Was it the ski instructor? Had he left Gina stranded in Lucerne? Or Dev's Byzantine medallion? Had she tried to sell it and smacked up against some law against peddling antiquities on the black market?

Her stomach was twisted into knots by the time they landed in Zurich, and she rushed to the airport's Europcar desk. Fifteen minutes later she was behind the wheel of a rented Peugeot and zipping out of the airport. Once she hit the main motorway, she fumbled her phone out of her purse and speed-dialed her sister.

"I just landed in Zurich," Sarah informed her. "I'm in a rental car and should be there within an hour."

"Okay. Thanks for coming, Sarah. I'll call down to reception and tell them to expect you."

To her profound relief, Gina sounded much calmer. Probably because she knew the cavalry was on the way.

"I'll see you shortly."

Once Sarah left the lights of Zurich behind, she zoomed south on the six-lane E41. Speed limits in Switzerland didn't approach the insanity of those in Germany, but the 120 kilometers per hour max got her to the shores of Lake Lucerne in a little over forty minutes.

The city of Lucerne sat on the western arm of the lake. A modern metropolis with an ancient center, its proximity to the Alps had made it a favorite destination for tourists from the earliest days of the Hapsburg Empire. The Duchy of Karlenburgh had once constituted a minuscule part of that vast Hapsburg empire. As the lights of the city glowed in the distance, Sarah remembered that Grandmama had shared some of the less painful stories from the St. Sebastians' past during their stay in Lucerne.

She wasn't thinking of the past as she wound through the narrow streets of the Old Town. Only of her sister and whether whatever trouble Gina was in might impact their grandmother's health. The old worries she'd carried for so long—the worries she'd let herself slough off when she'd gotten so tangled up with Dev—came crashing back.

It was almost 3:00 a.m. when she pulled up at the entrance to the Hotel zum Rebstock. Subdued lighting illuminated its half-timbered red-and-white exterior. Three stories tall, with a turreted tower anchoring one end of the building, the hotel had a history dating back to the 1300s.

Even this early in the season, geraniums filled its window boxes and ivy-covered trellises defined the tiny terrace that served as an outdoor restaurant and *biergarten*.

Weary beyond words, Sarah grabbed her tote and purse and left the car parked on the street. She'd have a valet move it to the public garage on the next block tomorrow. Right now all she cared about was getting to her sister.

As promised, Gina had notified reception of a late arrival. Good thing, since a sign on the entrance informed guests that for safety purposes a key card was required for entry after midnight. A sleepy attendant answered Sarah's knock and welcomed her to the Rebstock.

"Lady Eugenia asked that we give you a key. She is in room 212. The elevator is just down the hall. Or you may take the stairs."

"Thank you."

She decided the stairs would be quicker and would also work out the kinks in her back from the flight and the drive. The ancient wooden stairs creaked beneath their carpeted runner. So did the boards of the second-floor hallway as Sarah counted room numbers until she reached the one at the far end of the hall. A corner turret room, judging by the way its door was wedged between two others.

She slid the key card into the lock and let herself into a narrow, dimly lit entryway.

"Gina?"

The door whooshed shut behind her. Sarah rounded the corner of the entryway, found herself in a charming bedroom with a sitting area occupying the octagonal turret and came to a dead stop. Her sister was tucked under the double bed's downy duvet, sound asleep.

A rueful smile curved Sarah's lips. She'd raced halfway across Europe in response to a desperate plea. Yet whatever was troubling Gina didn't appear to be giving her nightmares. She lay on one side, curled in a tight ball with a hand under her cheek and her blond curls spilling across the pillow.

Shaking her head in amused affection, Sarah dropped her tote and purse on the sofa in the sitting area and plunked down on the side of the bed.

"Hey!" She poked her sister in the shoulder. "Wake up!"

"Huh?" Gina raised her head and blinked open blurry eyes. "Oh, good," she muttered, her voice thick with sleep. "You made it."

"Finally."

"You've got to be totally wiped," she mumbled. Scooting over a few inches, she dragged up a corner of the comforter. "Crawl in."

"Oh, for…!"

Sarah swallowed the rest of the exasperated exclamation. Gina's head had already plopped back to the pillow. Her lids fluttered shut and her raised arm sank like a stone.

The elder sister sat on the edge of the bed for a few moments longer, caught in a wash of relief and bone-deep love for the younger. Then she got up long enough to kick off her boots and unbelt the cherry-red sweater coat. Shrugging it off, she slid under the comforter.

As exhausted as she was from her frantic dash across Europe, it took Sarah longer than she would have believed possible to fall asleep. She lay in the half darkness, listening to her sister's steady breathing, trying yet again to guess what had sparked her panic. Gradually, her thoughts shifted to Dev and their last exchange.

She'd overreacted to his criticism of Gina. She knew that now. At the time, though, her one driving thought had been to get to the airport. She'd apologize tomorrow. He had sisters of his own. Surely he'd understand.

Fifteen

Sarah came awake to blinding sunshine and the fuzziness that results from too little sleep. She rolled over, grimacing at the scratchy pull of her slept-in slacks and turtleneck, and squinted at the empty spot beside her.

No Gina.

And no note, she discovered when she crawled out of bed and checked the sunny sitting room. More than a little annoyed, she padded into the bathroom. Face scrubbed, she appropriated her sister's hairbrush and found a complimentary toothbrush in the basket of amenities provided by the hotel.

Luckily, she and Gina wore the same size, if not the same style. While she was content to adapt her grandmother's vintage classics, her sister preferred a trendier, splashier look. Sarah raided Gina's underwear for a pair of silky black hipsters and matching demibra, then wiggled into a chartreuse leotard patterned in a wild Alice In Wonderland motif. She topped them with a long-sleeved, thigh-skimming wool jumper in electric blue and a three-inch-wide elaborately studded belt that rode low on her hips.

No way was she wearing her red sweater coat with these

eye-popping colors. She'd look like a clown-school dropout. She flicked a denim jacket off a hangar instead, hitched her purse over her shoulder and went in search of her sister.

She found Gina outside on the terrace, chatting with an elderly couple at the next table. She'd gathered her blond curls into a one-sided cascade and looked impossibly chic in pencil-legged jeans, a shimmering metallic tank and a fur-trimmed Michael Kors blazer. When she spotted Sarah, she jumped up and rushed over with her arms outstretched.

"You're finally up! You got in so late last night I... Omigod! What happened to your face?"

Sarah was more anxious to hear her sister's story than tell her own. "I got crosswise of a metal strut."

"I'm so sorry! Does it hurt?"

"Not anymore."

"Thank goodness. We'll have to cover it with foundation when we go back upstairs. Do you want some coffee?"

"God, yes!"

Sarah followed her back to the table and smiled politely when Gina introduced her to the elderly couple. They were from Düsseldorf, were both retired schoolteachers and had three children, all grown now.

"They've been coming to Lake Lucerne every spring for forty-seven years to celebrate their anniversary," Gina related as she filled a cup from the carafe on her table. "Isn't that sweet?"

"Very sweet."

Sarah splashed milk into the cup and took two, quick lifesaving gulps while Gina carried on a cheerful conversation with the teachers. As she listened to the chatter, Sarah began to feel much like the tumbling, upside-down Alices on the leotard. Had she fallen down some rabbit hole? Imagined the panic in her sister's voice last night? Dreamed the sobs?

The unreal feeling persisted until Gina saw that she'd downed most of her coffee. "I told the chambermaid to wait until you were up to do the room. She's probably in there now. Why don't we take a walk and…and talk?"

The small stutter and flicker of nervousness told Sarah she hadn't entered some alternate universe. With a smile for the older couple, Gina pushed her chair back. Sarah did the same.

"Let's go down to Chapel Bridge," she suggested. "We can talk there."

The Rebstock sat directly across the street from Lucerne's centuries-old Church of Leodegar, named for the city's patron saint. Just beyond the needle-spired church, the cobbled street angled downward, following the Reuss River as it flowed into the impossibly blue lake. Since the Reuss bisected the city, Lucerne could claim almost as many bridges as Venice. The most famous of them was the Chapel Bridge, or *Kapellbrücke*. Reputed to be the oldest covered wooden bridge in Europe, it was constructed in the early 1300s. Some sections had to be rebuilt after a 1993 fire supposedly sparked by a discarded cigarette. But the octagonal watchtower halfway across was original, and the window boxes filled with spring flowers made it a favorite meandering spot for locals and tourists alike.

Zigzagging for more than six hundred feet across the river, it was decorated with paintings inside that depicted Lucerne's history and offered wooden benches with stunning views of the town, the lake and the snowcapped Alps. Gina sank onto a bench some yards from the watchtower. Sarah settled beside her and waited while her sister gnawed on her lower lip and stared at the snowy peaks in uncharacteristic silence.

"You might as well tell me," she said gently after several moments. "Whatever's happened, we'll find a way to fix it."

Gina exhaled a long, shuddering breath. Twisting around on the bench, she reached for Sarah's hands.

"That's the problem. I came here to fix it. But at the last minute, I couldn't go through with it."

"Go through with what?"

"Terminating the pregnancy."

Sarah managed not to gasp or groan or mangle the fingers entwined with hers, but it took a fierce struggle.

"You're pregnant?"

"Barely. I peed on the stick even before I missed my period. I thought... I was sure we were safe. He wore a condom." She gave a short, dry laugh. "Actually, we went through a whole box of condoms that weekend."

"For God's sake, I don't need the details. Except maybe his name. I assume we're talking about your ski instructor."

"Who?"

"The cuddly ski instructor you texted me about."

"Oh. There isn't any ski instructor. I just needed an excuse for my sudden trip to Switzerland."

That arrowed straight to Sarah's heart. Never, *ever* would she have imagined that her sister would keep a secret like this from her.

"Oh, Gina, why did you need an excuse? Why didn't you just tell me about the baby?"

"I couldn't. You've been so worried about Grandmama and the doctor bills. I couldn't dump this problem on you, too."

She crunched Sarah's fingers, tears shimmering in her eyes.

"But last night... After I canceled my appointment at the clinic...it all sort of came down on me. I had to call you, had to talk to you. Then, when I heard your voice, I just lost it."

When she burst into wrenching sobs, Sarah wiggled a hand free of her bone-crushing grip and threw an arm around her.

"I'm *glad* you lost it," she said fiercely as Gina cried into her shoulder. "I'm *glad* I was close enough to come when you needed me."

They rocked together, letting the tears flow, until Gina finally raised a tear-streaked face.

"You okay?" Sarah asked, fishing a tissue out of her purse.

"No, but...but I will be."

Thank God. She heard the old Gina in that defiant sniff. She handed her the tissue and hid a grin when her sister honked like a Canadian goose.

"I meant to ask you about that, Sarah."

"About what?"

"How you could get here so fast. What were you doing in Paris?"

"I'll tell you later. Let's focus on you right now. And the baby. Who's the father, Gina, and does he know he is one?"

"Yes, to the second part. I was so wigged-out last night, I called him before I called you." She scrunched up her nose. "He didn't take it well."

"Bastard!"

"And then some." Her tears completely gone now, Gina gave an indignant sniff. "You wouldn't believe how obnoxious and overbearing he is. And I can't believe I fell for him, even for one weekend. Although in my defense, he gives new meaning to the phrase sex on the hoof."

"Who *is* this character?"

"No one you know. I met him in L.A. My company catered a party for him."

The bottom dropped out of Sarah's stomach. She could have sworn she heard it splat into the weathered boards. She stared at the snow-covered peaks in the distance, but all she could see was the surveillance video of Gina. At Dev's house in L.A. Catering a private party.

"What's...?" She dragged her tongue over suddenly dry lips. Her voice sounded hollow in her ears, as though it came from the bottom of a well. "What's his name?"

"Jack Mason." Gina's lip curled. "Excuse me, John Harris Mason, the third."

For a dizzying moment, Sarah couldn't catch her breath. She only half heard the diatribe her sister proceeded to pour out concerning the man. She caught that he was some kind of ambassador, however, and that he worked out of the State Department.

"How in the world did you hook up with someone from the State Department?"

"He was in L.A. for a benefit. A friend introduced us."

"Oh. Well…"

Since Gina seemed to have finally run out of steam, Sarah asked if she'd eaten breakfast.

"No, I was waiting for you to wake up."

"The baby…" She gestured at her sister's still-flat stomach. "You need to eat, and I'm starved. Why don't you go back to the hotel and order us a gargantuan breakfast? I'll join you after I make a few calls."

"You're not going to call Grandmama?" Alarm put a squeak in Gina's voice. "We can't drop this on her long-distance."

"Good Lord, no! I need to call Paris. I raced out so fast last night, I didn't pack my things or check out of the hotel."

Or wait for Dev to hotfoot it back to the Hôtel Verneuil. Sarah didn't regret that hasty decision. She wouldn't have made the Swiss Air flight if she'd waited. But she did regret the anger that had flared between them.

No need to tell Gina about Dev right now. Not when she and Sarah were both still dealing with the emotional whammy of her pregnancy. She'd tell her later, after things had calmed down a bit.

Which was why she waited until her sister was almost to the exit of the wooden tunnel to whip out her phone. And why frustration put a scowl on her face when Dev didn't answer his cell.

She left a brief message. Just a quick apology for her spurt of temper last night and a request for him to return her call as soon as possible. She started to slip the phone back into her purse, but decided to try his hotel room. The house phone rang six times before switching to the hotel operator, as it had last night.

"May I help you?"

"This is Sarah St. Sebastian. I'm trying to reach Monsieur Hunter."

"I'm sorry, Lady Sarah. Monsieur Hunter has checked out."

"What! When?"

"Early this morning. He told Monsieur LeBon an urgent business matter had come up at home that required his immediate attention. He also instructed us to hold your room for you until you return."

For the second time in less than ten minutes, Sarah's stomach took a dive.

"Did he…? Did he leave a message for me?"

"No, ma'am."

"Are you sure?"

"Quite sure, ma'am."

"I see. Thank you."

The hand holding the phone dropped to her lap. Once again she stared blindly at the dazzling white peak. Long moments later, she gave her head a little shake and pushed off the bench.

Gina needed her. They'd work on her problem first. Then, maybe, work on Sarah's. When she was calmer and could put this business with Dev in some kind of perspective.

The scene that greeted her when she walked into the Rebstock's lobby did nothing to promote a sense of calm. If anything, she was jolted into instant outrage by the sight of a tawny-haired stranger brutally gripping one of Gina's wrists. She was hammering at him with her free fist. The receptionist dithered ineffectually behind the counter.

"What are you doing?"

Sarah flew across the lobby, her hands curled into talons. She attacked from the side while Gina continued to assault the front. Between them, they forced the stranger to hunch his shoulders and shield his face from fifteen painted, raking fingernails.

"Hey! Back off, lady."

"Let her go!"

Sarah got in a vicious swipe that drew blood. The man, whom she now suspected was the overbearing, obnoxious ambassador, cursed.

"Jesus! Back off, I said!"

"Not until you let Gina go."

"The hell I will! She's got some explaining to do, and I'm not letting her out of my sight until..."

He broke off, as startled as Sarah when she was thrust aside by 180 pounds of savage male.

"What the...?"

That was all Mason got out before a fist slammed into his jaw. He stumbled back a few steps, dragging Gina with him, then took a vicious blow to the midsection that sent him to his knees.

Still, he wouldn't release Gina's wrist. But instead of fighting and twisting, she was now on her knees beside him and waving her free hand frantically.

"Dev! Stop!"

Sarah was terrified her sister might be hurt in the melee. Or the baby. Dear God, the baby. She leaped forward and hung like a monkey from Dev's arm.

"For God's sake, be careful! She's pregnant!"

The frantic shout backed Dev off but produced the opposite reaction in Mason. His brown eyes blazing, he wrenched Gina around to face him.

"Pregnant? What the hell is this? When you called me last night, all weepy and hysterical, you said you'd just come back from the clinic."

"I *had* just come back from the clinic!"

"Then what…?" His glance shot to her stomach, ripped back to her face. "You didn't do it?"

"I…I couldn't."

"But you couldn't be bothered to mention that little fact before I walked out on a critical floor vote, jumped a plane and flew all night to help you through a crisis you *also* didn't bother to tell me about until last night."

"So I didn't choose my words well," Gina threw back. "I was upset."

"Upset? You were damned near incoherent."

"And you were your usual arrogant self. Let me go, dammit."

She wrenched her wrist free and scrambled to her feet. Mason followed her up, his angry glance going from her to their small but intensely interested audience. His eyes narrowed on Sarah.

"You must be the sister."

"I… Yes."

His jaw working, he shifted to Dev. "Who the hell are you?"

"The sister's fiancé."

"What!" Gina's shriek ricocheted off the walls. "Since when?"

"It's a long story," Sarah said weakly. "Why don't we, uh, go someplace a little more private and I'll explain."

"Let's go." Gina hooked an arm through Sarah's, then whirled to glare at the two men. "Not you. Not either of you. This is between me and my sister."

It wasn't, but Dev yielded ground. Mason was forced to follow suit, although he had to vent his feelings first.

"You, Eugenia Amalia Therése St. Sebastian, are the most irresponsible, irritating, thickheaded female I've ever met."

Her nostrils flaring, Gina tilted her chin in a way that would have made the duchess proud. "Then aren't you fortunate, Ambassador, that I refused to marry you."

* * *

Her regal hauteur carried her as far as the stairwell. Abandoning it on the first step, she yanked on Sarah's arm to hurry her up to their room. Once inside, she let the door slam and thrust her sister toward the sofa wedged into the turret sitting room.

"Sit." She pointed a stern finger. "Talk. Now."

Sarah sat, but talking didn't come easy. "It's a little difficult to explain."

"No, it's not. Start at the beginning. When and where did you meet Dev?"

"In New York. At my office. When he came to show me the surveillance video of you lifting his Byzantine medallion."

Gina's jaw sagged. "What Byzantine...? Oh! Wait! Do you mean that little gold-and-blue thingy?"

"That little gold-and-blue thingy is worth more than a hundred thousand pounds."

"You're kidding!"

"I wish I was. What did you do with it, Gina?"

"I didn't do anything with it."

"Dev's surveillance video shows the medallion sitting on its stand when you sashay up to the display shelves. When you sashay away, the medallion's gone."

"Good grief, Sarah, you don't think I stole it, do you?"

"No, and that's what I told him from day one."

"*He* thinks I stole it?"

The fury that flashed in her eyes didn't bode well for Devon Hunter.

"It doesn't matter what he thinks," Sarah lied. "What matters is that the medallion's missing. Think, sweetie, think. Did you lift it off its stand? Or knock it off by accident, so it fell behind the shelves, maybe?"

"I did lift it, but I just wanted to feel the surface. You know, rub a thumb over that deep blue enamel." Her forehead creased in concentration. "Then I heard someone coming and... Oh, damn! I must have slipped it into my pocket. It's probably still there."

"Gina!" The two syllables came out on a screech. "How could you not remember slipping a twelfth-century Byzantine medallion in your pocket?"

"Hey, I didn't know it was a twelfth-century *anything*. And I'd just taken the pregnancy test that morning, okay? I was a little rattled. I'm surprised I made it to work that evening, much less managed to smile and orchestrate Hunter's damned dinner."

She whirled and headed for the door. Sarah jumped up to follow.

"I'm going to rip him a new one," Gina fumed. "How *dare* he accuse me of..." She yanked open the door and instantly switched pronouns. "How *dare* you accuse me of stealing?"

The two men in the hall returned distinctly different frowns. Jack Mason's was quick and confused. Dev's was slower and more puzzled.

"You didn't take it?"

"No, Mr. High-and-Mighty Hunter, I didn't."

"Take what?" Mason wanted to know.

"Then where is it?"

"I'm guessing it's in the pocket of the jacket I wore that evening."

"So you *did* take it?"

"Take what?"

Sarah cut in. "Gina was just running a hand over the surface when she heard footsteps. She didn't want to be caught fingering it, so she slipped it into her pocket."

"Dammit!" the ambassador exploded. "What the hell are you three talking about it?"

"Nothing that concerns you," Gina returned icily. "Why are you in my room, anyway? I have nothing more to say to you."

"Tough. I've still got plenty to say to you."

Sarah had had enough. A night of gut-wrenching worry, little sleep, no breakfast and now all this shouting was giving her a world-class headache. Before she could tell everyone to please shut up, Dev hooked her elbow and edged her out the door. With his other hand, he pushed Mason inside.

"You take care of your woman. I'll take care of mine."

"Wait a minute!" Thoroughly frustrated, Gina stamped a foot. "I still don't know how or when or why you two got engaged. You can't just…"

Dev closed the door in her face.

"Ooh," Sarah breathed. "She'll make you pay for that."

He braced both hands against the wall, caging her in. "Do I look worried?"

What he looked was unshaven, red-eyed and pissed.

"What are you doing here?" she asked a little breathlessly. "When I called the Hôtel Verneuil a while ago, they told me you had some kind of crisis in your business and had to fly home."

"I had a crisis, all right, but it was here. We need to get something straight, Lady Sarah. From now on, it's not *my* sister or *your* business. We're in this together. Forever. Or at least until we deliver on that promise to give kid number four a cruise on the Seine."

Sixteen

The prewedding dinner was held on the evening of May 3 at Avery's, where Dev had first "proposed" to Sarah. He reserved the entire restaurant for the event. The wedding ceremony and reception took place at the Plaza the following evening.

Gina, who'd emerged from a private session with the duchess white-faced and shaking, had regained both her composure and some of her effervescence. She then proceeded to astonish both her sister and her grandmother by taking charge of the dinner, the wedding ceremony and the reception.

To pull them off, she'd enlisted the assistance of Andrew at the Plaza, who'd aged with immense dignity since that long-ago day he'd discreetly taken care of an inebriated presidential aide during Grandmama's soirée for the Sultan of Oman. Gina also formed a close alliance with Patrick Donovan, Dev's incredibly capable and supremely confident executive assistant.

All Sarah had to do was draw up her guest list and select her dress. She kept the list small. She wanted to *enjoy* her wedding, not feel as though she was participating in a carefully scripted media event. Besides, she didn't have any family other than Grandmama, Gina and Maria.

She did invite a number of close friends and coworkers—including Alexis. *Beguile*'s executive editor had admitted the Paris thing was a mistake of epic proportions, but swore she'd never intended to publish a single photo without Sarah's permission. As a peace offering/wedding present, she'd had the photos printed and inserted into a beautifully inscribed, gilt-edged scrapbook. Just to be safe, Sarah had also had her hand over the disk with the complete set of JPEGs.

Dev's guest list was considerably longer than his bride's. His parents, sisters, their spouses and various offspring had flown to New York four days before the wedding. Dev had arranged a whirlwind trip to New Mexico so Sarah could meet most of them. She'd gotten to know them better while playing Big Apple tour guide. She'd also gained more insight into her complex, fascinating, handsome fiancé as more of his friends and associates arrived, some from his Air Force days, some from the years afterward.

Elise and Jean-Jacques Girault had flown in from Paris the afternoon before the wedding, just in time for dinner at the Avery. Sarah wasn't surprised that Elise and Alexis formed an instant bond, but the sight of Madame Girault snuggled against one of Dev's friends during predinner cocktails made her a tad nervous.

"Uh-oh," she murmured to Dev. "Do you think she's trying to seduce him?"

"Probably."

She searched the crowded restaurant, spotted Monsieur Girault happily chatting with Gina and relaxed.

Her wedding day dawned sunny and bright. Gina once again assumed charge. She'd accepted Dev's offer of payment without a qualm and arranged a full day at a spa for the women in the wedding party. She, Sarah, the duchess,

Maria, Dev's mother and sisters and the two little nieces who would serve as flower girls all got the works. The adults indulged in massages, facials, manicures, pedicures and hair treatments. The giggling little girls had their hair done and their fingernails and toenails painted pale lavender.

Sarah had enjoyed every moment of it, but especially treasured the half hour lying next to her sister on side-by-side massage tables while their facial masks cleaned and tightened their pores. According to the attendant, the masks were made of New Zealand Manuka honey, lavender oils and shea butter, with the additive of bee venom, which reputedly gave Kate Middleton her glowing complexion.

"At fifty-five thousand dollars per bottle, the venom better produce results," Gina muttered.

Only the fact that their masks contained a single drop of venom each, thus reducing the treatment price to just a little over a hundred dollars, kept Sarah from having a heart attack. Reaching across the space between the tables, she took Gina's hand.

"Thanks for doing all this."

"You're welcome." Her sister's mouth turned up in one of her irrepressible grins. "It's easy to throw great parties when you're spending someone else's money."

"You're good at it."

"Yes," she said smugly, "I am."

Her grin slowly faded and her fingers tightened around Sarah's.

"It's one of the few things I *am* good at. I'm going to get serious about it, Sarah. I intend to learn everything I can about the event-planning business before the baby's born. That way, I can support us both."

"What about Jack Mason? How does he figure in this plan?"

"He doesn't."

"It's his child, too, Gina."

"He'll have as much involvement in the baby's life as he wants," she said stubbornly, "but not mine. It's time—past time—I took responsibility for myself."

Sarah couldn't argue with that, but she had to suppress a few doubts as she squeezed Gina's hand. "You know I'll help you any way I can. Dev, too."

"I know, but I've got to do this on my own. And you're going to have your hands full figuring how to meld your life with his. Have you decided yet where you're going to live?"

"In L.A., if we can convince Grandmama to move out there with us. Maria, too."

"They'll hate leaving New York."

"I know."

Sarah's joy in her special day dimmed. She'd had several conversations with the duchess about a possible move. None of them had ended satisfactorily. As an alternative, Dev had offered to temporarily move his base of operations to New York and commute to L.A.

"I just can't bear to think of Grandmama alone in that huge apartment."

"Well…" Gina hesitated, indecision written all over her face. "I know I just made a big speech about standing on my own two feet, but I hate the thought of her being alone, too. I could…I could move in with her until I land a job. Or maybe until the baby's born. If she'll have me, that is, which isn't a sure thing after the scathing lecture she delivered when I got back from Switzerland."

"Oh, Gina, she'll have you! You know she will. She loves you." Sarah's eyes misted. "Almost as much as I do."

"Stop," Gina pleaded, her own tears spouting. "You can't walk down the aisle with your eyes all swollen and red. Dev'll strangle me."

As Dev took his place under the arch of gauzy netting lit by a thousand tiny, sparkling lights, strangling his soon-to-be sister-in-law was the furthest thing from his mind.

He was as surprised as Sarah and the duchess at the way Gina had pulled everything together. So when the maid of honor followed two giggling flower girls down the aisle, he gave Gina a warm smile.

She returned it, but Dev could tell the sight of the unexpected, uninvited guest at the back of the room had shaken her. Mason stood with his arms folded and an expression on his face that suggested he didn't intend to return to Washington until he'd sorted some things out with the mother of his child.

Then the music swelled and Dev's gaze locked on the two women coming down the aisle arm in arm. Sarah matched her step to that of the duchess, who'd stated bluntly she did *not* require a cane to walk a few yards and give her granddaughter away. Spine straight, chin high, eyes glowing with pride, she did just that.

"I hope you understand what a gift I'm giving you, Devon."

"Yes, ma'am, I do."

With a small harrumph, the duchess kissed her granddaughter's cheek and took her seat. Then Sarah turned to Dev, and he felt himself fall into her smile. She was so luminous, so elegant. So gut-wrenchingly beautiful.

He still couldn't claim to know anything about haute couture, but she'd told him she would be wearing a Dior gown her grandmother had bought in Paris in the '60s. The body-clinging sheath of cream-colored satin gave Dev a whole new appreciation of what Sarah termed vintage. The neckline fell in a soft drape and was caught at each shoulder by a clasp adorned with soft, floating feathers. The same downy feathers circled her tiny pillbox cap with its short veil.

Taking the hand she held out to him, he tucked it close to his heart and grinned down at her.

"Are you ready for phase three, Lady Sarah?"

"I am," she laughed. "So very, very ready."

Epilogue

I must admit I approve of Sarah's choice of husband. I should, since I decided Devon Hunter was right for her even before he blackmailed her into posing as his fiancée. How absurd that they still think I don't know about the deception.

Almost as absurd as Eugenia's stubborn refusal to marry the father of her child. I would respect her decision except, to borrow the Bard's immortal words, the lady doth protest too much. I do so dislike the sordid, steaming cauldron of modern politics, but I shall have to learn more about this Jack Mason. In the meantime, I'll have the inestimable joy of watching Eugenia mature into motherhood—hopefully!

From the diary of Charlotte,
Grand Duchess of Karlenburgh

* * * * *

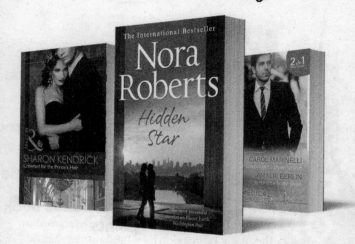
16